# THE
# FALLEN
## 2

*AERIE* AND *RECKONING*

THOMAS E. SNIEGOSKI

**SIMON AND SCHUSTER**

A simon pulse book

First published in Great Britain in 2010 by Simon & Schuster UK Ltd,
1st Floor, 222 Gray's Inn Road, London WC1X 8HB
A CBS COMPANY

Published in the USA in 2010 by Simon Pulse,
an imprint of Simon & Schuster Children's Division, New York.

*Aerie* copyright © Thomas E. Sniegoski, 2003
*Reckoning* copyright ©, Thomas E. Sniegoski, 2004
These titles were originally published individually in the USA by Simon Pulse.

A CIP catalogue record for this book is available from the British Library

ISBN  978-0-85707-274-0

10 9 8 7 6 5 4 3 2

Printed in the UK by CPI Cox & Wyman, Reading RG1 8EX

# CONTENTS

*AERIE*

*For Launey Fogg. His words of encouragement will be treasured forever, as will his memory.*

Thank you, as always, to my loving and oh-so-patient wife, LeeAnne, and my four-legged pally, Mulder.

Lots of special thanks with sprinkles to my brother, separated at birth, Christopher Golden, and to the Termineditor with a vengeance, Lisa Clancy, and her assistant to the stars, Lisa Gribbin.

And special thanks minus the sprinkles must go to: Mom and Dad, Eric Powell, Dave Kraus, David Carroll, Doctor Kris, Tom and Lori Stanley, Paul Griffin, Tim Cole, and the usual suspects, Jon and Flo, Bob and Pat, Don Kramer, Pete Donaldson, Ken Curtis, and Zach Howard. And remember, folks, be good to your parents; they've been good to you.

# PROLOGUE

I t never seems to rest, Alastor reflected as he shoveled the last bit of a hearty breakfast of eggs, bacon, and toast into his yawning maw. He belched powerfully, speckling his ample front with flecks of chewed food, and dropped the greasy paper plate to the floor beside his leather recliner. It was nine o'clock in the morning, and what the fallen angel had hidden in the basement of the Bourbonnais, Illinois, home was already calling out to him.

"*Alastor,*" it whispered like the buzzing of a housefly. "*Come, Alastor. Look upon what you have cast away.*"

Alastor chose to ignore it. *The monkeys, Reggie and Katie,* he thought as his eyes caught the clock on the wall, *they're often amusing.* He snatched up the remote control in a meaty hand, scattering potato chip bags and candy bar wrappers from atop the coffee table before him. He would lose himself in the trifle of morning television, a distraction from the incessant whispers in the cellar.

*"Do you remember what it was like before the war—before you listened to the seductive reasonings of the Morningstar? Do you remember, Alastor?"*

"Quiet!" the angel spat. He jabbed a sausage-thick finger down onto the remote to turn up the volume, settling his excessive bulk back into the recliner. It was a cooking segment, which he enjoyed, as mouthwatering meals were prepared by world-renowned chefs with the assistance of the program's hosts.

Reggie dropped an egg on the floor and the studio audience went wild with laughter. Alastor joined in the hilarity, captivated by the antics of the human monkeys. If the Creator had ever bothered to mention how thoroughly entertaining these fragile creatures could be, he would never have pledged allegiance to the Son of the Morning.

*"Remember what you once were, Alastor of the heavenly host Virtues. Come and recall your former glory."*

The audience was laughing again and Alastor seethed. He had missed the latest morsel of primitive humor.

"Damn you, be quiet!" he screamed, driving a fleshy fist down onto the chair's worn armrest. "I looked at you yesterday—and the day before that. I have no desire to see you now."

The chef produced a soufflé from the oven and the audience showed their approval with a burst of applause. Feigning exuberance, Katie explained how to acquire the recipe for the delectable dish, and he thought about writing the information down, but the whispers from the cellar beckoned for his attention.

*"A chance to remember how you once were—the beauty and the power . . ."*

Alastor hauled his bulky mass up out of the chair, a rain of crumbs from his last meal sprinkling down to the refuse-strewn floor. "I am still beautiful and still powerful," he bellowed, one eye fixed on the morning program, lest he miss something of importance. The *Reggie and Katie* show broke to a commercial about adult diapers and the angel turned his full attention to the taunting voice.

"What will it take to shut you up?" he growled, knowing full well what the answer would be, what the answer always was.

*"Look at me,"* the whispers hissed. *"Look at me and remember our time together."*

Alastor turned back to the television. A dog food commercial was showing—a small human child playing with puppies.

"No matter how often I see you, it never satisfies your need," the fallen angel grumbled, wondering offhandedly how the dog food would taste.

*"And it never shall. I will not allow you to forget what we once were."*

"Even if that is what *I* desire?" he asked, his attention drawn to an ad for the talk show that would follow *Reggie and Katie*. The show's topic would be crib death, and he smiled with the secret knowledge of things that the simple human brain could barely begin to perceive. If he were so inclined, he could tell them all why their babies die in the night. If he were so inclined.

*"I have no interest in your desire,"* said the voice from the basement. *"Come and look upon me or I shall taunt you all the rest of the day and well into the night."*

Reggie and Katie returned, and it took all the strength that Alastor could muster to pull his eyes from the entertaining visuals. "If I spend time with you now, you'll not bother me for the remainder of this day?" he asked, shambling closer to the kitchen.

*"Yes, come and look."*

Alastor lurched into the kitchen, gasping for breath as he propelled himself toward the cellar door, eager for the promise of blissful silence.

"Anything for some peace," he growled, in his mind planning his television viewing for the remainder of the day.

His sweatpants began to slip below his middle, and he reached down to pull the elastic waistband up over his protruding stomach.

*"Peace. An unattainable pursuit since our fall from Heaven; do you ever think we'll experience its bliss again?"* the bothersome voice asked through the door as Alastor took hold of the knob and turned it, a cool dampness wafting up from below as he pulled the cellar door open.

"I've found my own peace," he said irritably, leaning on the rail to carefully descend the wooden steps that creaked in protest beneath his weight. "Is it what I knew in Heaven? No, but I will never see the likes of that again."

He stood at the bottom of the stairs and glanced around, surveying his accumulation of goods, items he had acquired in the years since deciding he would live as a human. There was furniture, enough to fill multiple dwellings; boxes of books, clothes, and kitchen implements; tools; cans of paint; three lawnmowers; at least four televisions still in their boxes; and so much more stored away out of sight.

Alastor remembered when he had made the choice. The Powers were on the hunt, and he knew that it was only a matter of time before they found him. It was all about survival, so he did the unthinkable.

*"That was your second fall,"* the creeping voice spoke from within the room, pulling him from the past. *"When you attempted to sever our bond."*

Alastor lurched forward toward the source of his irritation, his slippered feet scuffling across the cool, concrete floor. Carefully he maneuvered around an ancient bureau. "There was no other way," he said, almost losing his balance as he stepped over a wooden milk crate filled with old toys made from tin. "It was that, or die." The fallen angel steadied himself with the help of a foldaway bed, and continued on toward the object of his torment. "I had no choice," he said again, perhaps more to convince himself. "How many times must I tell you?"

Everything that had defined him had been lost during the war. Alastor had fled to Earth with others of his ilk, the fearsome Powers in pursuit. For countless centuries he wandered the planet, purposeless, hiding from his would-be punishers. He had almost decided to give up and accept his fate, when it came to him: He would hide amongst the natives. He would become one of them, renouncing everything that defined him as a being of Heaven.

It was a perfect plan. By giving up his angel's ways and surrounding himself with all things human, Alastor hoped to mask his scent from the Powers that hunted him. The angel glanced across the basement, catching his reflection in a mirror against the wall.

*"Look at you,"* the voice said from close by, dripping with disdain. *"Look at what has become of you."*

Alastor was fat, morbidly so, but that was all part of the mask he wore. "I've explained why I must be this way," the angel said, eyes fixed upon the mirror.

For millienia the angel had found the concept of humanity revolting and then had been shocked at how easy it was to be one of them—how simply he slipped into the role of humanity—and he found the experience to be quite enjoyable most of the time. Alastor had grown particularly fond of eating and television.

The fallen angel looked away from the mirror, suddenly unnerved by his grotesque appearance. "I tell you there was no other way." He continued through the basement, drawing closer to the source of his tribulation.

"I'm here," he announced, his breath coming in wheezing gasps as he stopped before a large wooden table bolted to the wall. The top of the workplace had been cleared away, the only uncluttered surface in the entire room, and resting on it was a long, cardboard box.

*"Do you miss us?"* asked the voice in a sibilant whisper that tickled his ears.

Alastor felt the scars on his back begin to burn and itch beneath his heavy, cotton sweatshirt—slightly at first, but growing to the point where he wished he could tear the flesh from his back to make it stop. He gripped the ends of the table and squeezed.

"Of course I miss you, but . . ."

*"Take us back,"* the voice commanded, hissing. *"Make us whole again. It was never supposed to be this way."*

The fallen angel shook his head sadly, the flesh of his face and neck wobbling with his repressed emotion. "If I were to do that, I would most certainly be destroyed," he said, fighting back tears.

He reached for the box flaps that hid the artifacts of his past and pried them apart, the scars upon his shoulder blades screaming for his attention.

*"But we would be together again,"* the whisper from within the box cajoled. *"As we are meant to be."*

Alastor had wrapped them in sheets of plastic to protect them from the dampness. He gasped as he always did when he looked upon them, never fully remembering the extent of his sacrifice. He started to close up the box, not wanting to be reminded.

*"Look at me,"* the voice within the box demanded.

"I have looked," he responded slowly. "And as usual, I am filled with an overwhelming sadness."

*"Unwrap us,"* it ordered. *"Look upon us and remember."*

Alastor found himself doing as the voice requested, pulling back the plastic wrap to expose the box's contents. He remembered the pain—the decision, as well as the act itself—to sever from his body the final remnant of what separated him from the monkeys.

To be human, they had to be cut off.

Alastor mournfully gazed upon his severed wings. He had reasoned that without them, it would be easier to assume the human role, and it had most certainly helped, but that was before they began to speak to him.

With a trembling hand, the fallen angel gently stroked the downy soft surface of the wings and a faint smell of decay wafted up from them. He knew that it was impossible for the appendages to actually communicate with him, and defined the oddity as fallout from his attempt at being human. He had seen talk shows about situations just like this. The experts would say that he was delusional. Alastor smiled. To be human and insane; he had achieved far more success than he ever imagined.

*"Put us on,"* the wings whispered seductively. *"Shed the grotesque shell that adorns you and wear us again."*

Alastor began to close the wrappings.

*"What are you doing?"* they asked, panic in their sound.

"I have done as you asked," he responded to his psychosis, continuing to place the sheets of plastic over the severed limbs of flight. "I can do no more than that."

*"Please,"* the wings begged as he began to close the box.

His body wracked with guilt, Alastor ignored the plaintive cries. "I'm sorry," he managed.

The angel secured the box and stepped quickly back, listening for the sounds of protest that did not come. *Perhaps they are honoring their bargain after all.* He turned from the table, longing for the comfort of his chair, the television, and a large slice of pie. He smiled. *It's odd how much better things always are with pie.*

The laughter seemed to come from all around him.

Alastor whirled, startled by the harshness of the sound. His eyes immediately went to the box, but something told him that the sound did not come from there. Had his psychosis manifested in another way, or was he no longer alone? The angel's mind raced as he scanned the cluttered basement area before him.

A figure clad in crimson armor emerged from behind the curtain of coats hanging on pipes that ran across the cellar ceiling. Alastor gasped. The way the figure moved—stealthy and silent, almost as if he were watching something created by the madness of his own mind. Was it possible? Had his troubled thoughts created this specter in red? Something else to torment him?

But then it spoke, pointing a gauntlet-covered hand. "You try to hide, covering your pretty angel stink with the smell of man." The crimson figure shook its helmeted head, an odd clicking sound escaping from beneath the face mask. "You don't do the magick, and you cut away your wings," the man said, making a hacking gesture with one of his armored hands.

"The Powers . . . ," Alastor croaked, forcing the words from his corpulent mouth. "You serve the Powers."

He knew the answer, even before the figure clad in armor the color of blood nodded. He knew, for senses long atrophied had kicked in, the scent of Heaven's most aggressive host filling his nostrils with its fetid aroma of bloodshed.

"And you've come for me?"

Again the creature nodded.

Alastor studied the agent of the Powers, a part of him marveling at the beauty of the fearsome suit of metal that adorned his foe. The armor had been forged by Heaven's hands, of that there was no doubt. The faint light thrown by the cellar's single bulb played lovingly off the intricate details of the metal skin;

it made him remember days long past, of brethren that died beneath his sword, of his fall from grace.

Panic gripped the fallen angel. He did not want to die. From within he summoned a glimmer of strength, a spark of angelic fury untapped since he had fought beside the Son of the Morning. In his mind he saw an ax and tried to bring it into the world.

The spark of heavenly fire exploded to life in the palm of his hand—and Alastor began to scream. It had been so long that it burned him. His flesh had become as that of a human, and the fires of Heaven began to consume the delicate skin. The stench of frying meat filled the basement, and the fallen angel perversely realized that he was hungry, his swollen stomach grumbling to be fed.

He tried to concentrate on the weapon he saw in his mind's eye: a battle-ax like one he had wielded in the war. In his charred hand the flames began to take shape, and Alastor felt a wave of optimism the likes of which he had not felt since devising the plan that almost made him human. He brandished the ax, fearsome and complete, at his attacker.

The figure in red giggled; an eerie sound made all the more strange filtered through the mask that hid his face.

"You find me amusing, slave of the Powers host?" Alastor asked, attempting to block out the throbbing pain in his burned hand. "We'll see how comical I am when my ax takes your head from your shoulders."

Again the armored warrior laughed, reminding Alastor of some demented child. They continued to stare at each other across the cellar space, the fires of Heaven still burning in the fallen angel's fragile grasp. The pale, doughy skin of his arm had begun to bubble and smolder. The pain was excruciating, but it helped him to focus.

"You gave it all up for this?" the red-armored horror asked, looking around at the clutter of the basement before turning his gaze back to Alastor.

The eyes within the helmet were intense, boring into his own like daggers of ice. The servant to the Powers shook his head slowly in disgust.

This act of condescension only served to inflame Alastor's rage all the more. *How dare this lowly servant look down upon me? Does he not realize the courage and fortitude my sacrifice has required?*

From deep within, Alastor dredged up the final remnants of what remained of his long inactive angelic traits. The fallen angel bellowed his disdain and threw his massive bulk across the cellar floor, scattering his accumulated belongings in his wake. He hefted the battle-ax of fire above his head, ready to cleave his enemy in twain. The flaming ax descended, passing through the coats and sports jackets that hung from the ceiling pipes, and continuing its destructive course into a musty, cardboard box filled with pots and pans.

The fallen angel spun himself around, the burning ax

handle still clutched in his blackened grasp. The flaming weapon decimated a box of letters and tax records, sending burning pieces of paper up into the air, then drifting down upon him like burning snow. But despite the savagery of his assault, the weapon had yet to find its mark.

Through the burning refuse Alastor scanned the cellar in search of his adversary, weapon ready to strike yet again. He found the armored man standing before the worktable, his scarlet glove resting atop the box that contained the precious wings.

"How much did it hurt, Alastor?" the invader asked. "How great was the pain to murder what you were?"

Alastor relived the shrieking agony as he hacked his beautiful wings from his back; how he had blacked out after cutting away the first, only to return to consciousness and do away with the other. The pain had been excruciating, and was second only to his betrayal of the Creator.

The sight of the armored creature near his wings stoked the fires of his fury to maddening heights. Barely able to contain his rage, Alastor propelled himself at the figure, a cry like that of a hungry hawk erupting from his open mouth as he moved with a speed contrary to his bulk. He lifted the flaming ax above his head, but unexpectedly the intruder surged forward to meet his attack. The warrior struck quickly, fiercely, and just as fast leaped out of the fallen angel's path.

Alastor crashed into the long, wooden worktable, practically ripping it from the granite wall. The box fell, and he watched it open, spilling its precious contents as he slowly turned to face his attacker. The armored intruder stood perfectly still, his cold, predator's gaze watching him.

A terrible numbness had begun to spread from his chest, traveling to all his extremities. Alastor gazed down at his body gone to seed with the sweet indulgences of humanity, and saw the pommel of an ornate knife sticking out from the center of his chest. His strength suddenly leaving him, he watched helplessly as the ax of fire fell from his grasp to evaporate in a flash before it could hit the floor.

"What . . . what have you done to me?"

The fearsome figure shrugged its shoulders of metal. "Pretty little symbols etched into the metal of the blade," he said, drawing the same symbols in the air with his finger. "Symbols to take away strength—to make you easier to kill."

His legs no longer capable of supporting his enormous mass, Alastor pitched forward atop his wings. The aroma of their rot choked his senses, and he was overcome with a crushing sense of loss.

"I'm so sorry," he whispered to them through the plastic cover. He felt his body being turned and gazed up into the disturbing visage that straddled him.

"How? . . ." Alastor slurred, the magicks carved upon the knife blade affecting even his ability to speak.

His attacker reached down, taking hold of the knife that protruded from the center of Alastor's body.

"How?" the attacker asked, gripping the hilt.

"How did . . . how did you find me?" Alastor gasped.

The figure standing over him again began to laugh, that horrible sound of a demented child. "Find you?" it repeated, exerting pressure on the blade, cutting down through the flesh and bone of the fallen angel's chest. He completed his jagged incision, then extracted the blade and replaced it somewhere beneath the layers of his armor. "We did not need to find you," the Powers' servant said as it dug the fingers of both hands into the wound. "We knew where you were all along."

Alastor closed his eyes to his inevitable fate, focusing all his attention on the rapid-fire beating of his heart. It reminded him of the sound of flight, of his beautiful wings as they beat against the air.

And then what Alastor had sacrificed so much to keep was stolen away as the visage of death clad in scarlet tore his still-beating heart from his chest.

# CHAPTER ONE

"Can I take your order, sir?" asked the cute girl with the blond ponytail and a smile wide enough to split her face in two.

Aaron Corbet shook himself from his reverie and tried to focus on the menu board behind her. "Uh, yeah, thanks," he said, attempting to generate interest in yet another fast-food order. His eyes were strained from hours of driving, and the writing on the menu blurred as he tried to read it. "Give me a Whopper-with-cheese value meal, and four large fries to go."

Aaron hoped the four orders of fries would be enough to satisfy Camael's strange new craving for the greasy fast food. Just a few days ago the angel had given him a song and dance about how creatures of Heaven didn't need to eat—but that had been before he sampled some of the golden fried potatoes. *Angels addicted to French fries,* Aaron thought with a wry shake of his head. *Who'da thunk it?*

But then again, who could have predicted this crazy turn his life had taken? he thought as he waited for his order to be filled. The angel Camael had become his companion and mentor since Aaron's realization that he was born a Nephilim. He remembered how insane it had all sounded at first—the hybrid offspring of the mating between a human woman and an angelic being. Aaron thought he was losing his mind. And then people he cared about started dying, and he realized there was much more at stake than just his sanity.

Aaron turned away from the counter and looked out over the dining room. He noticed a couple with a little boy who appeared to be no more than four years old. The child was playing with a blue plastic top that he must have gotten as a prize with his kid's meal. Aaron immediately thought of Stevie, his foster brother, and a weighty feeling of unease washed over him. He recalled the last time he had seen his little brother. The seven-year-old autistic child was being dragged from their home in the clutches of an angel—a soldier in the service of a murderous host of angels called the Powers. The Powers wanted Aaron dead, for he was not just a Nephilim, he was also supposed to be the chosen one spoken of in an angelic prophecy written over a millennium ago, promising redemption to the fallen angels.

At first it had been an awful lot to swallow, but lately Aaron had begrudgingly come to accept the bizarre twists and turns that life seemed to have in store for him. Camael said that it was all part of his destiny, which had been pre-determined long before he was born.

The child had managed to make the top spin and, much to his parents' amusement, clapped his hands together as the plastic toy careened about the table top.

The prophecy predicted that someone very much like Aaron would be responsible for bringing forgiveness to the angels hiding on Earth since the Great War in Heaven, that he would be the one to reunite the fallen with God. It's a big job for an eighteen-year-old foster kid from Lynn, Massachusetts, but who was he to argue with destiny?

The spinning top flew from the table and the little boy began to scream in panic. Again Aaron was bombarded with painful memories of the recent past, of his foster brother's cries as he was stolen away. "I think I'll keep him," the Powers leader, Verchiel, had said as he handled the little boy like some kind of house pet. Aaron's blood seethed with the memory. Perhaps he *was* some kind of savior, but there was nothing he wanted more than to find his brother. Everything else would have to wait until Stevie was safe again.

The child continued to wail while his panicked parents scrambled to find the lost toy. On hands and knees the boy's father retrieved the top from beneath a nearby table and brought the child's sadness to an abrupt end by returning the toy to him. Though his face was still streaked with tears, the boy was smiling broadly now. *If only my task could be as simple,* Aaron thought wearily.

"Do you want ketchup?" he heard someone say close by, as he turned his thoughts to how much farther he'd be able to drive tonight. He was tired, and for a brief moment he considered teaching Camael how to drive, but that thought was stricken from his mind by the image of the heavenly warrior in the midst of a minor traffic altercation, cutting another driver in two with a flaming sword.

Aaron felt a hand upon his shoulder and spun around to see the girl with the ponytail and the incredibly wide smile holding out his bags of food. "Ketchup?" she asked again.

"Were you talking to me?" he asked, embarrassed, as he took the bags. "I'm sorry, I'm just a bit dazed from driving all day and . . ."

He froze. His foster mom would have described the strange feeling as somebody walking over his grave, whatever the hell that meant. He never did understand the strange superstitions she often shared, but for some reason, the imagery of that one always stuck with him. Aaron missed his foster parents, who had been mercilessly slain by Verchiel, and it made his desire to find his brother all the more urgent. He turned away from the counter to see a man hurriedly going out a back door, two others in pursuit.

The angelic nature that had been a part of him since his eighteenth birthday screamed to be noticed, and senses far beyond the human norm kicked into action. There was a trace of something in the air that marked the men's passing as they left the store. It was an aroma that Aaron could discern even over the prominent smells of hot vegetable oil and frying meat. The air was tainted with the rich smell of spice—and of blood.

With a polite thank-you he took his food and left the store, quickly heading to the metallic blue Toyota Corolla parked at the back of the lot. He could see the eager face of his dog in the back window. Gabriel began to bark happily as he reached the car, not so much that his master had returned, but that he had returned with food.

*"What took so long?"* the dog asked as Aaron placed the bags on the driver's seat. *"I didn't think you were ever coming out."*

Being able to understand and speak any form of language, including the vocalizations of animals, was yet another strange manifestation of Aaron's angelic talents, and one that was both a blessing and a curse when it came to his canine friend.

*"I'm starved, Aaron,"* the dog said eagerly, hoping that there would be something in one of the bags to satisfy what seemed to be a Labrador retriever's insatiable urge to eat.

Gabriel also loved to talk, and after Aaron had used his unique abilities to save the dog after a car accident, the Lab had suddenly become much smarter, making him quite the dynamic personality. Aaron loved the dog more than just about anything else, but there were days that he wished Gabriel was *only* a dog.

*"I'd really like to eat,"* he said from the backseat, licking his chops.

"Not now, Gabe," Aaron responded, directing his attention to the large man sitting with his eyes closed in the passenger seat. "I have to speak with Camael." The angel ignored him, but that didn't stop Aaron from talking. "Inside the restaurant," he said. "I think three angels just went out the back door and . . ."

Camael slowly turned his head and opened his steely blue eyes. "Two of them are of the Powers; the other, a fallen angel"—he tilted back his head of silvery white hair and sniffed, the mustache of his goatee twitching—"of the host Cherubim, I believe. I was aware of their presence when we pulled into the lot."

"And you didn't think it was important to say anything?" Aaron asked, annoyed. "This could be the break we've been waiting for. They might know where Stevie is."

The angel stared at him without emotion, the plight of Aaron's little brother obviously the furthest thing from his mind. With Camael, it was all about fulfilling the prophecy—that and finding a mysterious haven for fallen angels called Aerie.

"We have to go after them," Aaron said forcefully. "This is the first contact we've had with anything remotely angelic since we left Maine."

Gabriel stuck his head between the front seats. *"Then we*

*really should eat first. Right, Camael?"* he asked, eyeing the bags resting on the seat. *"Can't go after angels on an empty stomach, that's what I always say."* The dog had begun to drool, spattering the emergency break.

Camael moved his arm so as not to be splashed and glared at the animal. "I do not need to eat," he snarled, apparently very sensitive to the recent craving he had developed for French fries.

Aaron opened the back door of the car and motioned for Gabriel to get out. "C'mon," he said to them both. "We have to hurry or we'll lose them."

*"May I have a few fries before we go?"* the dog asked as he leaped from the car to the parking lot. *"Just to hold me over until we get back."*

Aaron ignored his dog and slammed the door closed, anxious to be on his way.

"Do you think this wise?" Camael asked as he removed himself from the front seat of the car. "To draw attention to ourselves in such a way?"

Aaron knew there was a risk in confronting the angels, but if they were ever going to find his brother they had to take the chance. "The Powers answer to Verchiel, and he's the one who took Stevie," Aaron said, hoping that the angel would understand. "I don't think I could live with myself if I didn't at least try to find out what they know."

Camael moved around the car casually buttoning his dark

suit jacket, impeccable as always. "You do realize that this will likely end in death."

"Tell me something I don't know," Aaron said as he turned away from his companions and followed the dwindling trail of angel scents into the dense woods behind the fast-food restaurant.

No matter how he tried to distract himself, Verchiel found himself drawn to the classroom within the St. Athanasius Orphanage where the prisoner was held.

Standing in the shadows of the room, the angel stared at the huddled figure feigning sleep within his prison, and marveled at how a mere cage of iron could contain an evil so vast. Verchiel would destroy the prisoner if he could, but even he was loath to admit that he did not have the power to accomplish such a task. He would have to take a level of satisfaction from the evil one's containment, at least for now. When matters with the Nephilim and the accursed prophecy were properly settled, then he could concentrate on an appropriate punishment for the captive.

"Am I that fascinating a specimen?" the prisoner asked from his cage. He slowly brought himself to a sitting position, his back against the bars. In his hand he held a gray furred mouse and gently stroked its tiny skull with an index finger. "I don't believe we saw this much of each other when we still lived in Heaven."

Verchiel bristled at the mention of his former home; it had been too long since last he looked upon its glorious spires and the memory of its beauty was almost too painful to bear. "Those were different times," he said coldly. "And we . . . different beings." The leader of the Powers suddenly wanted to leave the room, to be away from the criminal responsible for so much misery, but he stayed, both revolted and mesmerized by the fallen angel and all he had come to embody.

"Call me crazy," the prisoner said conversationally as he gestured with his chin beyond the confines of his prison, "but even locked away in here I can feel that something is happening."

Verchiel found himself drawn toward the cage. "Go on."

"You know how it feels before a summer storm?" the prisoner asked. "How the air is charged with an energy that tells you something big is on the way? That's how it feels to me. That something really big is coming." The prisoner continued to pet the vermin's head, waiting for some kind of confirmation. "Well, what do you think, Verchiel?" he asked. "Is there a storm on the way?"

The angel could not help but boast. His plans were reaching fruition and he felt confident. "More deluge than storm," Verchiel responded as he turned his back upon the captive. "When the Nephilim—this Aaron Corbet—is finally put down, a time of change will be upon us." He strode to a haphazardly boarded window and peered through the cracks at the New England summer night with eyes that saw through darkness as if it were day.

"With the savior of their blasphemous prophecy dead, all of the unpunished criminals of the Great War, driven to despair by the realization that their Lord of Lords will *not* forgive them, will at last be hunted down and executed." Verchiel turned from the window to gaze at his prize. "That is what you are feeling in the air, Son of the Morning. The victory of the Powers—my victory."

The prisoner brought the mouse up to his mouth and gently laid a kiss upon its tiny pointed head. "If you say so, but it doesn't feel like that to me. Feels more special than that," he said. The mouse nuzzled his chin and the prisoner chuckled, amused by the tiny creature's show of affection.

Verchiel glided toward the cage, a cold smile forming on his colorless lips. "And what could be more special than the Nephilim dying at the hands of his sibling?" he asked the prisoner cruelly. "We have spared nothing in our pursuit to destroy him."

The prisoner shook his head disapprovingly. "You're going to use this kid's brother to kill him? That's cold, Verchiel— even for someone with my reputation."

The angel smiled, pleased by the twisted compliment. "The child was a defective, a burden to the world in which he was born—that is, until I transformed him, forged him into a weapon with only one purpose: to kill the Nephilim and every tainted ideal that he represents." He paused for dramatic effect, studying the expression of unease upon the captive's gaunt face. "Cold?" Verchiel asked. "Most assuredly, for to bring about the end of this conflict I must be the coldest one there is."

The mouse had defecated in the prisoner's hand and he casually wiped it upon his robe of heavy brown cloth. "What makes this Nephilim—this Aaron Corbet—any different from the thousands of others you've killed over the millennia?"

Verchiel recalled his battle with this supposed savior, the ancient angelic sigils that covered his flesh, his ebony wings, the savagery of his combat skills. "There is nothing special about this one," he sneered. "And those of the fallen who cling to the belief that he is the savior of prophecy must be shown this."

He remembered how they battled within the storm he himself had conjured, weapons of heavenly fire searing the very air. It was to be a killing blow; his sword of fire poised to sever the blasphemer's head from his body. And then, inexplicably, lightning struck at Verchiel, and he fell from the sky in flames. The burns on his body had yet to heal, the pain a constant reminder of the Nephilim, and how much was at stake. "With his death," Verchiel continued, "they will be shown that the prophecy is a lie, that there will be no forgiveness from the Creator."

The prisoner leaned his head of shaggy black hair against the iron bars of his prison as the mouse crawled freely in his lap. "Why does the idea of the prophecy threaten you so?" he asked. "After all this time, is absolution such a terrible thing?"

Verchiel felt his anger blaze. His mighty wings unfurled from his back, stirring the dust and stagnant air of the room. "It is an affront to God! Those who fought against the Lord of Lords should be punished for their crimes, not forgiven."

The prisoner closed his eyes. "But think of it, Verchiel: to have the past cleared away. Personally I think it would be pretty sweet." He opened his eyes and smiled a beatific smile that again reminded Verchiel of how it had been in Heaven—and how much had been lost to them all. "Who knows," the prisoner added, "it might even clear up that complexion of yours."

It was a notion that had crossed Verchiel's mind as well— that his lack of healing was a sign that the Creator was not pleased with his actions—but to have it suggested by one so vilified, so foul, was enough to test his sanity. The leader of the Powers surged toward the cage, grabbing the bars of iron.

"If I have incurred the wrath of my heavenly sire, it is for what I failed to do, rather than what I have done." Verchiel felt the power of his angelic glory course through his body, down his arms, and into his hands. "I did not succeed in kill-ing the Nephilim, but I have every intention of correcting that oversight."

The metal of the cage began to glow a fiery orange with the heat of heavenly fire, and the prisoner moved to its center. His robes and the soles of his sandals began to smolder. "I deserve this," he said, a steely resolve in his dark eyes. "But *he* doesn't." He held the mouse out toward Verchiel and moved to the bars that now glowed a yellowish white. He thrust his arm between the barriers, his sleeve immediately bursting into flame, and let the mouse fall to the floor where it scurried off to hide among the shadows.

"How touching," Verchiel said, continuing to feed his unearthly energies into the metal bars of the prison. "It fills me with hope to see one as wicked as you showing such concern for one of the Father's lowliest creatures."

"It's called compassion, Verchiel," the prisoner said though gritted teeth, his simple clothing ablaze. "A divine trait, and one that you are severely lacking."

"How dare you," Verchiel growled, shaking the bars of the cage that now burned with a white-hot radiance. "I am, if nothing else, a spark of all that is the Creator; an extension of His divinity upon the world."

The prisoner fell, his body burning, his blackening skin sending wisps of oily smoke into the air as he writhed upon the blistering hot floor of the cage. "But what if it's true, Verchiel?" he asked in an impossibly calm voice. "What if . . . it's all part of His plan?"

"Blasphemy!" the angel bellowed, his anger making the bars burn all the brighter—all the hotter. "Do you seriously think that the Creator can forgive those who tried to usurp His reign?"

"I've heard tell," the prisoner whispered through lips blistered and oozing, "that He does work in mysterious ways."

Verchiel was enjoying his captive's suffering. "And what if it *is* true, Morningstar? What if the prophecy is some grand scheme of amnesty composed by God? Do you actually believe that *you* would be forgiven?"

The prisoner had curled into a tight ball, the flesh of his body aflame, but still he answered. "If I were to believe in the prophecy . . . then it would be up to the Nephilim . . . wouldn't it?"

"Yes," Verchiel answered. "Yes, it would. And it will never be allowed to happen."

The prisoner lifted his head, any semblance of discernable features burned away. "Is that why I'm here?" he croaked in a dry whisper. "Is that why you've captured me . . . locked me away . . . so that I will never be given that chance?"

Verchiel sent a final burst of energy through the metal of the cage. The prisoner thrashed like a fish pulled from a stream and tossed cruelly upon the land. Then he grew very still, the intensity of his injuries sending him into the embrace of unconsciousness.

The Powers' leader released the bars and stepped back. He knew that his captive would live, it would take far more than he could conjure to destroy something so powerful, but the injuries would cause him to suffer, and that was acceptable for now.

Verchiel turned from the cage and walked toward the door. There was still much to be done; he had no more time to concern himself with prisoners of war.

"As does the Lord," he said to himself, "I too work in mysterious ways."

The power of Heaven, tainted by the poison of arrogance and insanity, flowed through his injured body, bringing with it the most debilitating pain—but also sweet oblivion.

The prisoner drifted in a cold sea of darkness and dreamed.

In his dreams he saw a boy, and somehow he knew that this was the Nephilim of prophecy. There was nothing special about the way he looked, or the way he carried himself, but the Powers captive knew that this was the One—this was Aaron Corbet. The boy was moving purposefully through a thicket of woods; and he wasn't alone. Deep within the womb of unconsciousness the prisoner smiled as he saw an angel walking at the boy's side.

*Camael,* he thought, remembering how he had long ago called the warrior "friend." But that was before the jealousy, before the war, before the fall.

And then he saw the dog; it had gone ahead into the woods, but now returned to tell its master what it had found. It was a beautiful animal, its fur the color of the purest sunshine. It loved its master, he could tell by the way it moved around the boy, the way it cocked its head as it communicated, the way its tail wagged.

It would be easy to like this boy, the prisoner guessed as the sharp pain of his injuries began to intrude upon his insensate state. He pulled himself deeper into the healing embrace of the void. *How could I not like someone who has caused Verchiel such distress?* the prisoner wondered. And besides, Aaron Corbet had a dog.

*I've always been a sucker for dogs.*

# CHAPTER TWO

Johiel was annoyed with Earth the moment he arrived over a millenium ago, but as the toe of his sneaker caught beneath an unearthed root, and he fell sprawling, face first, to the forest floor, the fallen angel felt his simple antipathy ripen to bitter hatred. He hit the ground hard, the air punched from his lungs in a wheezing grunt, and slid halfway down a small embankment before regaining enough of his composure to struggle to his feet. Yes, Johiel hated living upon the Earth. However, the alternative—far more permanent—was even less appealing.

He chanced a look behind him to see if they were still following. What a foolish thought. *They are soldiers of the Powers; of course they're still following.* The ground beneath his feet started to level off and in the distance he could hear the sounds of cars and trucks as they traveled along the highway. *I can make it to the road,* he thought, his mind abuzz. *Perhaps I can hitch a ride and escape.*

Stumbling through the darkness of the woods, Johiel chastised himself for his rabid stupidity. If he hadn't tried to make contact with the Powers, he would not be in this predicament. How could he have been so foolish as to think that they could be convinced to show even the slightest leniency toward their enemies, no matter what was offered? But he had grown so tired of living in fear; a constant cloud of oppression hanging over his head, never knowing which moment would be his last.

The sounds of the road were closer now and he began to think that they had grown tired of the pursuit. Perhaps they decided he just wasn't worth the effort, he thought, both relieved and a little insulted that the Powers wouldn't even attempt to learn the information he wanted to trade for his life. Johiel was certain that his knowledge would prove valuable to their leader, and he would have given it freely for a chance to live without fear.

The ground before him suddenly exploded in a roiling ball of fire, and Johiel was thrown backward to the cool, moist forest floor.

"Is it something we said, little fallen brother?" said a cold, cruel voice behind him.

"Or something we didn't say, perhaps?" asked another, equally malevolent.

Johiel scrambled to his feet and turned to see two

immaculately dressed and smiling angels strolling through the woods toward him. He knew he had three choices, two of which would likely end in his own excruciating demise: He could run and be cut down like a lowly animal; he could fight and perish just the same; or he could carry through with his original plan. The notion of engaging the two Powers in conversation was terrifying, but he held his ground and summoned a sword of fire to defend himself if it proved necessary.

The warriors stopped in unison, the sparking flame of Johiel's weapon reflecting off the inky blackness of their eyes.

"I do not understand, Bethmael," said one to the other. "The criminal put word out that he wished to speak with us, yet flees when we approach. And now he brandishes a weapon?"

Bethmael sneered. "It is the world, brother Kyriel," he said, continuing to stare at the fallen angel. "They know they do not belong here, and the knowledge drives them mad."

Their wings gracefully expanded from their backs, reminding Johiel of king cobras unfurling their hoods before they strike.

"I wanted to speak with a representative of the Powers," he built up the courage to say. "Someone who has Lord Verchiel's ear. But instead I am attacked and forced to flee for my life."

Kyriel's wings languidly flapped and a sword sprang to life in his hand, lighting the darkened wood like dawn. "And what could a criminal possibly have to say that might interest Lord Verchiel?"

"I have information," Johiel began, suddenly unsure. The idea of betraying those who had once welcomed him into their fold filled him with trepidation, but not enough to hold his tongue. "The location of the place that you have desperately sought, but still cannot find."

"You wish an exchange of some kind?" Bethmael asked.

His large hands remained free of weapons and Johiel watched him with cautious eyes. He did not trust the Powers, but this was his last chance to be free of the fear that had plagued him since the war. He would either be free, or he would be dead.

"An exchange for my life," he explained. "I will give you the location of the secret haven, and you will grant me freedom."

"You're asking for immunity from our righteous wrath?" Kyriel asked, lowering his own mighty sword of fire.

"For what I give you, the life of one fallen angel is a bargain," Johiel answered.

The two Powers looked at each other, a communication passing between their gazes. Kyriel again raised his weapon. "Our fallen brother attempts to barter for his life," he said to Bethmael, bemused. Bethmael nodded, a humorless smile appearing on his beatific features. "Protection in exchange for information."

They were both smiling now, and Johiel began to believe that his gambit had actually paid off. He wished his weapon away as a sign of good faith, but he could not help thinking again of those who would die so that he could live. *I'll learn to live with that,* he thought. "Your word is your bond," he said aloud to Bethmael and Kyriel. "Do we have a deal?"

They laughed, a shrill, high-pitched sound that conjured images of a bird of prey as it dropped from the sky upon its kill. Johiel should have seen this for the warning that it was.

"The Powers do not bargain with criminals," Bethmael said as a weapon—a longbow—formed in his grasp, and in a matter of seconds he let fly a shaft of fire. It hissed as it cut through the air, as if warning its target of the excruciating pain of its bite.

The arrow of fire plunged deep into the flesh of Johiel's shoulder, the momentum carrying him backward, pinning him to the body of an ancient oak. Frantically Johiel tried to free himself. He gripped the shaft and the night air was suddenly filled with the sickly sweet fragrance of burning flesh. He screamed pathetically as he pulled his blistered hand away. Through eyes tearing with pain, he watched the two angels stalk closer.

"It is our turn to make a bargain with you, fallen one," Bethmael said. His bow had already been replaced with a dagger of fire that he held menacingly before Johiel. "You will tell us your secrets, and then you will be killed mercifully."

Johiel struggled to pull his shoulder from the tree, but the pain was too great. "I . . . I'll tell you nothing," he said, voice trembling with fear and agony. The fire of the arrow was beginning to eat at the flesh of his shoulder, beginning to spread voraciously down his arm.

"I was so hoping you would say that," Kyriel said, a knife coming to life in his grasp as well.

Johiel didn't want to die—especially not painfully. Perhaps a taste of his secret knowledge would grant him a small respite. "I know where the fallen hide," he proclaimed as the burning blades moved toward his flesh.

Bethmael stopped and motioned for Kyriel to halt as well. "Go on," the angel urged. "Unburden yourself."

"I . . . I can take you there . . . right to their doorstep," he stammered.

"He's bluffing," Kyriel snapped, and again started forward with knife in hand.

"I could tell you where . . . , but you won't find it without my help," Johiel whined, writhing in pain as the heavenly fire of the arrow in his shoulder continued to feed upon his flesh. "It's hidden with magick . . . , but I can show you where it is."

"I grow tired of his games, brother," Kyriel said, eager to inflict more pain. "We'll cut the flesh from his traitorous bones and—"

"Silence, Kyriel," Bethmael ordered, a look forming in his black gaze that told Johiel the Powers' soldier had begun to understand the importance of what he knew. "What is this place of which you speak?" Bethmael asked with intense curiosity.

Johiel looked to the arrow protruding from his shoulder, and then back to Bethmael. "Remove the arrow, and I'll share all that I know," he said, sensing that he was suddenly worth more to them alive than dead.

"What is the name of the place of which you speak?" Bethmael asked again.

Johiel was about to tell him when a rustle of brush and the snapping of twigs distracted them all from the business at hand.

The yellow-furred dog was the first to come upon them. It stopped, cocked its head to one side, and stared with deep brown eyes showing far more intelligence than expected from the average canine. A boy was next, followed by a familiar angel. Johiel believed his name to be Camael, a great angel warrior and traitor to the Powers host.

*"Told you I could find them first,"* the yellow dog said to the boy.

"And now that we have?" the angel warrior inquired.

The boy's appearance began to change, and Johiel thought he heard the Powers gasp. Sigils, angelic sigils appeared upon the boy's flesh. It was then that Johiel realized this was much more than a mere boy.

"And now that we've found them," the boy repeated, his voice dropping to a rumbling growl, "we kick their asses until they tell us what we want to know."

"I urge caution," Camael said quietly, placing his hand on

Aaron's shoulder. "Enter into battle without prudence, and have no one but yourself to blame for an untimely death."

Camael eyed the scene before him. It was typical: two agents of the Powers preparing to dispatch yet another fallen angel for crimes against Heaven. How many had died by his own hands in service to the Powers and their sacred mission, before he realized that the dispensing of death was not the answer.

"All right," Aaron said, impatience in his tone. "I'm being cautious. I haven't attacked yet—but how long should I be cautious before I get to kick butt?"

The two Powers stepped away from their prey, spreading their wings and puffing out their broad warriors' chests. The knives they each held changed, growing in size to something more formidable, something far more deadly.

"Do my eyes deceive me, brother Kyriel?" asked one soldier to the other. "Or is that former commander Camael I see before me?"

Camael was familiar with both Kyriel and Bethmael. They had served him well in his time as leader of the Powers host. It saddened him now to see the glint of madness in their eyes.

"But how can that be, Bethmael?" Kyriel asked mockingly. "The great Camael left the ways of violence to ascend to a higher level of being. I hear tell that he has taken up sides with a savior of sorts, a divine creature with the ability to bend the ear of God."

"Do tell," said Bethmael in response. "Then I am sorely mistaken, for those who stand before us now are neither higher beings nor saviors of any kind."

Camael would have welcomed a chance to explain his change of heart, his altered philosophy clarified by the reading of an ancient prophecy that foretold the coming of a Nephilim. This spawn of angel and mortal woman would bring absolution to those that had fled Heaven after the war. But he knew, in the core of his being, that the soldiers of the Powers would not listen. They had been changed over the millennia, poisoned by their mission of murder under the leadership of Verchiel.

"So you know these two, huh?" Aaron asked, still obliging Camael's warning of caution.

"They once served beneath me," he answered, his gaze never leaving the angelic soldiers. He recalled that the two had been ferocious warriors, their dedication to the cause unwavering. They would be formidable opponents indeed.

Bethmael pointed his awesome sword of flame at them. "Let us show you how we deal with traitors and mongrels," he said, a goading smile on his aquiline features.

"Have you heard enough of their crap yet?" Aaron asked.

Camael brought forth a blade of his own and readied himself for battle. "I believe I have."

Aaron suddenly turned to face him, placing a sigil-covered hand upon his chest. "Let me do this," he said forcefully. The young man's eyes glinted wetly, like two black pearls in a sea of unbridled emotion. "I have to learn to control it, you've said so yourself."

He could not argue with the boy, for it was what he had been attempting to teach Aaron all along. The angelic nature of the Nephilim was often a dangerous and tempestuous force. The human animal was not meant to wield such power, and it often drove them insane. Camael tried to recall the number of Nephilim driven mad by the power of their own angelic nature that he had been forced to put down. There were far more than he cared to remember.

"Don't worry," Aaron said confidently. "I'll give a yell if I need a hand."

The boy turned away and flexed his shoulders. Powerful wings of shiny black feathers sprouted from his back, tearing through his T-shirt. In his hand a sword of orange flame appeared and he hurled himself at the angelic opponents with a cry of abandon.

The power that resided within this boy was different than any other Camael had borne witness to; there was an intensity to it, something that hinted at the potential for greatness—or something devastatingly destructive. It was this that set him apart from the others, that made Camael believe that Aaron Corbet was indeed the one foretold of in prophecy, the one who could unite all of the fallen angels with Heaven. *Perhaps even . . .* He cut that thought off before it could go any further.

Camael watched with a cautious eye as the Nephilim

touched down before the Powers warriors. "Let me show you how I deal with a coupla assholes," he heard the boy say, goading the angels to attack.

At first the teenager had been afraid of his talents, but now Aaron was using his new abilities more and more frequently. Camael hoped that he would soon see the unification of human and angelic in the boy—and not a gradual descent into madness. He wished this not only for the sake of the boy, but for all fallen angels hiding on Earth, hungry for reunification with God and the kingdom of Heaven.

Bethmael was first to attack, bringing his blade down in a blazing arc, crackling and sparking as it cut through the air. Aaron spread wide his ebony wings and pushed off from the ground, evading the weapon as it bit into the underbrush and set it aflame.

"Fast, but not fast enough," the Nephilim said, lashing out with his own sword of fire. The blade cut a burning gash across Bethmael's chest and the angel cried out in shock and dismay.

Eyes riveted to the scene unfolding before him, Camael suddenly felt Gabriel's presence by his side.

*"I'm afraid,"* the dog said.

"Not to worry," Camael replied reassuringly. "Aaron will be fine."

There was silence for a moment, but then the animal spoke again.

*"Right now I'm not afraid* for *him, Camael,"* the dog said

with a slight tremble to his usually guttural voice. *"I'm afraid of him."*

As he struck at his enemies and watched the surprise and fear spread across their faces, Aaron wondered again why he had ever been so afraid.

Bethmael and Kyriel stepped away from him, cautious now that he had drawn first blood. He could still hear Bethmael's blood sizzling on the blade of his weapon. It was a wonderful sound that made the power within him yowl with delight.

This angelic essence was indeed a thing to be feared, but it was part of him now, and there was nothing he could do to change that. At first he had believed that the best way to deal with it was to suppress it, to keep the alien nature that had been awakened on his eighteenth birthday locked up inside, but that proved to be nearly impossible. The power wanted to be free to fulfill its purpose, and to be perfectly honest, Aaron knew he really wasn't strong enough to deny it. Self-control had been something he'd fought to learn for years in foster care. But his first confrontation with Verchiel over the burning remains of the only people who had ever treated him like family quickly taught him that he would have to occasionally free these newfound powers to stay alive.

"What's the matter? Scared?" Aaron asked the angels, a nasty grin spreading across his face. He imagined how he must look to them, and a chill of excitement ran up and down his spine. He *wanted* them to be afraid—he *wanted* them to fear him. They were agents of Verchiel, and that was all he needed to know. They didn't seek unification and peace. Only the merciless slaughter of those they considered "beneath" themselves.

That was it. They came at him with cries that reminded him of a bird's wail: an eagle, or a hawk perhaps. Bethmael's fiery blade passed dangerously close.

"Verchiel shall have your head," he heard the angel hiss. He felt the heat of heavenly flame streak by his face as he bent himself backward to avoid its destructive touch. Then he drove his foot into the angel's stomach, kicking him away.

Kyriel, working in unison with his brother, thrust his blade of fire toward Aaron's midsection. Aaron brought his own weapon down, swatting Kyriel's lunge aside, and carried through slashing his sword across the warrior's face. The angel stumbled back with a cry of surprise, a hand clutched to his now smoldering features.

"Bet that's gonna scar," Aaron taunted, feeling the ancient energy that he'd fought so hard to squelch course through his body. At that moment he felt as though there was nothing he couldn't do.

"He . . . he cut me," Kyriel said, gazing at the blood that covered his hand.

There wasn't much of it, the flames of the heavenly blades cauterizing the wounds, but Aaron wondered how long it had been since the angel had last seen even a little of his own blood. The Powers' soldier looked to his brother for support, though he too had been stung by Aaron's blade.

"Then we shall cut him back," Bethmael growled, spreading his wings of golden brown and springing from the ground, sword of fire ready for a taste of Nephilim blood.

Rallied by his brother, Kyriel forgot his wound and dove at Aaron.

Aaron watched them descending upon him as if in slow motion, the crackling flames of their burning swords growing louder as they drew closer. He tried to move, but found he could not. The angelic essence had grown tired of this particular battle, and was ready to bring it to an end. Aaron gave in, letting the divine power wash over him like a wave.

They were almost upon him, their angel scent filling his nostrils. There was arrogance in their stench. Even though he had held his own against their master, Verchiel, they still believed themselves superior. These angels would suffer for their conceit.

Kyriel was the first to meet his fate. His wicked blade of fire fell—its purpose to cleave Aaron in two, but the Nephilim was not there to meet the weapon's bite. With surprising speed, he moved beneath the descent of Kyriel's sword and thrust his own burning blade into the soldier's ribcage, thinking to pierce the creature's black heart.

Aaron had no time to cherish the look of sheer surprise that bled across his attacker's face, for he had the other to deal with now. He turned just as Bethmael slashed a painful bite from his shoulder. But he ignored the wound, following through with his own swing. His blade passed through the thick tendrils of sinew, muscle, and bone and severed Bethmael's head from his body. Aaron watched with a perverse wonder as the angel's head spun slowly in the air before falling to the ground. The body followed, the stump where its head had once been still smoldering from the cut of his weapon.

Aaron was surprised by his feelings as he gazed down at the astonished expression, frozen upon Bethmael's dead face. There was no revulsion, no surprise. It simply felt right.

He was suddenly distracted by a moan from behind and turned to see that Kyriel was still alive. The angel knelt upon the grass, clutching at his chest, a black oily smoke drifting from his wound. He was burning from within and the expression on his face was one of unbridled pain. Aaron looked upon his attacker and he felt no pity—only a cold, efficient need to see the job done.

"Aaron," he heard Camael call from close by. He ignored his mentor and prepared to finish what he had started.

"Aaron, what are you doing?" Camael cautiously questioned as the Nephilim brought his sword of fire up, and then down upon Kyriel's skull, ending his life and bringing the battle to a close.

He felt Camael's hand fall roughly upon his shoulder,

spinning him around to face his mentor. There was a split second when the power inside told him to lift his blade against the angel, but he managed to suppress the urge as he slowly emerged from the red haze of combat.

Camael was looking at him, eyes wide with dismay, although Aaron wasn't altogether sure what he had done to garner such a reaction. "What's the matter?" he asked, feeling the sigils upon his body start to fade, the wings upon his back furl beneath the flesh.

Gabriel had joined the angel and was looking up at him with an equal expression of shock. *"You killed them, Aaron,"* the dog said, disappointment in his tone.

"I did at that," Aaron replied, a smile tugging at the corners of his mouth as he remembered the remarkable feeling of letting the power inside him take control. "Bet they didn't think I'd be able to—"

*"But how are they going to help us find Stevie?"* Gabriel asked, and Aaron felt the world give way beneath him. He hadn't even thought of his brother during the fury of battle.

"What have I done?" he whispered, refusing to look at the accusatory gazes of his friends. Aaron focused his stare on the smoldering bodies of those he had vanquished, the horror of what he had done in the throes of battle, and what he had carelessly forgotten just then beginning to sink in.

And the power inside him rested, satisfied.

Sated for now.

\* \* \*

The hot orange flames burned higher and fiercer as they fed upon the corpses of the Powers' soldiers. Aaron could not pull his gaze from the sight as the unnatural fire consumed them, any chance of them sharing information about Stevie's fate silenced in a moment of gratuitous violence.

"What's wrong with me, Camael?" he asked as he watched the bones of angels burn to powder. "I didn't even think of Stevie," he said sadly. "It was like he didn't even matter."

"The power that is inside you can be a selfish thing," the angel said coldly. "It cares only to satisfy its needs. It is a wild thing and must be tamed. There must be unity between the human and angelic, or there can be only chaos."

A skull popped like a gunshot as it collapsed in upon itself in an explosion of fiery embers.

"I thought that when the power awakened in me . . . and when I talked to it that . . ."

"That was only the beginning of a much longer and difficult process," Camael said as he brushed the flying ash of his brethren from the sleeve of his suit jacket. "Unification must occur or . . ."

The angel trailed off, and Aaron finally looked away from the burning remains of the creatures he had killed. "Or what?" he asked, not sure if he really wanted to know the answer.

Camael met his gaze with eyes as cold as an arctic breeze, and Aaron felt the hair at the nape of his neck stand on end. "Or it will make you insane, and I will be forced to destroy you."

Aaron found he couldn't breathe. As if he didn't have enough to concern him; now he had to worry about losing his mind and being killed by someone he'd grown to trust. The angelic nature inside him was awake again and it cared very little for Camael's words. It wanted to be free, to confront Camael's threat, but Aaron struggled to keep it in check, defying its need for violence.

"Do you think I'm going insane?" he asked the angel.

Camael said nothing, averting his gaze to the stars. Aaron was about to press the question when Gabriel began to bark.

"What is it?" He looked down at his dog, whose hackles had risen ominously upon his neck.

*"I think we've got more trouble,"* the dog growled menacingly, padding past them in a crouch.

Aaron and Camael turned to see two figures standing before the tree where the Powers' original prey had been pinned by an arrow of fire. In the mayhem of battle, they had forgotten about the fallen angel, and now it appeared as though he had some friends after all. There was a man, dressed as though he had just walked off the set of a spaghetti western: cowboy boots and hat, black denim and a long brown duster that flowed around him in a nonexistent breeze. The woman, in denim as well, but wearing a more contemporary style of dress, stood out in the darkness, for her long, flowing hair was the color of freshly fallen snow.

"Who are . . . ?" Aaron began as the cowboy reached out and began to pull the arrow from the fallen angel's shoulder.

"Fallen," Camael announced, his nose twitching as he sniffed the air. "And the girl is Nephilim."

The angel cried out in pain as he was released, falling to his knees at the edge of the clearing.

"Looks as though they've come to rescue their friend," Aaron said, and then stopped.

The fallen angel that had removed the burning arrow from the Powers' victim had flipped back his coat, and from somewhere on his person had produced a pistol that would have been right at home in the old West, but this one seemed to be made of gold. He stepped back, aimed at the kneeling angel, and unmercifully shot him once in the forehead.

"Oh, shit," Aaron whispered, watching as the angel slumped to the ground, dead.

"I don't think they are his friends," Camael voiced, the echo of the single gunshot gradually fading.

Gabriel immediately began to bark, and the two new-comers spun to face them.

"I'd quiet that animal," said the cowboy as he turned his aim toward them. He was tall, his weathered features lined with age, long gray hair streaming out from beneath his Stetson. "Wouldn't want to make me nervous and have my gun go off accidentally," he said with a snarl.

*"Who's he calling an animal?"* Gabriel asked, barking and lunging forward threateningly.

"Quiet, Gabriel," Aaron said, placing the tips of his fingers reassuringly on the dog's rump.

A sword of fire ignited beside him, and he glanced over to see that Camael was preparing himself, just in case. He felt his own inner essence exert itself, and the strange markings again seared the surface of his flesh. Reluctantly he let the power come.

"We want no trouble," Camael's voice boomed. He held his sword at the ready. "Allow us to go our way, and this will be the end of it."

The two were silent. The woman casually combed the fingers of one hand through her long white hair, and Aaron realized that she probably wasn't much older than himself.

"Were they Verchiel's?" she asked, pointing to the still-smoldering remains behind them.

"Yes," Aaron answered. His wings had emerged and he slowly unfurled them, giving the potential attackers a glimpse of what would be in store for them if they started any trouble.

"Imagine that." The angel with the pistol squinted at them. "The likes of you taking down two of Verchiel's soldiers."

"I think we should bring them in," said the woman coldly.

She was a Nephilim, and Aaron felt a certain kinship with her, but he didn't care for what he was hearing. *Bring us in? Like we're criminals, or specimens, or something.*

"We're not going anywhere," Camael warned. "This can end in one of two ways—and one is not at all in your favor."

The angel with the pistol chuckled. "Not in our favor," he said. "I like that." And then he looked to the woman. "Lorelei, take 'em down."

"Right you are, Lehash," she said, and spread her arms, a strange guttural language spilling from her mouth.

Aaron heard the words and immediately knew that things were about to turn ugly. She was casting some kind of spell, calling upon the elements. He tensed, a sword suddenly in his hand.

"Camael, we have to—"

The air roared, like the largest of jungle cats, and jagged claws of lightning dropped down from the sky upon them. There was a brilliant flash, and then everything was black.

Aaron didn't even have a chance to finish his sentence.

# CHAPTER THREE

**M**alak's arrival was heralded by a tremble of the very air. It shook years of accumulated dust and dirt from the heating pipes and ducts spreading across the ceiling of the dormant boiler room in the sub-basement of the Saint Athanasius Orphanage. And then there came a tearing sound as a rip in the fabric of space appeared in the room and grew steadily larger to allow the servant of the Powers access to his place of solitude.

The fearsome figure, clad in ornate armor the color of drying blood and carrying a dripping sack, forced his body through the laceration in the flesh of reality. The armor, forged in the fires of Heaven and bestowed upon him by the chieftain of the Powers host, allowed him this fantastic mode of transportation. In an instant he could follow a scent wherever it might take him.

As his feet hit the concrete floor of his dwelling, the hovering wound behind him revealed a place of frigid, howling winds, covered with ice and snow. Gradually it healed and soon was no more.

Malak sniffed the air, searching for signs that anyone other than he had been within his den. The scent was all his and the hunter relaxed. He placed the satchel on the floor and pulled the helmet from his head, setting it down atop a stack of magazines tied with twine. His scalp tingled as it was exposed to the air, and he raised a gloved hand to his head, running metal-encased fingers through his shaggy blond hair. *It's good to be home,* he thought, gazing about the dank, dark room. His eyes fell upon the familiar sites: the piles of wooden desks, stacks of moldering textbooks. There were rows of file cabinets, their once important information now meaningless, and an ancient boiler, squatting in the darkness, its system of pipes and ducts reaching overhead like the tentacles of some long-extinct primordial beast. This was his place, a respite where he could gather his strength and concentrate on the hunts to come.

*Home . . .*

Malak retrieved his bag from the floor and headed across the sub-basement. The bag was dripping and left a serpentine trail upon the stones. He passed a dust-covered globe of the world and cheerfully gave it a spin.

Bolted to the wall at the back of the boiler room were rows of shelves that had once held supplies for the upkeep of the church buildings, but now held items of a decidedly different nature. Malak struck a match from a box and lit the candles placed about the shelves. The hunter's smile broadened as the flickering light illuminated his treasures, prizes from his hunts. He admired the leathery ears he had cut from the heads of a tribe of fallen hiding in the jungles of South America, and the glass jars with the eyes of those who did not recognize the heavenly authority of the Powers on Earth. The tongues he had pulled from the mouths of those fallen that had spoken ill of his lord and master, and the countless, bloodstained feathers he had plucked from the wings of those cast out of Heaven—all of this filled him with a burgeoning pride. *So many hunts,* he mused, recalling the death strikes to each and every one of his hapless prey.

Malak stepped closer to the shelves and pushed aside the blackened skull of a fallen angel who foolishly believed that God was by his side as he fought. He then reached into his dripping sack and removed a pair of severed hands, placing them in the space he had just cleared. In his mind he heard the screams of the angel as the appendages were taken from him only a short time ago, and he smiled, the pitiful cries of torment sweet music to his ears. He stepped back and again admired his growing collection. *Feet,* he suddenly thought. *My collection could use a pair of feet.*

Another stronger scent wafted up from the saturated bag in his hand and Malak pulled it open to peer inside. He licked his lips, feeling his stomach churn and gurgle with hunger as he gazed upon the most delectable prize still within. Carefully he withdrew the last item from the sack, the source of the soaking fluids staining its bottom—a dripping angel's heart.

"I trust your latest undertaking was a success?" said a voice from behind him, and the hunter turned quickly to gaze lovingly upon his master.

Verchiel casually strolled toward him, hands clasped behind his back, and Malak dropped to his knees, bowing his head in reverence.

"I hope I have made you proud," the hunter said.

"I am certain you did," the angel said as he walked past his kneeling servant to approach the trophy shelf.

"I see that there are many more . . . items since last I checked," Verchiel said, his eyes studying the hunter's display.

"Every day I hunt," Malak replied. "Sometimes two or three of the criminals die at my hand. I like the trophies to remind me of the glory of the moment."

"You most certainly do," Verchiel clucked, turning away from the shelves to look upon him. "And the scent of the Nephilim? Have you found it again?"

Malak bowed his head again, not wanting to endure the look of disappointment in his master's eyes. Two weeks ago he had found the scent of the half-breed in the lair of the sea beast. There had been a great battle there, and the Nephilim had stained the rocks with his blood. But Malak soon lost the trail. The Nephilim and his companion were taking no chances, masking their travels with powerful magicks.

"I have not," Malak said sadly. "But it is only a matter of time before I pick up the trail again and track him down—to the ends of the world if necessary."

Verchiel chuckled. "I'm sure you will, faithful Malak, but do not fret." The angel smiled down on him and the hunter was bathed in its radiance. "Losing the scent of our enemy has provided you with an opportunity to hone your special skills." He gestured toward the shelves filled with Malak's trophies. "Think of these as steps to prepare yourself for the final confrontation with the Nephilim."

Malak raised his head proudly and met his master's dark eyes. "I am ready now," he proclaimed.

"Yes, I do believe you are." Verchiel motioned for him to rise. "But we must have patience. Soon enough it will be the heart of Aaron Corbet that you have in your hand." Verchiel gestured to the dripping heart the hunter still held.

The hunter raised the angel heart in a toast to his master. "This will be the Nephilim's heart," he said, bringing the bloody muscle to his mouth and taking an enormous bite.

Verchiel nodded knowingly. "Far sooner than you imagine."

Mr. Arslanian's voice had become nothing more than a buzzing drone inside Vilma's head as she nervously glanced at the tree outside the second-story window. She flinched, for a moment expecting to see a man perched upon one of the branches watching her. *I've got to stop this craziness,* she warned herself, trying to refocus on her history teacher's lecture. She really had no idea what the day's topic was, although she was certain it had something to do with the Civil War—for when *didn't* a class of Mr. Arslanian's?

Vilma's eyes burned and she was sure they were bloodshot and red, despite the drops she constantly put in them. She needed sleep so badly, just a few good hours, and then she was sure she'd be good as new. But with sleep came the dreams, and the visions of men perched in the trees outside her bedroom windows. Images from her nighttime terrors flashed through her mind: fearsome angels, clad in golden armor, destroying an ancient city; a girl, very much like herself, fleeing through the desert as the creatures of Heaven pursued her; those same winged creatures descending upon the girl, dragging her up into the sky, ripping her apart, tearing the flesh from her—

"Miss Santiago?" beckoned a voice, and her entire body convulsed, sending her history book tumbling to the floor. The other students snickered, and she felt the warm flush of embarrassment spread across her face and down her neck. Vilma quickly retrieved her book from the floor, glancing to the front of the classroom where Judy Flannagan, the guidance office aide, was standing next to her teacher.

"Mrs. Beamis would like to see you," he said, looking annoyed.

"I'm sorry," she stammered as she gathered up her belongings and followed Judy from the room.

"It's okay," he responded, watching her go. "Didn't mean to startle you."

That also got a bit of a laugh from the class, adding a fresh bloom to her embarrassment as she closed the door behind her.

Book bag slung over her shoulder Vilma walked the now empty halls of Kenneth Curtis High School toward the guidance offices, wondering why Mrs. Beamis would want to see her now. She thought about the scholarship applications she'd completed over the past few months. *A little good news wouldn't hurt today,* she decided as she opened the door to the office and stepped into the small reception area.

Mrs. Vistorino, the office secretary, was busily working at her computer, clad in one of her usual pantsuits, this one a delicate powder blue. "Be with you in just a sec, hon." She finished her typing before tearing her attention away from the monitor. "What can I do for you, dear?" she asked, plucking her glasses from her face and letting them dangle from a gold chain around her neck.

"Mrs. Beamis wanted to see me?" Vilma said shyly, nervous anticipation beginning to grab hold of her.

"What's your name?" Mrs. Vistorino asked as she reached for the telephone next to her and pressed a button. Judy Flannagan came into the office behind her and gave her a polite smile before retrieving a stack of folders from

Mrs. Vistorino's desk and going to a filing cabinet in the corner.

"Vilma Santiago," she answered, mesmerized by the simple act of the girl filing. *I need sleep—badly.*

"Vilma Santiago out here to see you," Mrs. Vistorino said into the receiver. There was a slight pause, and Vilma suddenly found herself praying for some kind of mistake. "Will do," the receptionist responded as she hung up the phone. "Go on in. Mrs. Beamis is waiting."

Vilma walked to the door and knocked gently on the wooden frame. The counselor called out for her to enter, greeting her with a warm, friendly smile and motioning Vilma toward a chair in front of her desk. "Come in, Vilma," she said. "I'm sorry to pull you from class, but there's something I'd like to discuss with you and I'm afraid it couldn't wait."

Vilma lowered herself into the chair, taking the book bag from her shoulder and placing it on the floor beside her. "Nothing bad I hope," she said nervously. The office smelled of peppermint and she noticed that Mrs. Beamis had a piece of white-and-red-striped candy swishing around in her mouth as she studied an open file—hers, she imagined.

"No, nothing bad," she said, flipping through a few pages. "We're just a bit concerned right now." She looked up to meet Vilma's eyes.

Vilma's heart began to race. "What . . . what are you concerned about?"

The guidance counselor closed the folder and picked up a pen from the cluttered surface of her desk. "Since you transferred into Ken Curtis you've been one of our finest students, Vilma. Your teachers enjoy having you in their classes, and they say you're an excellent example for the other students. You're bright, articulate, and friendly; if we had a thousand more like you in this school, our jobs would be much easier."

Vilma found that she was blushing again. "Then why—"

"It's just that when a student such as yourself begins to act out of the ordinary, teachers notice, even students," she explained.

Vilma felt her heart sink. She had hoped she was hiding her problems well. But evidently she was only fooling herself. It was having a far more noticeable effect on her than she'd thought.

"Is there anything you want to talk about?" Mrs. Beamis asked. "A problem here at school, or maybe even at home?"

The urge to confess rose in Vilma's throat. Maybe it would be for the best to talk about the dreams—about the bizarre things she thought she was seeing.

"We want to help you in any way we can, Vilma," the counselor continued. "There is no problem too big, you do understand that, don't you?"

She nodded as images of herself in a straitjacket flashed through her mind. Mrs. Beamis would think she was crazy— and what if she was? What would she do then? "I've been very nervous about graduation," she lied. "About going off to college . . . It's been keeping me awake at night."

Mrs. Beamis tapped the pen tip on the cover of her folder. The woman's gaze was intense, as if she could see right through Vilma's ruse. "It is a very nerve-racking time of your life," she said, continuing to stare. "I can see where it might affect you."

Vilma laughed nervously. "It's just that I know how much my life is going to change, and it scares me."

"Are you sure that's the only thing bothering you?" the counselor asked, moving forward in her chair.

Vilma slowly nodded as a creeping feeling of dread spread throughout her body. She thought of going to bed that night. She wanted to sleep so badly, but the dreams were so terrifying.

"No relationship issues?" Mrs. Beamis added. "We can talk about anything, Vilma. I can't stress that enough."

Vilma thought of Aaron Corbet. It had been more than a week since his last e-mail. His typed words—*I miss you, love, Aaron*—were like a knife blade to her chest. She had no idea where these feelings for a mysterious boy she barely knew had come from, but she found them almost as disturbing as her dreams.

"Nope." Vilma again shook her head. "No problems with boys."

She would have done just about anything to have Aaron back with her, for somehow she was certain that he could help with her problem. But that wasn't to be, and sometimes when she thought she would never see him again, it felt as though a part of her were dying.

"With everything I've had on my mind lately I really don't have the time for them."

The end-of-period bell started to ring and Vilma reached for her book bag leaning against the chair. "Is that all, Mrs. Beamis?" she asked, desperate to be out from beneath the microscope. "I've got a quiz in chemistry and I was hoping to review my—"

The guidance counselor picked up Vilma's file and placed it in a stack on the lefthand corner of her desk. "Yes, Vilma, I think we're finished here," she said with a caring smile.

Vilma returned the smile and stood. "Thanks for the talk and everything," she said, slinging the bag over her shoulder and turning to leave.

"Remember, no problem is too big," Mrs. Beamis called after her.

*If only that were true,* Vilma thought, waving good-bye to Mrs. Vistorino on her way to chemistry.

Deep down in the darkness, the power was angry.

As Aaron drifted in the void between oblivion and consciousness, he felt its indignation. He floated buoyantly within the ocean of black, the rage of the angelic charging the very atmosphere of the unconscious environment with its fearsome electricity, and then there came a tug and he was drawn upward toward awareness.

*"I think he's waking up,"* he heard a familiar voice say as a wet tongue lapped his face, acting as a slimy lifeline to pull him farther from the depths of oblivion. Aaron opened his eyes and gazed up into Gabriel's looming face.

*"There he is,"* the dog said happily. *"You've been out for quite some time. I was starting to get worried."*

Aaron reached up and scratched his canine friend behind one of his floppy, yellow ears. "Sorry about that, pal. Where's—"

"I'm here," Camael said from someplace nearby.

Aaron sat up and the world began to spin. "Damn," he said, touching a hand to his head. "Is everybody all right?"

*"I'm hungry,"* Gabriel reported.

"You're always hungry," Aaron answered curtly. "What did she hit us with? Lightning?"

He noticed that his wrists were bound, encircled with manacles of golden metal, strange symbols scratched into their surface and a length of thick chain between them. There was a band of the same metal around his throat as well. "What the hell are these?" he asked, looking around.

It appeared that they were in the finished basement of a residential home. The Ping-Pong table, covered in what looked to be a couple of inches of dust and crammed into the far corner of the room, was a dead giveaway.

"The restraints were made by someone well versed in angel

magick," Camael said from across the room. He was manacled as well and sitting stiffly in the center of a black beanbag chair. "The characters inscribed on them are powerful, imbuing the bonds with the capacity to render our abilities inert."

"No wonder my angel half is so ticked off," Aaron said, struggling to stand. "Is it common for fallen angels to keep prisoners in a rec room?" he asked. There was a mustiness in the air that hinted of dampness and decay. Dark patches of mildew grew on the cream-colored walls. There was also a strong smell of chemicals.

Gabriel plopped down in the warm patch where Aaron had been lying. The dog was famous for stealing space after it had been warmed up. He'd always hated having to get up during the night, only to return and find Gabriel curled up, pretending to be fast asleep in his spot.

"The fallen hide from their pursuers in all manner of places," Camael said, still awkwardly perched atop his beanbag chair. "Usually locales that have been lost to the world, hidden pockets forgotten or abandoned by the human thrall."

"Who are these guys, Camael?" he asked, walking toward carpeted steps that led up to a closed door. "They're not Powers, right?"

The angel warrior thought for a moment and then struggled to stand. It was the first time Aaron had seen Camael show anything but supreme agility and grace.

"Need a hand?" Aaron asked, moving toward the angel.

"I do not," Camael proclaimed, awkwardly rising to his feet. "These particular fallen could be from any number of the various clans that inhabit this world, perhaps a particular band that wishes to endear themselves to the Powers by handing us over to Verchiel," he said with a hint of foreboding.

*"That would be very bad,"* Gabriel said from the floor, his snout nestled between his paws.

Aaron looked to the dog, but was distracted by the sound of the door opening above. He spun to face his captors as they slowly descended the stairs.

"Step away from the stairs, half-breed," said a low, rumbling voice with the slightest hint of a drawl. "I'd hate to put a bullet of fire in your brain before we had a chance to get acquainted and all."

Aaron heard a woman laugh and guessed it was the one who had brought the lightning down upon them. *Lorelei,* he remembered. *And . . . Lehash?*

He moved back and watched as the two they had confronted in the woods stepped into the basement, and this time they had brought someone else with them. The cowboy had his golden gun drawn, and it glowed in the semigloom. Aaron thought the sight particularly strange; he would never have thought of an angel looking this way. Actually he would never have imagined any of the angels he'd seen since his life had so dramatically changed, but an angelic gunslinger was certainly something he'd never considered.

THOMAS E. SNIEGOSKI

Camael and Gabriel now stood with him before the mysterious trio. The other of the three, an angel like the cowboy, stepped toward them, meeting Aaron's gaze with an icy stare.

"Why have we been brought here?" Aaron asked, trying to stay civil.

The cowboy laughed, a toothpick moving from one side of his mouth to the other. "Tell 'em, Scholar."

"As designated constables, Lehash and Lorelei have taken it upon themselves to detain you so that we may determine whether you pose a threat to those citizens we have sworn to protect," the newest addition said rather formally.

He was dressed in a pristine white shirt and dark slacks and looked as though he should have been working in an accounting firm, instead of hanging with angels. *With guns,* Aaron reminded himself.

The cowboy angel, Lehash, plucked the toothpick from his mouth, his eyes upon them unwavering. "He does have a way with the words, don't he, Lorelei? If the citizens ever decide to elect a mayor, I'm gonna be the first to nominate Scholar here."

They both laughed, but the angel they called Scholar scowled.

"You keep talking about citizens," Aaron said, still desperate to know what was going on. "Citizens of what? Where are we?"

Scholar was about to speak when Lehash cut him off. "Little piece a Heaven here on this godforsaken ball of mud."

Lorelei nodded, smiling beautifully, and Aaron was struck by how attractive she really was. "Aerie," she said in the softest of whispers.

"Damn straight," Lehash said, placing the toothpick back in his mouth.

Aaron turned to Camael and saw an expression of shock register on the angel's face.

"After all this time," the angel warrior said, "I did not find it—it found me."

*Can it be true?*

Camael's mind raced. He gazed at the rather sordid surroundings, then back to his captors. He lurched toward them eagerly.

Lehash aimed his weapon, pulling back the hammer on the gun. "Not so fast there, chief," he growled.

Camael halted, his thoughts afire. He had to know more, he had to know if this was truly the oasis of peace for which he had been searching. "This is Aerie?" he asked breathlessly, a tiny part of him hoping that he had misunderstood.

"That's what we said," Lehash snarled, his aim unwavering. "Why? You've been looking for us?"

Camael nodded slowly, his sad gaze never leaving the three before him. Had Paradise also been tainted by the infection of violence? he wondered. Had he found what he most eagerly sought, only to see it in the throes of decay? "Far longer than any of you can possibly imagine."

"You were close," Scholar spoke up, his tone serious. "Most of your kind don't get this far. It's a good thing we caught you when we did."

"Our kind?" Aaron asked. "What's that supposed to mean?"

Lorelei shrugged, glaring at him defiantly. "Scholar was being nice. I would have called you what you really are—assassins, killers of dreams."

"They know what they are," Lehash said, the toothpick in his mouth sliding from one side to the other.

"You are mistaken," Camael said in an attempt to be the voice of reason. "The Powers soldiers that were slain attacked us. We were merely defending ourselves."

"Were you merely defending yourselves against the others as well?" Scholar asked.

Camael shook his head. "I don't understand—"

"*You* killed one of your own," Aaron blurted out, cutting him off. All eyes turned to the boy. "I watched you put a bullet in that guy's head back in the woods, and you're calling *us* assassins?" he asked incredulously. "You've got some nerve."

Camael sighed. It was sad that someone with as much power as Aaron was so lacking in diplomatic skills.

"That one wasn't much better than you," the girl said, a sneer upon her face.

"Was looking to sell the location of Aerie to whoever would give him the best deal," Lehash added.

"But you're probably aware of that already," Scholar finished.

Camael analyzed the situation. The beings before them believed that they were killers, probably working for Verchiel, and had come to destroy Aerie. He attempted to formulate a solution, but realized that the only way to convince the three that they meant no harm would be to explain about Aaron and his connection to the prophecy, although he seriously doubted they would even begin to believe that the boy—

*"Aaron is the One in the prophecy,"* he heard Gabriel suddenly say. The dog had strolled away from them and now sat patiently before their captors.

"Gabriel, get back here," Aaron commanded.

Lorelei squatted down in front of the dog meeting him eye to eye. She reached out and rubbed one of his ears. "Is that what you think?" she asked affectionately. "You must think your master is pretty special."

"Gabriel, come," the boy called to the Lab, but he did not respond.

*"I'm not the only one,"* he explained. *"Camael thinks so, and so does Verchiel. Do you have anything to eat? I'm hungry."*

Lorelei rose slowly, eyeing Aaron as she did. "Is that what you think?" she asked, loathing in her voice.

Camael was silent, as was Aaron.

"Looks like we've got ourselves a celebrity," Lehash said with a grin that was absent of any humor whatsoever. "I say we finish this here and now before any more bull is slung." He drew another pistol of gold and aimed them both.

"No!" blurted out Scholar, as he reached over to push the weapons down. "We take them to the Founder and let him decide."

Gabriel turned to look at Aaron and Camael, his tail thumping happily on the concrete floor.

*"We're going to see the Founder,"* he said. *"Maybe he'll have something for us to eat."*

# CHAPTER FOUR

B elphegor pushed a wheelbarrow of dirt across the yard toward a row of blossoming rose bushes. A succession of summer rains had eroded some of the dirt at their base and he was eager to replace it before any of the plants' more delicate regions were exposed to the elements.

He set the barrow down, careful not to tip its contents, and picked up the shovel that was lying beside a rake in the sparse, brown grass. Belphegor plunged the shovel into the center of the mound of dirt and carried it to the rosebushes, where he ladled it onto the ground beneath them. The wheelbarrow was nearly empty of its load before he felt that the bushes were properly protected.

The angel leaned upon his shovel and studied his work. The chemical pollutants that laced the rich, dark soil wafted up into the air, invisible to the human eye. With an angel's vision, however, Belphegor watched the poisonous particles drift heavily upon the summer breeze before settling back down to the tainted ground.

He squatted, digging his fingers into the newly shoveled dirt, and withdrew the contaminants, taking them into his own body. Belphegor shuddered and began to cough. There had been a time when purifying a stretch of land four times this area would have been nothing more than a trifle. But now, after so many years upon Earth and so much poison, it was beginning to have its effects upon him.

*Is it worth it?* he wondered, stepping back to admire the beauty he had helped create from the corrupted ground, beautiful red buds opening to the warmth of the sun. In his mind he pictured other gardens he had sown and knew that there was no question.

Belphegor picked up the metal rake and began to spread the new soil evenly about the base of the roses. In these gardens, left untended, he saw a reflection of himself and those who had chosen to join his community. Outcasts, each and every one, tainted in some way, desperately wanting to grow toward the sun—toward Heaven—but hindered by the poison that impaired them all.

He tried to force the sudden images away, but they had been with him for countless millennia and would likely remain with him for countless more. He remembered the poison that drove him from the kingdom of God to the world of man—

the poison of indecision. The angel saw the war as if for the first time, no detail forgotten or fuzzy with the passage of time. His brethren locked in furious combat as he watched, lacking the courage within himself to take a side.

Belphegor stopped raking, forcing aside the painful remembrances to concentrate on the beauty he had helped to set free. Someday he hoped that he and all of Aerie's citizens would be as these roses: forgiven through penance and the fulfillment of an ancient prophecy, rising up out of the poisonous earth, reaching for the radiance of Heaven.

The sounds of voices, carried by the breeze, intruded on his thoughts, and reluctantly he turned from his roses to meet his visitors. He walked through the expanse of yard, and around to the front of the abandoned dwelling, its windows boarded up and covered with spray-painted graffiti. It had once been the home of a family of six, with hopes and dreams very much like many of the other families that had lived within the Ravenschild housing development. Belphegor could still feel their sadness radiating from the structures in the desolate neighborhood, the echoes of life silenced by a corporation's greedy little secret. The ChemCord chemical company had buried its waste here, poisoning the land and those who lived in homes built upon it. It was a sad place, this Ravenschild housing development, but it was now *their* home, the latest Aerie for those who awaited forgiveness.

Belphegor glanced down the sidewalk to see his constables

approaching with two others—and a dog. *These must be the ones suspected of murder,* he thought, recalling the sudden, violent increase in deaths of fallen angels scattered about the world. He would question these strangers, but he had already decided their fate. Earth was a dangerous place for the likes of the fallen, and he would do anything to keep his people and their community safe. With that in mind, he steeled himself to pass judgment, studying the captives as they approached.

Belphegor gasped as he suddenly realized that one of the strangers was not that at all. He knew the angel that walked with the boy. They had been friends once, before the war, before his own fall from grace.

"Camael," Belphegor whispered, his thoughts drifting to the last time he had seen his heavenly brother. "Have you finally come to finish what you failed to do so very long ago?"

## THE GARDEN OF EDEN,
## SOON AFTER THE GREAT WAR

Camael drew back his arm and brought down his sword of fire with the same devastating results as during the heavenly conflict. The impossibly thick wall of vegetation that had grown between the gates of Paradise was no match for his blazing weapon, the seemingly impenetrable barrier of tangled plant life parting with the descent of his lethal blade. It had not been long since the eviction of humans from the Garden, yet already the once perfect habitat for God's newest creations was falling prey to ruin.

Animals from every genus fled before him, sensing the murderous purpose that had brought him to this place. The war had finally been won by the armies of the Lord and the defeated—the legions of the Morningstar—had been driven from Heaven. As leader of the Powers host, it had fallen to him to track and destroy those who opposed the Almighty and brought the blight of war to the most sacred of places.

Camael had come to the Garden in search of one such criminal, one that had once served the glory of the Creator as devoutly as he—but that had been before the war, and things were no longer as they once were. Belphegor would pay for his crimes, as would all who took up arms against the Lord of Lords.

Camael stopped before another obstruction of root, tree, and vine, and with his patience on the wane, slashed out with his fiery blade, venting some of the rage that had been his constant companion since the war began. His fury poured forth in torrents as his sword cut a swath of flaming devastation through the Garden of Paradise, his roar of indignation mixing with the cries of panicked animals.

*How could they have done this to the Lord God—the Creator of all there is?* His thoughts raged as he lashed out at the thick vegetation, the vestiges of battles he had so recently fought still raw and bleeding upon his mind. His anger spent, Paradise burned around him and the barriers of growth fell away to smoldering ash. Camael beheld a clearing, void of life except for a single tree—and the one he was searching for.

Belphegor stood before what could only have been the Tree of Knowledge—large with golden bark, and carrying sparsely among its canopy of yellow leaves, a forbidden fruit that shone like a newly born star in the night sky.

"Belphegor," Camael said, stepping through the burning brush and into the clearing. In his hand he still clutched his weapon of fire, and it sparked and licked at the air, eager to be used.

Hand pressed to the tree's body, the angel Belphegor turned to glance at him and smiled sadly. "It's dying," he said, returning his attention to the tree. "And it will be only a matter of time before what is killing it spreads to the remainder of the Garden."

Camael stopped and glared at his fallen brethren. His anger, though abated by the destructive tantrum, still thrummed inside.

"It's His disappointment," Belphegor said, again looking at Camael. "The Creator's disappointment in the man and woman—it's acting as a poison, gradually killing everything that He made especially for them. I'm doing my best to slow the process, but I'm afraid it's only a matter of time before it is all lost."

Camael gripped his sword tighter and spoke the words that had been trapped in his throat. They spilled from his mouth, reeking of anger and despair. "I've come to kill you, Belphegor." He wasn't sure how he expected the fallen angel to react—perhaps to cower with fear, or suddenly flee deeper into the Garden—but it appeared that Belphegor had already accepted his lot.

"I'm glad it's you who has come for me," he said casually, moving away from the tree toward Camael.

Camael pointed his sword, halting the angelic fugitive's progress.

Belphegor stared at him over the sputtering blade of fire. "If it is time for me to die, then I accept my fate."

The Powers' commander seethed. *How dare such a sinner surrender without a fight. How dare he deny me the wrath of battle.* "You will summon a weapon and fight me," he snarled.

Belphegor slowly shook his head. "I did not fight in the war and I will not fight you, my friend," he said sadly. "If you are to take my life, do it now, for I am ready."

Camael wanted to strike the angel down, lift his fearsome blade above his head and cleave the traitor in two, but something stayed his hand—the question that had plagued his tortured thoughts since the war began. "Why, Belphegor?" he asked, his body trembling with repressed anger.

The fallen angel sighed and sat down in the shade of the Tree of Knowledge. Camael loomed above him, his blade of fire poised for attack.

"I did not want to fight," Belphegor said, picking up a

dry stalk of grass and twirling it between his fingers. "For either side."

"He is your Creator, Belphegor," Camael spat. "How could you not fight for Him?"

The fallen angel turned his gaze up to Camael and the look upon his face was one of resignation. "I could not even begin to think of raising a weapon against my brothers—or my Creator. If that makes me an enemy of Heaven, so be it."

"It makes you a coward," Camael said, tightening his grip upon his weapon's hilt.

"Is that really how you feel, Camael?" Belphegor asked without a hint of fear. "Have you come for me not because of what *I* did not do—but for what *you* did not have the courage to do yourself?"

The words were like a savage attack, weapons of truth hacking away at Camael to reveal the painful reality. There had been so much death, and he could see no end to it.

Camael swung his blade and buried it mere inches from Belphegor. The ground around the weapon began to burn.

"Damn you," he hissed, pulling the sword from the smoldering earth and stepping back, his steely stare still upon his foe. In his mind's eye he saw them, the faces of all he had slain in the battle for Heaven, a seemingly endless parade of death marching through his memories, and it chilled him to his core. Once they had been like him, serving the one true God—and then came dissension, sides were chosen and a war begun.

"You must be made to answer for your crimes," he said as Belphegor rose to his feet.

"Haven't we been punished enough?" the fallen angel asked. "Rejected, forced to abandon all we have ever known to live amongst animals—most, I think, already suffer a fate far worse than what awaits at your hands." Belphegor moved closer. "Death at your hands might even be considered an act of mercy."

Camael placed the tip of his sword beneath Belphegor's throat and the flesh there bubbled and burned—yet despite this, the fallen angel did not pull away.

"We were brothers once," Camael whispered, staring at Belphegor's face twisted in pain. "But no more," he said as he pulled the blade away. "It will be as if you were destroyed by my hand."

Belphegor gingerly touched the charred and oozing flesh beneath his chin. "Will this mercy be bestowed upon the others as well?" he asked, his voice a gentle whisper.

Camael turned and prepared to leave Eden.

"How many more will have to die?" Belphegor called after him as Camael reached the edge of the clearing. "When will it be enough, Camael?" the fallen angel asked. "And when will we finally be allowed to show our sorrow for what we have done?"

Camael left the Garden of Eden, never to look upon it again, Belphegor's questions reverberating through his mind.

He did not respond to his fallen brother, for he did not have the answers, and he had begun to wonder if ever he truly would.

## AERIE, PRESENT DAY

The sight of Belphegor stirred memories Camael had not experienced for millennia. Pictures of the past billowed and whirled, like desert sands agitated by the winds of storm. The angel warrior quickly suppressed them.

"Hello, Camael," Belphegor said, standing on the sidewalk in front of a boarded-up home. "It's been quite some time."

Camael looked closely at the fallen angel before him; he appeared old, almost sickly. It was common for angels that had fled to Earth to allow themselves to age, to fit in with their new environment, but Belphegor's look was more than that.

"I executed you," Camael said, remembering the day he had stormed from the Garden of Eden without completing his assignment.

"Is that what you told your Powers' comrades—did you actually tell them that I died at your hand?"

Camael recalled addressing his troops before their journey to Earth. He remembered telling them, the lie already beginning to eat at him, the doubts about their mission, seeded by Belphegor, already starting to sprout. "I was their leader, they would believe anything I told them."

"And now?" Belphegor asked.

"Now they would like to see me as dead as they believe you to be."

The old angel studied Camael's face, obviously searching for signs of untruth. "I had heard that you left them, but was still saddened that it took as long as it did."

"It was when I read the words of the prophecy that I realized it wasn't the way," Camael answered. "There had already been too much death. I began to believe that a new future for our kind rests in the hands of a half-breed—a Nephilim, chosen by God."

Camael looked at Aaron, who shifted his feet nervously at the attention now placed upon him.

"That would be me, I guess," he said.

The constables, who had been silent until that point, chuckled at the idea of this Nephilim boy being the Chosen One, but Camael waited to see how Belphegor would respond.

"You believe this one to be the Chosen?" he asked, pointing at Aaron with a long gnarled finger.

Camael noticed the dirt beneath his nails. "Yes, I believe it is so," he answered.

"Have you ever heard anything so foolish, Belphegor?" Lehash asked, scratching the side of his grizzled face with the golden barrel of his gun. "Next they'll be telling us that they ain't had nothin' to do with the rash a' killin's this last week."

Silently Belphegor moved closer to Aaron. "Are you?" he asked as he began to sniff him from head to toe.

"I have no idea what they're talking about," Aaron explained. "We tried to tell them that before, but—"

"There's quite a bit of violence locked up inside you," Belphegor said, stepping back and wiping his nose with a finger. "Powerful stuff, wild—wouldn't take much, I imagine, to set you on a killing spree."

Camael stepped forward to defend the boy. "Aaron has accomplished much since the angelic nature has awakened. I've seen him use his power, on more than one occasion, to send a fallen angel home."

Belphegor tilted his head to one side. "Home?" he questioned, deep crow's feet forming at the corners of his squinting eyes. "What do you mean?"

Camael nodded slowly, allowing the meaning of his words to sink in. *"Home,"* he said, still nodding. "He sent them home to Heaven."

Lehash began to laugh uproariously, looking to his fellow constables to join him. They smiled uneasily. Camael scowled, he did not care to have his motivations questioned and would have given everything to be free of the magickally augmented manacles.

The constable strode forward, puffing out his chest. "Go ahead, boy," he said, holding his arms out. "I'm ready. Send me home to God."

"It . . . it doesn't work that way," Aaron stammered. "I just can't do it—something inside tells me when it's time."

Lehash laughed again, as if he'd never heard anything as funny, and Camael seethed.

"Silence, Lehash," Belphegor ordered again, scrutinizing Aaron. "Is that true, boy?" he asked. "Have you sent fallen angels back to Heaven?"

Gabriel, who had been unusually quiet, suddenly padded toward Belphegor. *"I saw him do it,"* the dog said in all earnest. *"And he made me better after I was hurt. Do you have anything to eat? I'm very hungry."*

Belphegor studied the animal, whose tail wagged eagerly. "This animal has been altered," he said, looking first to Camael, and then to Aaron. "Who would do such a thing?"

"He was hurt very badly," Aaron explained. "I . . . I didn't even know what I was doing. I talked to the thing living inside me. . . . I begged it to save Gabriel and—"

Belphegor raised a hand to silence Aaron. "I've heard enough," he said. "The idea of such power in the hands of someone like you chills me to the bone."

"What should we do with them?" Lehash asked. There was a cruel look in his eyes, and Camael was convinced that he would do whatever Belphegor told him, no matter how dire.

"Take them back to the house," the old angel said, turning toward the fenced yard he had come from. "I need time to think."

"Listen to me, Belphegor," Camael again tried to explain. "No matter how wrong it may seem to you, Aaron *is* the one you've been waiting for. Even the Archangel Gabriel believed it to be so. You have to trust me on this."

The fallen angel returned his attention to Camael. "God's most holy messenger is not here to vouch for him, and I'm afraid trust is in very short supply here these days," Belphegor said sadly. "There's far too much at stake. I'm sorry." He looked to his people. "Take them back to the house, and be sure to keep the restraints on them."

Lehash grabbed hold of Aaron, but the boy fought against him.

"Listen," he cried out, and Belphegor stopped to stare at the Nephilim. "I'm trying to find my little brother—he's the only real family I have left."

Belphegor looked away, seemingly uninterested in the boy's plight.

"Please!" he yelled. "Verchiel has him and I have to get him back. Let us go, and we'll leave you alone, we promise."

The old fallen angel ignored the boy, continuing on his way. Lehash again gripped him by the arm and pulled. "C'mon, boy. He don't want to hear any more of your nonsense."

"Goddam it!" Aaron shouted. "If you're not going to listen, I'll *make* you listen!"

And then he did something he should not have been able to do with the magickal restraints in place.

Aaron Corbet began to change.

# CHAPTER FIVE

Aaron knew that time was of the essence and felt his patience stretched to its limits. The fallen angels, these citizens of Aerie, weren't listening to him. He didn't have time to be locked away in the playroom of some abandoned house. The Powers had Stevie, and the thought of his little brother still in the clutches of the murderous Verchiel acted like a key to unleash the power within him. Before he realized what he was doing, anger and guilt had unlocked the cage door, inviting the wild thing out to play. Aaron felt his transformation begin, and this time it hurt more than anything he could remember.

He turned to glare at Lehash, who still held his arm. "Let go of me," he snarled, and felt a certain amount of satisfaction when the fallen angel did as he was told.

The pain was incredible, and Aaron could only guess it

was because of the magickal restraints he still wore on his wrists and around his neck. He could feel the sigils burning upward from beneath his skin to decorate his flesh. They felt like small rodents with sharp, nasty claws, frantically digging to the surface. He screamed as sparks jumped from the golden manacles. The power within him wasn't about to back down, even if it killed him.

He found Belphegor's wide-eyed stare and held it with eyes as black as night. "Look at me!" Aaron cried. "Can't you see that we're telling the truth?"

He lurched toward the ancient fallen angel, crackling arcs of supernatural energy streaming from the enchanted restraints. From behind him he heard Camael and Gabriel call out for him to stop—but he couldn't. He had to make Belphegor realize that they meant the people of Aerie no harm.

The constables were beside him. Lehash was aiming his guns, pulling back the golden hammers, while Lorelei had raised her hands and was mumbling something that sounded incredibly old. The one called Scholar stood at Belphegor's side, ready to defend the wizened fallen angel if necessary.

"Give me the word, boss," Lehash sneered, "and I'll drop him where he stands."

"No!" Belphegor ordered, raising his hand.

The sigils had finally burned their way to the surface of Aaron's flesh, but there was no relief from the pain. His wings of ebony black had begun to expand on his back, but were hindered by the magick within the sparking bonds. The pain was just too much, and he fell to his knees upon the desiccated lawn in front of the abandoned home. "You've got to listen," he moaned.

"Could just any Nephilim override the magicks of the manacles, Belphegor?" he heard Camael ask above the roar of anguish deafening his ears.

"He is powerful, I'll grant him that," Belphegor replied. "But I've met powerful halflings in my time, and that doesn't make them prophets. Matter of fact, most are dead now, driven insane by power they couldn't begin to understand, never mind tame."

"And the markings?" Camael asked. "What do you make of them?"

Aaron opened his eyes to see the leader of Aerie kneeling beside him with Scholar. "I want to know what they mean," Belphegor said, gesturing to the archaic symbols decorating the Nephilim's face and arms. Scholar removed a pad of paper and pen from his back pocket and began to copy them.

"Do you believe me now?" Aaron asked weakly, exhausted from the battle between the angelic force and the magick within the golden restraints.

Belphegor stared at him with eyes ancient and inhuman, and he felt like some kind of new germ beneath a scientist's microscope. "The question is, boy, do *you* believe that you are the Chosen?" Belphegor asked.

Aaron wanted to tell him what he wanted to hear, what would allow them their freedom, but he couldn't. Although Camael and even the Archangel Gabriel believed he was the savior, the truth was, Aaron still saw himself as just a kid from Lynn, Massachusetts. Certainly he couldn't deny his power, but did that make him the Chosen One?

*I just don't know.*

"I . . . I'm not sure," he told Belphegor, and felt the power begin to recede.

The old angel smiled and rose to his feet.

"Should we take them back to the house?" Lorelei asked. She had moved up behind the older angel, and Aaron noticed that her fingertips still crackled with the residual of her unused spell.

"I don't think that will be necessary," Belphegor replied. "Let them have the run of the place, but the manacles stay on until I'm sure they can be trusted."

"Are you out of your mind, old man?" Lehash asked. The others looked uncomfortable with his outburst. "With so much going on out there, you're gonna give them free reign? They'll be murderin' us in our sleep before—"

"You heard me, Lehash," Belphegor said as he turned his back and strode through the yard. "Welcome to Aerie, folks," he said, and disappeared around the corner of the abandoned house.

\* \* \*

The prisoner's eyes opened with a sound very much like late fall leaves crackling underfoot, head bent and gazing down upon hands charred and blackened. He was sitting up against the bars of his cage, his entire body enveloped in a cocoon of sheer agony. His fingers slowly straightened, and through scorched and bleary eyes, he watched as flakes of burnt flesh rained on his lap.

He wasn't positive when Verchiel had left, but he was glad to see the Powers' leader gone, for as bored as he was, imprisoned within the cage, he did not care for the angel's company in the least. *High maintenance, that one,* he thought, shifting his position in an attempt to get comfortable and accomplishing nothing more than additional waves of excruciating pain. *Very temperamental.*

The smell of overcooked meat wafted about the inside of the cage and the prisoner was reminded of a feast he had attended in a Serbian village not long before taking up residence in the Crna Reka Monastery. They had been celebrating the birth of a child, and had cooked a pig on a spit over a roaring fire. They had welcomed him to their celebration; a total stranger invited to partake of their happiness. So he did, and for a brief moment was able to forget all that he was, and the horrors for which he was responsible. Moments like that were few and far between in his interminable existence, and he held onto each like the most precious of jewels.

From the corner of his eye he spied movement, a tiny, dark

shape scurrying along the wall toward the hanging cage. His friend the mouse had returned. The prisoner leaned back to see outside the cage, and some skin from his neck sloughed off between the bars to sprinkle the floor like black confetti. The air felt cool against his exposed flesh. He was healing, despite the hindering magicks in the metal of the cage.

"Hello," he croaked, his voice little more than a dry whisper.

The mouse responded with a succession of tiny squeaks.

"I'm fine," the prisoner answered. He leaned over until he was lying on his side and extended a blackened arm through the bars of the cage. The mouse began to squeak again, and he was touched by the tiny creature's concern.

"Don't worry about me," he told the mouse. "Pain and I have a very unique relationship."

The animal then sprung from the floor to land on the prisoner's upturned hand and scrambled up the length of his arm into the cage.

"That's it," he cooed, still lying on his side, the mouse squatting before his face, nose, and whiskers twitching curiously.

"I'll be fine, little one. A bit more time and I'll be good as new."

The mouse squeaked once and then again, tilting its head as it studied his condition.

"Yes, it hurts a great deal. But that's all part of the game. It's not as if I don't deserve every teeth-gritting twitch of pain."

The mouse squeaked, moving closer to his face. It nuzzled affectionately against the burned skin on his nose, gently rubbing it away to expose new flesh, pink and raw.

"No," the prisoner said. "You just *think* I'm a good man; you didn't know me before."

Memories of times he'd rather have forgotten danced past the theater of his mind, and the prisoner struggled to right himself. His furry companion dug its claws into his shoulder and held on as he braced himself against the bars of the cage.

"What kind of man was I before? Do you really want to know?" he asked with a dry chuckle. The mouse began to clean itself, comfortably perched upon the prisoner's shoulder.

"That's a good idea," he told his friend. "You're going to feel pretty dirty when I'm done."

The pain was no worse, and neither was it better, but this was old hat for him. He was a pro when it came to pain. It was always with him, whether his flesh was burned and blackened or he was sleeping peacefully on a woven mat in a Serbian monastery. It was his punishment, and he deserved it.

"You've got to promise that once you hear my story, you won't leave me for some other fallen angel."

The mouse gave him an encouraging squeak, and the prisoner's breath rattled in his seared, fluid-filled lungs as he took a deep breath.

"It all started in Heaven," he began, and the depth of his sorrow streamed from his mouth like blood from a mortal wound.

* * *

"So, where are all these citizens you guys keep talking about?" Aaron asked as they walked down the cracked and uneven sidewalk past one lifeless house after another.

"They're around," Lorelei answered with a flip of her snow-white locks. "After the business with that Johiel creep, I don't think they're too eager to roll out the red carpet for anybody new. I can't believe he was going to sell us out just to save his own butt." She shook her head in disgust as she crossed the street at a crosswalk. "Can't trust anyone these days," she said with a warning glance over her shoulder.

"How long has it been here?" Camael asked, scrutinizing the neighborhood with eyes more perceptive than a hawk's.

"What?" the girl asked. "Aerie? I've been here six years, and this is the only place I've ever known. Although I hear it's been in lots of different places: on the side of an active volcano, in an abandoned coal mine . . . one of the old-timers said he lived inside a sunken cruise ship at the bottom of the Atlantic Ocean. Aerie seems to be wherever the citizens are."

Camael nodded slowly. "That is why it was so difficult to find," he said, his eyes still taking it all in. "It does not stay in one location."

Gabriel was sniffing around the weatherbeaten front steps of one of the abandoned homes; he sounded like the clicks of a Geiger counter searching for radiation. On a house in front of them, a large piece of plywood had been nailed across the entryway where the front door should have been. Crudely spray-painted on the wood were the words MY FAMILY DIED FOR LIVING HERE.

"What happened here?" Aaron asked, the message affecting him far more than he would have imagined. It was as if he could feel the grief streaming from each of the painted words as thoughts of his foster parents, their horrible demise, and his own home destroyed by flames flashed through his mind.

Lorelei stopped and looked at the house with him. "During the 1940s and 1950s this property was owned by ChemCord. They were producers of industrial pesticides, acids, organic solvents, and whatnot, and they used to dump their waste here." She pointed to the street beneath her feet.

*"The place stinks, Aaron,"* Gabriel said as he relieved himself on the withered, brown remains of a bush in front of the house. *"The dirt smells bad—like poison."*

"And that's helping?" he asked the dog.

*"Can't hurt it,"* Gabriel responded haughtily, and continued his exploration.

"He's right, really," Lorelei said. "They dumped excess chemicals and by-products in metal drums that they buried all over this property; tons and tons of the stuff."

They continued to walk, each home taking on new meaning for Aaron. "Then how could they build houses—an entire neighborhood—here?" he asked.

"ChemCord went belly up in 1975 and they began to sell

off their assets—including undeveloped land. As far as the guys at ChemCord were concerned, the property was perfectly safe."

"There is much sadness here," Camael said from behind them. They turned to see that he was staring at another of the homes. A rusted tricycle lay on its side in front, a kind of marker for the sorrow that emanated from each of the homes. "It has saturated these structures; I can see why Belphegor and the others would be drawn to it."

"So let me guess," Aaron began. "They built on the land and people started to get sick."

Lorelei nodded. "They started construction of Ravenschild Estates in 1978, and the families began to move in during the spring of 1980. Everything was perfect bliss, until the first case of leukemia and then the second, and the third, and then came the birth defects."

"How many people died?" Aaron asked. The wind blew down the deserted street kicking up dust, and he could have sworn he heard the faint cries of the mournful in the breeze.

"I'm really not sure," the woman answered. "I know a lot of kids got sick before the state got involved in 1989. They investigated and forced the families to evacuate. They ended up purchasing more than three hundred and fifty homes and financing some of the relocation costs."

"So it's kind of like a ghost town," Aaron said, still listening to the haunted cries upon the wind.

"Yeah, it is," Lorelei answered.

"What did your friend Lehash call this place?" he asked, his nose wrinkled with displeasure. "A little piece of paradise? I'm not seeing that at all."

Lorelei looked about, a dreamy expression on her pale, attractive features. "It may not look like much," she said quietly, "but it's lots better than what I left behind. I'll take this over the nuthouse any day of the week." She abruptly turned and continued on her way.

Her words piqued Aaron's curiosity, and he sped up to walk beside her. "Did you say you were in a nuthouse?"

Lorelei didn't answer right away, as if she were deciding whether or not she wanted to talk about it. "A pretty good one too—or so I've been told," she finally said. "I was seventeen, on the verge of my eighteenth birthday, and everything I'd ever known turned to shit."

Aaron could hear the pain in her voice and immediately sympathized. He understood exactly what she was talking about. "It was the . . . the power inside you . . . the whole Nephilim thing."

She nodded. "I didn't know it then, but I finally figured it out after one of my last hospital stays. I was on the streets and had stopped taking my medications and things started to become clearer. 'Course that's what crazy people not taking their medicines always say." She laughed, but it was a laugh filled with bitterness.

Aaron suddenly saw in the young woman a kindred spirit and wondered if her story would have been his if not for the whole prophecy thing.

"I was drawn to this place," Lorelei continued. "As the drugs that I'd been pumped full of left my system I could feel the pull of Aerie—I was seeing it in my dreams, along with all kinds of other nonsense that I'm sure you're familiar with."

"Were there those that attempted to harm you?" Camael chimed in, making reference to the Powers. "Trying to keep you from reaching this destination?"

A lock of white hair drifted in front of her face, and she swept it away with the back of her hand. "I got really good at avoiding them." She turned to the angel. "At first I thought they were just manifestations of my paranoid delusions, but when one tried to burn me alive inside an old tenement house I was crashing in, I realized that wasn't the case."

"You were lucky to have survived."

Lorelei agreed. "I think that the power inside was helping me. Without the drugs, it was growing and helping me to find a place where I could be safe."

They passed an enormous mound of burned and blackened wood that had been piled in the center of the street. Aaron could see that some doors and windows, railings and banisters from some of the houses had made it onto the stack. He looked from the charred pyre to her.

"We had problems with some local kids," she explained. "Liked to use the place to party. We were afraid their little bonfires would eventually burn it down."

"What did you do?" Aaron asked.

Lorelei extended her hands and small sparks of radiant energy danced from one fingertip to the next. "After I finally got here and realized I wasn't crazy, that I was Nephilim, I learned that I had an affinity for angel magick. My father and I did some spells to scare the kids away. This place has a real reputation now, even worse than it had before."

"Your father? Who . . . ?"

"Lehash," she answered. "Pretty cool, huh? Not only was I not insane, but I hooked up with my dad the angel, and suddenly everything began to make a weird kind of sense."

The words of the Archangel Gabriel echoed through Aaron's mind—*You have your father's eyes*—and Aaron wondered if the mystery of his own parentage would ever be revealed to him.

On a tiny side street they stopped in front of a house with powder blue aluminum siding, strings of Christmas lights still dangling from the gutters.

"Is that my car?" Aaron asked, moving past Lorelei toward the vehicle parked in front.

Gabriel beat him there and gave the vehicle the once over. *"It's our car, Aaron,"* he said, tail wagging. *"I can smell our stuff."*

"One of the citizens retrieved it from the Burger King parking lot." Lorelei gestured toward the house. "This is where you'll be staying."

Aaron gave the house another look and felt his aggravation level rise. He didn't want to stay; he wanted to continue the search for his brother. They had done nothing wrong, and Belphegor had no right to keep them here. "How long are you planning to hold us?" he asked, staring down in growing anger at the manacles fastened around his wrist. "If I'm ever going to find my brother—"

"You'll stay as long as the Founder says you'll stay," Lorelei interrupted, crossing her arms in defiance. "As far as we're concerned, you're the ones responsible for all the killings. And, until we know otherwise, you're not going anywhere."

"That's crap and you know it," he growled, the angelic presence perking up within him. It would never miss an opportunity for conflict and he had to steel himself against the urge to let it free. He had no desire to feel the effects of the manacles' magicks again.

"If my father had his way," she interjected, "you'd still be locked in that basement, Chosen One or otherwise." Lorelei took a step closer, fists clenched by her side. "What makes you think you're so damn special anyway?" she demanded.

"I didn't ask for this!" Aaron pushed past the woman, heading in the opposite direction.

"Where are you going?"

He stopped, but didn't turn around. "I need to take a walk. Besides, Gabriel is hungry and I wouldn't mind a bite to eat myself. Is there anyplace around here where we can get some food?"

Lorelei didn't answer right away, as if she were considering not letting him go. Aaron decided that would be a very bad idea on her part, for his angelic nature was already coiled and ready to strike. Looking for trouble.

"You're heading in the right direction," she finally said. "Take a left onto Gagnon. You'll see the community center at the end of the street. Should be able to get a sandwich or something there."

"Thanks," he said, starting to walk again. Gabriel followed close at his side, but Camael remained with Lorelei. "I'll see you guys later."

"Yeah," Lorelei called after him. "You will, and as soon as you get used to the idea, things'll be a little easier for you."

# CHAPTER SIX

Camael watched Aaron leave and could not help but share some of the Nephilim's discontent.

"So, what do you *really* think?" Lorelei asked as they stood on the sidewalk before the shabby house. "Do you seriously believe that he's the Chosen One?"

He turned away from the boy and his dog walking off in the distance and met her gaze. "I believe there is something special about that one," he answered.

"I had a cat when I was eight that was pretty special, but it doesn't mean that she was the Messiah." Lorelei's tone dripped sarcasm.

Camael chose to ignore her jibes and instead addressed the dwelling before them. "This is where we will be staying then?" he asked, as if in need of clarification.

"This is it," she answered. "One of the sturdier homes, no

leaks and still unchristened by local youths brave enough to come here."

"It will do," he said, and then was quiet. He hoped that his silence would act as a dismissal to the female half-breed. The angel did not feel like talking; there was much he needed to reflect upon, and he found her presence distracting.

"You didn't answer my question," the Nephilim piped up, eager to press the sensitive issue. "Do you believe he's the One in the prophecy?"

"It matters not what I believe," he said, his pale blue eyes locked on hers, "for it appears you and yours have already made up your minds about the boy."

"We've seen a lot of so-called prophets here. Hell, I've seen at least two since I've been around. It takes more than the word of a former Powers' commander to convince us," she answered, arms folded across her chest. "Sorry to doubt you, but that's just the way it is."

He could sense that she wanted more, that she wanted him to convince her he was right. But as he stood on the desolate street, in the abandoned neighborhood that he had come to learn was the paradise he'd sought for centuries, Camael found that he just didn't have the strength.

"I have searched for this place far longer than even I can recall," he said, gesturing to the homes and the neighborhood around him. "If it is permitted, I would like to explore Aerie on my own."

Lorelei nodded slightly. There was disappointment in her look, and for that he was truly sorry. "Sure, it's permitted, knock yourself out." She placed her hands inside the pockets of her short jacket. "The manacles and choke collar should keep you out of trouble." She turned on her heel and crossed the street to leave him alone.

"It ain't much," he heard the Nephilim say as she slowly headed back in the direction they had come. "But it's home."

Camael wasn't sure what he had expected of Aerie but was certain, as he strolled down the deathly silent street with its houses in sad disrepair and the offensive aroma of chemical poisoning tainting the air, that this was not even remotely what he had imagined it would be.

*What did you think you would find?* he silently asked, the setting sun at his back. *An earthly version of a Heaven lost so long ago? Is that it?* he wondered. Was that why he was feeling so out of sorts?

In the distance before him, the angel could see the golden cross atop the steeple of a church, and found himself pulled to this human place of worship. Its architecture was far more contemporary than he cared for—simple, less ornate than many of the other places of worship he had visited in his long years upon the planet of man. Slowly he climbed the weathered concrete steps of the structure, feeling the residue of prayer left by the devout. He pulled open the door, and traces of the love these often primitive creatures felt for their Creator cascaded over him in waves.

Camael stepped inside the church, letting the door slowly close behind him. The structure had been stripped of its religious trappings; nowhere was there a crucifix or relic of a saint to be found. He guessed that such religious paraphernalia had been removed when the church was abandoned, but that did not change the feeling of the place. This was a place for worship, and no matter what iconic trappings had been taken from it, it could not change its original purpose.

Crudely constructed benches were lined up before the altar at the front of the building and Camael saw that he was not alone. A man, a Nephilim, sat at the front, his gaze intent upon an image that had been painted on the cream-colored wall at the back of the altar.

Camael walked closer. The artwork was crudely rendered, but there was no mistaking what it depicted—the joining of mortal woman and angel. A child hung in the air above its mismatched parents on wings of holy light, its tiny arms spread wide, the rays of light that haloed its head spreading upward to God, as well as drenching the world below them in its divine illumination. He found himself studying the artist's rendition of the child, searching for any similarity with his own charge, the boy Aaron Corbet. Of course there were none, and he felt foolish for looking.

The lone figure sitting before the altar turned with a start, his face contorting in wide-eyed astonishment as his gaze fell upon Camael. The angel considered speaking to the halfling, but before he could put the words together, the man leaped from his seat and fled through a nearby exit.

*These citizens certainly don't trust strangers,* Camael thought as he strode to the front of the old church and sat on the bench the Nephilim had vacated. The silence was comforting, and he closed his eyes, losing himself deep within his thoughts. It was not often that he had a chance to reflect.

He thought of the war in Heaven. It had seemed so black and white at the beginning: Those who opposed the Lord of Lords would be punished, it was as simple as that. Faces appeared before his eyes, brothers of the myriad heavenly hosts; some had been with him since their inception, but it mattered not, for they had to pay the price. And then it was too much for him, the smell of their blood choking his breath, their screams for mercy deafening his ears. There seemed to be no end, his existence had become one of vengeance and misery. He had become a messenger of death and he could stand it no more. *And then there was the prophecy. . . .*

Camael opened his eyes to look upon the image painted on the wall before him: the strange trinity that would herald the end of so much pain and suffering. He remembered when he had first heard the prophecy told by a human seer. He desperately wanted it to be true, for God's forgiveness to be bestowed upon those who had fallen, by a being that was an amalgam of His most precious creations.

From that moment, Camael had looked upon these

creatures—these Nephilim—as conduits of God's mercy, and he did everything in his power to keep them safe. These times had been long and filled with violence, but also salvation. He had taken it upon himself to find the Nephilim of prophecy, to help bring about the redemption of his fallen brethren, and at last it had brought him here.

To Aerie.

The angel looked around at the sparse environment in which he sat, and was overcome with feelings of disappointment. *Is this to be where the Lord's mercy is finally realized? A human neighborhood built upon a burial ground of toxic waste.* Camael was loath to admit it, but he was expecting more.

Even though lost in thought, he sensed their presence and rose from his seat to see that he was no longer alone. The Nephilim that had fled the church when he'd first arrived had returned, and brought others with him. They streamed into the place of worship, male and female of various ages—all of them the result of the joining of human and angel. They whispered and muttered among themselves as they stared at Camael.

He had no idea what they wanted of him and on reflex tried to conjure a sword of fire. But the magick that infused the manacles encircling his wrists and throat immediately kicked in. The angel shrieked in pain as daggers of ice plunged through his body. He fell to his knees, cursing his stupidity, and struggled to stay conscious as the waves of discomfort gradually abated.

The throng of Nephilim came at him then, and there was nothing he could do to stop them. They formed a circle around him, their buzzing whispers adding to the tension of the situation.

"What do you want?" he asked them. His voice sounded strained, tired.

An older woman, with eyes as green and deep as the Mediterranean, was the first to step forward, and reached a hand out to the angel warrior. He could see that there were tears in her eyes.

"We want to thank you," she said as she lay a cool palm against the side of his face, "for saving our lives."

He looked at her quizzically, her gentle touch soothing his pain.

"It was one of the fiercest blizzards I can remember," she whispered, tears streaming down her aged face, "and they had come to kill me, their swords of fire sizzling and hissing as the snow fell upon them. As long as I live I'll never forget that sound—or the sound of your voice as you ordered them away from me."

The woman's words gradually sank in. "I . . . I saved you," Camael said, gazing into her bottomless eyes, awash in a sea of emotion.

The woman nodded, a sad smile upon her trembling lips. "Me and so many more," she said, turning to look at the others that crowded behind her.

They all came forward then, hands touching him, the

unbridled emotion of their thanks almost intoxicating. How many times had he wondered what became of them; of those half-breeds he had saved from the murderous Powers? How often had he questioned the validity of his mission?

The Nephilim survivors surged around him, the warmth of their gratitude enveloping him in a cocoon of fulfillment.

*It wasn't for naught,* he thought as he welcomed each word of thanks, every loving touch. Camael, former leader of the Powers host, had at last found his peace, not only in place, but in spirit.

The prisoner curled himself tighter into a ball upon the floor of his cage, his body wracked with painful spasms brought about by the process of healing.

"It's kind of funny," he whispered to the mouse nestled in the crook of his neck, its gentle exhalations soothing in his ear. "Healing hurts almost as much as the injury itself." And again his body twitched and writhed in the throes of repairing itself. He waited for the agony to pass before continuing with his story.

"Sorry about the interruption," he said, trying to focus on something other than the sloughing of his old, dead flesh and the tenderness of the new pink skin beneath. "Where was I?"

The mouse snuffled gently.

"That's right," he answered. "My relationship with the Lord." Another wave of pain swept through his body, and he gritted his teeth and bore the bulk of it before he continued. "I was pretty high on His list of favorites; the mightiest and most beloved of all the angels in Heaven. He called me His Morningstar, and He loved me as much as I loved Him—or so I believed."

And though it was as torturous—even more so than having his burned flesh fall from his body—the prisoner remembered how beautiful it had been. "You should have seen it," he said dreamily, his memories transporting him back to his place of creation, back to Heaven. "It was everything you could possibly dream of—and more. It was Paradise."

He saw again the golden spires of Heaven's celestial mansions, reaching upward into infinity, culminating in the final, seventh Heaven, the place of the highest spiritual perfection. "And that was where He sat, on His throne of light, with me often by His side." The prisoner sighed, pain pulling his thoughts back to reality in his hanging prison.

The mouse was sleeping, but still he heard its voice, its questions about the past and his eventual downfall.

"Do you know I was by His side when He created humanity? The attention He languished on what appeared to us in the heavenly choirs as just another animal!" He remembered his anger, the uncontrollable emotion at the root of his fall so long ago. "He gave them their own paradise, a garden of incredible beauty and bounty. And He gave them something that we did not have. The Creator gave them a piece of Himself, a spark of His divinity—a soul."

The agony of his healing mixed with the recollection of his indignation caused the prisoner to sit bolt upright within the confines of his cage. His hand moved quickly to his bare shoulder, preventing the sleeping rodent from falling. "After all this time it can still get a rise out of me," he said, his voice less raspy, on the mend.

The mouse was in a panic, startled awake by the sudden movement. He could feel the racing beat of its tiny heart against the palm of his hand, the bars of the cage cold against the new flesh of his back.

"I was shocked and horrified, as were others of the various hosts. Why would He give such a priceless gift to a lowly animal? It was an insult to what we were."

The prisoner cupped the fragile creature in the palm of his hand and calmed its jangled nerves with the gentle attentions of his finger.

"Jealousy," he said, a deep sadness permeating the sound of his voice. "Every horrible act that followed was all because of jealousy." In his mind he saw them in the Garden of Eden, man and woman, basking in the light of His glory. "What fragile things they were. And how He loved them—which just made matters all the worse."

The mouse still trembled in his grasp, and the prisoner wondered if it was cold. He held it closer.

"As if things weren't bad enough, it wasn't long before He gathered us together and proclaimed that from that moment forth, we would bow to humanity, we would serve them as we served He who was the Creator of us all."

His scalp began to tingle unpleasantly and he suspected that his hair had begun to grow back.

"Needless to say, several of us were less than thrilled with this new spin on things." He remembered their angry faces again, their indignant fury, but none could match his own. His Lord and Creator had abandoned him, cast him aside for the love of something inferior, and he would not stand for it. "I was so blinded by jealousy and my wounded pride that I gathered an army of those who felt as I did, a third of Heaven's angels they say, and waged war against my heavenly father, my creator, and all those who defended His edict."

Glimpses of a battle fought countless millennia ago danced across his vision of the past. Not a day went by that he didn't relive it. He saw the faces of the elite soldiers, so beautiful and yet so full of rage, and he knew they believed in him, that the cause he fought for was just. "And as the Creator had done with the first humans, I touched them—each and every one of the army that swore their allegiance to me—and I gave them a piece of myself, a fragment of what had once made me the most powerful angel in Heaven." The tips of his fingers came alive with the recollection of those who had received his gift, a black mark—a symbol burned into their flesh, a sigil that spoke of their devotion to him, and to the cause.

"We presumed that the Almighty had no right to do what

He did to us—but we presumed too much," the prisoner said sadly. He was exhausted by the painful remembrances of his sordid past; he lowered his hands, and the mouse resting within them, to his lap.

"What were we trying to prove? What were our intentions?" He shook his head and smiled sadly. "Were we going to *force* the Creator to love us best?"

The mouse looked up from the nest within his hands, its dark eyes filled with what he read to be sympathy.

"It was a ferocious battle. I can't even tell you how long it lasted—days, weeks, years perhaps—time passed differently for me then. We fought valiantly, but in the end, it was all in vain."

The mouse nudged at his fingers, its tiny nose a pinprick of cold, and he began to gently pet it again.

"When the battle was finally over, when my elite were dead and myself in chains, I was brought before my Lord God, and finally began to realize the horror of what I had done."

The prisoner closed his eyes to the flood of emotions that filled them, tears streamed down the newly grown skin on his face. "I tried to apologize. I begged for His forgiveness and mercy, but He wouldn't hear it."

A stray tear splashed into his hand and the mouse gingerly licked at the salty fluid.

"I was banished from Heaven, cast down to Earth, and as my constant companion, I would forever experience the pain and suffering of what I had done."

The mouse looked up at him; its triangular head bent quizzically to one side.

"You want to know about the place called Hell?" he asked the curious animal. "There is no Hell," he said. "Hell is in here." He touched the raw, pink skin of his chest with the tips of his fingers. "And it will forever burn inside me for what I have done."

*"She said take a left onto Gagnon and there would be a community center where we could get food,"* Gabriel whined.

"That's what she said," Aaron replied, looking around as they walked. All he could see were homes, each more rundown and dilapidated than the next.

*"And what exactly is a community center?"* the dog asked pathetically. It was past his suppertime and he was beginning to panic.

Aaron stopped, glancing back in the direction from which they had just come. "This is still Gagnon, isn't it?" he asked more to himself than to his ravenous companion.

*"I don't know,"* Gabriel answered, his nose pressed to the sidewalk, searching for the scent of food. *"I'm so hungry I can't even think straight, and it's getting dark."*

They started walking again. A gentle wind blew down the street, rustling what few leaves remained in the skeletal trees.

"Well, let's keep going and see what we run into. Maybe it's at the far end."

*"What if it's not?"* the dog asked, a touch of panic in his guttural-sounding voice.

Aaron sighed with exasperation. "Don't worry, Gabe. If we can't find the community center we'll double back to the car, and you can have some of the dog food in the trunk."

*"I don't want that food,"* he said, stopping, ears flat against his blocky head. *"It gives me gas."*

Aaron could not hold back his frustration. "Look, I'm just trying to tell you that you won't starve, okay? You *will* be fed!"

Gabriel's tail began to wag. *"You're a good boy."*

Aaron laughed in spite of himself and motioned for the dog to follow him. "Gabriel, you're a pip!" he said. "C'mon, let's find this place before I starve to death too."

The dog thought for a moment, keeping pace alongside his master. *"I don't think anybody has ever called me a pip before. I've been called a good boy, a good dog, a best pally, but never a pip."*

"Well, there you go," Aaron answered. "Something new for the résumé."

*"Do you think we will ever find Stevie?"* Gabriel suddenly asked, changing the topic in an instant, as he was prone to do.

Aaron felt his mood suddenly darken. "As soon as we can leave here, we'll start looking again."

*"How long will that be?"*

Aaron felt himself growing angry again and took a series of deep breaths to calm down. "I don't know," he said flatly.

"We'll play by their rules for a while, but there might come a time when we'll have to take a stand."

*"I don't like the sound of that,"* Gabriel said.

"Neither do I," Aaron answered. "Let's just hope it doesn't come to that."

The two continued to walk in brooding silence, both thinking of the disturbing possibilities that waited in their future. They were near the end of the street when Gabriel stopped.

"What is it now?" Aaron snapped.

*"Do you smell that?"* Gabriel tilted his head back, nose twitching as it pulled something from the air.

Aaron sniffed at the air as well, at first sensing nothing, but then he too smelled it. Food— cooking food.

Gabriel was off in a flash, following the odor as if arrows had been put down on the street to lead them. *"This way,"* he cried excitedly.

Aaron had to quicken his pace to keep up with the hungry animal and watched as Gabriel darted suddenly to the left, moving onto the front lawn of one of the rundown homes.

"This isn't a community center, Gabe," he called, but the dog was in the grip of a food frenzy.

Gabriel followed the scent right up onto the porch and planted his nose at the bottom of the front door, sniffling and snuffling as if it were possible for him to pull some sustenance from beneath the door.

Aaron stood on the walkway. The smell was stronger and

more delicious. He felt his own stomach begin to gurgle. "Gabriel, c'mon down! This is somebody's house."

The Labrador reluctantly turned his head toward Aaron. *"But this house has food."*

Aaron moved closer to the front porch, feeling sorry for the famished animal. "I know there's food here, but we can't just invite ourselves in. Remember, we don't know these people and they probably wouldn't trust us anyway."

*"But you're the Chosen One,"* he said sadly. *"And I'm your dog, who's very hungry."*

If it weren't so pathetic, Aaron probably would have laughed, but the events of the day so far had chased away any chance for humor. "Gabriel, come down here this instant or—"

*"Can't we knock and ask where the community center is?"* the dog asked with a nervous wag of his muscular tail.

"I guess we could do that," Aaron answered, climbing the three rickety wooden steps to the porch. "But if nobody answers, we have to go. Deal?"

*"There's somebody in there, Aaron. I can smell him over the food."*

Aaron rapped on the door and waited. He listened for sounds from inside and could just make out the chatter of a television. "I don't think they want to—"

*"Knock again,"* the dog demanded, his tail wagging furiously.

Aaron knocked harder. "Remember what I said: If nobody comes to the door, we go."

Gabriel suddenly bolted down the steps and around the side of the house.

"Where are you going?" Aaron demanded, starting to follow.

*"There's somebody in there. Maybe he can hear the back door better,"* the Lab called excitedly, already out of sight.

Aaron reluctantly followed. He had no idea how the citizens would react if they found him skulking around somebody's home. An image of Lehash with his golden pistols drawn suddenly came to mind. He rounded the corner of the house, careful not to stumble in the growing darkness, and found Gabriel already on the back porch trying to turn the doorknob in his mouth. "What the hell do you think you're doing?"

*"I scratched at the door and somebody said come in,"* Gabriel replied as the door popped open and the rich, succulent smell of cooking food drifted out from the kitchen. Without waiting for an answer, he pushed through the door with his snout and disappeared.

"Gabriel!" Aaron called, climbing the steps and following his dog into the tiny kitchen. It was overly warm and the smell of cooking meat enveloped him like a blanket. Sounds of a television drifted in from the room beyond. "Gabriel, you can't just—"

*"I can't help it."* Gabriel was moving toward the stove as if

hypnotized, droplets of saliva raining from his mouth to the floor, nose twitching eagerly. *"Maybe he'll invite us to stay."*

"Or he'll call the constables and we'll really be in a fix," Aaron said nervously, half expecting the house's resident to fly into the kitchen screaming.

*"I told you he said to come in."*

Aaron moved toward the door that would take him out of the kitchen, the light of the television illuminating the room beyond. "Why don't I trust you," he hissed, his back to the animal.

*"I don't know."* Gabriel sounded hurt.

"Hello?" Aaron called softly as he wrapped his knuckles on the frame of the kitchen doorway. "I don't mean to bother you, but we're looking for the—"

"Come in, Aaron," said a voice from the living room.

Aaron turned back to Gabriel and must have looked surprised.

*"I told you he knew we were here,"* the dog said knowingly.

Aaron walked through a short corridor and into the living room beyond, the sound of Gabriel's toenails clicking on the hardwood floor behind him as he followed. The room was dark except for the flickering light of the television and Aaron could just about make out the older man sitting in a worn, leather recliner in front of an old-fashioned console. It was Belphegor. Aaron cleared his throat, but the old man did not respond, apparently engrossed in the television show.

Curious, he stepped farther into the room. The sound was turned down, but it looked as though the angel was watching home movies, the scenes jumping from one moment to the next. Suddenly Aaron saw himself on the screen.

He was dressed in a black tuxedo and carrying a flower—a corsage in a clear plastic container. He had just stepped out of his car and was approaching a house that seemed vaguely familiar. *What is this?* His mind was in a panic.

*"Aaron, what's wrong?"* Gabriel asked, obviously picking up on his panicked vibe.

Aaron could not pull his eyes from the scene unfolding before him. *Where had he seen that house before?* His thoughts raced as he watched himself on the television knocking on the house's front door. It hit him just as the door began to open. It was Belvidere Place back home in Lynn. He'd been there only once before.

The door opened, and Vilma stood there in a cream-colored gown, her hair up and decorated with baby's breath, and the smile on her face as she saw him made him want to cry. His tuxedoed version was in the process of giving her the flower he had brought, when he ripped his eyes from the screen to look at the old man placidly sitting in the oversized chair.

"What is this?" Aaron demanded.

He looked back to the screen briefly to see him and Vilma posing for pictures. Vilma seemed to be embarrassed by the whole thing, waving her family away and trying to drag him toward the car. He couldn't get over how beautiful she looked.

"It's how you wish things had been," Belphegor responded, his eyes never leaving the television. "I like this part . . . didn't take you for a dancer."

Aaron gazed at the set again and saw that he and Vilma were slow dancing among a crowd. He didn't recognize their surroundings, but it appeared to be someplace fancy. Vilma was whispering in his ear as they slowly twirled in a circle on the dance floor. Foolishly he found himself growing jealous of his television doppelgänger. He pulled his eyes away, wanting to look anywhere else but there. His eyes landed on the dark cord of the television lying upon the floor, curled like a resting snake.

"It's not plugged in," he said aloud, turning his full attention to Belphegor. "The television's not plugged in."

"This is what your life could have been if not for the power that awakened inside you."

He didn't want to, but Aaron found himself looking at the screen again. He saw himself in a cap and gown, a stupid-looking grin on his face, accepting his diploma from Mr. Costan.

The view suddenly turned to the auditorium audience. With a sickening feeling growing in the pit of his stomach, he watched his foster mom and dad proudly applaud his achievement. It was when he noticed Stevie sitting in the

chair beside his mother, smiling as if he didn't have a problem in the world, that he realized he'd had more than enough.

"Make it stop," he demanded, stepping farther into the
room, fists clenched. He felt the manacles around his wrists
and the collar about his neck grow warmer.

Belphegor didn't respond, smiling as he watched television.
Aaron couldn't help himself and chanced a quick glance. It was
like driving past a car accident. You didn't want to see—but
you just had to look. He appeared older now, sitting in a large
classroom taking notes as a professor lectured. He was in college, and a part of him longed to switch places with this version
of himself.

"I've seen enough," he said louder, more demanding. The
restraints were burning him, but he barely noticed, for his
angelic nature had been awakened by his anger and it coiled
within him, eager to strike.

"Isn't this what you wanted, Aaron?" Belphegor asked,
pointing to the TV.

Aaron didn't want to see, but it was as if he weren't in control of his movements. He was giving Vilma a ring. They were
on a beach at sunset. Gabriel, looking older but still active, was
happily chasing seagulls, and Vilma was sitting on a blanket
with him. There was love in her eyes—love for him—and even
though the sound was off, he knew his words at that moment.
*Will you marry me?*

The angelic nature within him screamed, hurling itself

against the restraints of the magicks within the golden metal that bound him. The pain was incredible, and he began to scream, but more from anger than hurt.

Gabriel began to panic and fled into the kitchen, barking as he ran.

"Turn it off! Turn it off! Turn it off!" Aaron demanded, his voice raw and filled with emotion. "I don't want to see this—I don't want to see what I can't ever have. Why are you doing this?"

He stumbled forward to block the set, catching sight of Vilma in a wedding gown as she walked down the aisle of a church. His skin was on fire, the alien symbols appearing upon his flesh, even though the magick within the restraints tried to stop it. The wings beneath the flesh of his back writhed in agitation, gradually moving to the surface, ready to unfurl.

"I have to see if it's true," Belphegor said calmly. "I have to see if you are indeed the One."

Something inside Aaron broke. There was a sound in his head like the scream of high-speed train, and his wings exploded from his back, as the power of an angel suddenly flowed unimpeded from his body. As if suddenly made ancient and brittle, the manacles upon his wrists and the collar about his neck broke, crumbling as dust to the floor. A sword of fire ignited in his hand and, gazing greedily upon its destructive potential, he spun around, bringing the burning blade down upon the wooden cabinet of the television console. The window into a life he would never know exploded in flames and a shower of glass, but not before he glimpsed a very pregnant Vilma, smiling as if she somehow knew he was watching.

The transformed Aaron, his wings of glistening black spread wide, turned back to glare at Belphegor, who still sat quietly in his recliner. Gabriel tentatively peered around the doorway from the kitchen, ears flat against his square head.

*"Are . . . are you all right, Aaron?"* the dog asked.

"I'm fine, Gabriel," Aaron growled in the voice of the Nephilim. He pointed his sword of orange flame at the fallen angel. "You wanted to know if I was the One," he said, voice booming about the confines of the room. "Well, what do you think?"

"I think that supper's just about ready," Belphegor responded with a soothing smile, rising from his chair. "Would you and your friend care to join me?"

Gabriel pushed the plate of mashed potatoes, gravy, and peas farther across the dining room floor with each consecutive lap of his muscular tongue. Before he wound up halfway across the house, Aaron reached down and took the plate away.

*"I'm not finished with that,"* the dog said, the remains of mashed potatoes decorating the top of his nose.

"Believe me, you're finished," Aaron said, setting the spotless plate on the tabletop. *The plate is so clean, Belphegor could put it away without washing it,* he thought. *No one would be the wiser.*

*"I would like some more,"* Gabriel said with a wag of his tail.

"You've had enough," Aaron responded, as he took a hearty bite of his own roast beef and gravy. Then, always the ultimate pushover, he picked up a piece of meat from his plate and fed it to his insatiable companion. "Watch the fingers!" he squealed as the animal snatched away his offering. "I still use those, thank you very much."

Belphegor walked in from the kitchen with another steaming bowl in his hands. "Here are some fresh green beans," he said as he placed it on the table. "I grew them myself."

"Here?" Aaron asked, shaking his head. "No, thank you. I'm not into toxic waste."

*"I like toxic waste,"* Gabriel said happily, attempting to lick the remains of potato from his nose.

"It's perfectly safe," Belphegor said as he pulled out a chair and sat down across from Aaron. "All the poisons have been removed. They're quite good."

Aaron was reaching for the beans when he realized that Belphegor did not have a plate. "Aren't you eating?"

The angel shook his head. "No, not tonight. I actually prefer preparing meals to eating them." The fallen angel smiled, watching as Aaron spooned a heaping portion of the rich green vegetable onto his plate.

"You are aware that we—of my kind—do not need to eat."

"I've heard," Aaron said, taking a careful bite of the beans and then eagerly having more. "Except that Camael has a thing for French fries now."

Belphegor sat back in his chair. "Does he? I would never have imagined that. Perhaps the years upon this world have indeed softened our Powers' commander."

"*Former* commander," Aaron corrected through a mouthful of food. "Verchiel's the commander now—and has been for quite some time."

"Of course," Belphegor answered, crossing his arms. "How foolish of me to forget."

His plate nearly as clean as Gabriel's bowl, Aaron had a drink of water from an old jelly jar, then pushed the utensils away. "That thing with the television," he asked. "How did you do that?"

Gabriel had finally settled down and lay beside Aaron's chair. Aaron reached down to pet his friend as he waited for an answer.

"You wouldn't believe it if I told you." Belphegor shook his head, arms still crossed.

"You'd be surprised at the things I believe in now," Aaron said. Gabriel rolled onto his side to expose his belly, and Aaron obliged the animal. "Were those . . . images, those scenes . . . were they from some future or—"

"They were taken from your head and manipulated," Belphegor answered, tapping a finger against his skull. "Things that you most desire, but will likely never achieve."

Aaron stopped scratching Gabriel's belly, earning a disappointed snuff, and leaned back in his chair. "I don't like to think that way," he said, eyes focused on his empty plate, but seeing something else—a future that could very well be like the one he'd seen on Belphegor's television. "I like to think that there's something more for me, after I find my brother and this whole prophecy thing gets straightened out."

Belphegor chuckled. "Don't worry yourself about the prophecy thing," he said as he stood up from his chair. He started to gather the dirty bowls and plates.

"Why's that?"

The old fallen angel used a spoon to scrape what remained of the mashed potatoes onto Aaron's dirty plate. "Because it doesn't concern you," he answered.

"Don't you think I'm the One?" Aaron asked curiously, leaning forward in his seat. "You heard what Camael said, and you saw what I did to your magick handcuffs."

"All very impressive." Belphegor nodded as he gave Gabriel a green bean from the plate of refuse. "I can honestly say that I've never seen power the likes of yours, and your control over it thus far is admirable, but I do not believe you are the One spoken of in prophecy."

Aaron was surprised by the disappointment he felt; a day ago he would have traded the whole angelic Chosen One thing for a bag of Doritos. *Now* . . . "Are you positive?" he asked. "How do you know? Camael said . . ."

"Camael has been separated from his kind for a very long

time," the angel explained, pausing in his cleanup to gaze intently at Aaron. "He is desperate to belong again—perhaps too desperate—and he saw something in you that really isn't there. I'm sorry."

There was something in Belphegor's attitude that suddenly annoyed Aaron. It reminded him of his childhood in foster care, before he moved to the Stanleys' and learned what being part of a family was all about. Before that he was looked on as being less than other kids, perceived as a failure before he even had a chance to try.

"The essence inside you is extremely powerful, and I fear that if a true merger were ever to occur between the angelic nature and your fragile human psyche, you would be driven out of your mind. And we of Aerie would be forced to do something about it."

Aaron remembered a teacher he'd had in the first grade, Mr. Laidon. The teacher had singled him out, telling the other students that he didn't have a family and that the state needed to take care of him. At that moment he had felt like a show-and-tell project, something less than the other kids in his class. Aaron's face flushed hot with the memory.

"Maybe I could be taught," he began. "Camael says that if a union occurs properly—"

The old angel chuckled, a condescending laugh that Aaron had heard so many times in his life.

"Teach you to be our messiah?" Belphegor asked. "No, Aaron.

The true One spoken of in our sacred writing will be coming, just not right now."

"But the Archangel Gabriel said that I was God's new messenger," Aaron argued.

"Then he was wrong," Belphegor emphatically stated, and picked up the dishes, signaling an end to the conversation.

Aaron felt empty, as if being the savior of the fallen had actually begun to mean something to him, warts and all. He was about to offer Belphegor some help when there came a frantic rapping at the front door. Gabriel immediately sprang to his feet and began to bark.

"Come in," Belphegor called out, turning toward the front door, arms loaded with dirty dishes.

They heard the sounds of the front door open and close, followed by rapid footsteps. Scholar rushed in through the living room clutching a notebook in one hand. "Belphegor, we need to speak at once. . . ." His eyes found Aaron's and he fell silent.

"Good evening, Scholar. Aaron and I were just having dinner. May I get you something? Some coffee, or maybe some pie?"

The silence was becoming uncomfortable when Scholar finally spoke. "I need to speak with you in private, Belphegor." He tore his eyes from Aaron's and raised the notebook toward the old angel.

"Come with me," Belphegor said. "Excuse us for a moment, Aaron."

The two left the dining room, leaving Aaron to wonder what had gotten the angel so riled.

"*So you're not the Chosen One, then?*" Gabriel said, distracting him from his thoughts.

"I thought you were asleep," Aaron said, leaning back in his chair and watching the doorway to the kitchen.

"*You'd be surprised what I hear when I'm asleep.*"

"He doesn't think that it's me. It's no big deal. I always knew there was a chance that Camael was full of it." He looked at his dog lying on the floor by his chair.

"*What does this mean for us now?*" Gabriel asked earnestly.

Aaron shrugged. "I don't really know," he said, for the first time in a long while considering a future that didn't involve the angelic prophecy. "I guess it means we can get out of here and get back to finding Stevie."

"*Do you think Camael will come with us?*"

Aaron didn't get a chance to answer, for at that moment Belphegor and Scholar returned to the room. There was a strange look upon the old angel's face and Aaron saw that he was holding Scholar's notebook. It was open and Aaron could see parts of drawings that he recognized, sketches of the symbols that appeared on his body when he allowed his angelic essence to emerge.

"Is everything all right?" Aaron asked. As of late, fearing the worst had become as natural to him as breathing. It wasn't the greatest way to be, but at least he was always prepared.

"Were you serious about being taught, about wanting to learn?" Belphegor questioned.

Aaron nodded, not quite sure what he was getting himself into.

Belphegor handed the notebook and its drawings back to Scholar. "We'll begin your training immediately."

# CHAPTER SEVEN

amael sat on the forest green, metal bench in the tiny playground, his angel eyes detecting the resonance of things long past—ghosts of children and families who had once played here. It had been seven days since he and Aaron first arrived in Aerie, and the former leader of the Powers was having to deal with ghosts of his own. He thought of those he had destroyed during the conflict in Heaven, and those slain after the war when he was performing his duty as commander of the Powers host—obliterating those who were an offense to the Creator. Since finding Aerie, he'd been thinking of them more and more, their faces and death cries haunting his every moment.

*Should I be allowed to stay here?* he wondered. For if he had found this place before his change of heart, before the realization that the killing had to stop, he would have razed it, burned it to ash in a rain of heavenly fire—and God have mercy upon those he found living within its confines.

A crow cried overhead as it circled a gnarled and diseased tree growing to the side of the play area. Its caws voiced its uneasiness with the area, despite the fact that it was tired and wanted to rest. The animals knew that the Ravenschild development was poisoned, Camael realized; they could taste its taint on the air rising up from the earth. The place had the stink of man's folly, and the blackbird, knowing it did not belong here, flew on in search of another place to rest its tired wings.

*Do I belong?* Camael deliberated. He had searched for Aerie for many hundreds of years, but had he actually earned a place here? The faces of those who fell before him were slowly pushed aside, replaced by those he had saved. He could still hear their plaintive words of thanks and feel their touches of gratitude. Despite the violence he had wrought in the ancient past, he had still managed to do some good, and he would need to hold on to that as a drowning man would latch on to debris adrift in storm-wracked seas.

*And what about the Creator?* His mind frothed with questions for which he did not have answers. *Does He look upon me with disdain, or pity? When the time comes, will I be permitted to go home?*

The sound of claws upon the tar path interrupted the angel's musings, and he turned to see Gabriel trotting toward him.

*"Camael, have you seen Aaron?"* the dog asked, stopping before the bench.

The angel shook his head. "Not since this morning. I believe he is still with Belphegor."

*"It figures,"* Gabriel responded morosely.

"Is there a problem?" Camael asked, curious in spite of himself.

The dog hopped up onto the bench and sat beside him. *"He's never around anymore. I see him early in the morning when he takes me out and gets my breakfast, but then he's gone all day and he's too tired to play when he gets back."*

Camael slid over on the bench, away from the dog. He and Gabriel had developed a grudging respect for each other, but he still did not like to be too close to the animal. "I believe that Belphegor is attempting to train Aaron in the use of his angelic abilities."

*"And that's something else I don't understand,"* said the dog indignantly. *"First they think Aaron is a lost cause and now they can't seem to get enough of him. Besides, I thought you were training Aaron."*

"It would seem that Belphegor and the others have at last seen in Aaron what I found several weeks ago," Camael explained. "What that something is I cannot tell you, but it was enough to gain their trust and free us from those damnable restraints." The angel unconsciously rubbed at his wrists where the magickal manacles had recently been removed.

They were silent for a moment, two unlikely comrades pondering a similar mystery.

*"I miss him, Camael,"* Gabriel said as he gazed into the playground. *"I feel as if I'm losing him."*

"If Aaron is indeed the One foretold of in prophecy, you are losing him to something far larger than your simple emotional needs. He will be the one that brings about our redemption—Heaven will open its arms to us again and welcome us home," Camael said.

Gabriel turned his head to look at the angel. His animal eyes seemed darker somehow, intense with worry. *"I don't care about redemption,"* the Labrador said with a tremble in his voice. *"He was mine first; Aaron belongs to me."*

The primitive bond between humans and their domesticated animals was something that Camael had always struggled to understand. How had Aaron defined it for him during one of their seemingly endless drives? Unconditional love, he believed was how the boy had phrased it. The master was the animal's whole world, and it would love its master no matter what. That was the strength of the bond. The angel found the level of loyalty quite amazing.

"Aaron does not belong to you alone, Gabriel," Camael explained. "There are those around us now who have waited for his arrival for thousands of years. Would you deny them his touch?"

The dog bowed his head, golden brown ears pressed flat

against his skull. *"No,"* Gabriel growled, *"but who will take care of me if something happens to him?"*

Camael had no idea how to respond. It was a variation of a question he had been wondering himself. If Aaron was indeed the Chosen, what fate would the fallen meet if Verchiel should succeed in his mad plans to see the Nephilim destroyed?

The two sat quietly on the bench, the weight of their questions heavy upon their thoughts, the answers as elusive as the future.

Lorelei stepped out the back door of the house she shared with Lehash, a steaming cup of coffee in one hand, searching for her father. She thought the constable had come outside, but he was nowhere to be seen. Since the strangers' arrival, Lehash had become distant, uncommunicative, immersed in his work of keeping the citizens of Aerie safe, and she was becoming concerned.

Over the sound of the gas-powered generator that provided their electricity, she heard the reports of his guns, like small claps of thunder, rolling up from somewhere beyond the thick brush that surrounded the backyard. She started toward the sound, dipping her head beneath young saplings, careful not to spill the coffee as she maneuvered through the woods. Stepping into a man-made clearing, probably meant for development in years past, Lorelei stared at her father's back as he fired at targets set up along the far side of the wide open space. The weapons discharged with a booming report, and several targets disintegrated in plumes of heavenly fire.

"Good shootin', Tex," she joked, letting him know that he was no longer alone.

Lehash slowly turned and regarded her with dark and somber eyes, smoking pistols of gold in each hand. It was a look common to the head constable of Aerie, a look that she herself was often accused of wearing. The angel Lehash took everything quite seriously.

"Practicing?" she asked, moving closer and holding out the steaming mug of coffee.

He pointed a pistol over his shoulder and fired. Lorelei jumped as an old teddy bear tied to a tree exploded in a cloud of burning stuffing.

"Well, it does make perfect," he said, the slightest hint of a Texas twang in his voice. It never ceased to amuse her how he insisted on hanging on to the mannerisms and style of the old West. He'd explained that it had been his favorite time period during his countless years on Earth, and she guessed it was better than if he'd fallen in love with the Bronze age.

The golden pistols shimmered and disappeared into the ether with a flash of flame, and Lehash took the mug from her.

"And here I thought you were already perfect," she said, placing her hands inside the front pockets of her jeans. "Guess you really do learn something new every day."

He sipped at the coffee carefully, ignoring her good-natured barb. Something was bothering him, and now was as good a time as any to find out what.

"What's the matter, Lehash?" she asked. "Something's got your dander up even more than usual."

The angel looked up into the early morning, powder blue sky, as if searching for something. "Belphegor's been talking 'bout how he thinks trouble's coming." He took another swig of coffee and glanced back to her. "I believe it's already here."

She was confused at first, but then realized the meaning of his words. "You can't blame Aaron and Camael anymore. The deaths of other fallen have continued around the world since they've been here. And besides, reports that have trickled in say that the killer wears armor—blood-red armor." Lorelei felt a chill creep down her spine and shivered.

"And our troubles are just beginning," Lehash said, finishing the last of his drink. "Kind of like the early tremors I felt that morning in San Francisco in 1906—and we know how that one turned out."

Lorelei sighed. Her father often used historical catastrophes to make his points; the *Hindenburg* and *Titanic* disasters were quite popular with him, as were the Boxer Rebellion and World War II.

"Did you ever stop to think that their coming might be the beginning of something good?" she asked. "Y'know there's talk among the citizens that . . ." Lorelei stopped, suddenly not sure if she should continue.

"Talk about what?" he asked, his voice a low rumble, its tone already telling her that he wasn't going to care for what she had to say.

"That Aaron . . . that he might really be the One."

Lehash scowled and handed her back the empty mug. The golden pistols formed in his hands again, and he turned away to resume his target practice.

"What's the matter?" she asked. "What could possibly be wrong if that were true?"

Lehash did not answer her in words. Instead he began to fire his weapons repeatedly, with barely a moment between each of the thunderous blasts. The remaining targets disintegrated, as did the trees and branches that they had been positioned upon.

Then, as quickly as he had begun to fire, he stopped, whirling around to face her. "You haven't seen what I've seen, Lore. I've been living for a very long time now, and the thought of some messiah suddenly making everything all better . . ." He shook his head.

Lorelei moved toward him, words of disbelief spilling from her lips. "Are you saying you don't believe in the prophecy?" she asked incredulously. "The whole reason that Aerie even exists, and you don't believe in it?"

He lowered the smoldering weapons, and held her in his

steely gaze. "Aerie and its people are about the only things I *do* believe in these days."

Lorelei was speechless. She had only learned of the prophecy on her arrival in Ravenschild, but the promise of something other than the harsh world that she'd grown up in had given her the strength to continue.

"I fought during the Great War, Lorelei," he tried to explain. "And not on the winning side. I can't believe that God—even one merciful and just—could ever begin to forgive us for the wrong we've done."

She didn't want to hear this; she didn't want the hope that she kept protected deep inside her to be diminished in any way.

"The prophecy says—"

"Fairy stories," he retorted. The guns had again disappeared, and he grasped her shoulders in a powerful grip. "What you've got to realize—what we've all got to realize—is the only thing we have to look forward to is a world of hurt, and not all the prophecies and teenage messiahs in the world are gonna keep it away."

"But what if you're wrong?" she asked, pulling away. "What if Aaron *is* the harbinger of better times?"

Lehash scowled. "If you believe that, then I have some serious doubts as to whether you really are my daughter."

The words of a powerful angelic spell that would have caused the ground to split beneath the fallen angel and swallow him whole danced at the edge of her mind. It was ready to spill from her lips, but Lorelei stopped herself, instead turning her back upon her parent and starting back to the house. As she made her way through the brush, a part of her wished for him to call after her, to apologize in a fatherly way for the harshness of his words, but the more realistic half got exactly what it expected.

He had begun his target practice again, the blasts of gunfire like the explosive precursor to an approaching storm.

Vilma Santiago felt her eyes grow increasingly heavy, the words in her literature book starting to blur. She refused to look at the clock, deluding herself into thinking that if she didn't know the time, her body wouldn't crave sleep as badly. She thought about taking another of the pills she had bought at the drugstore to keep herself awake, but she'd already had three, and the directions said no more than two were recommended.

She closed her literature book and slid it into the bag leaning against the side of her desk. *Maybe if I can get ahead on my physics assignments,* Vilma thought, pulling out the overly large book and placing it on the desk before her.

Vilma would do anything to stay awake, anything to avoid the dreams. Disturbing visions from her recurring nightmares flashed before her eyes, a staccato slideshow of images that seemed more like memories than the fantastic creations of a sleeping mind. She felt herself begin to slip into the fugue state that always preceded sleep, and spastically jumped from her chair. Pacing about her bedroom, she slapped at her cheeks, hoping that the sharp stabs of pain would give her a second wind. *Or would this be my third?* she wondered groggily.

"C'mon, Vilma," she said aloud. "Stay awake." From the corner of her eye she saw her bed and for a split second could have sworn that it was calling to her. "No," she said. "No bed, you know what it means when you go to bed." She continued to pace, swinging her arms and taking deep breaths.

As she walked around her room, Vilma saw that a pink envelope had fallen from her book bag when she'd removed her physics text. It was a birthday card from Tina, who wasn't going to be in school the next day and hadn't wanted to miss her friend's big day. Vilma was going to be eighteen years old, but if it hadn't been for Tina, she wouldn't have even remembered. She retrieved the envelope and opened it. It was a typical Tina card. "I know what would make your birthday happy!" read the caption over a picture of a man wearing only unzipped blue jeans, his abs and pecs spectacularly oiled.

"You think so?" Vilma asked the card as she studied the handsome figure. She immediately thought of Aaron. It had been two weeks since his last e-mail and she was beginning to fear that she'd never hear from him again, that maybe he had found a new life somewhere, and no longer wanted reminders of the past he had left behind.

Vilma pushed the horrible thought from her head as she tossed the card into the plastic barrel beside her desk. *He pro-*

*bably just hasn't had a chance to get to a computer.* In fact she wouldn't be surprised if there was a message from him now. She had checked her e-mail just a few hours ago, but something told her that *maybe* Aaron had been in touch since then.

Vilma returned to her desk and turned on the computer. As she waited for the system to boot up, her thoughts stayed on the boy who had captured her heart. She wondered how he would react if she told him about her awful dreams and her fear of sleep—and would she even share the information with him in the first place? The answer to that was a simple one: of course she would. The way she felt about Aaron Corbet, she would have told him anything. It was as if they shared some strange kind of bond.

Maneuvering her mouse she clicked on the icon to connect to the Internet. *Maybe he sent me an electronic greeting card,* she thought happily and then realized that he probably didn't even know that tomorrow was her birthday. From the living room downstairs, the old grandfather clock began to chime, and as she waited for her connection, Vilma found herself counting the tolls of the bell.

*Bong! Bong! Bong! Bong! Bong! Bong! Bong! Bong! Bong! Bong! Bong!*

The clock tolled midnight, and she saw that there were no messages from Aaron or anybody else. Vilma was overcome with disappointment and the realization that she was now a year older. She stared at the computer screen, wishing a message to appear, but it didn't happen. "Happy Birthday to me," she said sadly.

She prepared to disconnect from the Internet and her bleary eyes traveled to the right corner of the screen where it showed the time. The clock read 11:59 P.M. and she offhandedly wondered if the clock downstairs was fast, or her computer's clock slow. Then, just as the disconnect message came up, the clock on her screen changed to 12:00 A.M.—and every one of her senses inexplicably came alive at once.

Vilma tossed her head violently back and the chair tipped over, spilling her onto the floor. The assault came upon her in waves. The sounds in her ears were deafening, a cacophony of noise through which she could just hear the panicked beat of her own heart and the swishing of blood through her veins.

*What's happening to me?* Vilma thought as she struggled to her feet, her hands pressed tightly against the bludgeoning invasion of sound. *Is this some kind of bizarre reaction to my lack of sleep, or the drugs I've taken?* she frantically wondered. Smells were suddenly overpowering—cleaning products from the kitchen, wood stain from the basement, bags of garbage in the barrels outside. She gasped for breath. The light of the room was blinding, and she lashed out at the lamp on her desk, knocking it to the floor.

*I've got to get help!* Vilma panicked. She needed a hospital. . . . She would wake her aunt and uncle. . . .

Her hand was on the doorknob when she heard a voice

from somewhere in the room behind her. *"The seed of a seraph stirs to waking as the clock tolls twelve,"* it said in a language that she had never heard before and should not have been able to understand—but did. *"This new day is the day of your birth, I'd wager."*

The hairs at the back of Vilma's neck bristled. She didn't want to turn around, didn't want to acknowledge this latest bit of insanity, but she could not help herself. As she slowly began to turn, a strange odor suddenly permeated the air. It smelled of rich spice and something rotten. It smelled of decay.

Vilma saw that there was a man inside her bedroom. He was dressed in dark clothes and wore a long raincoat despite the fact that it had not rained in weeks. His hair was long and combed back upon his head. His skin was deathly pale and seemed to glow in the limited light, and his eyes, if he had any, were lost within dark shadows that sat upon his face. Vilma had seen this mysterious figment of her madness before, perched in the tree outside her window: watching, waiting.

"You're not real."

*"Think what you will,"* he answered in the ancient tongue as he started toward her. *"It is no concern of mine. My charge was to wait and watch for you to blossom—and that is exactly what you have started to do."*

She closed her eyes and wished the figure away, but still he moved toward her. A scream about to explode from her lips froze in her lungs, and Vilma watched in stunned silence as speckled wings of black and white gradually unfurled from the figure's back.

*"Come along, little Nephilim,"* said the man who could only have been an angel. *"My master has plans for you."*

He took her in his arms and the world around her began to spin. And as she fell into unconsciousness, Vilma Santiago wondered if she was being taken to meet with God.

# CHAPTER EIGHT

Belphegor walked among his crops and in the primitive language of the bug, kindly asked them to leave his vegetables. Purging his gardens of toxic residue was like placing neon signs in front of all his plants, welcoming the various insects. But he hadn't forgotten them. There was an area of garden he had grown especially for the primitive life forms, and he invited them to partake of that particular bounty. The insects did as he asked, some flying into the air in a buzzing cloud, while others tumbled to the rich earth, heading for a more appropriate place to dine. The bugs did not care where they ate, as long as they were allowed to feed.

The angel thanked the simple creatures and turned his attention to a pitcher of iced tea that was waiting for him atop a rusted patio table in the center of the yard. He strolled casually through the grass, his bare feet enjoying the sensation of the new, healthy plant life. Removing the poisons from the backyards of Ravenschild brought him great pleasure, although those same toxins were beginning to wear upon his own body. The angel poured himself a glass from the pitcher of brown liquid and gazed out over his own little piece of paradise as he drank. This yard, of all the yards in Aerie, was one of his favorites. He had made it his own and it was good again. If only it was as simple for those who had fallen from God's grace.

And then came that odd feeling of excitement he'd experienced since first viewing the manifestation of Aaron Corbet's angelic self. *Is it possible?* Could he dare to believe that after all this time, after so many false hopes, the prophecy might actually come true?

Belphegor sipped his bitter brew, enjoying the sensation of the cold fluid as it traveled down his throat. He would not allow himself to be tricked; there was too much—too many—relying upon him, to be caught up in a wave of religious fervor. But he had to admit, there was something about this Nephilim, something wild, untamed, that inspired both excitement and fear.

The teaching had been going reasonably well. The boy was eager to learn, but his angelic nature was rough, rebellious, and if they were not careful, a deadly force could be unleashed upon them—upon the world. But that was a worry for another time.

The air in a far corner of the yard began to shimmer, a

dark patch forming at the center of the distress. There was sound, very much like the inhalation of breath, and the darkness blossomed to reveal its identity. Wings that seemed to be made from swaths of solid night unfurled, the shape of the boy nestled between them. He looked exhausted, yet exhilarated, a cocky smile on his young face.

"That took longer than I expected," Belphegor said, feigning disinterest as he reached for the pitcher of iced tea and refilled his glass. "Was there a problem?"

Aaron suppressed his angelic nature, the sigils fading, the wings shrinking to nothing upon his back. In his hand he held a rolled newspaper and whacked it against the palm of his other hand as he walked toward the old angel. "No problems," he said, tossing the paper onto the patio table where it unrolled to reveal the Chinese typesetting. It was *The People's Daily*. "I didn't have any Chinese money to buy one, so I had to wait until somebody threw this away."

The boy smiled, exuding a newfound confidence. He was learning fast, but there was still much to do—and so many ways in which things could go wrong.

"How was the travel?" Belphegor asked before taking another sip of tea. He had taught the youth a method of angelic travel requiring only the wings on his back and an idea of where he wanted to go.

"It was amazing," Aaron said. There was another glass on the table and he reached for it. "I did exactly what you said." He poured a full glass, almost spilling it in his excitement. "I pictured Beijing in my head, from those travel books and magazines, and I told myself that was where I wanted to be."

Belphegor nodded, secretly impressed. There had been many a Nephilim that couldn't even begin to grasp the concept, never mind actually do it.

"It was pretty cool," Aaron continued. "I saw it in my head, wrapped myself in my wings, and when I opened them up again, I was there." He gulped down his iced tea.

"And did anyone notice your arrival?"

Aaron tapped the remainder of the ice cubes in his glass into his open mouth and began to crunch noisily. "Nope," he said between crunches. "I didn't want anybody to see me—so they didn't."

Belphegor turned away and strolled back toward his plants and vegetables, leaving Aaron alone by the table. Absently he began to harvest some ripened cucumbers. The boy was advancing far more quickly than any Nephilim he had ever encountered. But the next phase of training was crucial, and the most dangerous. Despite his affinity, Belphegor wasn't sure if Aaron was ready.

"So what now?" he heard Aaron ask behind him.

Belphegor stopped and turned, cucumbers momentarily forgotten. "We're done for the day," he said dismissively.

"But it's still early," the Nephilim said, genuine eagerness in his voice. "Isn't there something more you can show me before—"

"The next phase of development is the investigation of your inner self," the angel interrupted.

"Okay," Aaron responded easily. "Let's do it."

"Do you think you're ready for a trip inside here?" Belphegor tapped Aaron's chest. "It's going to be a lot harder than a jaunt to Beijing."

Aaron's expression became more serious, as if the angel's cautioning words had stirred something—some shaded information hidden in the back of Aaron's mind, about to be dragged out into the light.

"If you think you're ready, prepared to find out who you are . . . what you are," Belphegor said cryptically, holding the boy in an unwavering gaze, "then we'll begin. But I'm not entirely sure you'll be happy with what you learn."

Verchiel gazed upon the unconscious female who had been laid on the floor before him. "Can you sense it as I can?" he asked the prisoner in the hanging cage across the room. "Like a newly emerging hatchling, fighting against the shell of its humanity. It wants so desperately to be free of its confines, to blossom and transform its fragile human vessel into the horror it is destined to be."

The leader of the Powers shifted his weight uncomfortably in the high-backed wooden chair. Though finally healing, the burns that he had received in his first confrontation with the Nephilim still caused him a great deal of discomfort. "It sickens me," Verchiel spat, his eyes riveted to the girl at his feet. "I should kill the wretched thing now."

"But you won't," wheezed the prisoner, still weak. "You took the trouble to bring her here, I gather she's going to play a part in whatever new trick you have up your sleeve. Maybe bait, to lure the Nephilim into a trap?"

Verchiel turned his attention from the girl to the prisoner. "Are you learning to think like me?" he asked with a humorless smile. "Or am I starting to think like you?"

The prisoner raised himself to a sitting position. "I'm not sure that even in my darkest days I could muster such disregard for innocent life."

"Innocent life?" the leader of the Powers asked as he studied the creature before him. "So simple—so defenseless—one can almost see why the Creator was so taken with them."

The female moaned softly in the grip of oblivion.

"But looks can be deceiving, can they not?" He nudged the girl with his foot. "There is a monster inside you just waiting to come out, isn't there, girl?"

The captive gripped the bars of his cage, hands pink with a fresh layer of skin. "A little bit of the pot calling the kettle black, don't you think, Verchiel?" he asked. "After all you've done of late, do you really believe she deserves the title of monster?"

Verchiel tilted his head in thought as he studied the girl lying before him. "I am not without a certain measure of pity for the misfortune of her birth. She cannot help what she is, but it does not change the fact that the likes of her kind should not exist."

"And who exactly provided you with this information?" the captive asked. "'Cause it looks as though I might have missed the announcement."

"It was never intended for our kind to lay with animals," Verchiel growled, the concept flooding him with feelings of revulsion. "The proof is in these monstrosities—animals with the power of the divine. I cannot imagine it was ever a part of the Creator's plan."

"And you being so close to God and all, you've taken it upon yourself to clear up the problem."

"As impudent as ever," Verchiel said, sliding from the chair to kneel beside the unconscious girl. "One would think that after all this time you would have learned some modicum of respect for the One you so horribly wronged."

"This has nothing to do with Him, Verchiel," the prisoner stressed, "and everything to do with your twisted perception of right and wrong."

Verchiel stifled the urge to lash out at his captive, focusing instead on the task at hand. "Right and wrong," he hissed, as he pushed up the girl's shirt to reveal the dark, delicate skin of her young stomach. "What is coming to fruition inside this poor creature is wrong."

The fingers of Verchiel's hand began to glow, and he lightly touched her stomach, burning her flesh in five places. Even within the hold of unconsciousness the female cried out, writhing in agony as her flesh sizzled and wisps of oily smoke curled up from the burns.

"I know what I do is right," he said. "There is a bond between the Nephilim and this female, a bond that will only be made stronger with the realization that they are of the same kind."

Verchiel could sense the essence of angel coiled inside the young woman, still not fully awake. The pain would draw it closer, forcing it to blossom sooner. He again reached down and touched her stomach, leaving his fingertips upon the fragile flesh just a bit longer. The fluids within the skin sputtered, crackled, and popped with his hellish caress.

The girl was moaning and crying now, still not fully awake, but the power inside her was growing stronger, calling out to others of its ilk for help.

"That's it," Verchiel cooed, inhaling the acrid aroma of burning skin. "Summon the great hero to your side so that I may destroy him and the dreams he inspires."

It was like the dreams. . . . No, *nightmares,* he had been having before the change.

But Aaron was not asleep.

Belphegor had done this. He had taken Aaron into his

home, telling him he had to learn the origins of the angelic essence that had become a part of him. He had made him drink a mug of some awful-tasting concoction from a boiling pot on the stove. It tasted like garbage and smelled even worse, but the old fallen angel had said that it would help Aaron to travel inside himself, to experience the genesis of the power that wanted so desperately to reshape him.

Aaron had choked down the foul liquid and sat upon the living-room floor, while Belphegor took his place in the recliner and began to read *The People's Daily*. At first Aaron was concerned that nothing was happening, but the old fallen angel had looked over the top of the paper and told him to wait for the poison to take effect.

*Poison?*

Yes, Belphegor had indeed given him poison—the impending death of his human aspect would allow his angelic nature to assume control, Belphegor explained before going back to the news of China.

A stabbing pain had begun in the pit of his stomach. An unnatural warmth radiated from the center of the intense agony and spread through his extremities, numbing them. Aaron found that he could no longer sit up and fell to his side on the cold wooden floor.

He was finding it hard to stay conscious, but could still hear Belphegor encouraging him to hold on, warning him not to succumb fully to the poison coursing through his body.

Aaron had to find the source of his essence's power; then wrest control away from the strengthening angelic might, and use it to complete the unification of the dual natures that existed within him.

*What if I'm not strong enough?* Aaron had asked. And the old angel had looked at him grimly and said that without the anchor of his humanity, the angelic essence within him would surely run amok and destroy them all.

At first there was only darkness and the burning warmth of the poison, but then he saw it there, writhing in the black sea of his gradual demise. When Aaron had last seen it, the power had taken the shapes of various creatures of creation. Now it had matured into a beautiful winged creature, humanoid in shape, with skin the color of the sun and eyes as cool and dark as the night. They were family in a strange kind of way, he thought, and it drew him close, wrapping him in its embrace, flowing over and into him as if liquid, and when he opened his eyes, he was somewhere else entirely.

The pain of the poison was gone and Aaron found himself standing in a vast field of tall grass the color of gold. A warm gentle breeze smelling of rich spice caressed the waving plains. Far off in the distance he could just about make out the shape of a vast city, but there were sounds nearby that pulled his attention away from the metropolis. He turned and walked toward a hill, the sound of a voice carried on the wind drawing him closer.

He reached the top of the rise and peered down into a

clearing, where an army had been gathered. They were angels, hundreds of angels garbed in armor polished to gleaming, and they stood unmoving, enraptured as they listened to one of their own. Clearly their leader, he paced before them, words of inspiration spilling from his mouth, and Aaron could see why they would have pledged their allegiance. There was something about him, a charisma that was impossible to deny.

*As beautiful as the morning stars,* he heard a voice whisper at the back of his mind, and he could not disagree.

And then the leader, the Morningstar, walked among his troops laying his hand upon each and every one of them, and as he touched them, bestowing upon them a special gift, weapons of fire sprang to life in their grasp, and they were ready to fight.

Ready for war.

Aaron experienced a sudden wave of vertigo, as if the world around him were being yanked away to be replaced by another time, another place, and he struggled to remain standing. He was on a battlefield now, surrounded by the unbridled carnage that was war. Soldiers he had watched rallied by the Morningstar were battling an army of equal savagery. He saw Camael and Verchiel fighting side by side against the Morningstar's army. The screams of the dying and the maimed filled the air as blazing swords hacked away limbs and snuffed out life, and angels fell helplessly from the sky, their wings consumed by flames of heavenly fire.

It was horrible; one of the most awesome yet disturbing

sights he had ever seen. He wanted to turn away, to pull his eyes from the scenes of brutality, the broken and burning bodies of angels, the golden grass trampled, the ground stained with the dark blood of the heavenly. But it was everywhere; no matter where he looked, there was death.

Aaron's eyes were suddenly drawn to the Morningstar, his sword of fire hacking a swath through the opposing forces. His army was vanquished, but still he fought on, flaxen wings spread wide, slashing his way toward a tower made of glass, crystal maybe, that seemed to go up into the sky forever. The angel was screaming and there were tears on his face. Aaron could feel his sadness, for the sorrow that permeated the atmosphere of this place was so strong as to be nearly palpable.

The Morningstar screamed up at the crystalline tower, shaking his armored fist and demanding that He who sits on high come down to face him. And with wings beating air ripe with the smells of bloodshed, he began to ascend. The skies grew dark, thick with roiling clouds of gunmetal gray, and thunder rumbled ominously, causing the very environment to tremble. But the Morningstar continued to rise, flying steadily upward, sword of fire brandished in his grip, unhindered by the threat of storm.

Aaron could feel it before it actually happened, as if the air itself had become charged with electricity. He wanted to warn the beautiful soldier, but it was too late. A bolt of lightning resembling a long, gnarled finger reached down from the gray, endless clouds and touched the warrior of Heaven. There was a flash of blinding light, and the Morningstar tumbled, burning, from the sky.

*Stay down,* Aaron whispered as he watched the figure twitch and then force himself to rise.

The Morningstar swayed upon legs charred black, and another blade of fire appeared in his hand. Again he looked up at the glass tower and raised his sword in defiance. *"How?"* he shrieked pitifully through a mouth now nothing more than a blackened hole. *"How can you love them more than us?"*

With wings still afire, he leaped back into the air, but his ascent was slower than before. The heavens growled with menace, as if displeased by his defiance, and birdlike shrieks filled the world. Aaron watched as the soldiers of the opposing army attacked the Morningstar, grabbing at his injured form, pulling him back to the ground, where they pitilessly set upon him with their weapons of fire.

He could feel the Morningstar's pain, every jab, every stab of the soldiers' searing blades, as if the attacks were being perpetrated upon him. Aaron fell to the ground, his eyes transfixed upon the violence before him, the blood of vanquished angels seeping through the knees of his pants.

Numbness had invaded his body, and he fought to stay conscious—to stay alive. But the darkness had him again in its grasp, and it pulled him below to a place where he could die in peace, the very same place that the angelic essence had resided before it had come awake on his eighteenth birthday. This was where he would slip from life, allowing the angelic power total mastery of his fragile human shell.

For a brief moment Aaron was convinced that this was the right thing for him to do. In this deep place of shadow there was no worry, no irritating mysteries of angelic powers, there was only comforting peace. Escape from the responsibilities heaped upon him by ancient prophecy.

*"Aaron! He's hurting me!"*

Aaron's tranquility was suddenly shattered by a cry for help, a desperate plea that echoed in the darkness. He tried to ignore it, but there was something about the voice that stirred within him a desire to live.

*"Where are you, Aaron? He'll keep hurting me unless you come."*

"Vilma," Aaron whispered within the constricting cocoon of shadow, and opened his eyes to a vision of the girl he believed he loved in the clutches of Verchiel. It was but a flash of sight, but it was enough to stir him from the comforting embrace of his impending death.

*"Please! Aaron!"*

The angelic essence fought to keep him submerged in the depths of oblivion, but Vilma needed him, Stevie and the fallen needed him, and he felt ashamed that he had even considered giving in. The closer he got to awareness, the more he felt the painful effects the poison had wrought upon his body, and he was reminded of, and inspired by, the Morningstar, burned black by the finger of God, but still he fought on.

Aaron came awake on his knees, now in the kitchen of Belphegor's home, his body wracked with bone-snapping convulsions. He pitched forward and vomited up the poison. Slowly he raised his head, wiping the remains of the revolting fluid that dribbled down his chin, to see Belphegor leaning forward on a wooden chair, offering him a white paper napkin.

"What did you see?" the angel asked, a gleam of excitement in his ancient eyes.

"Vilma." Aaron struggled to stand.

"Who?"

"I have to go to her," Aaron said, the familiar feeling of dread he'd been carrying since his life so dramatically changed replacing the nausea in his stomach.

"He has her. Verchiel has her."

# CHAPTER NINE

**V**ilma?" Belphegor asked, confused. "Who, may I ask, is Vilma?"

Aaron swayed upon legs that seemed to be made of rubber, grabbing hold of the kitchen doorframe to steady himself. "She's my girl . . ." He paused, rethinking his answer. "She's somebody from my old life, someone very important to me—and Verchiel has her." Images of the screaming girl flashed across his vision. He could hear her calling out to him.

"He is attempting to get to you through your friends," Belphegor commented matter-of-factly. "Typical behavior for one such as he."

Aaron didn't understand. Somehow Vilma had reached out and touched his mind.

*But how?*

"What did you see when you went inside, Aaron?" Belphegor questioned. "You must tell me everything—"

Aaron raised a hand to interrupt him. "She was inside my head." He stared hard at Belphegor. "How is that possible, unless . . . ?"

Belphegor slowly nodded, sensing that Aaron already suspected the answer. "Unless she is as you are," he finished.

It hit Aaron like a physical blow and he fell back against the doorframe, sliding to the floor as his knees gave out. "I can't believe it," he muttered in amazement. He remembered every moment, however brief, he had shared with her. There was no doubt of the attraction, but evidently the reason went far beyond raging hormones. They were of the same kind.

Nephilim.

"Just when I think I've seen it all," he said with an exasperated shake of his head.

Belphegor left the table and moved to Aaron's side. He seemed impatient, anxious. "Never mind your friend," he said. "What did you *see*, Aaron?"

"I don't have time for this," Aaron said, climbing to his feet. "She needs me."

Belphegor reached out and grabbed hold of his arm in a powerful grip. "I need to know what you saw," he stressed. "The people of Aerie need to know what you saw."

Aaron shook off the old angel's grasp. "I saw an angel—and he was one of the most beautiful things I have ever seen," he said, not without a little embarrassment, especially as he caught the look on Belphegor's face. "It's not sexual or anything," he explained. "It was just the way he carried himself. I could feel the devotion of his army in the air. I could feel how much they loved him."

"You . . . you saw the Morningstar?" Belphegor stammered, as if he were afraid of something.

Aaron nodded, a bit taken aback by the old angel's reaction. "And there was a battle," he said, the violent, disturbing imagery forever burned into his psyche. "It was horrible," he added. "And incredibly sad."

Belphegor stared off into space, thoughtfully stroking his chin.

"What does it mean, Belphegor?" Aaron asked cautiously. "What does all of this have to do with me?"

The old fallen slowly refocused his gaze on Aaron. "The pain and the sadness, the death and the violence—I believe that is the power from which you were born."

Aaron shook his head. "I don't understand."

"But you will," Belphegor said with authority. "We shall go to Scholar, and together we'll delve deeper into the mystery of your origin—"

"No," Aaron said emphatically. "You don't understand. Vilma is in trouble and I have to go to her." Aaron moved past the old angel, his resolve lending new strength to his legs. "I can't afford to waste any more time."

He had pulled open the kitchen door and was ready to step outside when Belphegor again grabbed him.

"We're close, Aaron," he said.

There was a tension in his voice that hadn't been there before, a veiled excitement hinting that the angel knew more than he was letting on. It almost drew Aaron back, but then he remembered Vilma's face—her beautiful face, twisted in pain and fear—and he knew he had no choice.

He shrugged Belphegor's hand away and started down the stairs. "I'm sorry, but I have to go," he said over his shoulder. "I'll come back just as soon as—"

Lehash stood in the street just outside the yard. A long, thin cigar dangled at the corner of his mouth, the smoke trailing from its tip forming a misty halo around his head. "Is there a problem, boy?" he asked in a grave voice, the cigar bobbing up and down like a conductor's baton as he spoke.

Aaron shook his head, fully feeling the menace that radiated from the Aerie constable. "Not yet," he answered, trying to keep the fear from his voice.

Belphegor came up behind him. "It's all right, Lehash," he said reassuringly. "Come back inside, Aaron. We'll talk."

"I'm going," Aaron said defiantly, and began to push past them.

Lehash came forward, and Aaron saw the shimmer of fire in his hands that signaled the arrival of his golden weapons.

"I'd listen to the boss if I was you," he said with a threatening hiss, blocking Aaron's path.

"It could be a trap, Aaron," Belphegor cautioned behind him. "Verchiel could be using your friend to strike, not only at you, but at us, at Aerie. I'm sorry, but we can't let you go, there's far too much at stake."

Lehash brandished his guns menacingly. "You heard 'im," he said, motioning for Aaron to return to the house. "Get back in there before things get serious."

"They already have," Aaron said, feeling the power come alive within him. It was like the world's biggest head rush, and he braced himself, not even trying to hold back its coming.

A crowd of citizens had started to gather, coming out of their decrepit homes as if drawn by the potential for violence. Aaron could see their nervous glances, hear their whispering.

"I knew he'd be trouble." "Him? He's not the One—I can't believe anyone could be so foolish as to think that." "Lehash will put him in his place."

The sigils emerged on Aaron's flesh, and he let his wings of solid black unfold. He heard gasps from the gathered, and even Lehash seemed genuinely taken aback as Aaron stepped past the constable and into the street. The citizens were in awe. He could see it in their eyes—or maybe it was something else they were seeing, he decided, as he heard the sharp click of twin gun hammers being pulled back from behind.

Aaron reacted purely on instinct; there was no inner

struggle, no attempt to keep the power at bay, he simply let it flow through him, guiding its might with a tempered hand. He spun around to face his potential foe, a feral snarl upon his lips. With a thunderous clap of sound, one of the gunslinger's pistols belched fire made solid, and it hurtled across the short expanse to burrow beneath the soft flesh of the Nephilim's shoulder.

Aaron fell backward, a scream upon his lips as he hit the street, his mighty wings cushioning the fall. The pain was bad, and his left side was growing numb as he lay gazing up at the early morning sky. Aaron knew that he should get up—for Stevie's sake, for Vilma's—but he wasn't sure he had the strength to do so.

The citizens' murmurs sounded to him like a swarm of bees roused to anger by a threat to their hive. Lehash stood over him, smoking pistol still in his grasp. There was cruelty in his steely gaze, a look that said so much more than words.

"Look at you," he said in a whisper meant only for Aaron's ears. "Can't even save yourself, never mind us." The gunslinger stared down his arm, down the length of his golden weapon. "How dare you fill their hearts with hope and then rip it away. Haven't we suffered enough without the likes of you?" Lehash came closer. "I should kill you now."

Aaron lay still, his gaze locked on the barrel of the pistol that hovered above him ominously like a black, unblinking eye. Lehash's finger twitched upon the trigger, and the

Nephilim's mind was assaulted with the brutal images of war. He again saw the Morningstar walking among his troops, laying his hand upon them, giving something of himself to each and every one. And he witnessed them in battle, fighting for their master's cause—dying for their master's cause—and he was filled with their purpose, with their power and strength.

The sigils on his body suddenly burned as if painted with acid, and Aaron sprang up from the street, a cry of rage from somewhere deep inside escaping his lips. The gunslinger fired, but this time the bullet did not find its target. Aaron lashed out with one of his wings, swatting the weapon from the constable's grasp. "No more guns," he commanded, grabbing the fallen angel's wrist and violently twisting his arm so that he dropped the second of the golden guns.

Aaron looked into the constable's eyes and saw that something new had taken the place of steely cruelty. He saw the beginnings of fear, but he did not want that. Effortlessly he hurled Lehash away. All he wanted was to save the people he loved.

Lehash landed in the street about six feet away, scattering citizens that had gathered there. A hush had fallen over the crowd, and they watched him in pregnant silence. Belphegor came forward to help Lehash as sparks danced in the constable's hands. Aaron tensed, a weapon of his own ready to surge to life.

"No," Belphegor commanded in a powerful voice.

Lehash stared at his superior, confusion on his grizzled face. "Let him go."

Lehash's eyes went wide in shock. "You can't do this," he sputtered. "He'll bring Verchiel and his bloodthirsty rabble down on our heads for sure!"

Belphegor raised a hand and closed his eyes. "You heard me, let the boy go."

From across the street Aaron met Belphegor's eyes and a jolt like electricity passed through his body.

"If you're going to go," Belphegor said, "then go now."

Aaron found it difficult to look away from the angel's intense gaze. *Am I doing the right thing?* he fretted. Doubt crept into his thoughts, but then images of Vilma and the still-missing Stevie filled his mind, and it didn't matter anymore if it was right or wrong. He had to go. "I'll come back," he said as he spread his wings.

"I hope you do," Belphegor replied, a scowling Lehash at his side.

Aaron took one final look about Aerie and saw Camael, Gabriel, and Lorelei heading toward him. He wanted to tell them what he was doing—what he had to do—but he didn't want to stop, unsure if he would have the courage to recommence if he did. They would have to understand.

The image of his destination fresh inside his head, Aaron folded his wings about himself and was gone.

\* \* \*

*"Maybe he didn't see us,"* Gabriel said forlornly.

But Camael knew differently. He had looked into the boy's eyes before he departed.

The fallen angel had known that it was only a matter of time before the violence in his life again reared its ugly head and his brief respite would end. It had been pleasurable while it lasted.

"What's going on?" Lorelei was asking an older woman whom Camael recognized as Marjorie. He had saved her from one of Verchiel's hunting parties sometime in the 1950s, and she still bore a red, ragged scar upon her cheek to commemorate the Powers' ruthless attack.

The woman wrung her hands nervously, staring off in the direction from which Aaron had departed. "He's gone," she said, her voice filled with concern. "There was a fight, and then he left us." Marjorie looked past Lorelei to Camael. "Is he coming back?" she asked pleadingly. "Can you tell me if the Chosen One is coming back?"

Lorelei turned to him as well, as though he might have some special insight into the situation unfolding.

"Let us find Belphegor," Camael said, ignoring the women's plaintive questions, and continuing down the street, Gabriel close at his heels.

The citizens of Aerie were abuzz, and as he passed, their eyes caught his, frantic for answers to assuage their fears. A hand shot out to grip his arm and Camael stared into the face of Scholar. He believed his true name to be Tumael, once a member of the host called Principalities. He was wild eyed, as anxious as the others around him.

"Do you know where he's gone—the boy?" Tumael asked nervously, his grip tight with desperation. "We have to get him back . . . we . . . we can't let him walk away from us, Camael. Do you understand the importance of what I'm saying?"

Camael knew exactly, but until he found out what had happened, he could offer no words of solace. "Belphegor. I need to speak with him."

The fallen angel pointed toward a house not far from where they stood.

"Come, Gabriel," Camael said to the dog that waited obediently by his side.

They approached the home, catching sight of Lorelei disappearing into the backyard. As they rounded the corner of the house, they were met by voices raised in panicked fury. Lehash and his daughter were in the midst of a heated argument, arms flailing as they railed against each other. Belphegor was across the yard, removed from the commotion, examining the branches of a young sapling.

"Why don't you go and talk with Belphegor," Camael told the Labrador at his side. "Maybe he can tell you where Aaron has gone."

Tail wagging, Gabriel trotted toward Aerie's Founder, while Camael turned his attention to the angry constable.

"You," Lehash growled, raising an accusatory hand as Camael approached. "This is your fault!"

"Lehash, stop," Lorelei pleaded.

"Would anyone care to tell me what has happened?" Camael asked, carefully watching Lehash's hands for signs of his golden weaponry.

"Your Nephilim will be the death of us all," the constable spat, fists clenched in barely suppressed rage. "Filling all their heads with foolishness . . . we'll see how much of a messiah they think he is when we have Verchiel's soldiers breathing down our necks."

"Dad, please," Lorelei said, again trying to calm him. She touched the sleeve of his coat, but he pulled away roughly.

"Is that what this is really about, Lehash?" Camael asked. "Your lack of belief?"

Lehash scowled. "Don't matter what I believe," he said with a sorrowful shake of his head. He glanced over at Belphegor and Gabriel. "Don't matter what any of us believes. Verchiel will have what he's been waiting for—a good whiff of Aerie, and that's all the son of a bitch will need to destroy us."

"Where has Aaron gone?"

"To rescue a friend—a female—from Verchiel," Lehash explained. He smiled, but the expression was void of any humor. "With the scent of where he's been these last weeks clinging to him like cheap perfume. Should have just handed a map to the Powers, get the slaughter over with all the quicker."

The fallen angel pushed past, his piece said, Lorelei close behind. Her eyes briefly touched Camael's. "I'm sorry," she said, and he wondered if she was apologizing for her father's behavior, or perhaps giving her condolences for what they believed to be Aerie's inevitable demise.

Camael joined Belphegor, who was leaning down to pet Gabriel.

*"Aaron's gone to find Vilma,"* the dog said, tipping his head back so the old angel would scratch beneath his throat. *"She's the one he talks to on the computer sometimes."*

"I believe that she, too, is a Nephilim." Belphegor spoke as he obliged the animal's wants. "Her angelic nature cried out to him as he was exploring his own." He stopped patting Gabriel, much to the dog's disappointment, and turned his attention to Camael. "Verchiel has her." He looked out to the neighborhood beyond the yard. "It's truly amazing how quickly things change, Camael," Belphegor said with a wistful smile. "You never really see it coming; it's just suddenly there, the eye of the speeding locomotive bearing down upon you."

"You could have stopped him," Camael said. "Or you could have found me and I would have—"

Again Belphegor smiled sadly. "It doesn't really matter that he's gone." He began to stroll from the yard, Gabriel and Camael following at his side. "Change is coming to Aerie, and whether it be the machinations of prophecy, or just plain fate, there's nothing we can do to stop it."

Aerie's citizens were still milling about the street, their gazes haunted.

"They can sense it as much as you and I," Belphegor said, gesturing at the crowd.

He stopped in the middle of the street and closed his eyes. With a soft grunt of exertion, his wings sprang from his back, sad-looking things of dingy gray and missing feathers. "Join me for a moment," he said, motioning for Camael to follow as he launched himself into the air, the wings, surprisingly, having the strength to lift him.

"Wait for me here," Camael told Gabriel, his own mighty wings sweeping from his back and taking him heavenward.

*"Like I have a choice,"* he heard the dog mumble as he ascended.

It was early morning, the sun just starting to rise above the horizon, illuminating the dilapidated neighborhood below.

"Take a good long look, Camael," Belphegor said, gesticulating with a hand to Aerie beneath him as his wings pounded the air. "For soon, it's all going to change."

Camael looked below, at the run-down houses, the cracked and untended streets, the high barbed-wire fence that encircled it, and felt the pangs of something he had not experienced since he first left heavenly paradise on a mission of murder. He had not had a home—a true place of belonging—in countless millenia. The troubling thought of losing this one filled him with great sorrow.

And then, hovering above the neighborhood, the former leader of the Powers suddenly knew what was required of him. It was his way of giving thanks to those who had accepted him into their community, despite his loathsome past.

Camael would do everything within his strength to see that Aerie lived on, and may Heaven have pity on any who dared try to keep him from his task.

Aaron had recognized Vilma's location in the vision almost immediately: the red metal lockers, the cracked plaster walls painted eggshell white, a handmade poster that should have been taken down months ago asking for canned donations for a Thanksgiving food drive. He opened his wings to an empty parking lot, for it was still quite early in the morning, and gazed at Kenneth Curtis High School. A pang of nostalgia spread through him; memories, both good and bad, flooded his thoughts.

As he crossed the lot to the redbrick-and-concrete building, his wings receded and the fearsome marks upon his flesh faded. As an afterthought, he willed himself invisible, not wanting an early riser to see him going into the building, and call the police. He climbed the steps leading to the large, double doors, thinking of how much his life had changed in such a brief amount of time. A little over a month ago he had been a student here, a senior, preparing to graduate and begin the next phase of his life. *The next phase happened all right, but not how I would have planned it.* He reached the top of the stairs and pulled on one of the doors. It was unlocked and his flesh tingled with the sensation of caution.

The smells of the old building wafted out to greet him. He remembered his first day at Ken Curtis. He hadn't wanted to return for a second, but he did, and each day he went back, it got a little easier. He also recalled the first day he had seen Vilma, and with that recollection came the realization of how much was now at stake.

He stepped into the school, and the door closed gradually behind him. Ahead, standing near the doorway of the principal's office, stood an angel. He was clothed as Aaron had come to expect: dark suit, trench coat—as if he'd just come from a funeral—and in his hand he held a flaming sword.

Expecting a fight, Aaron created a weapon of his own and felt the strange symbols return to his flesh. It was amazing how easily the transformation came now. *Maybe I'm finally getting the hang of this thing,* he thought absently.

Instead of brandishing his weapon, the Powers' soldier turned away and approached a set of swinging doors. With his free hand he pushed one side open and bowed his head.

Aaron cautiously proceeded down the hallway toward the doors, the angel watching, quelled anger in his dark eyes. But he remained silent, still holding the door for him. Aaron strode through defiantly. He could feel the angel's stare upon his back, cold and murderous, but did not give him the satisfaction of turning to meet his gaze. More angels emerged from the class-rooms along the hall, motioning with a flourish of their flaming blades for him to proceed past them.

At the top of the stairs leading down into the basement, another angel waited and gestured for him to descend. Of course he had to descend; his brain raced. Wasn't that one of the first things he had learned in freshman English? That the protagonist must always descend to confront what plagues him before his victory and eventual ascension.

As with the others in the corridor behind him, the angel warrior at the stairs said nothing as he passed. Aaron went down the steps to the first landing and chanced a look back. The angel was watching him, a cruel smile on its thin, blood-less lips. "Catch you on the way back," Aaron called. He had no idea what the Powers had in store for him below, but he wasn't about to give them the satisfaction of believing he was afraid.

He continued down into the basement, the illumination thrown by his flaming blade lighting the way. The air below was thick with the smell of chlorine, and at the foot of the stairs he stopped, trying to decide if he should head toward the school's pool or the gymnasium.

It didn't take long for another of Verchiel's soldiers to appear and motion him toward the gym. Aaron had never particularly enjoyed phys ed, and found it strangely fitting that the Powers would summon him there. His teacher had been a jock from way back and didn't much care for anyone who wasn't on the football team. "Abandon hope all ye who enter," the Nephilim muttered as he walked through the door and into the gymnasium, the strange and disturbing vision of angels playing a game of shirts-versus-skins basketball running through his head.

But those images were soon dispelled. The room was dark, red exit signs and the swords of the angelic army that awaited him providing the only light. Aaron felt his heart sink, even with the essence inside him. *How can I ever hope to fight so many?* They were everywhere: on the bleachers, perched atop the basketball rims, and up above in the girder-latticed ceiling. They reminded him of pigeons, only these birds were far more dangerous.

"We've been waiting for you," said a voice that made his flesh tingle as if covered with ants.

Immediately Aaron felt the wings on his back begin to stir. On cue, a group of angels atop the bleachers stepped aside to reveal Verchiel. He was reclining in the wooden seats, as if watching a game, the unconscious Vilma lying beside him. Aaron was disappointed to see that Stevie was not there as well. His pulse quickened as his wings sprang from his back. *This is it,* he thought, and the power inside him writhed in antici-pation. The Powers' leader watched him with eyes like shiny black marbles, and Aaron noticed that the angel's face still bore the angry scars from their first confrontation back in Lynn.

"Let her go, Verchiel," he said, raising his blade of fire. "She's done nothing to you. It's me that you want."

The Powers' leader gazed with disgust at the unconscious young woman. "That is where you are wrong, animal," he said in a voice filled with contempt. "My problem has grown far larger than you." He touched Vilma then, a gentle caress with fingertips that glowed like white-hot metal, and she cried out in pain.

Aaron surged forward, wings spread wide to lift him into the air, but something moved in the periphery of his sight, something that was beside him before his brain even had a chance to react. It lashed out at him, a gauntlet of metal connecting with the side of his face, sending him crashing to the slick wooden floor in a heap.

"What you are, what you represent, is a virulent disease," Verchiel said from the bleachers above, "a disease that has infected this world."

Aaron's head was ringing and he was finding it difficult to focus. But the power of the Nephilim coursed through his body, urging him to his feet. Sensing his attacker close by, Aaron lashed out with his sword of flame. The blade touched nothing.

"But I believe I have found a cure for this epidemic." Aaron could hear Verchiel descending the wooden bleachers a step at a time.

Another blow fell on the back of his neck with such force

that he wondered if it had been broken. He rolled onto his back and gazed up into the fearsome visage of a warrior clad entirely in armor of red—the color of spilled blood.

"This is Malak," he heard Verchiel say from somewhere nearby. "And he will be your death, body and spirit."

And as Aaron studied the armored figure looming menacingly above him, he had a sneaking suspicion that Verchiel might very well be right.

# CHAPTER TEN

The armored warrior called Malak reached into the air, and from some hidden pocket in space, removed a sword of dark metal. The light of the Powers' flaming weapons illuminated strange etchings on the blade, similar to those on the manacles Aaron had worn in Aerie. But he had little time to consider that, as Malak brought the weapon down, intending to cleave his skull in two.

Aaron rolled to the side, then flexing his powerful wings, propelled himself upward and lashed out with his own sword. The burning blade clipped Malak's shoulder, sending a shower of sparks into the air. Malak was already moving to counter the attack, his sword gone, replaced with a long spear made of the same dark, etched metal. He struck out with the shaft of the spear, catching Aaron on the chin. The Nephilim stumbled to the side and watched from the corner of his eye as the armored warrior lunged forward, the spear's tip searching for something vital.

His actions almost reflex, Aaron swatted the spearhead away with his sword of fire, severing it from the body of the shaft. He spun around, the weapon in his hand now seeking Malak's heart, momentarily amazed by the fluidity of his thoughts and movements. No longer did he feel the struggle inside him between what was angelic and what was human. But now wasn't the time for reflection.

Malak had dropped what was left of his spear and grabbed hold of Aaron's fiery blade, halting its deadly progress less than a half inch from his ornate chest plate. Aaron bore down upon the blade with all his might, but Malak's strength was incredible, his armored hand glowing white hot with the heat of heavenly fire. Suddenly there was a blinding flash, and the combatants were thrown apart by the force of the powerful concussion. Aaron shook away the cotton that seemed to fill his head, coming to a disturbing realization: Malak had broken his blade. The warrior had actually destroyed his sword of fire. He quickly scrambled to his feet. Malak was already standing, flexing the hand that had held back Aaron's sword of fire. The armored glove had already cooled, returning to its original color of ore.

A strange sound filled the air. Malak was laughing—a high-pitched titter that reminded Aaron more of a small child amused by cartoon antics on television than the laugh of a blood-thirsty warrior. Then, as abruptly as it had begun, Malak's laughter ended, and where there had been nothing in his armored hand, there were suddenly razor-sharp throwing stars. Aaron heard their metal surfaces grinding together as Malak bent forward and let the blades fly. He spread his wings and took to the air, the stars finding targets instead in the bodies of the Powers' angels that were unlucky enough to be standing nearby watching the conflict unfold.

He glided backward, keeping a cautious eye on the armored warrior already on the move. Not paying attention to his surroundings, his back hit up against something solid and instinctively a sword grew in his hand. He spun, hacking at what was behind him. Angels scattered in a flutter of wings and trench coats, hissing menacingly, as Aaron's blade passed through the steel poles of a basketball hoop, sending the backboard crashing to the gymnasium floor.

Distracted, Aaron didn't notice Malak until it was too late. The armored warrior tossed a net made of thin, flexible strands of the same black metal as his weapons and ensnared the Nephilim. The weighted ends of the net restricted Aaron's wings, and he fell to the floor atop the downed backboard. Eager to vanquish his prey, Malak charged; a dagger caked with the blood of earlier kills clutched in his armored hand.

Aaron concentrated on a new weapon, and another sword came to be in his grasp, melting through the tight weave of the net. But before he could free himself completely, Malak was upon him. He tried to turn away, but his movement was hindered by the net and the weight of his armored assailant, and the dagger's blade bit deep into his already wounded shoulder. Aaron cried out, thrashing violently beneath Malak's attack and managing to knock him to one side. With his sword of fire, he sliced upward through the metal mesh, cutting an opening big enough to crawl through.

As he sloughed off the net Aaron watched with muted horror: His armored attacker brought the knife blade to the face of his helmet, the tip of a pink tongue snaked from the mask and licked the Nephilim's blood from the weapon's edge. For an instant he wondered what kind of creature resided behind the concealing helmet of scarlet, recalling Camael's haunting explanation of the Powers' use of the handicapped. He thought of his foster brother, steeling his resolve against his foe and the others he would eventually have to face. Though his shoulder burned as if on fire, Aaron held his sword tightly and slowly pointed the fiery blade across the gym where his opponent waited.

"You," Aaron said in a booming voice filled with authority. "Let's finish this."

Malak giggled again. His knife disappeared and he withdrew a double-bladed battle-ax from the air to replace it. The warrior hefted the heavy weapon in one hand. "Bootiful," he said through his mask of red metal.

\* \* \*

*Bootiful.*

The word hit him like one of Lehash's flaming bullets, and Aaron lowered his weapon in shock.

"What did you say?" he asked the scarlet-garbed warrior.

Again Malak giggled, that high-pitched titter that put his nerves on edge.

"What's the matter, Nephilim?" he heard Verchiel ask with mock concern.

Aaron chanced a glance at the heavenly monster. He was standing before the bleachers, hands clasped behind his back, a throng of angel soldiers surrounding him. One of them had Vilma slung over its shoulder, as if she were nothing more than an afterthought.

"Has something plucked a chord of familiarity?"

Malak was suddenly before him, swinging the blade of his double-headed ax. Aaron sprang back from the vicious blade, studying his attacker's movement, the single word still echoing dangerously in his head.

*Bootiful.*

The ax buried itself deep into the shiny, hardwood floor, but Malak quickly retrieved it, coming at him again. The warrior swung his weapon of war, and this time Aaron responded in kind, deflecting the ax with his sword of fire.

"Why did you say that word?" he hissed, launching his own assault against Malak.

The warrior giggled, childlike, as he ducked beneath the swipe of Aaron's blade.

"Why did you say it?" he shouted frantically, an idea almost too horrible for him to comprehend beginning to form in his mind. His attack upon the Powers' assassin grew wilder, driving Malak back across the gym.

Malak countered as fast as Aaron struck, blocking and avoiding the weapon of heavenly fire with ease.

Verchiel was laughing, a grating sound, like the cawing of some carrion bird.

Aaron hacked downward with all his might, but Malak stepped aside, bringing his armored foot down upon the blade, trapping it against the floor as he lashed out with his ax. Aaron felt the bite of the razor-sharp blade as it cut through the fabric of his shirt and the skin beneath. He jumped back, leaving his pinned sword to disperse in a flash. Slowly he lowered his hand to his stomach, then brought it up to his face. His fingertips were stained the color of his attacker's armor.

The sight of his own blood and the unsettling sound of Verchiel's laughter served only to inflame his rage. He felt the power of the Nephilim inside him and it coursed through his muscles—through the entire fiber of his being. If he were to survive this conflict, he had to trust the warrior's nature he had inherited. He had to defeat this armored foe, but still he could not get past the implication of Verchiel's words.

*Has something plucked a chord of familiarity?*

Malak came at him again, battle-ax at the ready, and Aaron sprang forward to meet the attack. He dove low, connecting with the warrior's armor-plated legs, and they crashed to the floor in a thrashing pile. Malak held on to his ax and tried to use it to drive his opponent from atop him, but Aaron kept close, rendering the weapon useless. The power of the Nephilim shrieked a cry of battle, and Aaron found himself caught up in a wave of might that flooded his body, his every sense. *This must be what Camael was talking about, the unification of the human and the angelic.* It was wonderful, and for the first time since learning of his angelic heritage, Aaron Corbet felt truly complete.

He fought to his feet and wrenched the battle-ax from Malak's grasp.

"This is over," he growled, looming over the armored warrior, ax in hand, glaring at Verchiel and his followers around the gym. The sigils upon his body pulsed with a life all their own, and he spread his wings to their full span. *What a sight I must be,* he thought, inundated by feelings of perfection.

"Yes, you are right," Verchiel agreed with a casual nod. "I tire of these games. Malak, show your face."

Aaron almost screamed for the warrior to stop, not wanting to see what he already suspected. Malak reached up and yanked the scarlet helmet from his head.

"Do you see who you have been fighting, Nephilim?" Verchiel asked, moving closer with his angelic throng.

"No," Aaron cried, unable to tear his gaze away from the familiar features of the young man lying before him. He did not know this person, but then again, he did. "You son of bitch, what have you done?"

"With the magick of the Archons, we have transformed what by human standards was considered limited in its usefulness into a precision weapon."

Malak looked up at Aaron with eyes that once held the innocence of a special child, but now were filled with something else, something deadly. These eyes told a story of death; they were the eyes of a killer. The revelation was even worse than he'd imagined.

The ax slipped from Aaron's hands and clattered upon the floor. "Stevie?" he asked in a trembling whisper, giving credence to what should have been impossible. He willed away the sigils and his formidable wings. "It's me," he said, touching his chest with a trembling, blood-stained hand. Images of a past that seemed thousands of years ago, of the autistic child as he should have been, flashed through Aaron's mind. "It's me— it's Aaron," he said, offering the young man his hand.

At first there was nothing that showed even the slightest hint of humanity in the gaze that met Aaron's. It was like looking into the eyes of a wild animal, but then there came a spark and Malak's eyes twinkled with recognition.

"Aaron?" Stevie asked in a voice very much like that of a child, and his armored hand took hold of his brother's.

Every instinct screamed for Aaron to pull away. "Stevie," he began.

The warrior in red shook his head crazily from side to side, an idiot's grin spreading across his dull features. "Not Stevie," he said as Aaron watched him reach into a pocket of air with his free hand and withdraw a fearsome medieval mace. "Malak!" he shouted, and bludgeoned Aaron across the face with its studded head before the Nephilim had an opportunity to react.

Aaron fell to the floor, the world spinning and his every sense scrambled. He shook his head and slowly rose to his knees, the smell of his own blood wafting up into his nostrils. His scalp was bleeding. As his vision cleared, he could see that Verchiel and his soldiers were standing in a circle around them. The room was eerily quiet, the only sound the armored footfalls of Malak's approach. Aaron summoned another sword of fire.

He gazed into the face of his little brother, his murderous countenance filling the Nephilim with an overwhelming despair. He didn't want to think about what the Powers had done to the child, did not want to know the horror and pain his little brother had endured. But he felt the guilt of not being there to protect him from harm just the same.

Halfheartedly, he raised his weapon of heavenly flame. "I . . . I don't want to do this," he said.

Malak responded with a horrible smile, and Aaron was

reminded of a raccoon with rabies that had once been brought to the veterinary hospital where he used to work. Nothing could be done for the animal, and with a heavy heart, he realized the same was true now.

"I'm so sorry," he whispered as Malak rushed toward him, mace raised to strike. Aaron deflected the blow, but hesitated in his own attack. The warrior swung again, and this time the mace connected with Aaron's injured shoulder. He cried out and tried to back away, but came up against a living wall of Powers' soldiers.

"It ends here, Nephilim," Verchiel barked from across the circle. "It's time to remove from this world the sickness you represent." The Powers' commander looked to the unconscious Vilma, draped over the shoulder of the angel standing beside him, and sneered as he reached out to touch her raven black hair. "Let us hope it can survive the cleansing."

Aaron's arm throbbed with every staccato beat of his heart, and he was finding it difficult to hold on to his sword. The niggling idea that perhaps he should have listened to Belphegor played at the corner of his thoughts, but it was too late now for second guesses. He had already failed his brother; he wasn't about to fail Vilma as well.

Verchiel's emotionless black eyes fell upon his champion. "Kill the abomination and be done with it," he ordered.

Malak charged at Aaron, weapon raised, his features twisted in bloodlust. They were about to continue their dance of battle, when the gymnasium was suddenly filled with the sound of a booming voice.

"The Nephilim is under my protection."

Malak's attack came to a screeching halt, and the Powers searched for the source of the authoritative proclamation. The angels' circle broke to reveal the striking figure of Camael standing in the gymnasium doorway, Gabriel attentively at his side.

*"And mine too,"* said the dog in a throaty growl.

"Then it is only fitting that you all die together," Verchiel said, a sword igniting in his hand.

Everything became incredibly still, a tension so thick in the air that it seemed to have substance. And then Vilma began to scream, an anguished wail of terror that alluded to the violence that was yet to come.

Still slung over the shoulder of a Powers' soldier, Vilma Santiago had come noisily awake. Her scream was bloodcurdling, born out of sheer terror, and Aaron's heart nearly broke in sympathy. But he had little time to consider her fear, for her cry had acted as a kind of starter's pistol, signaling the beginning of an inevitable conflict.

The Powers were the first to react. With birdlike squawks, they leaped into the air, wings pounding, weapons of fire clenched in their hands. Camael reacted in kind, propelling himself up to confront his attackers above the gym floor.

Malak turned to Aaron, a malicious grin gracing his pale features. He began to lift the mace, but this time, Aaron was faster. He brought forth his wings, and as the mighty append-ages unfurled, the body of his right wing caught his attacker, swatting him aside. Through the chaos, Aaron set his sights on Vilma, who was thrashing wildly in the clutches of her angelic keeper. Desperately trying to ignore the throbbing pain in his head and shoulder, he began to make his way toward the girl and her captor, carefully avoiding the burning bodies of angels as they fell from the air, victims of Camael's battle prowess.

From the corner of his eye, Aaron glimpsed movement and turned just in time to avoid the blade of a broadsword as it attempted to split his skull. He stared into the still-grinning face of Malak. The armored warrior was already bringing the enormous sword around for another strike, but Aaron brought his own blade up to counter the attack before it could cut him in two. Malak stepped in close and drove a metal-clad knee up into the Nephilim's ribs. Aaron cried out in pain, but responded in kind, throwing an elbow into the bridge of Malak's nose.

The warrior of the Powers stumbled back, blood gushing from his nostrils. He brought his gloved hand to his nose and stared dumbfounded at the blood, and then Malak began to laugh. He plunged both hands into his magickal arsenal and emerged with two curved blades of Middle Eastern origin. "Pretty," he said through a spray of blood dripping from his nose. He brandished the unusual weapons and came toward Aaron again, his level of ferociousness seemingly endless.

Suddenly there was a rumbling growl, and a yellow blur

moved between Aaron and his attacker. He watched stunned as Malak took the full weight of Gabriel's pounce and was knocked backward to the gym floor.

*"Save Vilma,"* the dog barked, slamming the top of his thick skull down into the forehead of the Powers' assassin.

Across the gym floor littered with angelic dead, Aaron could see Vilma struggling with her captor. The Powers' angel was holding her wrist in one hand, while in the other was a dagger of flame. Aaron darted forward, but froze as the fearsome visage of Verchiel crossed his path.

"I've not forgotten you, animal," he snarled, the mottled scars on his once flawless features beaming a ruddy red. Like some great prehistoric bird, Verchiel opened his wings to their fullest and advanced. "I rather like the idea of killing you myself," he said with a predatory grin.

Aaron glanced quickly toward Vilma and back to his newest adversary. Taking a combat stance, he held his heavenly weapon high. "Let's do it then," he said, determined that nothing would keep him from the girl.

Then, as if Heaven had decided to answer his prayers, an angel fell from above, its body engulfed in flames. It landed atop Verchiel, knocking him to the ground. Aaron looked up to see Camael hovering above him, his suit tattered and torn, his exposed skin spattered with the blood of the vanquished. "Save the girl!" he ordered, before turning to defend himself against another wave of Powers' soldiers.

Vilma's captor had driven her to the floor, a fiery blade beginning to take form dangerously close to the delicate flesh of her throat. There was murder in the angel's face, and Aaron knew there was a chance that he would not reach her in time. But the image of a weapon took form in his mind—and a spear made from the heavenly fire that lived inside him became a thing of reality. Solid in his hand, he let the weapon fly and watched with great satisfaction as the razor-sharp tip plunged into the neck of the Powers' angel, knocking him away from the struggling girl and pinning his thrashing body to the bleachers.

Aaron was on the move again. "Vilma!" he shouted. The girl was in shock, stumbling about as she gazed around at the nightmarish visions unfolding before her. He called her name again, and she turned to look in his direction with fear-filled eyes.

He stopped before her and held out his hands. "It's me," he said in his most soothing voice. She stared at him, an expression of surprise gradually creeping across her features. He was pretty sure that at the moment he didn't look like the boy she'd said good-bye to in the hallway of Kenneth Curtis High School a few weeks ago, but now was not the time for explanations, all he cared about was keeping her alive. "It's Aaron," he continued, slowly reaching for her.

Vilma blinked, then turned and made a run for the door. Aaron dove for her, his powerful wings allowing him to glide the short distance and take her into his arms. "Please," he said, holding her tightly. "Listen to me."

She fought, punching, screaming, and kicking. She turned in his embrace and began to pound his chest with her fists. "No! No! No!"

*"Vilma, it's really me,"* Aaron said in her native Portuguese. *"I've come to help you."*

For an instant she stopped fighting, looking into his eyes as if searching for lies in his words.

*"Please, Vilma,"* he said again. *"You have to trust me."*

She sagged in his arms, the fight draining out of her. "I want to wake up," she said in a voice groggy with shock. "Just let me wake—"

There was an explosion from the center of the gymnasium, and Verchiel emerged from the conflagration, face twisted in madness as smoldering body parts of soldiers once in his service rained down around him.

"Aaron," Camael cried from above as he pitched another victim of his flaming swordplay at the Powers' commander. "Take the girl and leave!"

Gabriel charged across the gym. *"Yeah, let's get out of here."*

The yellow fur of the dog's face was spattered with blood, and Aaron wondered what it had taken to keep the armored Malak down. He gazed upward looking for Camael. The number of Powers' soldiers had diminished to five and still the warrior that he had learned to call friend fought on. "Camael!" he cried, Vilma slumped in his arms, his dog at his side. He gestured wildly for the angel to join them.

"Leave me!" the former leader of the Powers shouted as he swung his sword in a blazing arc, dispatching two more attackers.

"Nephilim!" Verchiel screamed as he strode across the bodies of his soldiers.

If they were going to leave together, it had to be now. Aaron again gazed up at his mentor. "Camael, please."

"Get out of here now," Camael commanded. "Too much depends upon your survival. Go. Now!" Then he spread his wings and hurled himself at Verchiel.

Aaron wanted to stay, but as he looked at the trembling girl in his arms, the realization of Camael's words slowly sank in. The citizens of Aerie were depending on him, and if he was indeed the Chosen One, he owed it to them to make their prophecy a reality. As much as it pained him, he knew that Camael was right. He had to leave.

*"Aaron, we should go,"* Gabriel said from his side, his warm body tightly pressed against his leg.

"I think you're right," Aaron answered. He took one last look at Verchiel and Camael locked in deadly combat, then spread his ebony wings wide to enfold them all.

"Nephilim!" Verchiel screamed as Aaron pictured Aerie in his mind. "You will not escape me!" And they were gone.

# CHAPTER ELEVEN

S words of fire came together with a deafening sound that reminded Camael of the birth cries of Creation. Slivers of heavenly flame leaped from the blades, burning shrapnel that eerily illuminated their twisted faces as he and Verchiel clashed.

Camael gazed sorrowfully at the scarred features of the creature before him, a once beatific being that had served the will of God, but had somewhere lost his way. He too bore scars, but his were deep inside, still-bleeding wounds of sacrifice for his chosen mission—for a path traveled alone. But this was not the time for philosophical musings, and Camael quickly returned his attention to the task at hand, the total annihilation of his foe.

"Surrender, Camael, and I shall see that you are treated fairly," Verchiel snarled over their locked blades. "It is the least I can do for one I once called friend."

Camael thrust his opponent away and propelled himself backward with the aid of his golden wings. "*Friend*, Verchiel?" he asked, landing in a crouch five feet away. "If this is how you treat your friends, I shudder to think of what you do to your enemies."

Thick black smoke from the burning bodies of Powers' soldiers billowed about the room, triggering the fire alarms and sprinkler systems.

"Humor?" Verchiel asked above the tolling bell as he took to the air with a powerful flap of his wings. "You *have* been amongst the monkeys too long," he observed coldly. "In matters of God and Heaven, there is no place for humor."

Camael propelled himself toward his adversary. "Aaron has often said that I lack a sense of humor," he said, pressing his attack. "I do so like to prove him wrong."

Verchiel parried a thrust from Camael's sword and carried through with a furious strike of his own, cutting a burning gash through Camael's shoulder.

"Listen to you," he said. "Proving yourself to the animals? You disgust me."

Driven by anger and pain, Camael attacked, a snarl of ferocity upon his lips, the swordplay driving Verchiel back through the rising smoke.

"Do you not remember what it was like?" Verchiel asked, his movements a blur as he blocked Camael's relentless rain of blows. "Side by side, meting out the word of God. Nothing could oppose us. We were Order incarnate, and Chaos bent to our every whim."

Camael leaned back as a swipe of Verchiel's sword narrowly missed his throat. "Until we became what we professed to fight." He stopped his attack, hoping that Verchiel would hear his words. "Bringers of destruction and fear. Chaos incarnate."

Verchiel's eyes widened in disbelief. "Are you so blinded by your insane beliefs that you cannot see what I'm trying to achieve?"

A whip took shape in his hand, and he lashed out with its tail of flame. The burning cord wrapped itself tightly around Camael's neck and instantly began to sear its way through his flesh. The pain was all-consuming as Camael felt himself pulled toward his enemy with a mighty yank.

"It was that accursed prophecy that brought pandemonium to the world," Verchiel said as he fought to pull Camael closer. "This belief in the Nephilim's redemptive powers has created bedlam; I only seek to stem the flow of madness."

The stench of his own burning sickened Camael. His wings frantically beat the air to maintain his distance from his adversary as he brought his sword up and severed the whip's embrace. "Why can you not face the reality of the prophecy?" he rasped. "The harder you try to stop it, the more it seems to fight to become true."

Camael dove backward, down into the densest smoke. He could no longer hear the clang of the fire alarm, but the water raining down from the sprinklers felt comforting upon his wounded throat. He touched down upon the wooden floor and willed himself to heal faster. There was so little time. The human authorities were certainly on their way; the battle would need to be brought promptly to a close, for Verchiel would think nothing of ending innocent lives in the pursuit of his goals.

Searching the wafting smoke above him for signs of his adversary, Camael thought of Aaron, of Aerie, of all he had saved from Verchiel's murderous throngs. *Has it been enough?* The unspeakable acts he had once perpetrated in the name of God as leader of the Powers filled him with self-loathing, and he wondered if he could ever forgive himself. *Will killing Verchiel and allowing the prophecy to be fulfilled finally be enough?* He stepped over bodies of angels burned black by his ferocity, continuing to scan the smoke-choked room for signs of movement.

"Have I told you my plan for this world, Camael?" asked Verchiel from somewhere nearby.

Camael tensed, sword ready. He tried to attune his senses to the environment, but the fire alarm and the fall of the sprinkler's artificial rain interfered with their acuity.

"I see a world of obedience." Verchiel's voice seemed to be shifting positions within the smoke. "A world where *my* word is law."

Camael's eyes scanned the billowing smoke. "Don't you mean God's word?"

The smoke to his right suddenly parted to reveal the formidable sight of his former second in command, a spear of orange fire in his grasp. "You heard me right the first time," Verchiel said, and let the weapon fly.

Camael reared back and brought his sword of fire to bear. He blocked the spear with the burning blade, but as it disintegrated in a flash of light, he felt another presence behind him. Still moving, he tossed his sword from right hand to left, spinning around to confront this new assailant.

Camael's blade struck armor the color of a blood-soaked battlefield and shattered. *Magick,* he thought, momentarily taken aback. He was about to formulate another weapon when he was struck from behind. A sword entered his body through his back; the white-hot blade exiting just below his ribcage in a geyser of steaming blood before being brutally pulled back.

Camael turned, a ferocious roar born of pain and rage escaping his lips. *How could I have been so reckless as to forget the hunter?* he thought, bringing his new sword of flame up to bite back at the coward who had struck from behind. Verchiel blocked his swipe with the sword he had pulled from the angel's back.

"Do you know what I think, Camael?" Verchiel asked in a voice that dripped with madness.

Camael gasped as another blade, this one made of iron, was plunged into his back, and he felt himself grow suddenly weaker, the magicks infused within the knife sapping away his

THOMAS E. SNIEGOSKI

strength. He heard the armored warrior breathe heavily behind him, as if aroused by this craven act of savagery.

"I believe that the Creator has lost His mind," Verchiel said in a conspiratorial whisper. "Driven mad by the infectious disease of this virulent prophecy."

He stepped closer as Camael fell to his knees. The bleeding angel tried to stand, to carry on with the fight, but the metal blade had made that impossible.

"It has touched His mind in such a way that He actually believes what is happening here is right. How else can you explain it?" the demented angel asked. "God has become infected, as you were infected, and so many other pathetic beings that we so mercifully dispatched over the centuries."

Camael could taste his own blood and suspected that his time was at an end. He had always known that it would come to this; that his final battle would be against the one that had so twisted the will of God. "Will you attempt to mercifully dispatch the Creator as well?" he asked, disturbed by how weak his voice sounded.

The Powers' leader seemed horrified by this query. "You speak blasphemy," he proclaimed. "When my job is done, I will return to Heaven and see to the affairs of both Heaven and Earth until our Lord and Master is well enough to see to the ministrations of the universe on His own."

Camael could not hold back his laughter, although it wracked his body with painful spasms. "Do you hear yourself?" he asked through bloody coughs that flecked his bearded chin with gore. "You presume to know the grand schemes of He who created all things—He who created *us*." He averted his gaze, no longer able to look upon the foul creature before him. "If Lucifer could hear you now, he would embrace you as a like-minded brother," Camael added with a disgusted shake of his head.

"How dare you speak his name to me," Verchiel raged, falling down upon his own knees and grabbing Camael's face. "Everything I do, I do for the glory of His name. When this is done, and things have returned to the way they once were, I shall sit by His side, and all shall know that my actions were just."

Camael stared into Verchiel's dark eyes, falling into the depths of their insanity. "Things will never be as they were," he whispered, shaking Verchiel's hand from his face. "And they will call you monster."

Verchiel jumped to his feet, his scarred features twisted in fury. "Then monster I shall be," he shrieked as he raised his flaming sword and brought it down toward Camael's head.

Camael had been saving his strength, a small pocket of might that he hoped would enable him to return to Aerie. He reached behind himself, finding the knife that still protruded from his flesh. His hand closed around the hilt and he yanked the offending object from his back, bringing it around and up to meet the sword's deadly arc. Verchiel's weapon shattered on contact with the mystical metal, and the Powers' commander cried out, stumbling back as burning shrapnel showered his exposed flesh.

Camael unfurled his wings, thrusting them outward, hurling the scarlet-armored warrior away from him. His body screamed in protest, blood filling his mouth, but he did not let it deter him.

"You cannot hope to escape me, traitor!" Verchiel screamed, the mottled flesh of his face decorated with fresh burns. "You're already dead!"

Camael enfolded himself in the comforting embrace of his wings and willed himself away from the school, with Verchiel's furious words echoing through the recesses of his mind.

"Not quite yet," said the warrior on his way to the place hidden from him for so long, the place he now called home.

Verchiel stood in the gymnasium at Kenneth Curtis High School surrounded by the burning bodies of his soldiers. "We're close," he said to his fallen comrades, now nothing more than smoking heaps of ash.

Malak had retrieved his helmet and stood by his master's side, his face bruised and spattered with blood. The alarm bell continued to toll and the sprinklers rained down upon them. The wails of fire trucks could be heard from outside, and Malak howled softly in response to the sirens' cries. Verchiel turned to him and the warrior abruptly stopped.

"You've failed me," Verchiel told him, and the warrior

cowered in the shadow of his disappointment.

"There is something in him, this Nephilim, that was not there in the others that I have hunted," Malak said in an attempt to explain his failure. He shook his head slowly, as if attempting to understand the perception himself. "A fire burns inside this one—a will to live." Malak looked up into the eyes of his master. "A purpose."

"Do you have it?" Verchiel asked, ignoring the ramblings of his servant. "Do you have the scent of our enemies?"

Malak nodded, a simpleton's grin of accomplishment spreading across his face. "They cannot hide from me anymore," he said, eyes twinkling mischievously. "Like blood in the white, white snow; I can follow them."

"Excellent," Verchiel hissed. He would remember this day, this very point in time when his plan fell neatly into place.

Through the billowing smoke, he saw shapes moving into the room, firefighters, their bodies covered in heavy, protective layers of clothing. In their hands they carried the tools of their trade: high-powered flashlights, axes, and thick hoses. Verchiel felt Malak bristle beside him.

"There's somebody in here," he heard one of the firefighters say, his voice muffled by the oxygen mask that covered his face.

A powerful flashlight illuminated the angel and his servant. Verchiel did not hide himself, instead he unfurled his wings and held his arms out so they might gaze upon his magnificence. Through the thick smoke and the clear masks that covered their faces, he could see their eyes bulge with fear and wonder, and reveled in their awe of him.

Malak growled and from the air plucked a fearsome sword, still encrusted with the blood of a previous kill. He started toward the humans, but Verchiel reached out, grabbing hold of his armored shoulder.

"Leave them be," he proclaimed for all to hear.

Two of the firemen had fallen to their knees in supplication, while another fled in sheer panic. Verchiel could hear their prayers.

"Let them look upon me and know that a time is approaching when the sight of my kind will be as common, and as welcome, as the sunrise." Verchiel's voice boomed above the sound of the fire alarm. "There are snakes living amongst you," he proclaimed as he closed his wings about himself and his servant. "And there shall come a time of cleansing."

And as Verchiel willed himself away, he left the firefighters with a final pronouncement.

"That time is now."

Aaron did as he was taught. He saw Aerie in his head; the high, chain-link fence that ran around its perimeter, the run-down homes, the weeds pushing up through the cracks in the sidewalks. In the beginning there was complete and utter darkness, and then a sense of movement. It was like traveling through a long, dark tunnel. He opened his wings, pushing back the stygian black that enveloped them and saw that they had suc-cessfully arrived. He had rescued Vilma—but at what price?

He looked around. They were standing in front of Belphegor's home, and nearly every citizen was waiting. The old fallen angel was sitting in a beach chair at the sidewalk's edge, a sweating glass of iced tea in his hand. Lehash, looking none too pleased, and Lorelei stood on either side of the multi-colored chair. It was quiet in Aerie, quiet as the grave.

Aaron felt Vilma shiver in his arms and pulled her closer, gazing into her wide, dark eyes. "It's going to be all right," he whispered, holding her tighter.

*"Is she hurt?"* Gabriel asked, sniffing at her body.

Vilma writhed and her shirt rose up to reveal the angry burns on her belly.

"Oh, my God," Aaron said, starting to panic. "Somebody help me." He looked frantically at the people around him.

Lorelei moved forward and placed a hand on Vilma's brow.

"He hurt her . . . tried to trigger the change," Aaron said. "There are burns on her stomach and I . . . I think she's sick."

"I'll take her from here," Lorelei said, and gently began to pry the girl from his arms.

"Will she be okay?" He didn't want to let her go.

"She's been with Verchiel," Lorelei responded coldly as she removed her dungaree jacket, wrapping it around the shiver-ing Vilma's shoulders. "I can only guess what that monster has done to her."

Lorelei began to lead Vilma away, and Aaron reached out to take hold of her arm. "Thank you."

She turned slowly to look at him; there was fear in her eyes. "Does that mean that you owe me?" Lorelei asked.

Aaron nodded as he let go of her arm. "Anything."

"Don't let them down," she whispered. "They've waited so long—sacrificed too much—to have it all taken away."

He had no idea how to respond, but Lorelei had already turned and was leading Vilma away. "C'mon, honey, let's see about getting you fixed up."

"Aaron?" Vilma suddenly protested.

He was going to her when Gabriel cut across his path. *"It's going to be just fine,"* the animal said to the girl, and the expression on her face told Aaron that she could understand the dog as well as he. Gabriel stretched his neck and nuzzled her hand lovingly. *"We'll go with Lorelei and she'll make you feel better, you'll see."* Gabriel looked back at Aaron. *"I'll go with her."*

Aaron nodded in approval and watched the threesome proceed down the street, Gabriel chatting reassuringly all the while. If only he could have the same level of confidence as his dog. He thought of Camael, who had yet to return, and icy fingers of dread took hold of his heart. He had to go back, back to Ken Curtis to help his friend. He turned to Belphegor. "I have to leave again; I have to help Camael."

He unfurled his wings, but pain shot through his body, driving him to his knees. His head throbbed and the stab wound in his shoulder was bleeding again, he could feel the snaking trail of warmth beneath his shirt.

"You need to rest," he heard Belphegor say evenly. "You're no good to anyone now."

"But he needs help!" Aaron said, fighting to get to his feet.

"Camael can take care of himself," Lehash barked. "He's fought many a battle without your help, Nephilim. You've done enough."

Aaron stared across the street at the gunslinger and Belphegor. Their faces were blank, insensate, as if they'd used up their lifetime allotment of emotion long ago. But it was in the faces of the others, the citizens, that he saw what he was responsible for. They milled about, eyes darting here and there, waiting for answers, waiting to have their fears put to rest. He could feel the anxiety coming off them in waves.

"I couldn't just leave her," he said to them. "I had to do something." He managed to get to his feet and lurched toward them, his angelic trappings fading as he drew closer. "I'm so sorry. It seemed right at the time, but now I . . ." He felt his strength wane and he suddenly sat down in the street, burying his face in his hands. "I just don't know what to think."

An aluminum chair leg scraped across the concrete sidewalk and he lifted his face to see that Belphegor was standing. The old fallen angel handed his nearly empty glass to Lehash, who stared at it with contempt. "Hold on to this," he told the constable, and moved toward Aaron.

It hurt to think. It felt as though Verchiel had touched his brain with a burning hand; his thoughts were a firestorm. There was so much he had to do—so much responsibility. Why did *he* have to be the Chosen One? he anguished. In his mind all he could see were the faces of those he had failed: his mom and dad, Dr. Jonas, Vilma . . . Stevie.

"They . . . he changed my little brother into a monster," Aaron said, gazing up into the elderly visage of Belphegor. "How could they do that to a kid?" he asked desperately as he ran a hand through his tangle of dark hair. "How could a creature of Heaven be so cruel?"

"Verchiel and his followers have not been creatures of Heaven for quite some time," Belphegor replied. "They lost sight of that special place a long time ago."

"Why can't he just leave me alone?" Aaron asked, the weight of his responsibilities beginning to wear upon him. "Why does it have to be this way?"

Belphegor sighed as he looked up at the early morning sky above Aerie. "Verchiel's still fighting the war, I think," he said after a bit of thought. "So caught up in righting a wrong, that he can't accept the idea that the battle is over. There's a new age dawning, Aaron." Belphegor slowly squatted down, and Aaron could hear the popping of his ancient joints. "Whether he likes it or not."

Aaron looked into the old angel's eyes, searching for a bit of strength he could borrow.

"And you're the harbinger," he continued. "Whether *you* like it or not."

"But I'm responsible for ruining this," Aaron said, motioning toward the neighborhood around them. "Verchiel and his Powers are probably coming here because of me."

"Looks that way," Belphegor said, calmly straightening up. "But we never expected it to be easy."

Lehash left the crowd of citizens and came to them. The constable's eyes had turned to dark, shiny marbles in the recesses of his shadowed brow. "Is this how he's going to save us?" he asked Belphegor, speaking loud enough for everyone to hear. "Crying in the street? I always expected that a savior would have more balls than that, but I guess I was wrong."

It couldn't have hurt worse if Lehash had pulled out his pistols and shot him again. The constable's words cut deep, and Aaron felt the power of angels surge through his body again. The sigils rose up on his flesh, his body afire as he leaped to his feet, his wings of shadow propelling him at the angel who had hurt him so.

"Do you want to see balls, Lehash?" he asked in a voice more animal than man. A sword of fire had materialized in his hand, and he stood ready to strike.

Lehash had drawn his golden guns. "Show me what you're gonna do when the Powers come for us, Nephilim," the gunslinger demanded, his thumbs playing with the hammers of his supernatural weapons. "Show me how powerful you are when they start to burn us alive."

Belphegor stepped between them, placing a hand on each of their chests. With little effort, he pushed them both apart. "This isn't going to help anything," the Founder of Aerie said, giving each a piece of his icy stare. "There's a storm coming, and no matter how much we rail against it—or one another—it doesn't change the fact that the rain is going to fall."

Aaron felt it at the nape of his neck, a slight tingle that made the hair stand at attention. He turned to see that something was taking shape in the air across the street from them.

"Camael?" Aaron asked, starting toward the disturbance.

Belphegor grabbed hold of his arm. "Wait," he demanded.

Aaron pulled away, certain that it was his friend who had returned. Camael's wings spread wide to reveal him, and Aaron gasped at the sight. The angel clutched his stomach, blood flowing from a wound to stain the streets of Aerie. Camael pitched forward as Aaron ran to him.

"It comes," he heard Belphegor say in a foreboding whisper at his back. "The storm comes."

# CHAPTER TWELVE

There was so much blood.

Aaron cradled the body of the angel warrior in his arms, feeling Camael's life force ebbing away. He was reminded of that horrible day he had knelt in the middle of the street holding a dying Gabriel. He had never wanted to feel that way again, but here it was, as painful as the last time.

"I can do something," he said to his friend in an attempt to rally some confidence not only for Camael, but also for himself. Aaron reached deep within, searching for that spark of the divine that would allow him to save his mentor as he had his pet.

Camael took Aaron's hand in his. "Do not waste your strength on a lost cause, boy," he said, his grip firm, but weakening.

Aaron held the angel to him, gazing in mute horror at the

stab wounds in his friend's back. One was a blackened hole characteristic of a heavenly weapon's bite, but the other showed no sign of cauterization and bled profusely. "We'll stop the bleeding and you'll be all right," he told his friend, pressing his hand firmly against the wound.

Camael shuddered, and a fresh geyser of dark blood sprayed from the wound. The blood was warm, its smell pungent. "It will not stop." He struggled to sit up. "The enchanted metal and Verchiel's sword," he strained, "I fear it was a most lethal combination."

"Lie still, we can—"

Camael still held Aaron's hand and rallied his strength to squeeze it all the harder. "I did not return to have you save my pathetic life," the angel said, the intensity of his stare grabbing Aaron's attention and holding it firm. "I never considered that the prophecy would apply to me . . . that I could be forgiven."

"Stop talking like that," Aaron said, dismissing the fatalistic words of his mentor.

Many of the citizens who had gathered in front of Belphegor's home now stood in a tight circle around Aaron and Camael, watching the drama unfold. One of the men stripped off his T-shirt and offered it to Aaron to use as a compress against the angel's bleeding wound.

"I've saved many lives in my time on this world," Camael reflected. "But I don't believe it will ever balance the scales against the lives I took as leader of the Powers."

"How can you be sure, Camael?" Aaron asked in an attempt to keep his friend with him, to keep him focused. He gestured at the circle around them. "Most of them wouldn't be here. *I* wouldn't be here if it weren't for you."

Camael looked at him with eyes that had grown tired, eyes that had seen so much. "Deep down I knew that it was wrong, but still I kept on with the killing, for I believed that it was what *He* wanted of me. How sad that it took the writings of a human seer to force me to come to my senses." He laughed and dark blood spilled from his mouth to stain his silver goatee. "Imagine that," he said with a weary smile. "It took a lowly human to show me the error of my ways."

Aaron chuckled sadly. "Yeah, imagine that."

The angel warrior's body was suddenly wracked with spasms of coughing that threatened to shake away what little life there still was in his dying frame. Time, as it always seemed to be, was running out.

"Is he going to die?" one of the citizens, a girl probably only a few years older than Aaron, asked. There were tears in her eyes, and in the eyes of all present. He could not bring himself to answer, even though the inevitable seemed obvious.

"That is the burning question of the day," Camael answered, looking at Aaron. "Will I die here on the street of the place I sought so long to find?" He pulled Aaron closer as he asked the question, the source of the strength that had allowed him to return to Aerie. "Or might I actually be forgiven?" the angel asked wistfully. "Only you have the answer."

Aaron could sense that his friend's time was short. "Shall we find out?" he asked Camael, reaching down into the center of his being to find the gift of redemption. It was there, waiting for him as he imagined it would be. He called forth the heavenly essence, drawing upon it, feeling its might rise up and flow down his arm into one of his hands. The facility to redeem danced upon his fingertips, and Aaron looked compassionately to the angel that had shown him the road to his destiny. He wrestled with feelings of intense emotion: sadness, for he would not be seeing his friend again, and great happiness, for Camael would be going home.

Camael began to pray, his weary eyes tightly closed. "Have mercy upon me, O God. With the multitude of Your tender mercies, blot out my offenses."

Aaron brought his hand closer, the power contained within glowing like a small sun.

"Cleanse me from my sins. For I acknowledge my offenses, and they are ever before me."

His touch lighted upon Camael's chest and Aaron felt the energy of his special gift swell and begin to flow from him. This was it. "You are forgiven," Aaron declared as his hand eerily slipped beneath the flesh of the angel's breast.

Camael gasped, his body arching as Aaron let go of the force collecting in his fingertips, releasing the power of redemption inside him. The angel's flesh began to fume. The skin grew brittle and fractured as the human shell that he had been wearing since his personal fall from grace began to flake away. Camael writhed upon the ground, like a snake sloughing off its skin, as the glory of what he once had been was revealed.

There came a jubilant cry of release, followed by a dazzling flash of brilliance, and Aaron instinctively turned away, the flash of the angel's rebirth blinding to the earthly eye. Aaron listened to the gasps and cries of awe from those that had gathered around them, and he turned his gaze back to the latest recipient of his heavenly gift.

*Awesome,* was all Aaron could think of as he watched the beautiful, fearsome creature floating on wings seemingly made from feathers of gossamer and sunlight. Camael's hair moved about his head like a halo of fire. His flesh was nearly translucent and he was adorned in armor that could easily have been forged from the rays of the sun. The angel noticed him then, and Aaron finally understood the enormity of his responsibility. As he gazed at the magnificent entity before him, he knew it was his right and his alone. He *was* the One, and this was his burden and his joy.

"It must have been something," Aaron said to the transformed Camael, thinking of a time in Heaven before the strife . . . and wondering how it would be now when his friend returned.

"Maybe it will be something again," Camael said in a

voice like the surge of ocean waves upon a beach, and turned his attention to the open sky above.

Aaron prepared himself for the being's ascension, but the angel seemed to hesitate, as if something was preventing him from moving on. "What's wrong, Camael?" he asked him.

"I . . . I do not wish to leave you with the burden of this responsibility," Camael said, longingly returning his gaze to the sky above him.

"I'll be fine," Aaron reassured him. "This is how it's supposed to be."

The two again exchanged looks, and Aaron could see that the angel was torn.

"Go, Camael," he said in a powerful voice that he hoped brimmed with authority. "Your job is done; it's time for you to go home."

With those words, Camael spread wide his wings and began his ascent to a world beyond this one. His wings of light and fire stirred the air, filling it with the gentle sounds of the wind. Aaron could not help but think that it sounded like the voices of small children singing.

"Say good-bye to Gabriel," the angel said. "I do believe I'll miss him."

"He has that effect," Aaron replied, and watched the glimmer of a smile cross the angel's blissful features.

Then Camael turned his full attention to the yawning space above him, raised his arms to the sky, and in a flash of light that seemed to warm Aaron to the depths of his soul, the angel that was his friend was gone.

Aaron stumbled back, the beauty of Camael's ascent still dancing before his eyes. He was on his own now, but he knew what needed to be done.

The Nephilim turned to face Belphegor and Lehash and was astonished to see that the citizens were kneeling on the street behind them, heads bowed in reverence. "What's all this?" he asked.

"They know the truth now," Belphegor said, a smile tugging at the corners of his mouth.

"Son of bitch," Lehash growled as he pulled the worn Stetson from his head. "You are the One."

Aaron walked toward Lorelei's house, wondering about Vilma's condition and how Gabriel would take the news of Camael's passing. At first meeting, the angel and the dog hadn't really gotten along, but recently, a strange, begrudging friendship seemed to have developed between the two.

He chanced a casual glance over his shoulder to see if he was still being followed, and sure enough, a sizeable number of Aerie's population trailed a respectful distance behind. Lehash, in the lead, politely tipped his hat. Aaron knew they were there because they believed he was something special—something many of them had been waiting for most of their lives—but the adoration made him uncomfortable. He wished they would admire him from their own homes.

He headed up the walk and climbed the few steps to the front door. As he pulled open the screen, he noted that the crowd had stopped at the street, watching him from a distance.

"I'll be right here if you need anything," the constable confirmed, taking up a guardian's stance at the beginning of the walk.

Aaron waved and stepped into the small hallway inside Lorelei's house. To the right was the living room. Vilma was lying on the overstuffed couch. She was asleep, her limp hand resting on Gabriel's side as he sat near her on the floor, resting his chin on the edge of the sofa. Lorelei sat at the edge of the rickety coffee table, applying tape to a bandage on Vilma's exposed stomach.

"Hey," Aaron said as he came into the room. "How's she doing?"

Gabriel lifted his head from the couch to look at Aaron. *"Hello,"* the dog said.

Lorelei finished her ministrations and gently pulled Vilma's shirt down to cover the dressing. "The burns were pretty bad," she said, packing up her supplies. "Looks like Verchiel had a good time with her," she added, jaw tightly clenched. "I've cleaned and dressed them using some special oils to help her heal faster. Physically, I'd say she's going to be fine."

"And mentally?" Aaron asked, struggling to contain his

guilt. It was exactly what he had feared, one of the reasons he had left Lynn to begin with. Verchiel had used someone else to get at him.

Lorelei looked at the sleeping girl on the couch. "Remember, the whole process of becoming a Nephilim does quite the job on your head, and some of us are stronger than others."

Aaron nodded, knowing full well the painful truth of Lorelei's words.

"We'll just have to wait and see," she said, taking the leftover medical supplies back to the kitchen.

Aaron found himself staring at Vilma's face. He could see her eyes moving beneath her lids. *Dreaming,* he thought as he watched her, *and hopefully only the good kind.*

*"Did Camael come back yet?"* Gabriel asked as he stood up and stretched, lowering his front body down to the ground while sticking his butt up into the air.

Aaron hesitated, not a good thing when dealing with a dog like Gabriel.

*"He hasn't come back yet, Aaron?"* the dog asked, showing concern as he completed his stretch. *"We should go look for him."*

Aaron squatted down, taking the yellow dog's head in his hands and rubbing behind his floppy ears.

*"What's wrong?"* the Labrador asked. *"I can sense that something isn't right."*

"Camael did come back, Gabe, and—"

*"Then where is he?"* the dog interrupted.

"Gabriel, please," Aaron said exasperated. "Let me finish."

Gabriel sat; his blocky head cocked quizzically to the side.

"Camael did come back," Aaron continued. "But he was hurt."

*"Like I was hurt before you made me better?"* the dog asked.

Aaron nodded, reaching down to stroke his friend's thick neck. "Yeah, like that, only I couldn't fix him."

Gabriel stared at his master, his chocolate brown eyes filled with a special intensity. *"What are we going to do?"*

He thought of how to explain this to the animal. Sometimes communicating with Gabriel was like talking to a little kid, and other times like an old soul with knowledge beyond his years. "Do you remember Zeke?" he asked, referring to the fallen angel who had first tried to tell him he was a Nephilim. Zeke had been mortally wounded during their first battle with Verchiel and his Powers.

*"I liked Zeke,"* Gabriel said with a wag of his tail. *"But you did something to him and he went away. Where did Zeke go again, Aaron?"*

"I sent Zeke home," he explained. "I sent him back to Heaven."

*"Just like the other Gabriel,"* his best friend said, referring to the archangel they had encountered in Maine a few weeks ago, whom Aaron had also released from his confines upon the Earth.

"Exactly," Aaron answered, petting the dog.

*"Did you have to send Camael home, Aaron?"* Gabriel asked, his guttural voice coming out as a cautious whisper.

Aaron nodded, continuing to scratch his four-legged friend behind his soft ears. "Yes, I did," Aaron said. "It was the only thing I could do for him." Of all the breeds of dogs that he had encountered while working at the veterinary clinic, it never ceased to amaze him how expressive the face of a Labrador retriever could be. He could tell that the dog was taking his news quite hard. "He told me to tell you good-bye—and that he'd miss you."

Gabriel slowly lowered himself to the floor, avoiding his master's watchful gaze. He placed his long face between his two front paws and sighed heavily.

Aaron reached out to stroke his head. "You okay, Gabe?" he asked tenderly, sharing the dog's sadness.

*"I didn't get a chance to say good-bye to him,"* Gabriel said softly, his ears lowered in a mournful show of feelings.

Aaron lay down beside the big, yellow dog and put his arm around him. "I said good-bye for the both of us," he said, hugging the Lab tightly. And they lay there for a little while longer, both of them remembering a friend now gone from their lives.

The leader of the Powers host flew in the predawn sky, circling high above the Saint Athanasius Church and Orphanage.

He could feel it in the atmosphere around him—change was imminent, and he reveled in it as the cool caress of the morning breeze soothed his healing flesh. *He* would be the harbinger of a new and glorious age.

Verchiel took his body earthward, gliding down toward the towering church steeple, where he clung to its side like some great predator of the air. He gazed down from his perch at the open space of the schoolyard below. *It is time,* he thought, time to call his army, to gather his troops for the impending war. Verchiel tilted back his head and let loose a wail that drifted on the winds, calling forth those that had sworn their allegiance to him and his holy mission. The cry moved through the air, beyond the confines of Saint Athanasius, to affect those still held tightly in the embrace of sleep.

A child of three awakened, screaming so long and hard that he ruptured a blood vessel in his throat, vomiting blood onto his Scooby Doo sheets. On the way to the emergency room, all he could tell his parents was that the bird men were coming and would kill everyone.

A middle-aged computer software specialist, recently separated from his wife, awoke from a disturbing dream, in his cold, one-bedroom apartment, determined that today would be the day he took his life.

A mother squirrel ensconced in her treetop nest of leaves, woke from a fitful rest and senselessly began to consume her young.

Verchiel ceased his ululating lament, watching with eager eyes as his army began to gather, their wings pounding the air. They circled above him like carrion birds waiting for the coming of death, then one by one began their descent. Some found purchase upon the weatherworn pieces of playground equipment, others roosted on the eaves of the administration building, and the remainder stood uncomfortably on the ground, hands clasped behind their backs.

Verchiel was both saddened and enraged by how their numbers had dwindled; victims of the Nephilim and those that believed in the validity of the prophecy. *They will not have died in vain,* he swore, spreading his wings, dropping from the steeple to land on the rusted swingset, scattering his warriors in a flurry of beating wings. All eyes were upon him as he raised himself to his full height, balanced on the horizontal metal pole. Today victory would belong to him. He raised his arm, and in his outstretched hand formed a magnificent sword of fire, the Bringer of Sorrow.

"Look upon this sword," the leader of the Powers proclaimed, "for it shall be your beacon." He felt their adoration, their belief in him and his mission. "Its mighty light will shine before us, illuminating the darkness to rout out evil. And it will be smited," he roared, holding out the sword to each of them.

Their own weapons of war took shape in the hands of those gathered before him, and they returned the gesture, reestablishing a camaraderie that was first forged during the

Great War in Heaven. A buzz like the crackle of an electrical current moved through the gathering, and he saw that Malak had arrived, bloodred armor polished and glistening in the light. *What a spectacular sight,* Verchiel thought. No finer weapon had he ever created.

Malak walked among the angels, an air of confidence surrounding him like a fog. Their eyes were upon him, filled with a mixture of awe and disdain. Some of the angels did not approve of the power that had been bestowed upon the human animal, but they dared not speak their disfavor to Verchiel. They did not understand human emotions, and were not able to see the psychological advantage he now held over his accursed enemy. But when Malak rendered helpless the one called Aaron Corbet, and the Nephilim's life was brought to an end, they would have no choice but to concede to the hunter's superiority.

"The smell of our enemy calls out to me," Malak declared, his voice cruel, echoing through the cold metal of his helmet.

"Then let us answer that call," Verchiel ordered from his roost.

With those words Malak spun around, an imposing sword of black metal in his grasp. As if delivering a deathblow to an opponent, he sliced through the air, creating a doorway to another place, the place where their final battle would be fought.

"Onward," the Powers' leader exclaimed. "It is the beginning of the end."

The angels of the Powers' host cried out as one, their mighty wings taking them aloft, through the tear in reality.

And as Verchiel watched them depart, he remembered something he had once read in the monkeys' holy book, written by one called Isaiah, he believed. *"They shall have no pity on the fruit of the womb; their eye shall not spare children.*

Verchiel smiled. He couldn't have voiced it better himself.

# CHAPTER THIRTEEN

Gabriel was feeling sad.

No matter how hard he tried, with pleasant thoughts of delicious things to eat, chasing after balls, and long naps in warm patches of sunshine, the dog could not shake the unhappy state of mind. How he wished the human idea that animals didn't experience emotion was not just a myth.

As he trotted beside Aaron down the center of an Aerie street, Gabriel thought of the long and difficult night they had just passed. Neither had slept much as they watched over Vilma and shared the pain of Camael's passing. The dog gazed up at his friend, studying the young man's face in the early morning light. His expression was intense, determined, but Gabriel could sense the pain that hovered just beneath the surface.

Their lives had suddenly become so hard. Gabriel thought

longingly of days—*Could it have only been just weeks ago?*—spent going for long walks, licking cookie crumbs from Stevie's face, cuddling with the Stanleys as they rubbed his belly.

The sound of a door slamming roused the Lab from his reflection, and he turned his blocky head to see another of Aerie's citizens leaving his home to join the crowd already on their way to the gathering.

Gabriel felt his hackles begin to rise. Verchiel was coming and he would probably be bringing Stevie along with him. He was no longer the little boy Gabriel so fondly remembered, but something that filled him with fear. Images of his battle with the armored monster at the school gym flooded his thoughts. It hadn't taken more than a moment for him to realize who he was facing; the scent of the boy—of Stevie—was there in the form of the one called Malak, but the smell was wrong. It had been changed, made foul. Last night Gabriel had struggled with a way in which to express to his master what his senses perceived, but Aaron already knew that Stevie had become Malak. Although Gabriel couldn't understand exactly what had happened to Stevie, he shared Aaron's deep shock at the little boy's transformation.

A sudden, nagging question formed in the Lab's mind and he stopped walking, waiting for Aaron to notice that he was no longer at his side. Finally Aaron turned.

"What's up?" the boy asked him.

Gabriel shook his head sadly, his golden brown ears

flopping around his long face. *"Stevie's been poisoned. It's like this place,"* he said. *"It was nice before, but something bad has happened to it. Do you understand what I'm trying to say?"*

Aaron walked back and laid a gentle hand on the dog's head. "I get it," he said.

Citizens passed on their way to the meeting place, but the two friends paid them no mind.

Gabriel licked Aaron's hand, then looked nervously into his eyes. *"It's Stevie, but it's not. His smell is all wrong."*

Aaron nodded quickly. "I understand," he said, a troubled expression on his face as he turned to join the others heading toward the church at the end of the street. "C'mon, we better get going."

Gabriel followed at his side, struggling with the dark question he did not want to ask. But it was one he knew that Aaron had to confront. *"What will you do if he tries to kill you again, Aaron?"* Gabriel asked gently.

Aaron did not answer, choosing to remain silent, but the expression upon his master's face told Gabriel everything he needed to know, and it just made the dog all the sadder.

Lehash stood nervously in Aerie's old church, where he had never stood before, attempting to communicate with a higher being he had not wanted to speak with for many a millennium.

He studied the crude picture of the savior painted on the altar wall. The child did not look like Aaron Corbet, with its bald head and bulging white eyes, but there was no doubt in the angel's mind of the boy's true identity. He had witnessed Aaron's power with his own eyes, and had been forever changed by it.

Lehash turned the Stetson nervously in his hands. "I . . . I don't know what to say," he stammered, his voice like sandpaper rubbing on wood. "I never imagined the day that I would speak to You again—never mind *want* to speak to You."

The fallen angel didn't care for what he heard in his voice: It sounded weak, scared, but at the moment, that was exactly what he was. "I never imagined You to have so much mercy," he said to the silence of the church. "To pardon what we did."

Lehash chuckled, looking about the room, then at the hat in his hands. "I used to feel sorry for the others—that they actually believed that You were going to forgive us. So many times I wanted to grab them by the shoulders and give 'em a good shake. *Don't you remember what we did?* I wanted to scream at them. But I kept my mouth shut."

Lehash slowly dropped to his knees and focused his gaze on the painting above the altar. "But I was wrong," he said, his voice filled with a sudden strength. "All these years here and I still don't know anything more than when I decided to join up with the Morningstar."

The fallen angel bowed his head and summoned forth

wings that had not unfurled since his fall from Heaven. It was painful at first and he gritted his teeth as the atrophied appendages gradually emerged.

"What I'm trying to say is that I'm sorry for what I did in the past and what I'm going to do—and if I should die in battle today, I hope You can find it in Your heart to forgive me."

He had summoned forth his guns of gold and crossed them over his chest, spreading his wings as wide as he could. "But if not, I understand, 'cause for what I intend to do to Verchiel and his lapdogs, I wouldn't let me back into Heaven either."

The church door opened behind him and he quickly stood, wishing away the wings that had not touched the sky since his descent. "I said I didn't want to be disturbed," he barked, before realizing that it was Belphegor striding down the center aisle toward him. "Oh, sorry," Lehash said quickly as he reached for his hat that had dropped to the floor.

"Quite all right," Belphegor said, looking at the altar painting. "Did you find what you were looking for?"

The constable thought for a moment. He had no idea if the Creator had been listening, but for the first time in longer than he could remember, he felt a certain sense of hope. "Y'know, I think I might have," he finally answered as he slipped the black Stetson down upon his head.

"That's good," Belphegor replied, and said no more.

And the two of them walked together toward the exit, and the gathering that awaited them beyond it.

* * *

Lorelei studied her reflection in the cracked, full-length mirror hanging on the back of her closet door. The vertical break in the reflective surface split the image of her, the two sides slightly out of sync with each other. She'd always thought about replacing it, but never seemed to have the time. She found the duality of the reflection depicted there strangely accurate, for since the emergence of her other half, the Nephilim side, struggle had been a constant in her life.

Lorelei ran a brush through her long, snow-white hair and wondered why she was bothering. *Have to look good for the slaughter, I guess,* she thought sardonically. Since arriving in Aerie she had known this day would come, the day that the Powers would try to kill them all. She shuddered, racked by a sudden chill of unease. She had seen what Verchiel and his kind were capable of, and the thought of facing them in battle filled her with dread.

She tossed her brush onto the bed and looked upon her trembling hands. Lorelei was afraid of what was to come. Part of her—some primitive, selfish part—wanted to run, to hide, but that side cared nothing for the future, for destiny. All that it concerned itself with was its continued survival. Taking some deep breaths, she attempted to calm the scared, animal side—the human nature—a single thought running through her head. *I am Nephilim and I have a destiny to fulfill.*

Lorelei grabbed her jacket from the bed and slipped it on, flipping out the snow-white hair from beneath her collar. "So what do you think?" she asked her cracked reflection as she adjusted the coat's fit. "Do you think he's really the One?" She had no idea, and doubted that the image looking back at her was any more knowledgeable. What she did know was that Aaron was something very special, and that was exactly what Aerie needed to survive this day. She only hoped that she would be strong enough to help him.

Leaving her bedroom, on the way to the gathering, she stopped in the living room to check on her patient. Lorelei sat on the couch next to the still-sleeping Vilma, and carefully checked beneath the bandage on her stomach. She was pleased; Verchiel had hurt the girl badly, but it looked like she was going to be all right, although she still had to survive the process of becoming a Nephilim.

Gently Lorelei placed her hand against the girl's perspiring brow, and Vilma's large, dark eyes suddenly opened. Her gaze darted about the room, then focused on Lorelei.

"I'm safe?" she asked groggily.

"Yes, you are," Lorelei answered in a soothing voice. "No one will hurt you anymore." She hoped that she was telling the truth, remembering the battle still to come.

A smile spread across the young woman's face. "He saved me," she said, obviously talking of Aaron, and Lorelei took strength from the moment.

"I think he's going to save us all," she told Vilma, suddenly confident that they would live to see tomorrow.

Aaron and Gabriel approached the crowd gathered before the Church of Aerie.

*"It looks like everyone is here,"* Gabriel said as he looked around at the waiting crowd.

There was a nervous tension in the air as fallen angels and Nephilim stood side by side, the first generation of heavenly beings rubbing elbows with the next. For the first time Aaron truly understood what Aerie was all about. It was about change, for the Nephilim would be what remained upon Earth after the fallen angels were finally forgiven and allowed to return to Heaven. *A changing of the guard,* Aaron thought.

The crowd started to notice his arrival and stepped back, bowing their heads in respect, opening a path for him to the steps of the church.

*"That's very nice of them,"* Gabriel commented as they walked past the citizens.

Some of those gathered gingerly reached out and touched his arms, his shoulders and back, barely audible words of thanks leaving their mouths. He wanted to tell them to stop. He wanted to tell them that he had done nothing that they should be thanking him for—in fact, they should be chewing his head off for drawing Verchiel's attention to Aerie's location.

A murmur passed through the crowd, and Aaron saw that

Belphegor and Lehash had come out of the building and now waited for him at the top of the church steps.

*This is it,* he thought, starting his ascent.

*"I'll wait for you down here,"* Gabriel said with a wag of his tail.

As he reached the top of the stairs, the two fallen angels bowed their heads as well. "Don't do that," he told them uncomfortably.

"Just showin' the proper respect," Lehash said as he clasped his hands in front of himself.

Belphegor placed a firm hand upon his shoulder and looked into Aaron's eyes. "They know what is coming," he said, nodding toward the crowd gathered below them. "But they need to hear it from you—they need to know your intentions."

Aaron could feel their eyes upon him, the intensity of their gazes boring into his back. "Wouldn't it be better if you talked to them?" he suggested. "They trust you."

"Don't sell yourself short, boy," Lehash told him. "They know the real thing when they see it. It's you they've been waitin' for."

Aaron looked back to Belphegor, hoping the old angel would help him out. He'd never been comfortable with public speaking.

"The citizens are waiting" was all Belphegor said as he stepped back.

And Aaron knew there was only one thing left for him to do. Slowly he turned to face the throng and his breath was taken away by the sight of them; every eye fixed upon him, every ear attuned, waiting for what he was about to say. His mind went blank and all he could do was to return their stare. *Who am I kidding?* he asked himself, sheer panic setting in. They were insane to be depending on him. He wasn't a savior; he couldn't even help his family or his friends.

He looked into the crowd and saw Gabriel staring up at him from the throng, the gaze of his dark brown eyes touching Aaron's, helping to bring a sense of calm to him. Farther back he noticed a distinct head of beautiful, white hair, and Lorelei giving him the thumbs-up.

"I don't want to disappoint you," Aaron said, his voice tenuous as the words began to spill from his mouth. "Some of you believe that I'm a savior, someone who's come to save the day." Aaron paused, looking out over the citizens of Aerie. "Am I the Chosen One?" he asked, feeling strength come into his words as he spoke from his heart. "I don't really know. But I do know that I have a power—a power that seems to set me apart from everyone else. And we'll never get to know what I am and what I'm capable of if Verchiel has anything to say about it."

A rumbling murmur went up from the crowd and Aaron could only imagine the fear that many of them had lived with during their lives, dreading the day when the leader of the Powers host would turn his attention to them, and the place of peace that they had built for themselves.

"This morning I'm asking you to fight," Aaron told them.

"To fight for your future—for your redemption, and your right to go home." He tried to look each in the eye. "This is what I intend to do," he told them. "It's time that I confronted my destiny—and I would be honored to have you all fight by my side."

The silence was deafening. Aaron wasn't exactly sure what he had expected, but a void of response was not necessarily what he'd hoped for. He was about to turn to Belphegor, when a sword of fire sprang to life within the crowd. It was raised high in the air, and was followed by another, and then another still. Aaron was speechless, looking out over the crowd, as every one of them raised a weapon of heavenly fire in salute to him.

"Guess that's a vote of confidence," Aaron heard Lehash say. He turned to find the constable wielding his golden pistols. "They're not swords, but they do pack a pretty good wallop," he said, crossing the weapons in front of his chest. "And I would be honored to fight in your name."

Belphegor smiled as Aaron looked back to the citizens.

*Maybe we do have a chance,* he thought, his faith roused by the sight of those gathered below him, and he wondered if Camael would have been proud. His musings on his absent friend were cut off, as there came a sound, abrupt in its intensity, painful to the ears. It was like the crack of an enormous bullwhip, and it was followed by a terrible ripping as a hole opened in the air above the crowd. Aaron watched with increasing horror as a red-garbed warrior dropped from the wound in space to the ground below. The crowd pulled back as Malak raised his spear, pointing it toward the Nephilim. Above the armored warrior, the gash pulsed and sparked as the sound of flapping wings began to fill the air.

*This is it,* Aaron thought as Lehash pushed past him down the stairs, pistols of heavenly fire in each hand. Gabriel had come up the stairs to Aaron's side, barking and baring his teeth in a display of savagery uncommon to the normally docile animal.

"I want you to go to Vilma," Aaron told him.

*"But I want to stay with—"*

"Don't argue, Gabriel," he ordered the dog. The sounds of angels' wings grew louder. "Protect Vilma." He knew that his friend would have preferred to stay at his side, but Vilma needed a guardian, and he could think of no one that he trusted more.

With no further argument, the dog bounded down the stairs and up the street.

And then an army of angels, bloodthirsty screams upon their lips, weapons of war in their hands, spewed forth from the hole, like biblical locusts preparing to blight the land.

# CHAPTER FOURTEEN

Aaron had begrudgingly accepted his inhumanity, and now attempted to wear it with pride. There was very little pain as the sigils appeared on his flesh and his powerful wings burst from his shoulder blades. A spectacular sword of fire ignited in his hand, and he welcomed the rush of power that engorged every fiber of his being.

The last of the Powers' soldiers emerged from the tear in the fabric of space, and they began their assault, dropping down from the sky, their weapons of flame seeking to end the lives of Aerie's citizens. He wanted to help them, but he could not take his eyes from Malak—his little brother—still standing before the fissure.

*What are you waiting for?* Aaron wondered. The report of Lehash's pistols echoed like thunder through the normally still air, and then Malak knelt on one knee, bowing his helmeted head before the opening. Aaron tried to see into the rip, certain that the surprises from the other side were not yet over.

A sudden chill filled the air, and Aaron felt his presence before seeing him. Verchiel emerged into Aerie as if he were its savior, and not its destroyer. Wings of the purest white spread full, he glided from the darkness of the fissure, a look of contentment on his pale, aquiline features.

Just seeing the leader of the Powers there in the citizens' place of solace filled Aaron with a barely controlled fury. It was all he could do not to launch himself at the villain, but caution was the victor, and he waited for his enemy to make the first move.

"And so it ends," the Powers' leader proclaimed, his voice booming over the cries of battle. Verchiel glanced at his soldiers in the midst of violence, at the citizens fighting for their lives, and then his dark, hawklike eyes fell upon Aaron. "You couldn't possibly have believed it would end any other way!" Verchiel roared, smiling with anticipation.

Aaron leaped from the church's steps and landed on the sidewalk, sword of fire at the ready. "It's not over yet," he said to the angel, beckoning to him with an outstretched hand.

Verchiel shook his head with great amusement. "No, Nephilim," he said, touching his long, spidery fingertips to the top of the kneeling Malak's helmet. "Another wants the honor of ending your life."

Malak slowly stood to face Aaron, a lance of black metal clutched in his armored hands.

"I believe he wants to eat your heart," the angel said, lovingly brushing imaginary dust from the shoulder of the warrior's scarlet armor. "And I do not wish to deny my pet his desire." Verchiel brought his hand to his mouth, kissed his fingertips, and placed them on Malak's head. "Kill him," the angel declared.

And with his master's blessing, Malak attacked.

Lehash had known the angels that now attacked him and the citizens of Aerie. Once they had been soldiers of Heaven, protecting the sanctity of the Creator's desires, but now they were something altogether different. These were not beings of purity and righteousness, but shadows of their former glory, twisted by the malignant beliefs of their leader.

He fired his weapon into the screaming face of one attacker, spinning around to kill another before the first could fall to the ground. It had been quite some time since he'd delivered violence on such a level, and he found that he had developed a distaste for it. Aerie had been good for him, calming what seemed to be an eternally angry spirit. He had found a place to belong, a home to replace the one that was lost to him.

But now there was a chance, a slim possibility, that he might see Heaven again, and somebody wanted to take that from him—from all of them who called Aerie their home. Lehash was not about to surrender that chance no matter how small. That was what fueled him.

He shot his bullets of fire, hoping that each enemy falling dead from the sky would bring him closer to forgiveness— closer to Heaven. But there were so many, and the air was soon filled with the stink of burning flesh and spilled blood.

*What a terrible thing,* the fallen angel thought as he unleashed the full fury of his terrible weapons, and watched as both friends and foes died around him.

*What a terrible price to pay for forgiveness.*

"Do you remember me, Stevie?" Aaron asked the creature before him. "Do you remember who I am?"

Malak thrust his spear forward with blinding speed, and Aaron reacted barely in time to angle his body away from its razor-sharp metal tip.

"I remember," Malak said, his voice cold and menacing as it echoed from inside the horned helmet. "I remember the pain you caused, the misery you have brought to the world."

He spun around gracefully, the spearhead slashing across the front of Aaron's body with an ominous whisper. The Nephilim moved too slowly and the tip of the spear passed through his shirt to cut a fine line from his left shoulder down to the right side of his stomach. He leaped back, feeling warm blood seeping from the open wound. First blood was to Malak, and Aaron doubted it would be the last of it spilled in this battle.

"I'm your brother," he tried again, preparing himself for

the next assault. "Verchiel killed our parents. He took you, changed you, turned you into something—"

Like a rampaging bull Malak charged, the spear suddenly gone, replaced by a fearsome club, its surface studded with spikes. "He made me a hunter," he growled. "A killer of Heaven's criminals."

Aaron dove beneath the club's pass, discarding his own sword of fire and lunging forward to grab his attacker's weapon. They struggled for control of the instrument of death, but then Malak slammed his armored face into the bridge of Aaron's nose. Aaron heard a wet snap and blood exploded from his nostrils. It felt as though his head was about shatter, but he maintained his grip on the club.

Malak violently wrenched the weapon away, watching as Aaron stumbled backward, wiping the blood from his face. There was no pause in the creature's reaction, not the slightest hint of mercy. The armored warrior came at him again, and Aaron called upon a sword of fire to defend himself. The club had become a two-handed ax, and it descended on him with incredible force. He brought his own blade up and the collision of heavenly fire with enchanted metal rang in Aaron's ears like the crack of doom.

Both combatants leaped back, a brief respite before continuing their skirmish. Aaron became aware of the battles going on around him. The streets of Aerie echoed with the sounds of strife, and he wondered if it would have been the same if he had listened to Belphegor and not gone to Vilma's aid.

Feelings of guilt fueling him, Aaron took the offensive, charging at Malak, the tip of his fiery sword tracing a sparking line across the enchanted chest armor. Malak stepped back, discarding his ax and reaching for another instrument of death from his seemingly endless magickal arsenal. Aaron did not wait to see what the warrior would choose. With the aid of his flapping wings, he propelled himself forward and relentlessly rained blows upon his enemy with his own sword of fire.

"I don't know what he's told you!" Aaron shouted, desperate to reach some trace of his brother, even as he drove Malak back. "But it isn't true."

"You are a master of deceit," Malak said, drawing his own sword of dark metal to parry Aaron's blows. The warrior moved with inhuman speed, his movements registering as little more than a scarlet blur. "Lies flow from your mouth like blood from a mortal wound."

"Listen to me, Stevie!" Aaron yelled, on the defensive again, barely stopping the unremitting fall of the enchanted black blade.

*"Malak,"* his attacker bellowed, enraged. "I am Malak!" The savagery of his attack intensified. "I kill you now in *his* name," Malak growled, preparing to deliver a final deadly strike.

And as Aaron primed himself to counter this killing blow, the question of futility echoed through his frenzied thoughts.

*Is it possible?* He caught sight of the warrior's eyes through the slits of the horned helmet—murderer's eyes, void of any trace of humanity—and wondered if there was even a slight chance that Stevie was still somewhere inside the monster that was Malak.

Verchiel grinned, pleased by the ferocity of his pet's attack. Everything was proceeding as planned. He looked out over the dilapidated human neighborhood, at the battles being fought in his name. The vermin would be routed from their place of concealment, and the process of purging the last believers of the prophecy from the world of God could begin. After Aerie was wiped from existence, it would only be a matter of time before all the Creator's offenders were destroyed. And on that day he would return to Heaven, to the accolades of the Almighty, and he would take his place at God's side.

The Powers' leader breathed in the stench of violence, his memories taking him back to a time when his purpose was defined for him. He remembered the war in Heaven and how even when it appeared to be over, the followers of the Morningstar defeated, the true struggle had yet to begin. They took their audacity, their insolence, and fled to the Earth, hoping to escape the Creator's wrath. *To think that they actually believed they would be forgiven,* the angel mused.

"Lost in thought, Verchiel?" A voice distracted him from his reflection.

Verchiel looked toward the entrance of the church and gazed upon the living dead. "Belphegor," the Powers' commander hissed. "Camael told us that he had taken your life in the Garden."

"I think he may have exaggerated the truth a bit," the Founder of Aerie commented.

His disappointment in Camael strengthened all the more, Verchiel started up the church steps two at a time. "What is it the humans say?" he muttered, murder on his mind. "If you want a job done right . . ."

Belphegor did not respond. Instead he opened the door of the church and slipped inside.

Verchiel suspected a trap, but the idea that one he believed destroyed so long ago was still among the living drove him forth. He summoned his weapon of choice, and the Bringer of Sorrow came to burning life in his hand as he took hold of the cold metal of the handle and yanked the door wide, plunging himself into the place of worship with the hunger of bloodlust beating in his chest. The church was enshrouded in darkness, the only light from candles burning before a makeshift altar in the front of the building. Belphegor waited for him there.

"Come in, come in," the old angel said as he motioned Verchiel closer. "I was hoping to have a discussion with you before things got out of hand." He shrugged. "I guess we're a little late."

Verchiel began moving cautiously down the center aisle; the flames of his sword illuminating the church's interior with its wavering light. "I have nothing to discuss with the likes of you," he snarled as he surveyed the offensive surroundings.

Belphegor smiled as if privy to some secret knowledge. "That is where you're wrong, Verchiel," he corrected. "There is much to talk about." He turned to the mural painted upon the wall. "Have you seen this?" the fallen angel asked, gesturing to the depiction of an unholy trinity.

Verchiel sneered. "I have borne witness to myriad representations of this repugnant prediction in my pursuits. I cannot begin to tell you how it disgusts me."

Belphegor nodded. "I figured that would be your answer."

"It is heresy to even think that the Lord God would allow—"

"He has, Verchiel," Belphegor interrupted. "He *has* allowed it. The prophecy has come true—you've seen it with your own eyes, but you're too damn stubborn to accept it."

The leader of the Powers seethed, the fallen angel's barbed words stoking the fires of his wrath. "The Creator has entrusted me with a mission that I intend to fulfill; those who sinned against Him will be held accountable for their crimes."

Belphegor moved toward him, defiance in his ancient eyes. "And what of our greatest sinner?" the fallen asked. "How is it that the first of the fallen was allowed to sire the savior of us all? Doesn't that tell you something, Verchiel? Doesn't that convince you that there might be some truth in the ancient writings?"

Sounds of the violence outside drifted into the place of worship, but it was nothing compared to the deafening din inside the angel's head. "The first of the fallen sired nothing," Verchiel roared, startled by his own fury. "We saw to that. Any woman who lay with him was destroyed. There was no chance of his seed taking root—"

"Not only did the seed root, but it bore fruit," Belphegor said, his voice firm with certainty.

Verchiel steeled himself, gripping his weapon all the tighter. "It cannot be," he whispered incredulously.

Belphegor shrugged again. "Mysterious ways and all that." He smiled and turned his gaze back to the mural. "Don't you see, Verchiel, it must be what *He* wanted—and if the Morningstar can be forgiven, there's hope for us all."

The church walls seemed to be closing in upon Verchiel, the revelation of the Nephilim's sire testing his limits. Did he have the might to hold on to his sacred mission? He felt it begin to slip from his grasp. *How could this have happened?* The question reverberated in his skull.

"Is it so outrageous to believe that we can be forgiven?" Belphegor asked him, the question like a dagger strike to his chest.

"Lies!" Verchiel shrieked, his wings unfurling as he strode down the remainder of the aisle toward the altar.

He pointed his blade toward the mural and the fire from his weapon streamed forth to scorch the painted image black. And then Belphegor's hands were suddenly upon his shoulders, and he was hurled backward into the rough benches, reducing them to kindling.

"You must face the truth!" Belphegor shouted, the altar burning behind him. "You are going against *His* wishes!"

Verchiel rose from the small pile of rubble, the power of his righteous fury building inside him. He remained silent, knowing what he must do.

"But it's not too late . . . ," Belphegor continued.

Verchiel's body began to glow, his clothing burning away to reveal flesh like cold, white marble. The floor beneath him began to smolder and the wood ignited.

"You, too, could be forgiven for your sins."

The Powers' commander spread open his wings and the fire of his heavenly being emanated from his body in waves.

"We could all go home, Verchiel," Belphegor pleaded, as his own flesh began to blister.

Then Belphegor burned.

As would they all.

Malak wielded two daggers, slashing and darting forward with the murderous grace of a venomous serpent. He seemed tireless in his pursuit of Aaron's demise, and the Nephilim found his defenses beginning to wane.

He didn't want to remember his little brother as the monster attacking him now, so he kept the memories of the child he loved at the forefront of his thoughts, drawing strength from emotion. With both hands he brandished a large broadsword of pulsing orange flame, swinging it around as opportunity presented itself. The flat of the blade connected with Malak's wrist, knocking one of the knives from his grasp in a flash of sparks as heavenly fire met magickally fortified armor.

Aaron heard a hiss of pain and anger from beneath the crimson face mask as Malak clutched his wrist to his chest. Although the blade could not penetrate the armor, the fragile flesh beneath would certainly suffer with the powerful force of the blow.

"It doesn't have to be like this, Stevie," Aaron said desperately. He just couldn't bring himself to give up.

But Aaron's futile attempts only served to enflame Malak's anger all the more, and the armored warrior came at him yet again. As he ducked and wove beneath the assassin's blows, Aaron knew a part of him was holding back. He also knew that if he didn't wise up fast, that part would get him killed. Malak was *not* Stevie. He had to accept that before he could bring this battle to a close.

Aaron sailed up into the air as Malak swiped at him with a short-bladed sword. He reached down and grabbed the armored warrior beneath the arms, ebony wings pounding the air to hold them aloft. Malak struggled in his clutches as the

Nephilim strained to carry him higher and higher still. When the Powers' assassin violently threw back his head, jabbing one of the horns on his helmet into the tender flesh of Aaron's stomach, the young man lost his grip, letting Malak plummet to the street below. Aaron watched the scarlet figure fall, fighting the urge to swoop down and save him. Malak hit the ground with a sickening clatter, his limp form tumbling to a stop in the center of the street.

The Nephilim swooped down from above to land beside the motionless body. Feeling the pangs of guilt, wishing he could hate the armored warrior, he reached out with both hands to pull the fearsome metal mask from the assassin's head. Aaron wanted to see the killer's face again, to look into his eyes, to find his little brother still alive somewhere within. He pulled off the horned helmet and discarded it, carefully placing a hand behind his neck and lifting his head. A single stream of red trickled from Malak's left nostril.

Malak's eyes slowly opened and Aaron tensed. The man's body shuddered and then coughed. "Aaron?" he said in a voice that sounded as if it came from a hundred miles away.

It was weak, but there was something in it that Aaron recognized. He pulled the young man closer, daring to believe there could be a chance, no matter how small. "I'm here," he told him, enfolding them both in the great expanse of his wings.

"Aaron . . . ," Malak said again, his voice strained and full of pain.

"Hold on now, we'll fix you," Aaron reassured him, certain now that Stevie was still in there somewhere, fighting for his identity, fighting against the pain and misery that Verchiel had used to distort him. He could see the struggle behind the man's deep blue eyes and Aaron held him tighter, lending him his strength. "Belphegor and Lorelei—they'll have the answers. We'll make it right, you'll see. Hang on, Stevie," he urged.

Slowly Stevie reached up to touch his brother's face, his gauntleted fingers tracing the black sigils.

"We'll be a family again, me and you . . . and Gabriel." Aaron laughed desperately, overcome with emotion. "Can't forget him."

He saw it in the man's eyes before he had a chance to react. Stevie had lost his battle. Malak closed his hand around Aaron's throat and started to squeeze. The grip was remarkable, cutting off his air supply completely as the metal-clad fingers dug into the tender flesh of his throat.

"Aaron," Malak said again, only this time it was more like a reptilian hiss, absent of any emotion.

The Nephilim grabbed Malak's wrist with both hands, struggling to break his grip. But Malak held fast, giggling maniacally. Explosions of color blossomed before his eyes and Aaron knew that it wouldn't be long before he blacked out. He spread his wings and began to beat the air, stirring up a storm of dirt and rock as he fought to be free, but it did nothing to loosen the hunter's grip upon his neck. Malak seemed to be enjoying the struggle, as if he too knew it was only a matter of time now.

Aaron's wings faltered and a trembling weakness spread through his arms. He gazed into the cold, dead eyes of the thing that used to be his brother and opened his mouth to scream. It was nothing more than a croak, but to the Nephilim's ears, it was a cry of mourning, a cry of rage for what had been done to an innocent little boy.

Malak smiled as Aaron let one of his hands fall away from the monster's wrist.

But the Nephilim wasn't giving up yet. From the arsenal inside his head, he selected a knife, a sleek and deadly object with the sharpest of blades. The weapon sparked to life in his free hand and he saw Malak's eyes drawn to it. The killer's armor was impervious to weapons of Heaven, but the flesh inside the shell was not. Aaron plunged the flaming dagger into the chink at the bend of Malak's arm where the armor separated into two pieces.

Malak screeched in pain, sounding more like a wounded animal than anything remotely human, and pulled away his arm, releasing Aaron's throat from his death grip. Aaron scrambled back across the ground, rubbing at his bruised windpipe, greedily taking in gulps of air.

"That hurt," Malak whined, sounding a bit like the little boy that he should have been. But Aaron now knew that wasn't the case at all.

With his other arm, the scarlet-garbed warrior raked his hand across an area of open air in front of him, and tore a hole in space. For the first time Aaron took note of the sound that it made, and it reminded him of the ripping of heavy fabric. From his neverending arsenal, the killer produced a loaded crossbow.

The fight was taking its toll. Wearily Aaron summoned another sword of fire, but his nemesis was faster. As his blade took form, Malak let fly a bolt. Aaron lashed out at the shaft of black metal, deflecting the projectile in a shower of sparks. With nimble fingers, Malak loaded another bolt and fired it. This time the Nephilim wasn't fast enough and the bolt buried itself deep in the flesh of his thigh.

The pain drove him to his knee. He tried to pull it from his leg, but the shaft was greasy with his own blood. He heard the clatter of armor on the move and saw that Malak was moving toward him, holding a sword as he came in for the kill. Aaron struggled to stand, hefting his own weapon of fire.

It was then that the church exploded. There was a flash from somewhere within the holy structure, and then it blew apart with a deafening roar, spewing hungry orange flames into the sky. Glass, metal, and wood rained down upon the battle-field.

"Master," Malak cried pitifully, his attention focused entirely on the blackened, smoking hole that was Aerie's place of worship.

Malak's show of concern for the monster that had brought nothing but pain and misery was all Aaron needed to spur him to action. This was the moment he had both dreaded and longed for, the opportunity to finally bring the battle to a close. Time slowed and his leg screeched in protest as he threw himself toward his distracted enemy. With both hands Aaron brought the blazing sword up over his shoulder and then swung it with all the force he could muster. As he watched the blade cut through the air on course to its target, his thoughts were filled with images of the past—frozen moments of time that seemed so very long ago.

He saw the little boy he'd loved sleeping peacefully in his bed, Gabriel curled into a tight ball at his side.

The blade was closer now, and Malak began to turn, suddenly aware.

The child rocking before the television set, the image upon the screen nothing more than static.

"I'm sorry, Stevie," Aaron whispered as the heavenly blade reached its destination, cutting through the thick muscle and bone of Malak's neck, severing his head from his armored body.

Aaron fell to his knees before the body of his foe—his brother—and bowed his head. He felt drained of life, as if this last, violent act had sucked away his final reserves of strength.

But then he heard something move within the rubble

of the church and lifted his head to gaze at the smoldering wreckage. There was a brilliant flash of light, and a warm breeze caressed his face as a figure rose up from beneath the detritus, carried into the air on wings composed of heavenly light.

"Murderer," Verchiel pronounced, his accusation rumbling through the air.

# CHAPTER FIFTEEN

No matter how hard she tried, Lorelei could not keep
the man from dying.

The attack by the Powers was unrelenting,
brutal, and she watched stunned as people who she had come
to know as friends were slain before her eyes. Lorelei did what
she could, using angelic magicks to repel the attackers, but it
wasn't enough. Citizens were still dying.

She did not know him well, but thought his name was
Mike. He too was a Nephilim, and had come to Aerie not
long after she'd first arrived. He'd had the look—pale skin,
close-cropped hair, an unusual amount of scar tissue around
the wrists. Like her, he had been institutionalized as the angelic
birthright came to life inside him, turning his day-to-day existence on its ear.

Lorelei had seen him struck down. A Powers' angel had

come swooping down out of the sky and impaled him on the end of a flaming spear before moving on to find murder and mayhem elsewhere. There was a flash of recognition in his eyes as she approached him, a glimmer of hope that this was not the end for him despite the gaping wound in his chest. If only she had the power. Using all her strength, she dragged him from the street, away from the battle that would decide their fate. On a front lawn more dirt than grass, she knelt down beside him and took his hand in hers.

In the past she'd tried to make small talk with Mike. Whenever she saw him out walking or at the group meetings, she always made it a point to smile and say hello. But Mike had kept to himself. She'd heard that he wasn't adjusting well to his transformation. Right now, it didn't really matter. Mike was dying and there was nothing she could do to save him. All she could do was be with him when he passed.

*We're not doing very well,* she thought as she gave Mike's hand a gentle squeeze. The dying Nephilim squeezed back weakly. His wound was still smoking, as if burning somewhere deep within, and she placed her other hand over the hole in his chest hoping to smother it.

Her father's guns boomed somewhere in the distance, and she was certain that another Powers' angel had met its fate, but it wasn't enough. Most of the citizens weren't soldiers, and the Powers had sworn their existences to wiping Aerie's kind from the world. Lorelei could sense her fellow Nephilim dying, like tiny pieces of herself floating away on the wind.

She returned her attention to Mike and saw that he had passed away. His eyes were wide in death, staring up into the sky toward what she hoped was a better place, a place where he could be at peace. And wasn't that what they were all fighting for?

She rose and moved to return to the battle. The ground was littered with the corpses of citizens and Powers alike. A Powers' soldier, one of his wings twisted and bent, came at her from across the street. There was a dagger of flame in one hand and the look of murder in his glistening black eyes. She must have looked like an easy target.

"Hate to disappoint you," she said before beginning to mutter a spell of defense. She felt the charge of angelic energy building inside her. The angel was almost upon her, but she held her ground. She could smell the stink of his fury oozing from his flesh; it smelled of spice and something akin to burning rubber. It made her want to vomit.

Lorelei was getting tired. Her body was not used to manipulating these kinds of energies for this length of time, and the magicks were slow to respond. The strain was painful as she called forth a blast of crackling energy. Bolts of energy emanated from her fingertips and met in the air to form a ball. The energy rolled across the space between them, striking the Powers' angel in the face, stopping him in his tracks. The angel screamed pitifully as the flesh on his face turned to ash. He fell to his knees, dead before his body even touched the ground.

Her head swam and the tips of her fingers ached as if frostbitten. She wondered if she'd be able to find the strength to defend herself again, when she felt an uncomfortable tingling in the pit of her stomach and looked past the battles to the church of Aerie. It was Belphegor she sensed, and he was in great pain. But as Lorelei started for the holy place, it exploded in a blast of orange flame and a scorching wind that picked her up and tossed her back. She struggled to her feet and wound her way across the battlefield to the smoking pile of rubble. Not even the destruction of the church could stop their battle.

"Belphegor!" she cried, the heat of the ruins on which she walked burning through the soles of her boots.

It was then that she felt him, a twinge of his once powerful life force calling from nearby. A hand, charred and blackened, beckoned to her from beneath a section of collapsed wall and she went to it. Using all her strength, Lorelei moved the rubble aside, managing to expose Belphegor's upper body. He was hurt beyond imagining, and she hadn't the slightest idea how he was still living. His breathing was a grating rasp, and his eyes—his beautiful, soulful eyes—opened as she laid her hand upon his blackened cheek.

"Belphegor," she whispered, scalding tears of sadness raining down from her eyes. "What have they done to you?"

The fallen angel closed his eyes again, as if attempting to muster the strength to speak. "I have lost my battle," he said in a strained whisper, his voice like the rustling of dry leaves. "But the war is far from over."

"They're killing us," she said, bowing her head, feeling the grip of despair upon her.

His charred hand brushed against the side of her head, and she raised her gaze to him. "As long as *he* still lives," the Founder stressed, "there is hope."

She wanted to believe in the savior, in Aaron Corbet, but at the moment it all seemed so unrealistic. Instead Lorelei began to move away more of the debris. "Let's see about getting you free—"

"Stop," he commanded, his voice stronger. "It is too late for me," he said with finality.

She didn't want to hear that, she didn't want to hear that he had given up. If he had managed to survive thus far, maybe there was something she could do to help him heal faster. Her thoughts raced with spells of healing. "You can't die." She continued to frantically try to free him. "You have to hold on . . . you have to hold on until the savior forgives you."

"That is not to be my fate," Belphegor responded sadly, his head resting on a pillow of rubble.

And though it pained her, something deep down inside told her that it was true.

"My many years of tending these gardens has left my constitution weak." He shook his head feebly from side to side. "Do not despair for me," he told her. "For I have lived far longer than even I expected. From the moment Camael spared my life in Eden, I knew that I was living on borrowed time, and swore that when the moment finally did arrive, I would not fight, but would welcome it—for it was due me long ago."

Belphegor paused, his eyes closing, and for a brief moment she wondered if he had slipped away. But then the old angel sighed, a sound suffused with disappointment. "The only thing that pains me is that I will not survive to see the outcome," he said.

Lorelei said nothing, and the Founder read her silence.

"You believe all is lost?" he asked, and still she did not respond.

The sounds of battle drifted up to them, Lehash's guns booming, screams of rage, cries of fear. Lorelei didn't have to see it to know that they were losing the war, she could feel it in the depths of her soul. She could feel them dying.

"Even with Aaron, we're not strong enough," she whispered, nearly overcome with hopelessness.

"So you believe," Belphegor said. "Do you even understand the true nature of what you are?" he asked, straining upon every word. "The merging of God's two most fabulous creations into one fantastic form of life."

She felt another of the citizens die as she listened to Belphegor's words.

"Do you think that the Powers kill you because they think you inferior?" he asked. "They hunt you because they *fear* you—fear what you have the potential to become." Painfully he raised an arm to point a blackened finger at her. "You, all the Nephilim, are the next phase in our evolution . . . the next best thing. But to survive—to make the prophecy a reality— you must fight. It is the last of the trials we must face to achieve absolution."

There was strength in the old angel's words, and Lorelei felt the power of her birthright stir. *The next best thing,* she repeated to herself as she watched the Founder's eyes begin to close.

"Show them what it means to be Nephilim . . . ," he said, his words trailing off in a weakening rattle.

Lorelei felt his life slip away, and the world suddenly seemed to be a much colder place. "Sleep well, old man," she said, and leaned down to place a kiss upon his blackened brow.

Then she climbed to her feet upon the shifting rubble and gazed out over the streets made into a battleground, the citizens fighting to make their dreams of a prophecy come true. *The next best thing,* she heard the Founder of Aerie say again, and knew that it was now her place to prove him right.

"This is for you," she said, reaching within herself to stir a power she had believed to be nearly depleted, and she gazed up into the cloudless sky, beckoning to the elements in the language of the messengers.

And the heavens answered.

With a vengeance.

* * *

The fear was gone.

Aaron climbed to his feet, crossbow shaft still protruding from his leg, the sword of fire he had just used to end his brother's life still in his hand. He looked upon his enemy with disdain.

Verchiel hovered over the remains of the citizens' church, his mighty wings fanning the pockets of flame that still burned amid the rubble. As Aaron studied the creature of Heaven, a monster that had fallen farther than any of the poor beings that had taken up residence on this poisoned land, he felt only anger.

Verchiel gracefully set down upon the rubble-strewn sidewalk, his armor still glistening resplendently in the smoky, early morning sunshine. He too was holding a sword, a truly magnificent blade that Aaron had seen once before when they battled in the sky above his home, on the night his parents were murdered and Stevie was taken.

*What was it Popeye always said?* his addled brain tried to remember. And then it came to him, and he heard it echo through his head in the odd, gravelly voice of the popular cartoon character. *I had all I can stands, I can't stands no more.* Aaron caught himself smiling, the words of the animated sailor summing up his emotions perfectly. He had been pushed beyond fear of the vengeful creatures of Heaven, and after all he had experienced in the last few hours, he did not have the ability to care.

Verchiel walked toward him slowly, a predator's gait, full of graceful strength and self-assurance. It was obvious that he believed himself the victor. *He can't be more wrong,* Aaron thought as he spread his wings wide and leaped at his foe, sword poised to strike. His body screamed, the numerous wounds recently inflicted upon it crying out in protest.

"I'll show you a murderer," he growled, his voice filled with the fury of the angelic essence that had become part of his nature.

"Look at what you've caused," Verchiel taunted as he parried Aaron's strike and pressed an assault of his own.

Aaron was driven back farther into the street. He had to be careful, as the angel's savage blows rained down upon him, not to listen to Verchiel's jibes, for they were there only to weaken his resolve and make him doubt his purpose. The heel of his shoe bumped up against something in the street and he chanced a look down to see that he'd almost tripped over Stevie's headless corpse.

Verchiel used this moment of distraction to savagely hack through Aaron's defenses, his sword cutting a deep swathe down the Nephilim's cheek. Aaron cried out in pain and surprise. He had been lucky though, the wound numbed the left side of his face, but Verchiel's blade could very easily have taken away an eye.

The Powers' leader was laughing, toying with him like a cat playing with a mouse. *Time for the mouse to give the cat a taste of his own medicine,* Aaron thought. He unfurled his wings and sprang from the ground, ignoring the blaring pain of the crossbow bolt still imbedded in the thick muscle of his thigh. He flew into the Powers' commander; his shoulder connecting with the angel's armored midsection, and the two tumbled backward to the street in a heap of flapping wings.

"The savior of them all," Verchiel sneered through bared teeth as they wrestled. "They actually believed that you would be the one that brought them God's forgiveness."

Aaron bore down on him, rage and pain fueling his strength as he held Verchiel's wrist in a steely grip, preventing the angel from using his sword. He looked into the monster's black, bottomless eyes, searching for even the slightest hint that this creature once served a loving God. He saw nothing but his own look of revulsion reflected in the void of Verchiel's stare.

"Look around you, Nephilim," the Powers' commander said, struggling to break Aaron's grip. "It is not forgiveness that you bring, but death and destruction."

"No!" Aaron shouted. He reached down and pulled the blood-caked metal shaft from his leg. "I'll show you death and destruction, you son of a bitch," he growled through gritted teeth.

A look of utter shock spread over Verchiel's face as Aaron drove the body of the magickally imbued bolt down into the chest plate of the angel's armor. The pointed head pierced the armor with ease, continuing on into the angelic flesh beneath. Verchiel wailed, his pain-filled thrashings so violent that Aaron was thrown away from him.

Aaron wasted no time in pressing the advantage. Though the wound in his leg throbbed, he scrambled toward his enemy, a scream of battle on his lips, a sword of heavenly fire ready to strike. He didn't want to give the monster even the smallest chance to recover. But Verchiel moved quickly, ignoring the shaft of metal in his chest. He summoned his blade and blocked the arc of Aaron's weapon.

"You've actually begun to believe what they say," Verchiel said, his voice dripping with contempt.

He twisted his body to the side, one of his wings suddenly snapping out, swiping Aaron across the face and knocking him away. The Powers' commander charged, his fiery blade slicing through the air in search of a kill. Aaron moved just as quickly and felt the heat of Verchiel's sword as it narrowly missed him.

"You're as delusional as the monstrosity that sired you," Verchiel retorted, hissing, his blade melting its way into the blacktop of the street on which they battled. He soared up into the air, his wings spread to their full impressive span. Fluidly he spun around and angled down like a hawk descending upon unsuspecting prey.

Aaron did not shy away, swinging the blade of flame with all his might. "What do you know about my father?" he yelled as their blades connected.

The Nephilim's sword exploded with the force of the blow

and he was thrown back across the street, ears ringing. He scrambled to his feet to find the Powers' leader untouched by the volatile contact. The black metal bolt still protruded from his chest, a trail of black blood staining his golden armor.

"Your weapon is as fragile as the idea that one such as you could best me in combat," the angel spat. He raised his fearsome blade of fire. "Bringer of Sorrow shall drink deeply of your blood this day."

"I *did* best you in combat, Verchiel," Aaron angrily retorted. "Did my father as well?"

The angel recoiled as if slapped, and then a cruel smile, oozing with malice, crept across his face. "You don't know, do you. You are ignorant to the identity of the one who sired you." And then he began to laugh.

Aaron reacted instinctively, a weapon unlike any he had conjured before taking shape in his hand. It was a baseball bat—a Louisville Slugger formed of heavenly fire. If things hadn't been so dire at the moment, he would have been amused.

The adversaries swept toward each other. Mere inches apart, Aaron swung his flaming club and swatted aside Verchiel's blazing weapon. He followed with a blow at the angel's face, the club connecting with his chin. Knocked off balance, the Powers' leader fought to stay afloat, his wings wildly flapping. Aaron didn't give him the chance. He brought the club down upon Verchiel's head and watched as the angel fell to the street, wings barely softening his fall.

Aaron was beyond anger now; the idea that Verchiel might know the identity of his father spurred him on. He would have this knowledge—this missing piece of the puzzle—even if he had to beat the angel within an inch of his life to get it. He landed in a crouch before Verchiel, who was just climbing to his feet, the so-called Bringer of Sorrow still clutched in his hand. Aaron did not hesitate, swinging the bat of fire savagely down upon the angel's wrist, forcing him to drop his weapon. The sword fell, evaporating in an implosion of fire, wisps of smoke the only evidence it had ever existed.

"You've taken so much from me," Aaron spat, looming before the angel, weapon at the ready. "It's time you gave me something in return."

Verchiel bristled like a cornered animal. "I'll give you nothing," he growled, his perfect teeth stained black from his wounded mouth.

Aaron brought the bat of fire down again, driving the Powers' commander to the street. He wanted to deliver the fatal blow, but restrained himself, keeping at bay the killer's instinct yowling for vengeance inside him. It wasn't easy. Here was the monster responsible for the death of his parents, of his little brother, of Zeke and Camael, broken and driven to his knees, and he longed to show the angel the same amount of mercy that had been afforded his loved ones. But not until he received the answer to the question that haunted him.

"It's over, Verchiel," he said, a tremble of suppressed rage in his voice. "All the misery and death you've been responsible for—it's come back to bite you on the ass."

Verchiel glared at the burning club against his armored chest, keeping him pinned to the ground. "The Creator will—"

"The Creator will what?" Aaron screamed. "What will it take for you to realize that you're on your own?" he asked the Powers' commander. "God isn't protecting you!"

An expression of horror gradually crossed Verchiel's face. And then the angel began to laugh, a high-pitched sound tainted with a hint of insanity. "Very good, Nephilim." Verchiel giggled, looking up into Aaron's eyes. "You almost had me. It appears that you have your father's gift for twisting the truth."

Aaron couldn't stand it anymore, his fury overflowing as he lifted the bat and prepared to deliver another blow. "Who is my father?" he demanded.

But the Powers' commander proved himself more wily than Aaron anticipated, re-igniting his sword of sorrow and abruptly stopping Aaron's weapon. "You'll die with the knowledge filling your ears," Verchiel hissed as he sprang to his feet, a dagger of orange flame in his injured hand. The knife cut a course through the air on its way to the tender flesh of Aaron's throat. "He is the one who started it all. Without his selfish act none of us would have fallen."

The knife was coming for him, but Aaron was frozen in place by anticipation.

"Your father is . . . ," the angel began, but never got the chance to finish.

Tremendous bolts of lightning rained down from a roiling sky, a deluge of destructive force, incinerating everything they touched.

In the midst of combat with a Powers' soldier, Lehash was thrown backward as a jagged strike of icy blue turned his opponent to a screaming cinder, melting the street with the heat of its touch.

It was like nothing he had ever experienced. Bolts of electrical force snapping down from the sky, striking at anything that moved. *No,* he corrected himself as he climbed to his feet and picked up his hat. *Not anything. The Powers . . . the lightning was singling out the Powers host.* For a brief moment he entertained the concept of divine intervention, that this was the Creator's way of telling them that they were forgiven, but then in flash of searing white he saw her silhouette atop the rubble that had been the church.

"Lorelei," Lehash said aloud. He watched her wield the spell of the elements, her head tossed back, arms reaching up to the sky. Tendrils of magickal power leaked from the tips of her fingers, trailing up into the heavens, into the bodies of the low hanging clouds. He had seen her weave the spell of angelic magick before, but never like this.

The lightning continued to fall, lashing out at those who

attempted to escape, their ashes scattering on the blowing winds. The surviving citizens ran for cover against the electrical onslaught, but Lehash turned in the direction of his daughter. He summoned a pistol of golden fire and discharged a shot into the air, hoping to capture Lorelei's attention. The Nephilim sorceress didn't even flinch, continuing to stare up into the heavens, arms outstretched as she drew down the fury of the elements.

As a new succession of lightning bolts rained down from above, Lehash felt a tremor beneath his boots. The intensity of the power his daughter was unleashing, it permeated the very earth. And he remembered the tons of toxic waste buried beneath the Ravenschild Estates. He sprinted toward his daughter as he felt another vibration. He had to get her attention; he had to get her to stop before—

The air was filled with the sounds of explosions and the ground trembled beneath Gabriel's paws. Plumes of flame, the color of tarnished sunset rose up into the sky in the distance, as if attempting to rival the perilous fury of the lightning bolts that continued to emanate from the pregnant clouds in the distance.

He had feared something like this; it was why he hadn't wanted to leave Aaron's side, but he couldn't have denied his master's wishes. Aaron had said he should protect Vilma and that was what he was going to do. The three Powers' soldiers that had been advancing on the house stopped their progress and anxiously gazed off in the direction of the sounds of destruction, Gabriel and the girl inside temporarily forgotten.

Above the rumble of thunder, Gabriel heard Vilma's pitiful cries from inside the house behind him. When he had reached the home earlier, he'd found the girl in the grip of what he thought to be a nightmare. But as he listened to the words she spoke, the dog came to realize that even in the midst of sleep, the girl was seeing the war being waged between the Powers and the citizens. It was her plaintive murmurings of what was happening to his friends that drove the dog from the house, and it was a good thing, too, for he would never have known they were about to be attacked.

The angels looked back to him, weapons of fire held in their hands. *They must have been drawn to Vilma's scent,* he thought, to the scent of her newly awakening abilities. Gabriel crouched low and emitted a fearsome growl. Hackles rose around his neck and tail, and the power that had been inside since Aaron brought him back from the brink of death let its presence be known. Gabriel knew that he was different now, and accepted it. As Aaron had a special purpose upon the world, the dog decided that he did as well. It was his job to protect his master and to do his bidding. Vilma would be protected, or he would die trying.

The Powers stopped, studying the dog that blocked their advance.

"It is the animal," said one of the angels. "The one the Nephilim altered."

"You are correct, brother," said the second. "And it has been made savage by the Nephilim's poisonous taint."

"We would be showing it a great mercy if we were to end its life," said the last, and he crept closer. The others cautiously followed.

*"Don't think I'm going to make this easy,"* Gabriel growled, his large, blocky head moving slowly from side to side, keeping his eyes on all three of his adversaries.

There were more explosions in the distance, blasts that sent powerful shock waves through the ground and shattered the windows of homes around them. Geysers of flame erupted into the sky followed by billowing clouds of oily, black smoke.

The angels were distracted. Bolts of electricity continued to drop from the sky, and wherever lightning fell, an explosion that shook the neighborhood followed. Gabriel held his ground uneasily, fearing for his master's safety.

They looked back to him, but he could see in their eyes that the angels had lost interest. Each continued to gaze longingly in the direction from whence they had come.

*"I think your brothers might need your help,"* Gabriel said, hoping he could convince them to leave.

They looked at one another. The sounds of explosions filled the air.

*"Are you going to waste your time fighting an* animal, *or are you going to help your brothers?"*

The angels suddenly screamed, their cries like those of the seagulls he used to chase on Lynn beach, and Gabriel thought he had made a mistake. But they didn't attack; instead each opened his wings and they flew off to join their brethren. Gabriel watched them glide through the air and had to fight the urge to follow. He was worried about Aaron and about the citizens, but he had made a promise that he would not break.

The dog heard a noise behind him and turned to see the front door slowly open. Vilma stood there, wrapped in the knitted afghan that had been thrown over the back of the couch. She appeared cold, her body racked with chills. Her eyes were wide, as if awakened by something that had truly terrified her. The smell of sickly sweat wafted from her body in waves.

Gabriel padded back up the concrete path toward her. *"What's the matter, Vilma?"*

On bare feet she stepped out of the house and proceeded down the path. She seemed drawn to the sounds of the explosions and looked off in the direction where the angels had just gone.

*"Vilma,"* Gabriel said, standing by her side. *"What did you see, Vilma?"* he asked her softly, not sure he wanted the answer.

"He's still alive," Vilma said softly, a tremble in her voice. "Aaron's alive."

And, overcome with relief and happiness that his master was safe, Gabriel tilted back his head and howled with joy.

Aaron regained consciousness gradually, his brain fumbling for connections to his senses. Hearing was first, but that only caught his own labored breathing and the rapid-fire beating of his heart. Pain came next, a thousand aches, bruises, and cuts. He wiggled toes and fingers, flexed muscles in his arms, back, and legs. They all hurt, but everything seemed to be working.

As he opened his eyes, he recalled the battle he had been fighting before . . . *before what?*

His blurred vision gradually cleared to reveal the obscene level of devastation that had befallen Aerie. He remembered fighting Verchiel. The last thing he recalled was the Powers' leader attacking, a blade of fire destined for his throat. He was about to reveal the identity of the angel that had sired him— Verchiel was about to say his father's name when there was a blinding flash, and an explosion that tossed the angel aside like a rag doll.

The air was thick with acrid smoke, but it did not hide the corpses that littered the ground. On weakened legs Aaron walked among them, his eyes falling upon bodies so badly burned that their identities were a mystery. Friend or foe, he had no way of telling, and an incredible sadness washed over him.

*"Verchiel,"* he whispered with disdain, somehow knowing

that his enemy's body was not among the blackened corpses at his feet. Aaron knew that somehow Verchiel had survived the cataclysm that had ravaged this place.

He heard an awkward approach behind him and whirled, a sword of flame coming to life in hand. He was exhausted, emotionally and physically, but he was ready to fight again if necessary. From the thick smoke they came, a bedraggled Lehash supporting a weakened Lorelei, followed by other residents that had survived the Powers' attack.

"You're alive," Aaron said, beaming as the gunslinger and his Nephilim daughter lurched toward him.

"Appears that way," Lehash responded. His clothes, face, and hands were covered in a thick mixture of dirt, dust, and dried blood. "Can't say that would've been the case if it weren't for Lorelei here," he said, his attention upon the young woman at his side. Lorelei looked the way he felt, drained of all strength. "She brought the wrath of Heaven down on them sons a' bitches," Lehash said proudly, and Aaron then knew that it had been angel magick that rained down upon Aerie that day.

Lorelei slowly lifted her head, her blank, exhausted stare suddenly focusing on Aaron. "He's gone," she whispered. "He never got a chance to see it all come together." Tears streamed from her eyes, leaving trails down her dirt-covered face. "Belphegor's dead."

Aaron's body began to tremble. It was a feeling he had

experienced before and he knew what it meant. "Where is he?" he asked, a sense of urgency to his tone. "Where's Belphegor's body?"

Lorelei feebly pointed to what remained of the church behind them. "He's there," she said. "In the rubble of the church. He died trying to defend it from Verchiel."

As before, Aaron felt the power building at the center of his being and he spread his wings to fly, soaring over the heads of the surviving citizens, and then above the ruin that had once been their place of worship. He had to act quickly before the opportunity passed.

The Founder's body lay half buried beneath the debris of the church, and Aaron touched down to kneel before his lifeless form. As he leaned closer to the fallen angel's corpse his suspicions were verified. Belphegor's angelic essence was faint, but it still lived.

The power swelled inside Aaron, flowing up and out of his center to pool in his hand. "You are forgiven," he said to Belphegor, and laid his hand upon the fallen angel's brow. There was a blinding flash, like a thousand and one photographs being taken at once, and a creature of the purest white light emerged from the rubble of the church to hover above him.

Aaron sensed the presence of the citizens nearby as they struggled to climb the debris, and heard their collective gasp as they looked upon what he had done.

"It's time to go home, Belphegor," he told the being of light.

And the angel, once again in its purest form, looked up to the heavens, toward what had been denied it for countless millennia. The heavenly creature then spread its gossamer wings of radiance, and in a silent flash, was gone.

Aaron knelt upon the rubble, awash in the relief of Belphegor's release. But this time, he felt no satisfaction, as if he had not yet completed the task at hand. And then he understood, for it was true that he had not yet finished his work.

He stood, turning to those around him. "Gather the remains of those fallen in battle," he stated firmly. "*All* of them, Powers' soldiers included.

"I have work to do."

# EPILOGUE

Aaron had marked his brother's grave with a rosebush. It was taken from one of Belphegor's many gardens scattered about the property that was Aerie, and it appeared to be doing quite well within its new patch of earth.

A warm presummer wind ruffled his hair, and he could barely smell the stink of devastation it carried. After three days the aroma of burning buildings and charred flesh had finally begun to fade. He had been surprised that no one in the outside world took notice of the destruction that plagued the abandoned neighborhood, but when dealing with angels and the magicks they wielded, nothing should have surprised him.

He knelt in the damp, freshly turned soil to inspect the red buds. An insect that he could not identify—some kind of green-shelled beetle—alighted on one of the rosebush's leaves and looked as though it might be ready for a little snack. In the language of the beetle, he asked it to please find somewhere else to dine, and to pass the word to his fellow bugs that this particular bush was off limits. The bug obliged with an irritated buzz and a flutter of its wings.

Aaron looked up from his brother's grave to see Lehash and Lorelei crossing the yard toward him.

"Did you check it for bugs?" Lorelei asked him, gesturing with her chin toward the rosebush.

"The bugs and I have an understanding," he answered as he stood, leaning over to wipe the damp earth from his knees. "But I'm keeping my eyes open."

Lehash removed his Stetson and combed his fingers through his white hair. "And speaking of keeping an eye out," he said, placing the hat back atop his head, "we got our feelers out to see if anyone's caught sight of our wayward Powers' commander."

Aaron looked back to the grave, imagining that he could see beneath the earth to his brother buried there. It turned his stomach to think that he was the one who put him there. Yet again he saw the blade of his sword slicing toward Stevie's—*Malak's*—neck, and a savage chill coursed down his spine.

"Anything?" Aaron asked.

Lehash shook his head. "Nope," he said. "Are you sure that Verchiel wasn't killed—that one of Lorelei's lightning strikes didn't turn his sorry carcass to ash?"

Gabriel's sudden burst of barking distracted them and

they looked to the far corner of the yard. Vilma was holding a tennis ball, pretending to throw it, whipping the Labrador into an excited frenzy.

"How's she doing?" Lorelei asked.

Aaron watched as she threw the ball and Gabriel eagerly bounded across the sparse grass in pursuit.

"She's doing all right," he said. The dog had snatched the ball up and was returning for another round. Besides eating, there was nothing Gabriel enjoyed more than a game of fetch. "I think it's going to take her some time to adjust, but I think she's going to be okay."

They were silent, watching the dog as he tirelessly chased the tennis ball and dropped the slobbered toy at Vilma's feet. She laughed out loud at the dog's antics and Aaron couldn't imagine a nicer sound. He remembered how lucky she was—how lucky he was—that Vilma had survived the ordeal with Verchiel.

"He's still out there," Aaron suddenly said. "I can feel him, biding his time." He shook his head slowly. "But I'm not going to give him the opportunity. I've got some questions, so this time I'm taking the fight to him."

There was a wooden picnic table in the yard, and the trio headed over to sit in the spring sunshine, a little breather from the violence that seemed to be an integral part of their lives lately.

"What kind of questions, Aaron?" Lorelei asked, pulling

her snow-white hair back on her head and using an elastic band from her pocket to tie it in place.

They sat on the wooden benches, Lehash and Lorelei across from Aaron. Since the invasion of Aerie and Lorelei's attack on the Powers, father and daughter seemed much closer, as if Lehash were developing a whole new respect for Nephilim.

"Belphegor told me that he had some information about the source of my powers—and Verchiel was going to tell me who my father was before the lightning strikes started to fall."

"Sorry about that," Lorelei said sheepishly.

Lehash chuckled. "Hell, boy, you don't need to track down Verchiel to tell you that," he said, a twinkle in his eyes. "I know all about the one that sired you. Scholar worked it out."

Gabriel was happily barking in the distance, but all Aaron could hear was the thrumming of his own heart.

"It makes perfect sense when you think of it," Lehash said, casually scratching his chin. "It's all about absolution."

Aaron stood. "Tell me," he demanded.

"Maybe you should sit down for this," Lorelei suggested.

"Is there anybody besides me who doesn't know who my father is?" Aaron asked, annoyed. He fixed Lehash in a steely gaze. "No more games. Tell me, who my father—"

"Lucifer."

Aaron felt as if the world had fallen away beneath him and he had to sit down. "What . . . what are you saying?" he stammered.

"Can't get any clearer than that, boy," Lehash answered with the slightest hint of a smile. "Your daddy's the Devil."

Verchiel strode through the abandoned Saint Athanasius School, his heavy footfalls echoing ominously. The five remaining Archons followed close behind. The Powers had been diminished greatly in the devastating battle at Aerie and a part of him wished he had died that day as well. Opening the Nephilim's throat with his burning blade before his own life was taken by the elemental forces unleashed there would have been a satisfying end. But it was not to be. The Archons had been watching, and they conjured a doorway to retrieve him. At the time he had been enraged by their audacity and had lashed out at his loyal magick wielders, killing two of them before finally succumbing to his injuries.

Verchiel reached the classroom at the end of the hallway and entered.

The blind healer, Kraus, was changing a bandage on the prisoner's arm. It had been this same human servant who had also helped Verchiel to heal after the battle at Aerie, and during his recovery he realized that the Archons had been correct. It was not yet time for him to die. There were things that he still had to do.

The leader of the Powers seethed at the sight of the imprisoned angel. Here was the source of all his misery, the reason for the fall. He thought of the Nephilim and the prophecy he personified; it too was because of him—the first of the fallen. The depravities this creature was responsible for appeared limitless, and Verchiel would rather bring about an end to all things than see this one forgiven by God.

"Hey, there," his captive said in a voice that oozed with disrespect. "I was having a bit of a problem with the burns on my arms, and Kraus here said he could help me out."

Verchiel stifled the urge to smother the human servant in fire. He had to remind himself that humans were merely animals. Most of the time they meant no offense, but to see his servant caring for the needs of his prisoner was almost more than he could tolerate.

"Away from the cage," he ordered the sightless creature, and watched as Kraus obediently gathered up his supplies, and using the wall to guide him, scurried from the room.

"Nice guy, that Kraus," the angel in the cage said, admiring the bandage that covered his arm. "He thinks the world of you."

Mere days ago the prisoner's flesh had been charred to black, but now, other than a few stubborn patches, he had completely healed. Verchiel recalled the burns that he had suffered as a result of his first battle with the Nephilim, and how they still had not completely healed.

A tiny pair of eyes stared at him hostilely from the bare shoulder of his adversary. Verchiel would have found it strangely compelling that the mouse had chosen to remain with the prisoner, but there were things of a far more important nature for him to ponder than the actions of vermin. The first of the fallen was the Creator's greatest failure, and to have him absolved of his sins would mean that all Verchiel had dedicated himself to had been a lie, that what he had achieved in the name of the Father was all for nothing. It was enough to drive him mad.

Verchiel stared at the angel imprisoned behind bars of magickally imbued metal, and felt his hatred bubble forth. "Open the cage," he ordered the Archons behind him.

Archon Jaldabaoth raised a long, spidery hand, and uttered a spell of release. The door of the prisoner's confines slowly swung open with a high-pitched whine. But the prisoner did not move.

The absolution of the Morningstar would be a devastating blow to his cause. Verchiel could not allow that to happen. He would complete his sacred mission, whether it be the will of God—or not. He would see it through, for it was what he believed to be right.

"Step out of your cage . . . Lucifer," Verchiel said the name as though there were pieces of glass lodged in his throat.

"That's the first time you've called me by name since we've been together," the prisoner said, still peering through the bars. "To what do I owe that?"

"Get out of the cage!" Verchiel shouted, the rage inside him becoming more difficult to contain.

All the pain, sorrow, and misery that Lucifer had caused was collected by the power of the Almighty and placed inside the vessel that was the Morningstar's corporeal form. For as long as he existed, he would suffer the magnitude of what he had done. This was the first of the fallen's punishment—his penance.

Lucifer carefully eased his naked frame from the prison. "What's this, Verchiel?" he asked. "Don't tell me you've seen the error of your ways and are letting me go."

Verchiel's wings snapped opened. "Silence!" he bellowed, raising a sword of fire above his head.

His sudden movement startled the mouse upon his captive's shoulder, and it leaped to the ground to scamper off to a hiding place.

The prisoner fixed him in an icy stare. "What's the matter?" he asked. "Bad couple of days?"

The Archons moved forward, ancient arcanum spilling from their mouths. They extended their arms toward Lucifer and he was enveloped in an aura of crackling energy. The prisoner screamed, a long, mournful wail that seemed to come from somewhere deep inside, and his body went rigidly stiff as he was lifted up by the power of the angel magicians.

"Is it there?" Verchiel asked as they swayed to some silent song of another's misery.

"The accumulated sorrow of the universe," Archon Oraios hissed, his body trembling.

"Locked away," added Archon Jao.

"Sealed away behind barricades fortified by His word," Archon Jaldabaoth explained.

Archon Domiel started to twitch, his body suddenly racked by convulsions. "Powerful magicks were used here," he said, his voice rising in pitch. "Powerful magicks that keep us at bay."

Verchiel did not want to hear this. The maelstrom of desolation locked away inside the first of the fallen was to be his weapon. Unleashed it would bring a veritable Hell to the world of God's favored creations.

"Tear them down!" Verchiel screamed. "Remove the obstructions and allow Heaven's suffering to flow free."

Archon Katspiel was the first to suffer for his arrogance. The angelic magick user cried out as his eyes exploded from his head in a geyser of steaming gore, and he crumpled to a moaning, quivering mass upon the floor. The other Archons broke contact with the first of the fallen, setting his body free from their hold.

"What has happened?" Vercheil bellowed, stalking toward them, murder in his gaze. "Why have you stopped?"

The Archons knelt before their injured brother, attempting to heal his wounds with incantations of healing.

"The barriers are too strong," Archon Domiel said with a shake of his head. "Katspiel attempted to peel away the layers and it gave him but a taste of what was locked behind them."

"You will remove these obstructions and set this force free," Verchiel demanded.

"But the word of God . . . ," Archon Oraios tried to explain.

"The word of God shall be broken," Verchiel spat. He would have victory at any cost.

"I'd do anything to be free of it," said the weakened voice of the angel that had started it all. Lucifer was picking his naked form up off the ground, his body shivering as if in the grip of unimaginable cold. "But even I know what it would do if it were ever set free—I could never be that selfish, to let it loose upon the world."

"It's what they deserve, really," Verchiel said with venom, leaving the huddled Archons and walking to him. "What *He* deserves for having abandoned me."

Lucifer laughed, shaking his head in disbelief. "You . . . you can't be serious."

"Can't I?" he asked, a cruel smile spreading across his face, and for a brief moment, Verchiel felt a special camaraderie with his prisoner.

With the first of the fallen.

*RECKONING*

*In loving memory of Carol A. Giordano.*
*I'm sure she has God laughing.*


To LeeAnne for inspiring me with her love, and to Mulder for always making me smile.

Great gobs of gooey thanks to my creepy little brother, Christopher Golden, and to the best dang editor a cowpoke could have, Lisa Clancy.

And thanks prepared in a delicious red wine sauce must be served to: Mom & Dad; Eric "The Goon" Powell; Dave "Fancy Britches" Kraus; David Carroll; Dr. Kris; Tom & Lori Stanley and their wonder twins; Paul Griffin; Tim Cole and the usual cast of crazies; Jon & Flo; Bob & Pat; Don Kramer; Pete Donaldson; Ken Curtis; Joan Reilly; Allie Costa; and Debra and Michael Sundin at the Hearts & Stars Bookshop.

It's been a great ride. Thank you, and good night.

# PROLOGUE

**M**aybe it's time to move on, the Malakim Peliel considered as he perched atop Mount Kilimanjaro, nineteen thousand feet above the arid African plains of Tanzania.

The angelic being could count on one hand the number of times he'd had this thought in his two-millennia stay upon the dormant volcanic mountain. But always something distracted him from these musings. The coming of so-called civilization as villages turned to cities, seeming to grow up from the earth to replace the primordial jungles. The vast springtime migrations of wildebeests, zebras, antelopes, gazelles, and lions as they made their way across the Serengeti's southern plains to greener pastures in nearby Kenya. *There is so much to see here,* he reminded himself. *So much to feel, to hear, to smell.* And wasn't that his purpose—the purpose of being Malakim? He and his brethren around the globe acted as God's senses, enabling the Supreme Being to experience the wonders of the world He created.

However, today was different. Something in the thin, frigid air of Kilimanjaro was telling him—warning him—that perhaps it would be wise to seek another roost.

Slowly, Peliel flexed millennial stiffness from his wings. The collected layers of dirt and ice that had clung to his stationary form over the thousands of years fell away to reveal a creature of Heaven in what had appeared to be just another natural formation dappling the frozen landscape.

"There you are," said a voice even colder than the winds blowing across the mountaintop.

The Malakim gracefully turned, finding himself in the presence of another of God's heavenly children. This one was dressed in human garb, accompanied by twenty of his ilk, and seemed to be the source of Peliel's unease. "What host are you?" Peliel asked, casually brushing dirt from his intricate armor.

"I am Verchiel," the intruder answered, bowing slightly, "of the heavenly host Powers."

Peliel studied the beings before him, taking note of the multitude of angry scars that adorned the exposed flesh of their bodies. This angelic army had been in battle against a foe that also wielded the power of the divine; there was no other way to explain the marks of conflict they carried. *What has transpired while my attentions were elsewhere?* the Malakim wondered.

"Ah yes, the hunters of the fallen," Peliel commented

aloud, the wind howling about him as if in warning. "You have been searching for me, Verchiel of the Powers?" To his own ears, his voice was gruff from millenia of non-use, like the grinding of tectonic plates within the earth's crust. "And why would that be?"

It pleased him to speak again, and his mind wandered back to the last time he had used his voice to communicate. Many centuries past, a jungle cat, a leopard, had inexplicably climbed close to the western summit of the great mountain. Curious of the creature's intent, Peliel had appeared before the animal. It was dying, the frigid climate of Kilimanjaro's winter season sapping the warmth from its lithe, spotted body, and in the language of its species, the Malakim had asked it why it had come to such an inhospitable place. As it lay down in the snow to die, the leopard had responded that it had been drawn up the mountain, tempted by the desire to bear witness to something greater than itself—lured by the powerful emanations of the Malakim. Peliel smiled, wondering if this was the reason these Powers had come, drawn by a sense of his omnipotence.

"I am in need of something you have in your possession," Verchiel interrupted the Malakim's musings.

Peliel chuckled, amused by this angel's arrogance. "And what could I have that would possibly interest you, little messenger?"

"You and the others of your kind are direct conduits to

God," Verchiel explained. "Extensions of His holy power—receptacles for His wisdom and knowledge."

Peliel crossed his arms across his broad chest, silently urging the angel to continue with a nod of his head.

"I require information concerning the deconstruction of God's Word . . . and I shall have it no matter the cost," Verchiel proclaimed.

Peliel's ire was rankled by the presumption. *How dare this angel think himself worthy to make demands of a Malakim?* "Tread carefully, Verchiel," the Malakim growled, "for it is within my might to see you punished for your conceit." He unfurled his great wings of gunmetal gray, the very air around him crackling with restrained supernatural energies.

"I'm sorry to say there is little you can subject me to, holy Malakim, that is any worse than what I have already endured," Verchiel replied, a vicious sneer appearing upon his pale, burn-mottled features. "Give me what I ask for and I shall leave you to your observation of this . . . *fascinating* continent." Malice dripped from his disrespectful words as he chanced a casual glance over the African horizon.

*There is a dangerous hate in this one,* the Malakim observed, and again wondered what could have transpired while his attentions were focused elsewhere. He had no choice but to put this imperious angel, and those who followed him, in their respective places. This reckless arrogance could not be allowed to continue unchecked.

"Insolent pup!" Peliel bellowed, his voice rumbling across the mountain like the roar of an avalanche. He reached up into the icy blue sky to draw from the heavens a weapon of crackling energy, a sword of divine might. And he slammed his weapon down upon the mountaintop. The ground heaved and split where it was struck, a fissure in Kilimanjaro's rocky flesh zigzagging haphazardly toward the Powers angels as the ground beneath their feet shook.

"Rail all you like, keeper of His Word," Verchiel said, taking flight, his powerful wings lifting him from the tremulous earth. "It will change nothing." And then he raised his hand and brought it down in a silent command to those who served him.

The angels of the Powers host surged toward the Malakim, screams of violence pouring from their open maws, weapons of flame materializing in their grasps.

Peliel responded in kind, his own weapon forged from the might of the storm, incinerating the first of the attacking heavenly warriors. They were no match for him, but still they came, one after another, unto their deaths. As the last of them cried out in failure and the ashes of their bodies drifted across the frozen mountaintop, Peliel turned to face their master.

Verchiel stood unmoving, his hands clasped behind his back. There was not the slightest hint of remorse for the fate of those who obeyed his command.

"You knew that they hadn't a chance against me," the

Malakim seethed, the lightning sword humming and flashing in his grip, eager to strike again.

The leader of the army so callously sent to their fates nodded in agreement.

"But still you ordered them to attack. Why? Is it your wish to die, Verchiel of the Powers host? Do you attempt to save face by being vanquished by one greater than you?"

The angel smiled, and in that instant Peliel of the Malakim was certain that the disease of madness had indeed infected this creature of Heaven. It was a smile that told him the angel was beyond caring, beyond fear of reprisal. And for the briefest of instants, the emissary of God feared the lowly messenger.

"What has happened to make you this way?" Peliel asked.

Verchiel's body grew straight and rigid. "I am what He has made me," the Powers leader growled. "The deaths of those in my charge have served a purpose." His eyes of solid black twinkled with the taint of insanity and he opened his wings as if to punctuate his mad statement. "A distraction was required."

Peliel sensed the presence of the Archons before their attack upon him, attuned as he was to the delicate thrum of angelic magicks—magicks that were taught by the Malakim. He turned to face the threat as a doorway into a place that reeked of death and decay closed behind them. There were only five Archons when there should have been seven, another sign that things were amiss. The Malakim began to ask his students what had befallen the world of God's man while he was preoccupied, but the words did not have a chance to leave his mouth.

Peliel knew the spells that flowed from their mouths, powerful magicks meant to immobilize prey of great strength, and he was preparing to counter their attack when he was viciously struck from behind. The ferocious heat of Verchiel's sword had melted through the metal of his armor and punctured the angelic flesh beneath. The Malakim whirled to confront the source of this latest affront as the last words of the Powers commander became frighteningly obvious.

*"A distraction was required."*

Verchiel had already leaped away and Peliel felt the spells of the Archons take hold. It was too late. He had missed his opportunity to fight back. The magick entered his body, worming its way beneath his flesh, into his muscles and bones, freezing him solid like the cold, rugged terrain on which he had dwelled these last two thousand years. His students had learned well the might of angel sorcery, and they encircled his immobilized form, gently lowering him to the icy ground as the winds swirled feverishly around them.

Peliel could feel nothing but was fully aware of all that transpired about him. Four of the Archons loomed above, muttering the incantations that kept him incapacitated. From inside his robes, the fifth of the magick users—whose eyes, Peliel noticed, had been removed from his skull—produced a tool, a knife that shimmered and glowed seductively. Its blade was curved and serrated, and the Malakim was certain that its bite would be fierce indeed.

The blind Archon plunged the blade down into Peliel's forehead with such force that his skull split wide. The world began to grow dim, and as the veil of unconsciousness drifted across his eyes, Peliel saw that Verchiel had taken his place beside his purveyors of angel magick.

"Do you see it?" he was asking over the droning repetition of the Archons' spell, a breathless impatience in his voice.

"It is there," said the magick user with a tilt of his hooded head, the vacant caverns of his eye sockets filled with swirling pools of bottomless darkness.

"Then get it for me," Verchiel demanded with a fervent hiss.

And with trembling fingers, the blind Archon reached inside the Malakim's skull to take the prize his master so desperately sought.

# CHAPTER ONE

Vilma Santiago pressed the phone to her ear, listening to the sounds of sadness and disappointment. She hated lying to her aunt and uncle—hated how it made her feel like a silly little girl—but the alternative was something that she herself had barely begun to comprehend, never mind her guardians.

*No, I didn't really run away from home to hook up with a boy I barely knew, but was convinced that I'd fallen in love with,* she wanted to tell them. *Nope, not at all. In fact I was kidnapped by real live angels as bait to lure Aaron—you know, that boy that I'm in love with—into a trap. The bad angels wanted to kill Aaron before some kind of ancient prophecy that he was supposed to represent came true. You see, Aaron is a Nephilim, the child of a human mother and an angel—and guess what, so am I. Isn't that awesome?*

She heard her aunt's voice suddenly asking if she was still there, and Vilma promptly pushed aside the truth in favor of the lies. At the moment, lies were far less trouble.

"I'm here," she said, trying to keep the tone in her voice cheerful and upbeat. "Sorry about that, I think we might have a bad connection."

The woman's questions droned on and on, the same questions that she had asked during Vilma's first call a week ago. Was she in trouble? Did she have a place to stay? When was she coming home? Vilma gazed through the glass partition in the back of the phone booth at the traffic whizzing past her on the highway across from the roadside stop. She wanted nothing more than to be in one of those cars, speeding away from her life—running from what she had learned about herself. But she knew that was impossible, because no matter how far she drove or how fast she ran, she could never escape what she truly was.

Nephilim. The word continued to haunt her. She had read about these offspring of angels and humans in the numerous books about heavenly beings she had enjoyed reading over the years, but she had never imagined that the knowledge she had gleaned would in any way, shape, or form pertain to her. It was just all so crazy.

"Are you sure you're all right?" her aunt asked yet again, and Vilma paused before allowing the lie to flow from her mouth.

The thing that made her a Nephilim—what Aaron described as an angelic essence—had awakened at the strike of midnight on her eighteenth birthday. With each passing day she could feel it growing stronger. And it scared her.

"I'm fine," she said into the phone. "I told you, I just need a little more time to figure out what I want to do with my life. As soon as I do, I'll come home. I promise."

*Is that really a lie?* she wondered, barely hearing her uncle's hundredth offer to come and get her wherever she was, any time of the day or night. All she had to do was call, let him know where to find her, and he would be there for her. *Will I ever be able to return to Lynn, Massachusetts—especially being the way I am now?*

Vilma felt the power stir inside her and offhandedly wondered if it was similar to the feelings women experienced when pregnant. She seriously doubted that having a baby growing inside her could ever scare her as much this. Besides, if she were having a child it would be because it was wanted. Vilma didn't want this angelic power, and sometimes she suspected that the thing inside her knew it. It was unpredictable, and she never knew when the essence would awaken and cause a fuss. She tried with all her might to keep it under control, but it was like trying to hold back a sneeze—except a sneeze didn't have the power of Heaven behind it. Every day it seemed just a little bit stronger than the day before, and Vilma worried that there would come a time when the force would be stronger than her.

Suddenly she didn't want to be on the phone anymore, just in case the power of the Nephilim decided to assert itself. Most of the time it was downright painful, and she didn't want to give her aunt and uncle any reason to be more concerned for her than they already were.

Vilma told them that she had to go and that she would call them again in a couple of days. She told them that she loved them and her niece and nephew very much, reminded them not to worry, and assured them that she would be back home soon.

And then, as the connection was broken, the power of angels thrummed through her body like the bass from a car stereo cranked to maximum, and Vilma wondered if this would be the time.

The time that she could not hold it back.

Aaron Corbet couldn't pull his eyes from the entrance to the diner across the parking lot. The elderly, families, and truck drivers—people of all shapes and sizes, heading in for breakfast and coming out satisfied. It was all so boring—so mundane.

What he wouldn't give for boring and mundane in his own life.

*"What do you think that big fat guy with the bald head ate?"* his Labrador retriever and best friend, Gabriel, asked from his side. *"I think he just burped; I can smell sausage. I love sausage, don't you, Aaron?"*

The young man didn't answer, still caught up in the flow of normal. For just a brief moment he wanted to remember what it was like to be them—the people coming and going from the diner, oblivious to the beings from Heaven, angels, who walked among them.

*"Are you thinking about sausage, Aaron?"* Gabriel suddenly asked him, chasing away his brief fantasy. *"Or maybe pancakes. What I wouldn't give for some of those. Are you sure we can't go in and have something to eat? I'm very hungry."*

"No, we can't," Aaron responded, feeling again the weight of the new responsibilities he had to bear. He had come to accept them, but that did not make them any easier to carry.

The fallen angels that had fled to Earth after the war in Heaven believed in an ancient prophecy, a revelation that an offspring of a mortal woman and angel would be born into the world of man. This amalgam of God's greatest creations, this Nephilim, would be special— different from others of its ilk— and would bring with it a way in which those who had fallen from grace could be forgiven their sins and reunited with their Holy Father in Heaven. Aaron Corbet was this Nephilim—the savior—whether he liked it or not.

A family exited the restaurant—mother, father, and little boy probably about seven years old. The boy held tightly to the string of a SpongeBob balloon, and at that moment looked to be the happiest kid in the world. Aaron watched them cross the parking lot to their car and couldn't help but think of the family that had been lost to him, violently torn away as a result of his angelic destiny.

After spending the first years of his life shuffled from one foster family to another, he was finally placed with the Stanleys, a truly loving couple, and their young, autistic son. They had accepted him as one of their own, and became the only family Aaron ever really knew. But they were all gone now, murdered by a host of angels—the Powers—hellbent on making sure that the prophecy of forgiveness would never come to pass. Their leader, a nasty piece of work called Verchiel, wanted him dead in the worst of ways, but Aaron just couldn't find it in his heart to oblige.

*"It's that no-dogs-allowed thing again, isn't it?"* the Lab interrupted Aaron's thoughts again, frustrated by the fact that he couldn't eat. Gabriel loved to eat—and to talk . . . and talk and talk. *"Is it because they think we smell, Aaron?"* the dog asked. *"I don't think I smell any worse than most babies do."*

Being able to understand the dog—being able to understand the language of all living things—was but one of the strengths of Aaron's Nephilim birthright. With the help of his angel mentor, Camael, and an old fallen angel called Belphegor, he had successfully merged with the power of Heaven that flowed through his body. This power provided him with the strength and skill he would need to achieve his destiny, as well as deal with the threat still posed by Verchiel and the Powers.

"I think you smell better than most babies too," he complimented the dog, "but they still won't let you eat inside. We'll have something when we get back to Aerie. Don't worry; I won't let you starve."

Aerie was their home now, a settlement of fallen angels and Nephilim dedicated to the belief in the ancient prophecy that Aaron was supposed to represent. Aerie had also become his responsibility.

The dog grumbled, not completely satisfied with the compromise, but knowing he had little choice. Aaron knew that feeling well enough. He could complain all he wanted, but it wouldn't change the fact that he had a destiny to fulfill. He tried not to allow his new duties to overwhelm him, but it was a challenge. Not only did he have to protect the citizens of Aerie, knowing that Verchiel was still out there looking for revenge, he also had to look after Vilma and deal with the most recent revelation that Lucifer was the angel who fathered him. *Who ever said that being a savior was all fun and games?*

Aaron turned away from the restaurant and looked toward the phone booth where Vilma appeared to be wrapping up her call.

*"I'm worried about her,"* Gabriel said, putting words to Aaron's sentiments as they both watched her hang up the phone and emerge from the glass-and-metal cubicle.

Vilma had been part of Aaron's old life, before the power

of the angels asserted itself and turned the world as he had known it on its ear. Although he had kept in contact through e-mail, he hadn't really thought he would ever see her again, yet another piece of his life that he was forced to abandon. But here she was, inexplicably made part of his new existence—a Nephilim too. He always felt he was in love with her, always knew there was some powerful connection, but that just made her involvement in the whirlwind that his life had become all the more scary.

"Is everything okay at home?" he asked as she approached them.

The girl shrugged, combing a nervous hand through her shiny, black shoulder-length hair. "As good as can be expected, I guess," she said, not looking at him.

She was sweating, even though the temperature wasn't above sixty degrees, and he also noticed the dark circles under her normally beautiful brown eyes.

Aaron reached out gingerly to touch Vilma's shoulder. "Are you all right?" he asked softly.

Vilma raised her face to look at him, eyes filled with emotion. "No," she answered, shaking her head as the tears began to tumble down the dark skin of her cheeks. "I've been taken away from my home and my school, been tortured by . . . monsters, I'm having dreams that make me afraid to go to sleep, and . . . and there's something coming alive inside me that I can't even begin to understand. No, Aaron, I am so *not* all right."

She was angry and scared, and he knew exactly how she felt, for it wasn't that long ago that he first experienced the awakening of the angelic essence within himself. He tried to think of the right things to say to reassure her, but he couldn't; he didn't want to lie. Aaron had no idea how things were going to be in the future—for her, for himself, for the fallen angels. Life was uncertain right now, and that was something that he was learning to live with. It was something Vilma was going to have to learn as well.

As if on cue, Gabriel leaned his large, yellow body against the girl, nudging her hand with his cold, damp nose. *"Don't cry, Vilma,"* he said consolingly, his dark eyes looking up into hers. *"Everything is going to be fine. Just you wait and see."*

She began to pat his blocky head, and Aaron could see the immediate calming effect that the dog's presence had upon her. In the week since they had saved her from Verchiel's grasp, Gabriel had become Vilma's anchor to sanity.

"I'm very tired," she said, her voice no louder than a whisper. "I think I'd like to go ho—" Vilma halted, the word catching in her throat before it could leave her mouth. She was going to say "home." But it wasn't home for her, although it would have to do until the threat of Verchiel and his Powers was ended once and for all.

"I'll take you back to Aerie," Aaron said quietly, putting his arm around her and gently pulling her close.

She nodded and said nothing more as Gabriel, too, stepped closer.

Using another of the gifts from his angelic nature, Aaron willed them all invisible, then allowed the massive, shiny black wings to unfurl from his back. He thought of Aerie, picturing in his mind the abandoned neighborhood built atop a burial ground for toxic waste, enfolded Vilma and Gabriel within his feathered embrace, and took them there.

Deep within the hold of oblivion, Lucifer had sought the escape of torment, and instead found memories of times preferred forgotten.

He saw it all as he always did when he closed his eyes: the crimes he committed against God, the war he waged in Heaven in the name of petty jealousy. But when those recollections were spent, the wounds of his past discretion reopened, the first of the fallen saw that the painful conjurings of his mind were not yet finished with him.

It had been years since he last dreamed of her—thought of her—and he moaned in protest as remembrances long suppressed played out upon his dreamscape. Her name was Taylor, and the memory of her was as painful as anything he'd been forced to endure since his capture by Verchiel and his followers.

He saw her as he had that very first time: a beautiful, human woman who emanated life and vitality, with rich, dark eyes the color of polished mahogany, and jet-black hair that curled seductively around her shoulders. She was wearing a flowing yellow sundress, leather sandals upon her delicate feet, and she was playing with a dog—a golden retriever named Brandy. There was something about her that drew him in, something that made him believe he might not be the monster his own kind had branded him to be.

In the brief time that he had been with her, Lucifer had almost been able to convince himself that he was just a man, not the leader of a rebellion against God. How beautifully mundane his life had become, the urge to wander the planet, as he had done for thousands of years, suddenly stifled by the love of an earthly woman. It was as if she had been touched by the Archons themselves; there was an inherent magick in her that seemed to calm his restless spirit and numb the pain of the curse he would forever carry as the inciter of Heaven's war.

Lucifer fought toward consciousness, but the current of the past was too strong, and he was drowned in further memories, pulled deeper. It was in fact the dreams that had been harbingers to the end of his happiness with the woman. He had begun to experience dreams of the turmoil for which he was responsible, of the blood and death—the faces of those who had died for his cause haunting his attempts at peace. The dreams were relentless. They reawakened in him the enormity of his sins, and he knew that he must move on. He had not yet earned the right to peace and happiness. How stupid he had been to think that his penance might be at an end. Though it pained him, he left her—the beautiful, magickal Taylor—and began his wanderings anew.

And in his fevered mind he saw her as he had that very last time, asleep in the bed they'd shared as man and woman. How beautiful she was. He had left her during the night, sneaking silently out into the darkness and out of her life. It was for the best, he had told himself, for he could bring her nothing but misery.

But this time the memory was different and he did not leave. Instead Taylor stirred upon the bed, as if feeling his gaze upon her, and she rolled over to look at him, a seductive smile spreading across her features, clad in the shadows of the early hour.

"Hello, Lucifer," she said in a voice filled with the huskiness of interrupted sleep, and he felt his love for the woman swell within him.

It was as if he had never left her.

# CHAPTER TWO

L orelei sighed as the commotion continued to escalate. She placed her hands flat atop the table, took a deep breath, and forced herself not to utter an incantation that would have called down lightning from the sky and permanently silenced the agitated citizens gathered in the meeting room of Aerie's community center.

"People, please," she said, raising her voice to be heard above their frenetic din. "We'll get absolutely nothing accomplished here if we're all talking at once."

The citizens ignored her and continued their excited chatter, the volume within the low-ceilinged room intensifying. She remembered how easy it had seemed for Belphegor to preside over these meetings. All the ancient fallen angel had to do was stand up from his chair and clear his throat, and immediately they would all fall silent, awaiting his words with rapt attention. And that was just one of the things she missed about their leader.

Belphegor had been mortally injured during the Powers' attack upon Aerie, in a violent duel with their commander, Verchiel. They had found him close to death, but Aaron Corbet had set him free from his shell of flesh and blood, forgiving him and all the others that had fallen in the devastating battle, allowing them to return to Heaven. Lorelei had been happy for them; it was what every one of the fallen inhabiting this place dreamed of, but Belphegor's absence was felt each and every day.

"There's been enough talk," said a fallen angel named Atliel. He was standing up beside his metal folding chair, his single eye and badly burned face commanding the attention of those around him. The angel had been scarred in the battle with the Powers, but at least he had survived when so many others of the citizenry had not.

Lorelei looked about the room and was reminded of how many had been lost trying to defend Aerie from Verchiel's soldiers. Not all of them died; Aaron had freed many fallen angels who had managed to hang on to a thread of life. Even still, their numbers had been cut easily by half, and that didn't count those Nephilim who had been seriously injured. They were still trying to heal, the question of their survival nowhere near certain.

"We must act at once or suffer the fate of our brothers,"

Atliel proclaimed, looking about the room, his scarred visage quieting the congregation far more effectively than had Lorelei's raised voice.

"And what do you propose?" the Nephilim asked, rising from her chair as she'd seen Belphegor do in the past, hoping she could regain some control of the meeting. She knew many of the citizens were not happy that she, a Nephilim, a half-breed, had assumed control of the angelic settlement with their founder's passing, but it had been Belphegor's wish. His confidence in her ability to lead had always surpassed her own. Even though the fallen angels and the Nephilim lived together in relative harmony, there was still a certain amount of prejudice—especially when it came to the decisions that would govern the future of Aerie.

Atliel turned to fix her in the gaze of his good eye. It was obvious that he didn't appreciate her interruption. "We must do what we have in the past when we've been threatened," he answered, a hint of petulance in his voice. "Aerie must be relocated. We cannot chance another Powers attack."

Lorelei watched the reactions of those before her. They were a mixture of shock, quiet acceptance, and complete despair. Aerie had been in many places throughout the millennia it had existed, moving from one secret location to the next as the Powers grew closer to finding them. To many of the sanctuary's newer residents, the abandoned neighborhood of the Ravenschild Estates was the only true home they had ever known, and that she knew from personal experience.

"Don't you think we've come too far for that?" she asked, stoking the fires of Atliel's ire. "Do you think that Belphegor and all the other citizens who fell during the battle did so only that we could run and hide again? I seriously doubt it."

Atliel gripped the edge of the chair in front of him, knuckles white with the force of his frustration. "Verchiel and his followers know where we are. They can return at any moment to finish what they started. Aerie must survive if we are ever to find forgiveness from our Father in Heaven. Nothing else matters."

Lorelei moved out from behind the table. She knew they were afraid, but she couldn't believe that they were so blinded by their fear that they didn't see the signs of change that were upon them, changes that had begun soon after Aaron Corbet had arrived in Aerie.

"I believe the time you've been waiting for, the forgiveness you've been seeking, is upon us, Atliel," she said, leaning back against the table edge and crossing her booted feet at the ankles.

"You're referring to that Nephilim, Aaron Corbet," the fallen angel responded, a sneer upon his damaged features.

"Yes," she replied emphatically, "I am."

Atliel slowly shook his head. "The savior of prophecy," he grumbled, looking at those gathered around him. "I'm having great difficulty believing that—"

"You saw what he can do," Lorelei cried, pushing away from the table to stress her point. "You saw what he did for Camael—what he did for Belphegor and all the others who fell in battle."

"Yes, but—"

"He *forgave* them," Lorelei continued over Atliel's protest. She didn't have the patience for his or any of the others' doubts. Aaron Corbet was the *One*, and she wasn't about to let a discordant voice among them detract from what was finally, after thousands and thousands of years, about to happen to them. "Aaron allowed them to return to Heaven, and I believe he'll do the same for you."

The room was suddenly quiet and Lorelei saw that all eyes were finally upon her. She was proud of herself for speaking out. The citizens of Aerie could no longer allow themselves to be governed by fear. These were new times ahead of them, and they needed a fresh perspective.

"And where is our savior?" Atliel posed his question to the room at large. "Was he not made aware of this gathering?"

"Yes, he was, but—"

It was Atliel's turn to interrupt as a low buzz moved through the crowd. "He was aware, but he chose not to attend. Is that what you're telling us, Lorelei? That the fate of our hopes and dreams is teetering on the edge of a precipice, and Aaron Corbet could not be bothered?"

"Look," she began, exasperated—by Aaron's unexplained

absence, by Atliel's persistent questioning, by her own lack of control. "All I'm saying is that we need to consider all our options before we turn tail and run. At least talk to Aaron, he might be able to give us—"

"And all *I'm* asking, Lorelei," Atliel said, cutting her off again, "is for our *savior* to start acting like one and offer us some guidance."

She didn't know how to respond, choosing instead to say nothing, and in a matter of moments the commotion was on the rise again, voices of fallen angels and Nephilim alike, all speaking at once, clamoring to be heard.

*Shit,* Aaron thought, suddenly remembering the meeting at Aerie's community center that he had promised Lorelei he would attend.

He was in the process of transporting Vilma, Gabriel, and himself back to their house in Aerie, traversing the void between *here* and *there*. It was one of the few angelic skills that he genuinely appreciated. All he had to do was picture in his mind the place he wished to be, wrap himself within his wings, and in a matter of seconds he was there. In this particular instant, though, he was forced to change his mind midtrip, and he opened his wings to emerge on the street in front of the community center.

"I'm really sorry about this," he apologized to his traveling companions as his wings receded beneath the flesh of his back.

"I just remembered that I promised Lorelei I'd go to the community meeting today and . . ."

Vilma smiled weakly, and he couldn't get over how tired she looked. "That's okay," she said. "I think I need to lie down anyway. I'm still feeling pretty exhausted."

Aaron glanced over at the entrance to the community center and caught Lehash sitting out front, watching them. The fallen angel in charge of Aerie's security tipped his cowboy hat in greeting, looking every inch as though he'd just walked out of an old spaghetti Western. Aaron smiled and waved briefly before turning his attention back to Vilma.

"Gabriel will go with you," he told the girl.

She reached down and scratched the top of the Lab's bony head. "Is that what you want to do, Gabe?" she asked him in the language of dogs.

*"Will you give me breakfast?"*

"Of course I will," she assured him.

*"Then let's go,"* Gabriel said, already beginning to walk in the direction of the house where they were staying. *"I'm starving."*

Vilma laughed, then paused to look back at Aaron.

"I'll see you later?" she asked, and he could hear the sadness permeating her voice.

It just about broke his heart. *But it won't last forever,* he tried to reassure himself. He stepped toward her and put his arms tentatively around her. "It's going to be all right," he whispered in her ear, squeezing her tightly.

Vilma hugged him back, but said nothing to prove that she believed in what he had told her.

*"C'mon, Vilma. Let's go,"* Gabriel called, his tail wagging eagerly as he urged her to follow.

She was the first to break the embrace, looking deeply into Aaron's eyes and forcing a smile before turning to join the dog.

*It's an enormous adjustment,* he told himself, watching as she walked away from him. *She just needs time.* He could sense the angelic essence inside her becoming stronger, and prayed for an easy merger. Hopefully it wouldn't take much longer for the process to complete itself.

Aaron turned and jogged toward the community center. "Lorelei is going to kill me," he said to the fallen angel that just happened to be her father.

Lehash had tipped his chair back on two legs and was leaning against the building's wall. "Not sure you want to be going in there right now," he said in the drawl of the Old West. "Folks are a mite riled up at the moment. Lorelei's attempting to calm 'em down."

"What are they upset about?"

"You," Lehash answered, lowering his chair legs to the ground.

"Me?" Aaron asked incredulously.

The fallen angel nodded. "Yep. They're worried that yer not taking the job of savior seriously enough." The angel gunslinger tilted back the brim of his hat and looked into Aaron's eyes. "They want to know why you haven't got around to savin' them yet."

"Son of a bitch," Aaron hissed as he grabbed hold of the handle and flung the door wide.

"What're you gonna do?" he heard Lehash call after him as he stormed inside.

"I'm going to have a little talk with the citizens of Aerie."

Lehash guffawed, his chair sliding across the ground as he abruptly stood, following the Nephilim into the building.

"This I gotta see," Aaron heard the angel say.

Aaron entered the meeting room through a door at the back and immediately felt as though he was in the midst of one of those bizarre go-to-school-naked dreams. He had heard them carrying on as he approached, each trying to be heard above the other and Lorelei shouting for order.

And they did quiet down, but only because they saw that he had arrived.

Every head swiveled in his direction, and every eye watched as he strode down the aisle to join Lorelei at the front. He didn't make eye contact with any of them, but could sense their hostility and their frustration. The feelings were mutual.

"Sorry I'm late," he said quietly to Lorelei as she stepped aside to allow him her space.

He faced the crowded room. Lehash was standing at the back, arms folded, leaning against the wall, a sly smile on his haggard features. They were all there—Nephilim and fallen angels both. And why shouldn't they be? The citizens of Aerie were concerned about their future, a future in which Aaron played a large part. It was a heavy responsibility, and he felt as though he was beginning to buckle beneath its tremendous weight. He was doing the best he could, but sometimes it just didn't seem to be enough.

"Sorry I'm late," he said again to the room at large.

But before he could continue, Atliel interrupted. "Aerie must be relocated," he declared, his single eye staring intensely. "We cannot risk any more lives. The dream of Aerie must survive, and it cannot if we stay here."

"I don't think we need to worry about Verchiel right now," Aaron tried to reassure the citizens. "He suffered casualties even greater than ours, thanks to Lorelei here. I believe we're safe for now." He looked to Lorelei for support, and saw that she was nodding in agreement.

"*You* believe we're safe?" Atliel said, pointing a long finger at him.

Aaron cringed. He didn't want this to turn into an argument. He had wanted to come in, tell them what he had planned for their future, and then spend the remainder of the day with Vilma. "Yes, *I* do."

The angel's expression turned to one of complete revulsion. "What right have you to tell us we'll be safe, when you know very well what Verchiel is capable of?"

He felt his heart rate quicken, his blood beginning to rush through his veins. He forced himself to stay calm. It was a democracy here in Aerie, and the citizens had every right to speak their minds.

"He killed your parents," Atliel snarled. "Turned your little brother into a monster. Killed your mentor and used your woman as bait to lure you to your death."

Aaron knew all this. It was with him every day, a constant reminder of how much his life had changed—of what his destiny as a savior had taken from him.

"Verchiel is an unpredictable force," Atliel continued. "All of us have feared his wrath since our fall from Heaven. Do not tell me that we're safe. It couldn't be further from the truth."

Aaron's anger was growing and he felt the power of his angelic heritage course through his blood and muscle, enflaming the very essence of his being. "I'm doing my best," he said through gritted teeth. He saw that Lehash had moved away from the wall and was approaching the front. The warrior angel obviously suspected that something was about to happen, and he couldn't have been more right.

"We of Aerie expect more from our savior than his *best*." And with those words, Atliel spread his wings, as did some others in the community center, and they began to flap gently in unison, the close confines of the meeting space filled with the sound of feathered wings striking the air. They did it to show their displeasure, to show their doubt that Aaron was capable of fulfilling the prophecy.

The sigils rose to the surface of his skin and Aaron knew that he could hold back his anger no longer. He let out a cry of rage as his ebony wings exploded from his back, and he too began to beat the air, harder, singularly drowning out the sounds of the others. He watched the expressions of shock and surprise spread across the faces of the citizens as he revealed to them the shape of their redeemer. His mighty wings continued to flap, forcing them back, tipping over their chairs and creating a mini-maelstrom of dust and dirt.

And as abruptly as he had started, he stopped, furling his appendages at his back and glaring at them all.

"Why don't you people just cut me some slack?" His voice rumbled like the growl of a dangerous, jungle beast, filled with the potential for violence. "Do you seriously believe that I understand what it means to be a savior? Well, in case you haven't figured it out yet, I don't have a clue."

Fallen angels and Nephilim alike were silent. Even Atliel had decided that it might be best to hold his tongue. Lehash stood nearby and Aaron could see sparks of golden fire dancing around his hands, the gunslinger ready to call forth his pistols of heavenly flame if necessary.

"All I'm asking is for you to give me a break. I know that you're scared—I'm scared too—but it isn't going to do anybody any good to come after me for not living up to your expectations."

Aaron made eye contact with them and they each looked away, accepting his position as top dog.

"I have no idea what tomorrow holds for me or for you. But I do know that to guarantee any future at all, we have to work together. We can't *run* from Verchiel; we have to *deal* with him." He let his wings recede beneath his flesh as the sigils began to fade.

"And that's exactly what I intend to do," he declared with finality as he strode from the room.

"Meeting adjourned."

# CHAPTER THREE

The tiny rodent cowered in a pocket of shadow, watching with wide, fear-filled eyes, as its friend was tortured.

It wanted to run, to flee the ugly scene, but for a reason its tiny brain could not begin to fathom, the mouse would not leave the man who had befriended it. *Man?* it questioned. Its primitive thought process grappled with the concept, for this being was far more than just a man.

It remembered the first time that it had seen him. It was living in a monastery in mountains far, far away, and Lucifer arrived in the midst of a terrific snowstorm. The brothers who dwelt in the monastery had no idea how he had made it to their door, but they welcomed him inside, inviting him to share their evening meal. He had claimed to be a traveler, grown weary from his wanderings, looking for a place to rest and reflect upon a life filled with regrets. The brothers offered their monastery as a refuge and Lucifer accepted their offer to stay.

The mouse watched as the five beings that abused its friend hoisted him up, naked, into the air, hanging him from thick black chains secured upon his wrists and ankles, his face pointed at the floor. They crouched beneath him, carefully examining his exposed underbelly.

When first they met, the stranger had asked of the mouse a favor. Lucifer spoke to it in the language of its species and gave it a delicious piece of bread as payment. He had simply asked it to keep its eyes open when wandering about the monastery, and to let him know if it saw any strangers like himself. A relationship was born that benefited them both greatly, and soon blossomed into something larger, a mutual admiration— a genuine friendship.

The tiny observer watched an Archon stand beneath its hanging friend, and in his hand, there formed a knife of flame. With one sudden, savage movement, the Archon cut open its friend, his blood raining down to puddle upon the floor.

It wanted to help its friend, but instead retreated farther into the darkness of the corner. For what could it possibly do?

It was only a mouse.

The rite was forbidden. Archon Oraios was sure of that. But here they were, making preparations to reverse the Word of God.

"Quickly!" Archon Jao screeched, crouching beneath the body of the first of the fallen as the prisoner's blood poured from the gash cut into his belly. "Bring me the bowl. We cannot waste a drop!"

Archon Domiel retrieved a golden ceremonial bowl from their belongings and carefully slid it beneath the dripping wound of the hanging Lucifer.

"Excellent," Jao said rubbing his long, spidery hands together as he watched the spattering of warm crimson begin to fill the bowl. "There is much to be done with this blood. Every drop must serve our master's cause."

Archon Oraios turned his gaze from the unconscious Lucifer to Jao beside him. "Is that what he is to us now, brother?" the angel asked. "When first we joined Verchiel's quest to rid the world of God's offenders, we did so as equals, sharing the Powers' abhorrence for those who had sinned against Heaven. But now it appears we are nothing more than servants to his rage."

"Careful, Oraios," Archon Jaldabaoth warned, on hands and knees, dipping his fingers into the bowl of gore upon the floor. "Remember the fate of our brothers, Sabaoth and Erathaol. Their actions did not please Verch . . . our master, and for that they paid a price most dear." Jaldabaoth began to paint a large circle of blood on the hardwood floor beneath the first of the fallen angels.

"Why can't you say it, brother?" Oraios asked. "Paid a

price most dear, indeed," he snarled. "Verchiel killed them in a fit of anger. It seems that our *master* has become quite enamored with the act of murder."

Archon Domiel turned away with a hiss. "I do not want to hear this," he said, shaking his head. "Sacrifices must be made to achieve one's ultimate goals. Verchiel's cause is a just one, a final attempt to right a grievous wrong."

The air was thick with the smell of blood as Jao joined Jaldabaoth on the floor. "This discussion is finished," he said, dipping his fingers in the collected blood of their enemy and completing the circle. "There is far too much to be done to debate this now."

"The killing of our Malakim pedagogue—with more to follow if we are to have what we need to complete the rite to unravel the words of the Most Holy and unleash Hell upon the world. Is that how a grievous wrong is righted, my Archon brothers?" Oraios asked, ignoring Jao.

"It is too late to be thinking of such things," Katspiel said quietly from the far corner. Slowly he lifted his head, the shadows of the room flowing to fill the empty sockets of his eyes like oil. In an earlier ritual he had attempted to look upon the Hell within Lucifer, and had paid the price with his sight. "Events have transpired beyond our abilities to control," he wheezed. "We are just cogs in the great mechanism that has been set in motion."

"So you say we are to continue as we are," Oraios asked his

eyeless brother, "carrying out the wants and desires of one who could very well damn us all."

"Yes," Katspiel said, his head slipping forward as he began to drift off into the meditative slumber that would allow him to locate the next of the Malakim. "But I would not concern yourself with potential damnation, Brother Oraios.

"For what we have done, and are about to do, we are already damned."

Verchiel stood naked before the healer, allowing the blind human to administer to his injuries, both old and new.

The rich smell of ancient oils wafted up as Kraus dipped cloths into his restorative medicament and gently applied them to the Powers leader's various lesions.

"I apologize for the pain I must be causing, my lord," the human said. "But I must try a stronger remedy if I am ever to mend your wounds completely."

Verchiel's injuries were extensive and were healing far more slowly than normal for an angel of such power. Some were not healing at all. *Another piece of evidence that the Holy Creator has indeed abandoned His most faithful soldier,* he thought bitterly, the agony of the healing oils nothing in comparison to being forsaken.

The leader of the Powers host shuddered as his servant applied more of the medicinal balm.

"If only I could share your pain, my master," Kraus said as

he bowed his head in sadness. "I would gladly bear the burden to lessen your suffering."

Verchiel gazed down upon the lesser being kneeling at his feet. "The path before us is fraught with danger," the angel said, laying his hand upon the human's head. "The potential for injuries most excruciating is great. Do you still wish to partake of my pain, little monkey?"

Kraus lifted his head to gaze upon Verchiel with sightless eyes bulging white, his old face twisted in adoration. "It would be the least I could do," Kraus said, his body trembling. "But since I cannot bear your pain, I will soothe your injuries and heal your wounds for as long as the gift of life still fills these bones and I am allowed to serve you."

Verchiel thought of his own master and what Verchiel had lost. How he had loved his Creator, but obviously it wasn't enough to prevent Him from turning away—from bestowing His blessings upon the most wretched of creations, the criminals and the mongrel abominations. The angel seethed with anger. He wanted to lash out—to rend and tear, to burn to ashes anything and everything that reminded him of his loss.

A faint wheeze pulled the leader of the Powers from his distraught reverie, and he saw that he had grabbed the blind human by the throat and was squeezing the life from his body. The monkey thrashed in his grip, but the look of rapture, of pure adoration, was still upon his face.

THOMAS E. SNIEGOSKI

Verchiel let the healer fall from his angry hand, for it was not the fault of this lowly life form that the Creator had chosen to desert him.

The blind healer struggled for breath as he lay upon the floor of the old classroom. "So sorry," he gasped over and over again, certain that he had done something to offend his master.

But the monkey's apologies—his solicitations for forgiveness—would not fall upon deaf ears, as Verchiel's had. He would hear his servant's pleadings, and he would answer.

Verchiel unfurled his wings and knelt beside his quivering supplicant. "I hear your pleas," he said as he took the frightened man into his arms and drew him close. "But you have nothing to be sorry for."

Kraus began to cry, moisture leaking from his sightless orbs.

"It was *my* rage, my own inner turmoil, that almost caused your death," Verchiel said to him. "And for that error *I* am sorry."

The pain of his injuries was suddenly gone and Verchiel was filled with the power of his own divinity. He knew then, truly understood what it was like to be a god—blessed with the power of damnation or absolution.

"I will show you the depth of my regret," the angel said, drawing the still trembling Kraus closer. Verchiel leaned his head forward and placed a gentle kiss upon each milky, cataract-covered orb.

And the healer began to scream.

* * *

The pain was like nothing Kraus had ever experienced.

He fell away from his master's embrace, stumbling about the classroom as the pain in his useless eyes intensified. He had memorized the layout of the room, as well as the entire abandoned Saint Athanasius Church and Orphanage where the Powers were gathered these days, but sheer panic and roiling pain made him careless. He ran headlong into a wall, falling to the floor in a quivering heap.

*Why would he do this to me?* Kraus's thoughts raced. *Have I insulted him?* He wanted to ask his master, but his distress was too great. It felt as though molten metal had been poured into his eye sockets, and instead of cooling with the passage of time, it was growing hotter and hotter still.

He thought he was going to die.

Kraus curled up on the floor and waited for death to take him. The torment was so great that he thought he might actually welcome the end to his pitiful existence. Eyes tightly clenched, a ball of shivering blood, bone, and flesh, he readied himself—and then he heard the voice of his master. It drifted upon the air like the notes of the most beautiful song he had ever heard.

"Open your eyes."

And Kraus did as he was told. The pain was gone, but he barely noticed.

*He could see!*

He was gazing at the floor. It was wood, covered with decades of dirt and dust. And Kraus was seeing it all for the very first time, the intricacies, patterns and colors of the wood, and the accumulated filth. Somehow, even though he had never seen before, having been blind since birth, he knew what he was looking at, the identity of each thing his new eyes fell upon filling his head.

"Lift your head from the ground and gaze upon the world," the angel Verchiel said, his voice booming around the room. "This is my gift to you."

Kraus looked up, his new sight landing on the wall above the floor. It was painted a dingy gray; and above that was a blackboard, the faint trace of the last lesson taught within the schoolroom still evident upon its dark surface. *Thou shalt not kill,* he read, despite never having learned to read.

Everything his new vision saw, all the colors, the shapes, the items left behind when the school was abandoned, he knew their identity, their purpose, and was filled with the wonder of it all.

The air stirred behind him and Kraus turned to *see* for the first time the creature that had given him this most wonderful gift. How blessed he was to serve an emissary of God, so merciful as to heal a lowly beast such as he. His master stood before him, naked, mighty wings spread wide so that he might gaze upon the full glory of the angel, of Heaven embodied.

And Kraus genuinely saw the master that he had served

these many years. The scars of battle, the burns—seeping and red—and the wings, now gone to seed, molted, and the color of grime.

"I am the glory of Heaven," Verchiel proclaimed.

But the healer, once blind, now saw his master for what he truly was.

He saw a monster.

# CHAPTER FOUR

aron stepped out of the community center, the lingering sensation of his transformation still causing his flesh to tingle. He remembered a time not too long ago when a change from his human form to the angelic would have caused him nothing but pain. Now it had become almost second nature, the two halves of his being, opposite sides to the same coin.

He took a few calming, deep breaths. The air was surprisingly cool, despite the fact that April was almost over. Yes, there had been some warm days, but it seemed that winter was having a difficult time abdicating its seasonal seat of power.

Gradually he began to feel the tension leaving his body. Aaron never expected being a savior was going to be easy, but he wished that the citizens of Aerie would give him a chance to

figure things out at his own speed. Decisions as gravely important as what to do about Verchiel just couldn't be rushed. There
was too much at stake.

"Damn," said a familiar voice from behind, and Aaron
turned to see Lehash approaching. "Guess you gave them a
little somethin' to chew on," he said, a big smile spreading
across his usually dour features as he motioned with his thumb
toward the door behind him.

"They made me mad," Aaron said, sounding trite and not
at all proud of his reaction.

"No kiddin'," Lehash said with a rumbling chuckle. "Wish
Belphegor was here to see you put old Atliel and his cronies in
their places. It would've made him happier than a pig in slop."

Aaron chuckled as well. "I guess it's not how you'd expect
a messiah to act."

The angel withdrew a thin cigar from inside his duster
pocket and lit it with the tip of his leather-gloved forefinger.
"Hell, boy, you put Verchiel down for the count and get us
back to Heaven, you can act any way you damn well please."

Sensing that they were no longer alone, both Aaron and
Lehash turned to see the citizens leaving the community center. Atliel and his cronies stood to the side of the building's
entrance glaring at them.

"I think somebody's gettin' the hairy eyeball," Lehash said,
sucking on the end of his cigar and blowing a cloud of smoke
up into the air. "And I don't think it's me."

"What do you think I should do?" Aaron asked the gunslinger, his voice at a whisper. "Should I apologize or just let it go?"

The fallen angel rolled the cigar around in his mouth. "Personally, I'd let 'em stew, but then again, I ain't no messiah. You're gonna haf'ta do what you think is right."

Aaron's foster dad had taught him that nine out of ten times it was easier to apologize and move past the problem. Tom Stanley had been a good man and a wonderful father, and Aaron missed him very much. He decided he would honor the memory of the only father he had ever known by doing what *he* would have thought was right.

Aaron moved around Lehash and walked toward the gaggle of fallen angels. "Look, I'm sorry for my behavior in there," he said with genuine sincerity. If he was going to be their leader, he guessed that it probably wouldn't hurt for them to see that he knew he wasn't infallible and could admit when he was wrong. "Things have been kind of crazy for me and I just wanted to—"

"Is it true what they're saying?" Atliel suddenly interrupted. "I thought it was only a wild rumor, but seeing you in there, the anger you wield, I can almost believe it to be true."

His three companions nodded their agreement.

"I don't understand," Aaron said. "What rumors are you talking about?"

Atliel looked to his brethren for support and then back to

Aaron, bolstered by their admiration. "That you are the son of the Morningstar—the spawn of Lucifer," he spat.

Aaron didn't know how to respond. He knew what he had been told, but he couldn't yet bring himself to believe it. "I . . . I'm not sure that . . . ," he stuttered.

"See how he responds," Atliel said to his comrades. "It *is* true that we are to be delivered to salvation by the progeny of the monster who led us to our fall."

Lehash moved forward, a pistol of heavenly fire glistening gold in his gloved hand. "That'll be enough of that, brother," the law of Aerie said, stepping between the Nephilim and the group of angels.

"It's okay, Lehash," Aaron said quickly. "They're right in their concern. How *are* they supposed to trust the son of the Devil to lead them to salvation?" he asked quietly as he turned away. Though he had no desire to, and had been avoiding it for days, Aaron Corbet knew that he had to confront the mystery of his heritage before he could finally assume his role as Aerie's savior.

Vilma mistook the sudden wave of panic as another example of the angelic essence awakening, but as she and Gabriel entered the ranch-style house she shared with Lorelei and Lehash, she remembered that this was senior finals week at school. The feeling was sudden, like an electrical jolt, and her entire body broke out in a tingling sweat. It didn't take her long to realize that this had nothing to do with the power residing inside her, and everything to do with her academic career crumbling to ruin.

She slammed the door behind her, and Gabriel started from the noise.

*"Are you okay?"* the Labrador asked, his head tilted to the right with concern.

"I'm fine," she answered with a sigh. "Sorry I slammed the door."

*"That's okay,"* he said, walking past her, toward the kitchen. He turned and looked at her. *"How about breakfast now?"*

Grateful for the distraction, Vilma filled the dog's bowl with food and got him some fresh water. "Here you go," she said, stepping back and watching him devour his meal in record time. He licked his chops, took a long, slurping drink, and then cleaned his bowl with his tongue.

"Happy?" she asked as she followed him into the living room.

*"Yes, thank you."* Gabriel hopped up onto the couch and turned once in a circle before settling down to rest. *"I need a nap, though."* He exhaled noisily and closed his eyes.

Vilma shook her head, watching him for a moment. She had never owned a dog and was amazed by how much Gabriel slept. This was but one of many naps he'd take during the day before going to bed and sleeping through the night. Aaron always joked that it was Gabriel's job to sleep, and if the animal could collect a check for snoozing, they'd both be millionaires.

She sat down in a large, overstuffed chair and pulled her knees up to her chin. She felt cold inside, but it had nothing to do with the actual temperature. She was afraid again. Until a month ago, she knew exactly what she was going to do with her life: finish high school, go on to college for a degree in education, and then teach, preferably first or second grade.

She smiled sadly, remembering how she would talk with her friends about the future, and how excited it made her. They thought she was a freak, never really understanding that this was the stuff that made her truly happy, that this was as exciting for her as they found dancing at the all-ages club or conning someone into buying them liquor. Her plans for the future were her hopes and dreams, and everything was going fabulously until she met Aaron Corbet.

Vilma's anger flared. She didn't want to blame him for her troubles, but it was so easy. What would have happened if she hadn't spoken to him that day at the library? She sat with her chin atop her knees, rocking from side to side, thinking about what her life would be like without him. She tried desperately to believe that it would have been better, but deep down she knew that wasn't true. She had felt a strange attraction to him the first time she noticed him at his locker across from hers, as if their being together was part of some bigger plan. And when Aaron had gone away after the deaths of his foster family, Vilma had never felt so lonely—so incomplete.

And now they were together again, but still she felt lonely

and frightened, although she knew Aaron was doing the best he could to help her adjust to the changes in her life.

Something stirred inside her, but this time the sensation had nothing to do with anxiety. The angelic power, stirred too quickly to maturity by the tortures of Verchiel, was awake again, and she felt it testing the confines of the flesh and blood that was its cage.

Aaron had tried to explain that the essence had been a part of her since her conception, that the power had simply lain dormant within her, waiting for her to come of age and embrace it. For most Nephilim the unification of the human and heavenly sides was a naturally occurring process, but for others . . .

Vilma didn't want to think about it anymore. The idea of the thing inside her was driving her insane. She dropped her feet to the floor and quickly stood, looking about the room for something, anything, that could distract her.

Gabriel came awake, lifting his head slowly to stare at her.

"I'm sorry, Gabriel," Vilma said, nervously biting at the cuticles of one of her fingers. "I'm feeling a bit antsy. I need to do something—to get my mind off things for a while." She remembered she'd only had a piece of toast earlier that morning, and thought that food would be as good a distraction as anything. "I'm going to get something to eat, want to come?" She knew it was a stupid question, for the Lab was *always* hungry.

*"Don't mind if I do,"* he said, quickly getting down from the sofa and following her to the small kitchen where he had eaten a full meal only minutes before.

Vilma went to the fridge and opened the door, peering inside at some vegetables and milk of questionable age. Gabriel squeezed his head past her leg to take a look for himself.

*"Hmmm,"* he grumbled. *"Nothing good in here."*

The power inside her had calmed, but it was still awake. She could feel it experiencing the world through her actions. She closed the refrigerator and looked around the kitchen. In a wicker basket by the sink she spotted some red delicious apples.

"How about an apple?" she asked the dog as she plucked the largest one from the basket.

*"I love apples."* Gabriel had already begun to drool.

Vilma grabbed a knife from a drawer and cut the apple in half. "Do you eat the skin or do you want me to peel it for you?"

*"The skin is fine,"* he said, wagging his tail, a puddle forming on the floor beneath his leaking mouth. *"Just take the core out, please. The seeds make me choke."*

Vilma held half of the apple in one hand and sank the tip of the knife into the fruit to cut away the core as she had done for her nieces and nephews countless times before. It was then that the angelic essence chose to exert itself, surging forward to throw itself against the prison of her body. She gasped aloud as the knife blade sank through the flesh of the apple and into the palm of her hand. Bleeding, she dropped both to the kitchen floor. But all she could do was tremble, watching as the scarlet fluid oozed from the wound in her palm, running down her arm.

The power was shrieking inside her, aroused by the spilling of her own blood, and no matter how many calming thoughts she tried to put into her head, the angelic force continued to build. She couldn't hold it back; it was exactly what she feared.

*"Vilma!"* Gabriel cried, moving toward her, trying to calm her as he'd done in the past. But he was too late, and the power was too strong.

God help her, it was free.

Aaron approached the rundown house with trepidation.

Scholar had been asking to see him for days, but Aaron always found some reason to avoid meeting with Aerie's keeper of information and the chronicler of its history. Aaron knew the angel was right. He had come a long way in the past few weeks, but he still had much to learn—about the prophecy that he embodied and the fallen angel that had sired him.

Lucifer.

He climbed the porch steps and knocked on the door. While he had come to accept his destiny, Aaron still didn't want to believe that his father was the Devil. But he owed it to the citizens of Aerie at least to hear the proof of his heritage. If he was going to lead and expect them to follow, he had to have all of his facts straight.

Aaron knocked a second time, but there was still no answer. He briefly entertained the idea of coming back later, but knew that if he left, the chances he'd be back any time soon were slim. *No*, he thought, grabbing the doorknob and turning it. *I have to do this now.*

The door opened and a cool gust of heavily scented air reached out to greet him. The air smelled of paper, of old books. It reminded him of the basement stacks at the Lynn Public Library. There was something strangely comforting about the aroma, bringing back memories of the days when finishing a term paper and getting a good grade were the most stressful things in his life.

Aaron stepped inside and stopped in disbelief. The single room in which he stood was huge. For as far as his eyes could see, there were bookcases and piles of books of every conceivable size and shape. He thought his eyes might be playing tricks on him, for it seemed as though the inside of this house was all one room and at least five times larger than it appeared to be on the outside. He considered going out the door and coming back in.

Scholar came out from behind one of the shelves, dressed in his customary crisp white shirt—buttoned to the collar—and black pants, his face buried in an ancient tome. "I thought I heard someone knocking," he said without looking up. He continued to walk through the room, somehow managing to avoid the precariously stacked books all around him. "Come in, come in," he urged, sounding impatient. "I should have known you'd come just when I'd gotten busy with something else."

Aaron moved farther into the enormous storeroom of knowledge. "Sorry," he apologized. "If you want, I'll come back another time, when you're not so busy."

Scholar finally tore his gaze from his book, a petulant smile on his pale, gaunt face. "Tell me, when will I ever *not* be busy?"

Aaron threw up his hands. "I don't know. I was just being polite."

"Savior to us all and manners to boot," Scholar said sharply as he closed his book and placed it atop a pile already nearly five feet tall. The pile teetered but did not fall. Strangely enough, it seemed that the laws of physics didn't apply here.

Aaron again looked about the enormous room, at the domed ceiling at least twenty feet high. "Is it me or is this place bigger than it looks outside?"

A teakettle's shrill whistle punctuated his question as Scholar motioned for him to follow. "Can't pull the wool over your eyes, can we, Aaron?" he chided. "Ancient angel magick," he explained as he walked to a small table in a far corner of the room. "Would you care for a cup?" he asked, unplugging the electric kettle and pouring the boiling water into a mug containing a tea bag. "I think there's enough water for another."

Aaron shook his head. "No, that's all right. Thanks, anyway." The last time he accepted a cup of tea from an angel it had been poisoned.

He couldn't get over the size of the room and the enormous number of books. "It's amazing how much you have here," he commented, looking back to Scholar. "I never would have guessed."

The angel turned toward Aaron, blowing on the steaming liquid in his mug. "We could have filled every house in Aerie and still not had a place for it all," he said between sips. "That's when angel magick can be put to good use."

Aaron didn't remember moving, but suddenly a stack of books tumbled over with a crash, sending three other stacks nearby to the floor as well. Scholar gasped.

"I didn't touch a thing," Aaron yelled. "Really, they just fell on their own." He made a move to start picking up the books and heard Scholar gasp all the louder.

"Please, just step away from the stacks," the fallen angel instructed, gesturing for the boy to move toward him. "That's it," he urged softly. "No sudden movements."

Aaron maneuvered himself carefully between the stacks, and noticed the angel breathe a sigh of relief as he reached him without further incident. "I'm really sorry about that," he said as Scholar helped himself to more tea.

"It's quite all right," he said with a strained smile on his pinched features. "Why don't we simply deal with the reason you have come, and then you can be on your way, hmm?"

If Aaron didn't hear it in his words, he could see in the angel's eyes that he regretted ever having invited him into his work place. But he pushed forward with his questions. "How do you know?" he asked. "How do you know for sure that . . . *he's* my father?" He didn't feel comfortable saying the name. It made him nervous, the evil connotations and all.

"Lucifer?" Scholar asked, seeming to take some kind of perverse pleasure in seeing Aaron's reaction to the name of the first of the fallen. "You showed us as much that first day we met," he explained, "when you manifested your angelic abilities, even through the manacles. Belphegor and I knew then that only an angel of enormous power could have sired one such as you."

"But aren't there other powerful angels out there that could have been with my mother? Why does it have to be—"

"The sigils," the angel interrupted, making reference to the markings that appeared on Aaron's flesh whenever he manifested the full power of his angelic heritage. "We believed that the sigils were significant to the angelic entity that sired you, but little did we imagine how much."

Aaron held out his arm and thought hard about the markings. The bare flesh began to smolder ever so slightly as the archaic shapes rose to the surface. He remembered Scholar making sketches of them at Belphegor's urgings on that first day in Aerie. Now he examined them in the flesh. "Okay, so what do they mean?" he asked.

"They are special symbols representing the names of the elite soldiers that swore their allegiance to your father and his cause," Scholar explained as he traced the shapes on Aaron's arm with the tip of his index finger. "Soldiers that died during the battle in Heaven."

Suddenly it all made sense to Aaron as he recalled the bizarre inner journey he had made with the assistance of Belphegor and a poisoned cup of tea. Within his mind, he had seen the consummation of the power that resided within him, represented by the most magnificent of angels as he bestowed his gift upon his gathered troops.

"I . . . I saw this," he stammered, looking into Scholar's intense eyes. "I saw Lucifer. . . . I saw my father. . . ."

Scholar nodded slowly, encouraging him to accept the truth. "Before the fighting began, the Morningstar gave each of his soldiers a special mark to show how important they were to him. It was with a piece of himself that he adorned them—a piece of his power."

Feeling suddenly weak, Aaron let go of the symbols and allowed them to fade from his flesh. "But why do *I* have them?" he asked, sitting down on the floor as his head swam with dizziness. "Why are they on *my* skin?"

Scholar turned away. "Belphegor and I were trying to figure that out right before Verchiel attacked," the scholarly angel said. "We believe that if Lucifer is indeed seeking absolution for his sins, then you represent his apology to God—and to all those who died for his insane cause."

Overwhelmed, Aaron buried his head in his hands as visions of the most splendorous angelic entity he could ever imagine again filled his mind. "How could anything so beautiful be responsible for so much horror?" he asked.

Scholar stood over him as Aaron sat on the floor, awash in the raw emotion of revelation. "He was afraid that he was no longer loved," he said softly, gazing off into space.

"As were we all."

# CHAPTER FIVE

"Where would we go?" Lorelei asked the angel that she had come to know as her father. The two walked down the center of the street toward the place that they called home. It was a little past noon, and on either side of them the citizens of Aerie were going about their usual business. Some were maintaining small gardens, bringing life up from the toxic soil; others simply sat in old lawn chairs, staring off into space, reflecting on all that had befallen them and what was to come.

Lehash puffed on a cigar, blowing a nasty cloud of smoke from the corner of his mouth. "What, Aerie?" he asked. "Hell if I know. Probably some abandoned wreck of a place like all the others we've picked over the millennia." He took another puff on the cheroot. "I don't know why we can't go someplace nice, like Montana, or maybe even

Texas," the gunslinger said, waxing poetic about places he had lived long ago.

"Hasn't it been a while since you've been to either of those places, Dad?" she asked, the hint of a smile tugging at the corners of her mouth.

"It's only been a couple'a hundred years or so," he commented, his eagle eyes scanning the streets of Aerie for any signs of trouble. "How much could they have changed?"

Lorelei couldn't help herself and laughed out loud. As far as Lehash was concerned, mail was still being delivered by Pony Express, and Butch Cassidy and his Wild Bunch were still robbing banks and escaping on horseback. Lorelei shook her head. She couldn't even begin to imagine the changes beings like her father had seen on Earth since their exile after Heaven's war.

"I don't want to leave here," she proclaimed, any trace of humor now gone from her voice. She motioned toward the others around them. "And I'm sure that they share my feelings as well."

The constable scratched the side of his face with his finger; it sounded as if it were made of sandpaper. "It ain't the side of an active volcano or the hull of a sunken ship, but it's served its purpose." Lehash looked about the desolate and forgotten neighborhood that was his responsibility to protect. "But if the boy manages to pull it all together, we won't be needin' to worry about whether we're gonna be stayin' here or not."

It seemed odd to hear her father talk of such things. For

years Lehash's only concern had been the protection of Aerie and its people, no matter the location. Aerie was his life and his world; there was no other place for him. Heaven was something he'd given up on a long, long time ago, but that was before Aaron Corbet. The Nephilim had made him believe that the prophecy was true, that there was a chance the fallen would be forgiven, that *he* would be forgiven.

"Don't worry about me," she said, bumping her shoulder against his. "You go off to Heaven, and we'll get along just fine without you."

The prophecy was vague about the fate of the Nephilim, only hinting at a special purpose for them upon the world of God's man. Lorelei felt a strange combination of fear and excitement when she thought of her own future, knowing full well that there was much to be dealt with in the present, before that long, unknown road could be traveled.

They had reached their house and were casually walking down the concrete path that led to the front door.

"I'm going to make myself a quick bite and check on Vilma. Do you want a cup of coffee or—"

Lehash had suddenly stopped, and he stood at the beginning of the path, eyes squinted as if sensing something in the air.

"Is everything okay?" she asked cautiously, moving a strand of her snow-white hair away from her face. She was beginning to feel something as well.

The door to the house blew off its hinges in an explosion

of roiling fire, taking the screen door along with it. Lorelei was blown backward by the force of the blast, her ears ringing as she struggled to get to her feet.

Lehash was already moving in slow motion toward her, weapons of golden fire taking shape in his hands. Then she saw Gabriel bound through the gaping hole where the door used to be, his yellow coat black in spots and smoldering, eyes wild in panic.

"Gabriel!" she screamed as the dog ran toward them.

*"Run!"* he barked, falling to the ground and rolling to extinguish his burning fur. *"There was nothing I could do to stop it,"* the Lab cried, panting wildly. *"It's out—it's taken control of her!"*

"Son of a bitch," Lorelei heard her father mutter beneath his breath, and she looked up at the front of the house.

Vilma Santiago stood there stiffly, a corona of unnatural flame radiating from her body. "Help me," she hissed as she slowly raised her hands, watching in the grip of terror as the fires of Heaven danced upon her fingertips. She was trying to hold it back, but it had already tasted freedom and clearly wanted more.

Then Vilma's body went suddenly rigid, her eyes a glistening black, like two shiny marbles floating within a contorted expression of misery. And then that too was gone, and Vilma Santiago was suddenly no longer with them, replaced by something else altogether.

Something wild and dangerous.

* * *

Now that he had the gift of vision, Kraus half expected that his other senses, augmented by a lifetime of blindness, would begin to decline. But that wasn't the case at all. They were all just as sharp as they had been, perhaps even a bit more so with the addition of sight.

And something else had taken its place among his five senses, another feeling that warned him of dire times to come, a sensation of foreboding had become the sixth of his senses.

The healer moved about them unnoticed, still beneath their regard. He stopped to check the stitches he had sewn into the arm of a Powers soldier that perched atop the ledge of the orphanage roof. Eight others were there as well, staring silently out across western Massachusetts with dark, unwavering gazes.

"Do you feel them, brothers?" asked the warrior whose arm Kraus carefully examined, his voice leaden, as if drained of vitality. "Stirring to be born, a bane to our holy cause."

The angel was talking of Nephilim. How the Powers hated these half-breed progeny, but as of late, they had not been allowed to hunt the accursed offspring of the fallen.

"Our master tells us that there are more important concerns these days, but I, too, feel the threat of the Nephilim on the rise," said another. "I ask you, what could be more important than the extermination of these abominations?"

Infection had found its way into the angel's wound and Kraus could smell the pungent aroma of decay.

"Verchiel has ordered us to stand down," an angel of the flock said, tilting his head strangely to one side as he addressed his brethren. "It is not our place to question."

"It is not our place to sit and allow the offenders of His will to go unpunished," another replied.

They all ruffled the feathers of their wings menacingly. Dissension was brewing in the ranks of the Powers, the likes of which Kraus had never perceived. *Is this the reason I feel such dread?* he wondered. *Or is there something more?* He thought of the enigmatic Archons and the mysterious prisoner they still held in the abandoned St. Athanasius Orphanage.

Then a shudder passed through the healer as he recalled the moment his new eyes first beheld their master—his master. Kraus felt ashamed, for here was the being that had given his miserable life purpose, given him the gift of sight, and rather than feeling love and gratitude, he experienced only an inexplicable revulsion and fear.

There came a disturbance in the sky above the rooftop, and Kraus watched in wonder as the air began to shimmer like water, growing increasingly darker as Verchiel appeared. The angel leader touched down upon the tar roof, opening his expansive wings to reveal the blind Archon, Katspiel, huddled within their folds. The magick user was bent over, his body twisted with fatigue. Kraus could hear him gasping for air, fluid rattling in his lungs. He was about to go to the Archon, to see if he could help, when Verchiel began to address what remained of his army.

"Rally yourselves, my brethren," their leader proclaimed, "for I have need of your warrior skills!"

The roosting angels spread their wings and leaped into the air to circle about their master, agitated cries of anticipation issuing from their mouths. The Archon raised his arm, a tremulous hand weaving the fabric of a magickal spell in the air, coalescing like drifting cobwebs to affix to their bodies.

"The last two Malakim have been found," Verchiel bellowed as the air around them began to distort. "The final fragments of the rite we seek will soon be in our grasp."

"Know as I know," Katspiel pronounced, still casting his spell. "See as I see."

One by one the angels nodded, knowing where they must go to obtain their master's prize. With nary a question, they wrapped themselves in their wings and were gone. Verchiel was the last to depart, closing his eyes and smiling as his feathered appendages slowly closed about him and the Archon.

"Closer and closer still," he said, his voice tainted with the thrill of anticipation, and then they, too, were gone.

The sense of foreboding was with Kraus again, stronger than any of the others, and a small part of him longed for the way things used to be, before he was given sight and truly began to see.

Things seemed so much clearer then.

* * *

Aaron sat on the cluttered floor and thumbed through a book of art. The book depicted various interpretations of Heaven and Hell by artists with names like Blake, Doré, and Bosch. He was paying close attention to the artists' renditions of Hell.

"So let me see if I understand this," he said, looking up from a particularly disturbing take on the underworld that showed the damned being mauled by demons and eaten by mutant animals in a landscape of mind-boggling chaos, painted by the Dutch artist Hieronymus Bosch. "According to you, there is no Hell."

Scholar was in the process of preparing himself yet another cup of tea. Aaron had noticed the many small tables set up throughout the expansive library so the fallen angel could enjoy his hot beverage wherever he happened to be working.

"Let's try this again, shall we? Hell is not a place, per se," the angel said, removing the dripping bag from his cup and dropping it onto a plate on the table. "It is more a state of being—an experience, if you will."

Aaron closed the heavy volume and climbed to his feet to return the book to its shelf. "But there is a Heaven?" he asked, just to be certain.

Scholar intercepted him before he could reach the bookcase, probably worried that the boy would put it back in the wrong place or maybe topple the bookcases. "Of course there is a Heaven," he answered sharply, exasperated that Aaron could even ask such a question. "Otherwise the whole reason for your conception wouldn't even exist." He pointedly returned the art text to its proper place.

Aaron shrugged, leaning back casually against one of the packed shelves. "I thought that one couldn't exist without the other."

Scholar returned to his steaming brew, picking up the mug to drink. "Humankind has been fascinated by the concept of an underworld, a Hell, since first leaving the trees—sitting around blazing campfires, speculating about the fate of their souls after death." He took a sip and closed his eyes, the warm fluid passing over his lips, seeming to bring the high-strung angel a certain amount of calm.

"They wondered what would happen when they were no more, struggling to unravel the vast mysteries of life in a strange and unknowable world. The early humans wove all manner of fantastic tales about underworld deities and perilous journeys to the afterlife. The stories were passed from parent to child by word of mouth, with every generation adding a little of its own spice to the mix. Organized religion fine-tuned these theories into elaborate cause-and-effect scenarios, but it always meant the same: good behavior meant salvation; evil, damnation."

"So if Hell isn't a place, what is it really?" Aaron asked.

Scholar chuckled, but there was no amusement in his response as he stared off into space. "If you asked each of us who has fallen, you would likely receive a different answer from each," he said. "To some, being banished from Heaven was the ultimate damnation." The angel paused and caught Aaron's eye before continuing. "But it was your sire, the son of the morning—Lucifer Morningstar—that experienced, and probably still endures, a level of Hell in which all others pale in comparison."

"It was his punishment," Aaron stated firmly, "for what he did to Heaven."

Scholar nodded slowly, and Aaron knew he was reliving the moment God bestowed His punishment upon the angel that was his own father. "All the pain, all the violence that he was responsible for, was collected in one seething mass of misery." The angel's face twisted. He held up his empty hand as if clutching a ball of something terrible. "And it was put inside him so that he would forever feel the extent of the suffering he caused." Scholar touched his chest, acting out Lucifer's fate. "He was the first of the fallen, and those who had taken up his cause followed him to Earth, sharing in his banishment from Heaven."

"Where did he go?" Aaron asked. *If there is no Hell, where does the Devil live?* he wondered, recalling some neighborhoods in his hometown of Lynn that the Devil would have been quite comfortable in.

"Lucifer wandered the globe. Some say he was so bitterly angry with God that he turned to evil, doing everything in his power to corrupt the world of which the Creator was so proud." Scholar finished what could have been his tenth cup of tea since Aaron arrived and set the used cup down on a tabletop.

"And what do you think?" Aaron asked. "Was he evil or was that just a bad rap that followed him because of what he did in Heaven?"

"If he was a creature of evil," Scholar began thoughtfully. "If he was the unrepenting scourge that your popular culture suggests, would it have been possible for him to conceive a being whose sole reason for living is to bring redemption not only for himself, but for all who were tempted by him? I think not."

"I can see why Verchiel and his Powers aren't so thrilled with me," Aaron said as things began to tumble into place in his mind. "If everything goes according to the prophecy, I'll be responsible for granting forgiveness to the ultimate sinner, one that Verchiel feels should suffer for his crimes for all eternity."

Scholar nodded in agreement. "Verchiel still believes in his mission, no matter how foul and twisted it has become. He still believes in the ultimate punishment for those who questioned the Word of God."

The enormity of his responsibility to the fallen angels, to his father, to God Himself, landed upon Aaron's shoulders like a ton of bricks. He was finally getting used to the idea of reuniting the fallen with God, but to repair a rift between God and the Devil? That was another thing entirely.

"Do you think he deserves to be forgiven?" Aaron asked Scholar.

The fallen angel smiled sadly and shrugged his shoulders. "That's not for me to decide."

"But if it *was*," Aaron persisted.

"Then yes, I would forgive him," Scholar said. "If we pathetic creatures can receive absolution, then so should he, for he did only what the others of us were not brave or strong enough to do ourselves."

Aaron thought for a moment. "Guess I'm going to have to find this Lucifer and see for myself," he said with a hint of a smile. "But not before I deal with a certain Powers commander."

He was about to ask Scholar if they had learned anything more about Verchiel's whereabouts, when from somewhere far off in the room he heard a door thrown violently open and his name being called. Aaron recognized the sound of Lehash's voice as well as the intensity in it and hurried to find Aerie's head of security, with a curious Scholar close behind.

Aaron ran around the corner of a wall of bookcases and nearly head-on into the gunslinger. "What's wrong?" he gasped, not liking the look he saw in Lehash's eyes.

"There's trouble at the house," the angel began. "It's Vilma, she . . ."

Aaron didn't wait for him to finish. Immediately the

image of the home in which the girl he loved was staying formed in his mind. His wings of solid black surged from his back, toppling stacks of books as they closed around him, Scholar's frantic gasps the last sound heard before he was gone in the blink of an eye.

# CHAPTER SIX

Traversing the void between the here and there, Verchiel listened to the fearsome shrieks of his soldiers. They sensed the battle to come, and reveled in the opportunity to honor him; their cries of war an inspiration to his cause.

Verchiel had never trusted the Malakim. He had always been suspicious of the level of knowledge and power that had been conferred on the angelic trinity by the Supreme Being. How ironic that these same gifts would be used against their most Holy Father. It almost amused him, but since the horrible realization that he had been cast adrift by the same Master he had most dutifully served since the beginning of time, there was very little room left for amusement.

They were close now; Verchiel could feel their presence, their complex magicks no longer able to hide them.

The Archon Katspiel had again proven his worth. Though it drained his life force like a thirsty desert nomad sucking greedily upon a canteen, the angelic magick user had managed to weave an intricate spell that revealed the secret location of the two surviving Malakim.

*What's that monkey expression I've heard so many times?* Verchiel mused. *Two birds with a single rock,* he thought as his wings parted to reveal his journey's end.

Two Malakim, clothed in shimmering robes seemingly woven from the purest sunlight, stood over the body of the first of their kind slain at Kilimanjaro. His armored body had been laid out upon an ancient stone altar and encircled with burning candles of various heights. The inscrutable creatures of Heaven, oft believed to be as close to God as any of His creations, were mourning their kindred's passing. *How quaintly . . . human,* Verchiel thought while he surveyed their whereabouts.

They had traveled to a vast cave, its walls dappled with man-size recesses filled with desiccated remains. The stink of the dead hung heavy in the stagnant air. Based upon the religious trappings around the cavern, Verchiel gathered that they were in some early Christian burial chamber, long forgotten and probably hidden deep beneath some sprawling metropolis. The Malakim had always been fascinated with the ways of the human monkeys, observing their every movement along the evolutionary path. Verchiel still believed the species to be little more than clever animals and saw no real future for them. And if he accomplished what he'd set out to do, there would indeed be none.

"You have not been bidden here, angel," one of the Malakim said, his voice dripping with conceit. "Take your host and depart. We respect your empathy, but wish to grieve for our departed brother alone."

Was that the slightest hint of fear Verchiel saw on the faces of these supposedly superior beings as they stood over the remains of their brother? How disturbing it must have been for them, to find one of their own brought down to ground, its most precious resource torn from its body.

"We didn't wish it to be this way," he said to the Malakim, moving closer. He noticed that they had cleaned the corpse, but it did little to hide the ravages of the Powers' search for their prize. "We begged him to surrender, but he chose instead to fight."

The two angelic beings shared a quick glance before looking back to Verchiel. It was exactly as it had been with the first of their ilk: so arrogant that they couldn't even begin to fathom the idea that they would soon be under siege.

"It was as if he wanted to die," Verchiel said, gazing down upon the corpse in mock sadness and then smiling a predator's smile.

At that moment, the Malakim finally understood, and the look upon their oh-so-superior faces was priceless. The Powers leader raised his hand. "Take them," he barked to his troops.

His warriors sprang at his command, weapons of flame appearing for battle. Startled by this overt display of hostility, the Malakim backed away from the stone altar on which their fallen comrade had been laid.

"The others have arrived," Archon Katspiel whispered, his sightless head tilted back, nose twitching, and Verchiel saw that he was correct. The air behind the distracted Malakim had begun to distort, a magickal entrance for the remaining Archons.

The Malakim were standing back to back, the blessed light of their divinity radiating from their bodies, illuminating the ugliness of the burial chamber around them, the heat thrown from their omnipotence igniting the remains of the interred. Weapons of crackling, blue force had appeared in their hands, and they fought Verchiel's soldiers with a ferocity that impressed the Powers leader greatly. If only they would give up their knowledge willingly and join him in his endeavor against a Creator that had gone mad. But Verchiel knew that it would never come to be, for he imagined they were still under the misconception that their God could do no wrong, and nothing would sway them from their faith.

*Poor deluded fools.*

His Powers did what was expected of them, their fury relentless, their numbers expendable for the greater good. Many had begun to burn, the intense heat radiating from the Malakim devouring their flesh with a ravenous hunger, but still they fought, the first wave of a two-pronged assault.

The Archons had taken up their positions behind the battle, their arms waving in the air as they recited incantations that would render their prey helpless. From Verchiel's side, Katspiel joined his voice to his fellow magicians as he removed the sacred blade of extraction from within the folds of his robe.

A high-pitched squeal echoed through the burial chamber, and one of the Malakim fell, writhing and twitching upon the mausoleum floor, fighting the Archon's magick. But the other acted as his partner fell, conjuring a shield, a protective bubble that kept out the spell of incapacitation, as well as the fury of the remaining Powers soldiers.

Verchiel spread his wings and leaped into the air, a sword coming to life in his grasp. "Step aside," he bellowed as he landed before the crackling sphere of magickal energy that contained his quarry. His surviving warriors, blackened and blistered, quickly scattered.

"Give me what I want, and I will let you live," Verchiel said as he placed his hand against the sphere. There was a flash of supernatural energies and the Powers commander pulled quickly away, his palm blackened by the discharge.

"We know what you took from brother Peliel," the Malakim said from within the bubble. He had fallen to his knees, exhausted from the expenditure. "You tamper with forces far beyond your capacity to understand. I ask you, angel of the Powers host, to abandon this madness before it is too late."

Verchiel smiled, more snarl than grin, and ran his tongue

over the tender flesh of his burned palm. He turned away from the sphere to look upon the Archon Katspiel. The blind sorcerer had found his way across the room and now stood over the body of the Malakim they had brought down, clutching the fearsome tool of extraction.

"Katspiel," Verchiel said, looking back to the magickally protected Malakim. "Take what I came for."

The blind Archon raised his arm, preparing to bring the dagger down.

"Please," the divine being begged from within his sphere of protective energy. "Allow us our lives and we'll give you what you want."

"Raphael, no!" shrieked the Malakim beneath the awful dagger, eyes wide in defiance.

"Silence!" Verchiel ordered, turning his attentions back to the Malakim Raphael. "Drop the spell of protection and I will consider your offer."

Raphael stared at the Powers commander for a moment, then did as he was ordered, the bubble of magickal energy dissipating in the air, like the smoke from the burning remains within the burial chamber. "It is done," he said.

"Yes. Yes, it is," Verchiel replied. "Katspiel."

The Archon brought the dagger down into the skull of the immobilized Malakim, the sound of splitting skull explosive in the quiet air of the tomb.

"Your offer is too costly," Verchiel said to the surviving

Malakim. "You and your brother are too dangerous to be left alive. I hope you can understand my position."

The angelic being nodded as the Archons surrounded him, the spell of immobilization beginning to spill from their lips. "As I hope you will understand mine," Raphael said. A sword of crackling energy sprang suddenly to life in his grasp and he spun around to plunge it into the chest of the nearest angelic magician.

Chaos erupted. The Archons began to scream, their concentration broken as Jaldabaoth slumped to the ground, the blade of light protruding from his chest. The surviving Powers soldiers surged forward in an attempt to apprehend the last of the Malakim. But Verchiel already knew it was too late. Raphael had taken advantage of the moment, and before they could put their hands upon him or recast their spells, he had sprouted wings of gold and taken flight.

Aaron felt the ground appear beneath his feet and opened his wings, his blood running cold with the sight before him. The girl he loved was attacking Lorelei and Gabriel. *No, not the girl I love,* he corrected himself, *but the ancient power that has spun out of control within her.*

Vilma was screaming, an ear-piercing mixture of anger and pain, as supernatural flame streamed from her fingertips to consume everything it touched. Lorelei had extended her arm, and a spell of defense spilled from her mouth as she attempted to restrain the rampant Nephilim. Tendrils of magickal force erupted from her outstretched hand, striking Vilma and knocking her violently to the ground. Aaron was moving to help her when the girl began to shriek—a scream he had heard before. A scream he himself had bellowed in times of battle. It was a cry of war.

Aaron opened his mouth to warn Lorelei of the impending danger, but it was too late. The flash was blinding, an explosion of heavenly fire that propelled the Nephilim sorceress backward, her body landing in a broken heap in the front yard. Vilma was on her feet again and she began to wander toward the street, but Gabriel surged forward to block her path.

*"C'mon, Vilma,"* he said to her. *"You've got to calm down before somebody really gets hurt."*

And Aaron noticed then that his dog was burned, patches of Gabriel's beautiful, golden yellow coat still smoldering from the bite of the angelic essence. He held his breath, watching as the girl gazed at the canine obstacle, her head tilting strangely to one side, the angelic essence peering out through her eyes.

*"That's it,"* the dog continued in a soothing, rumble of a voice. *"No need to be so upset, we can work it out."*

They were still unaware of his presence and Aaron remained perfectly still; at the moment Gabriel seemed to have the situation under control and he didn't want to disturb a thing if this had a chance of working. Since his rebirth, the dog had developed a number of rather unique abilities. It seemed that there was a strange psychic connection between the Labrador and all things Nephilim. If there was anybody that could calm the raging angelic essence, it was Gabriel.

"I'm . . . I'm trying," Vilma said, her voice small and trembling. She sounded very far away. "But it's fighting me."

Aaron saw the tears streaming down her face and his heart just about broke. He remembered how painful it had been for him when he had tried to hold back his own emerging angelic essence.

*"I'll help you,"* Gabriel said. *"Just let me inside your thoughts and we'll see if we can't put it back to sleep. That's it,"* the dog cooed.

The girl began to sway slowly, her eyes clamped tightly shut. Gabriel swayed as well, psychically connected, adding his own strength to hers. But suddenly her body stiffened and a gasp of agony escaped her lips. Gabriel yelped as well, recoiling from the psychic pain. And then Aaron heard the sound of something tearing.

"Gabriel, get away from her!" he screamed in warning, waving his arms as he ran toward them, his sneakered feet slipping on the wet grass, the smell of things burning assailing his nostrils.

Vilma cried out as the wings, hidden beneath the flesh of her back, began to grow. Her clothing tore as they slowly unfurled. If the moment hadn't been so intense, Aaron would have thought them the most beautiful wings he had ever seen;

fawn feathers, dappled with spots of white, brown, and black.

Her body shuddered with release, her new wings fanning the air. She gazed down upon Gabriel, a sneer of cruelty on her tear-stained face. The dog seemed stunned as he sat before the out of control Nephilim, furiously shaking his head.

The language of messengers—the language of angels—poured from Vilma's mouth. She extended her arms toward the helpless Lab and heavenly fire began to dance at her fingertips.

Aaron pushed his wings from his back and leaped the final few feet to his best friend. The flame cascaded off his back, over his wings of glistening black, and he cried out as he pulled Gabriel into his protective embrace.

"You're going to run now," he whispered into the dog's ear through gritted teeth as the fire lapped at his back.

Gabriel seemed to gather his wits about him, and he sprinted from his master's arms to safety behind a nearby tree.

Aaron whirled around, the stench of burning flesh and feathers choking the air. He sprang from the ground, propelling himself toward Vilma, his shoulder connecting with her midsection. He didn't want to hurt her, but she had to be stopped. The power inside her, if left unchecked, would threaten not only Aerie, but the human world outside as well.

He drove her backward into the front of the house. The force of their strike shattering the window above their heads.

"Listen to me, Vilma," he said, trying to pin her flailing

arms against the house. "Listen to the sound of my voice."

She cried out a shrill, birdlike shriek as she thrashed from side to side.

"You're stronger than this," he continued, trying to keep his voice calm, even though the burns on his back throbbed with his every movement. "You have to force it down where it belongs. It's not stronger than you; it just wants you to think it is."

She stopped struggling, her body growing slack, and Aaron mistakenly loosened his hold upon her. Still firmly in the grip of the angelic power, Vilma drove her knee up into his groin and he fell to the ground gasping for air.

She continued to rant and rave in the tongue of angels as she slowly beat the air with her wings, preparing for her first flight. One word stuck out from all the rest.

*"Escape!"*

But that was something Aaron couldn't allow. Through the haze of pain, he tried to straighten his body enough to grab at her—to keep her on the ground—but his fingers only brushed the hem of her jeans as she took to the air. And then a yellow blur moved past him, latching onto Vilma's leg with a furious grip. Gabriel growled as Vilma kicked at him, but he held firm, giving Aaron enough time to gather his wits and take to the air.

He managed to grab hold of the girl, but she beat her wings furiously and still they climbed higher. Gabriel released his hold on her, falling harmlessly to the ground, where he stood staring up at them, locked in a struggle above the rooftop.

Fire again shot from her outstretched hands, knocking Aaron away with its scouring blast. She was flying away from him now, frantically trying to flee, and he realized there was only one thing he could do to stop her. He summoned a sword of fire, watching as its deadly shape took form in his grasp. Then he poured on the speed cutting through the air, like a hungry shark zeroing in upon its hapless prey. *This is the only way,* he repeated in his mind as he flew above her and lashed out with his weapon, cutting into one of her beautiful new wings.

Her scream was piercing as she floundered in the air attempting to stay aloft, but the pain was too great, the injury too extensive, and Vilma began to fall from the sky. Aaron wished his sword away and dived to catch her flailing body. "Let me help," he pleaded.

But the essence roared its ire, flames exploding from her hands and driving him away. Helplessly, he followed her path of descent, watching as she landed on the street below, scattering a crowd of citizens who had gathered to watch the battle.

He crouched beside her and took her into his arms. She was alive but seemed to be in the grip of nightmare, moaning and thrashing in his embrace. It was only a matter of time before she regained consciousness and he didn't know what to do.

"You might want to step away from her," he heard Lehash

say from somewhere close by, and turned to see the angel aiming one of his golden weapons, hammer already cocked. "It's probably the most merciful thing to do."

Aaron pulled her closer, shielding her from harm. "You want to kill her?" he cried incredulously. "Are you out of your mind? Is that how you solve problems here, by putting bullets in them?"

Lehash lowered his weapon with a heavy sigh and stepped closer. "You know that's not what I'm about, boy," he said quietly. "The merger's just not happening right with her. She's a danger to herself—to us and the world." The gunslinger angel gripped Aaron's shoulder and squeezed. "Puttin' her down might just be the best thing for her."

"I can't let you do that," the boy said, looking from Lehash to Vilma. "I have to try and help her."

The gun in Lehash's hand disappeared in a flash of light, but Aaron knew it could be back in an instant. "And what if you can't? What if this is one that can't be saved?"

Aaron didn't answer the fallen angel. Instead he pulled the girl even closer, whispering softly in her ear that everything was going to be all right, and wishing with all his might for it to be true.

Deep within the realm of unconsciousness, Lucifer fled into a place of his own creation to escape the agonies of torture.

He lay upon the bed beside her, knowing full well that she

was but a figment from his past, a creation of his pain-addled mind. But he could not help but feel a spike of joy having Taylor beside him again.

"What?" she asked, looking into his eyes. "Is there something wrong?"

*Where to begin?* Lucifer pondered. He considered wishing it all away, to return to the darkness of oblivion, to the bleak reality of his situation, but he couldn't bring himself to do so.

"No," he finally said, feeling somewhat guilty for the lie, even though she was only a creation of his mind. "Everything's fine. Why don't you go back to sleep?"

Taylor sat up in bed, the strap of her nightgown sliding off her shoulder to expose the curves of her delicate flesh. "You're not a very good liar, you know that?" she said with a knowing smile. "Maybe if we talk about it, you'll feel better, come up with something that you didn't think of before."

He found it strangely amusing that he tried to lie to an invention of his own imagination, as if it wouldn't already be aware of the danger he was in.

Lucifer rolled away and climbed from the bed. "There's really nothing to talk about." His environment suddenly changed, like a scene-shift in a motion picture, the quiet darkness of the bedroom blurring into a park on a beautiful summer's day.

"Try me," Taylor said, her hand firmly clasped in his.

Her silk nightgown had been replaced with a simple sundress, sandals, and a floppy, wide-brimmed hat. It was the outfit she had been wearing when they'd first met so long ago. A dog, a golden retriever that he already knew was named Brandy, bounded toward them, a stick in its mouth, eager for a game of fetch.

It was an absolutely beautiful day, just as he remembered. The sky was bluer than he had ever seen it, wispy clouds like spider's silk stretching across the broad turquoise expanse. It was a day unlike any other he had spent upon the world of his banishment—the day when he first considered that he could be something *more* than the first of the fallen, the monster that had brought about a war in Paradise.

How foolish he had been.

Taylor took the stick from the dog and threw it. "Do you think he'll actually do it?" she asked, watching the dog bound across the green, green grass in pursuit of its prize.

She was speaking about Verchiel and the angel's intention to use Lucifer as an instrument of death to strike at the heart of the Creator—by destroying His world. He would have liked to believe that nothing that sprang from the loins of God could do such evil, but he had looked into the eyes of the Powers commander and saw something angry and twisted—something familiar—and he knew the answer.

"Yes, I think he will," Lucifer said.

Brandy returned happily with the stick, and he noticed that the sky had grown suddenly darker, as if there were a storm brewing. This had not been part of their original day and Lucifer grew wary.

"And do you think he'll succeed?" the woman asked, squatting down to pat the dog, running her nails through its long, golden brown fur and rubbing its ears.

The sky had turned the color of night and thunder rumbled ominously in the distance. "In order for Verchiel to destroy the world of man, he must somehow undo the Word of God," Lucifer replied as the darkness closed in around them. "And I doubt that even one as tenacious as he can concoct a way in which to do that."

The rain began to fall in drenching torrents, and he took her by the hand and pulled her to her feet, and they ran for cover. Brandy had already deserted them, fleeing into the permanent midnight that had consumed all evidence of the park.

He put his arm around Taylor, holding her close to him, fearing that he might lose her in the storm. She was soaked, and he felt her tremble as they stumbled through the dreamscape in search of shelter.

A cave was suddenly before them, like the open maw of the great whale ready to swallow Jonah, and as they approached, a feeling of unease swept over him and he recoiled.

"What's the matter?" Taylor asked, pushing her wet hair away from her face. "Do you know this place?" And he knew full well that she knew he did.

"It's not a place I care to visit," he said, staring into the Cimmerian space beyond the cave's entrance.

Taylor tugged at his hand, pulling him toward the cave.

"We should go inside," she suggested. "Just for a little while, to get out of the rain."

Every instinct screamed for him to run, but he allowed himself to be pulled along, and the darkness enveloped them in an embrace that chilled him to his very core.

Torches came to life as they walked deeper into the cave. There were crude drawings upon the walls depicting God's creation of the universe, of the beings that He would call His angels. He saw himself sitting at the Creator's right hand as the Earth formed beneath them.

"That really pissed you off, didn't it?" Taylor asked. The passage in which they walked angled steeply downward.

"Yes, it did," Lucifer admitted, eyeing the interpretation of Eden and its first human residents. He still felt the fury as if for the first time. "I was jealous of them. I thought that He was pushing us aside for the humans—that He loved them more than us."

They continued their descent, the passage opening wider, the paintings now dwarfing them with their size.

"Did you have to start a war?" She gave his hand a loving squeeze. "Couldn't you have just had a nice talk? Told Him how you were feeling?"

The pictures showed Lucifer gathering his army and giving them a gift of his inner strength.

"I was angry."

"No kidding," Taylor said, pointing out a particularly fearsome depiction of himself, flaming sword in hand as he led his troops into battle against the forces of Heaven.

The wall art that followed was of things that he didn't care to see. Paintings of his army's defeat, of the deaths of those that had sworn him allegiance, the survivors fleeing Heaven to hide upon the earth.

"I bet seeing it drawn out like this makes you feel pretty stupid," Taylor said with a sigh.

"You don't know the half of it," Lucifer answered. "But somehow you learn to live with and accept the mistakes that you made."

They had reached the end of the passage, the final drawing before them an image of himself, broken, beaten, skin blackened and charred, as the hand of God came down from the heavens to deliver His verdict upon him.

"And His punishment?" she asked, unconsciously rubbing her own chest at the point where God had touched him—where all the pain and sorrow that he had caused was placed. "Have you accepted that?"

Lucifer slowly nodded, his eyes riveted to the artistic representation of his fate. "It is what I deserved," he said, reaching out to place the palm of his hand upon the cool stone wall that marked the end of their journey.

And as his hand came in contact with the wall, a shudder went through the painted rock. Large cracks appeared, splitting the stone. Lucifer was quick to act, gripping Taylor by the arm and pulling her from the path of harm as the stone wall before them fell away to reveal something hidden behind it.

They stared in awe as the dust began to settle, and they looked upon an enormous door of metal. It reminded him of a bank vault, only far larger, its surface crisscrossed with thick chains and fortified with multiple locks of every imaginable size.

Instinctively he knew what he was looking at—what *they* were looking at—and was in awe of it. Here was the psychic representation of God's Word, the curse that kept the accumulated pain and sorrow of the War in Heaven locked away inside of him.

"And Verchiel would have to get through *that* to achieve his plans?" Taylor asked, pointing to the enormous door.

Lucifer was about to respond, to reassure her that nothing short of God Himself could access the obstacle that kept his hellish penance at bay, when he felt a tremor pass through the tunnel, and the great door rattled in its frame of ancient rock. They both watched in growing horror as a padlock connecting two links of a mighty chain sprang open, clattering to the floor.

"That's exactly what he would have to do," Lucifer said, an icy claw of dread closing upon his heart as another of the locks fell away.

# CHAPTER SEVEN

Aaron stifled a cry of discomfort as Lorelei dabbed some salve on the wounds he sustained during his altercation with Vilma. It smelled absolutely horrible and stung even worse. But she had already chastised him once about being a baby, embarrassing him in front of Lehash, so he gritted his teeth and endured the pain.

"Are you almost done back there?" he asked.

"Just about," she said as he felt her attach a dampened bandage to his shoulder. "That oughta take care of that." She gently pressed the bandage against his burned skin. It felt cool—almost soothing—but then the throbbing was back.

"Until she loses it again," Lehash added, pulling one of his foul-smelling cheroots from his duster pocket.

"That's not the least bit funny." Aaron glared at the angel.

"It wasn't meant to be, boy," the gunslinger said, lifting his index finger to the tip of the thin cigar in his mouth.

"Don't you dare light that filthy thing in here," Scholar bellowed from across the room. "The books will stink of it for months." The angel was sitting at a small wooden desk, his back to them, as he continued to peruse the books he had gathered, hoping to find a solution to Vilma's problem.

"And you wonder why I don't visit," Lehash grumbled, taking the cigar from his mouth and returning it to his pocket.

The mood was depressingly grim. Neither Lorelei nor Lehash held out much hope for Vilma, but Aaron wasn't about to give up that easily. If anyone in Aerie could help her, it was Scholar.

The fallen angel threw up his hands in exasperation and rose from his seat. "I've found nothing," he said, beginning to pace. "There's plenty about Nephilim, but nothing on how to control them once they're out of balance."

Lehash leaned back against a bookcase and crossed his arms. "And you know why that is?" he asked. "Because there *isn't* any way, and that's one of the reasons why the Powers started killing Nephilim. The angelic essence is sometimes too much for the human aspect to deal with; it's too strong and it takes control—makes 'em crazy, dangerous."

"She's not crazy *or* dangerous," Aaron grumbled, slipping on a fresh shirt.

"Right now she ain't, and that's only because we got her knocked out with one of Lorelei's special potions, and wearing a pair'a them magickal bracelets. Hell, we even got that dog of yours over there trying to keep her from getting her feathers ruffled."

Aaron's thoughts raced. He didn't like where this was going. There had to be something they could do to help her. "What about the ritual I went through with Belphegor?" he asked. "Wasn't that to help my two natures unify properly? Why couldn't we do that with—"

Scholar shook his head. "She'd never survive it. The angelic nature is already stronger than her human half. It would eat her alive and we'd have the same problem we started with: pure angelic power running amok."

"And we can't have that, Aaron," Lehash said grimly. "It may not be what you want, but somethin's got to be done before she gets outta hand again."

Aaron shook his head. They'd already given up on her. "I'm not hearing this," he said, turning to face them all. Lorelei wouldn't make eye contact, arranging her bottles and vials of healing remedies in a pink, plastic makeup case. "I refuse to believe that there's nothing we can do for Vilma, short of putting her down like some sick animal."

They said nothing, refusing to provide him with even the slightest glimmer of hope.

"Lorelei," Aaron said, watching as she visibly flinched, "with your angel magick, there's nothing you can do that might help?"

She shook her head, finally meeting his gaze. "You're talking about binding a divine essence. I haven't the training or the knowledge to—"

Aaron suddenly clapped his hands and whirled toward Scholar. "The knowledge," he repeated, moving toward the angel. "Lorelei doesn't have the knowledge, but maybe somebody else does." He stopped short before the scholarly angel. "Who would have more knowledge than Lorelei? How did she learn what she knows? Who taught the magick user?"

Scholar shrugged his shoulders and tugged at his ear nervously. "Belphegor taught her quite a bit, and then there are books and scrolls. But Vilma's problem, like I already told you, isn't addressed in—"

"Who taught Belphegor?" Aaron persisted. "Who wrote the books and the scrolls?" He gestured to them for help. "C'mon guys, give me something—anything."

"Most of what we have comes from the Archons," Scholar said slowly.

"But what's left of them hooked up with Verchiel and his Powers," Lehash said, stepping away from the bookcase.

Aaron felt his anger flare and struggled to prevent his wings from bursting forth and the sigils from rising upon his flesh. "Damn it," he swore beneath his breath, feeling his own ray of hope beginning to dim.

"Who taught the Archons?" Lorelei said softly and they

all looked at her, although Scholar and Lehash remained strangely silent.

"Well?" Aaron prodded. "The lady asked a question. Who taught the Archons?"

Scholar turned back to his books. "It's too much of a long shot," he said, stacking the texts. "I wouldn't want you to get your hopes up."

"Too late," Aaron said, walking to Scholar and gripping his arm. "Who are they?"

"You're clutching at straws here, boy," Lehash echoed. "We don't have the time to be wastin' on—"

Aaron whirled to glare at the gunslinger, this time letting the sigils of warriors that died serving the will of Lucifer appear on his flesh. "I don't want to hear that," he growled, and watched as Lehash backed down, averting his eyes.

"Who taught the Archons?" he asked Scholar firmly, and there would be no debate.

"They're called the Malakim," Scholar replied, an air of reverence in his tone. "And if you can't get a meeting with the Lord God Almighty, then they're the next best thing.

*Do we truly understand what we are doing?* Archon Oraios wondered as he lifted the lid of the golden chest containing the paraphernalia of their mystical art. *Or have we been blinded by the obsession of the one that commands us—drawn into the web of his madness, no longer able to escape?*

"Where is the dirt?" Archon Jao screeched, crouching within the circle of containment beneath Lucifer's hanging body. The angel frantically checked and rechecked the metal clamps affixed to the first of the fallen's chest to keep his incision pulled wide and taut. The bleeding had stopped sometime ago, and now the hint of a pulsing, red glow could be seen leaking from the splayed chest cavity. "I must have the dirt," Jao demanded.

Archon Oraios continued to search. The bag of sacred earth was crucial to their preparations. It was soil from the fields of Heaven, a powerful component of angelic sorceries, used to fortify and maintain the strength of more dangerous magicks. A small, frightened part of him hoped to never find it, forcing them to abandon this dangerous and blasphemous ritual.

But alas, there it was—in a place he had already checked twice. *Is a higher mystical force attempting to intervene, to prevent them from making a horrible mistake?* he pondered.

"Did you find it?" Archon Domiel prodded, tension filling his voice.

With the death of their brother Jaldabaoth at the hands of the Malakim Raphael, their numbers were fewer, and all were feeling the strain. Only one more Malakim remained, one final shard of forbidden information, and then they would do the unthinkable: reverse the Word of God. And a plague of despair, the likes of which the world had never known, would wash over the land.

"Here," Oraios said, pulling from the chest the purse, made from the skin of an animal that had thrived in the garden before the death of the Eden.

"Quickly now," Jao insisted, his outstretched hand beckoning for the precious, magickal component.

Oraios handed the pouch to his brother and watched as Jao carefully spilled a portion of the rich, black contents into his open palm. The scent of Heaven wafted through the stale air of the abandoned school, and Oraios found himself transported back to Paradise by the memories stored within the fragrant aroma of the blessed earth.

He'd always believed that he would return there someday, to again witness the towering crystal spires reaching up into forever, the endless fields of golden grass, whispering softly, caressed by the gentle winds, and to bask again in the radiance of His glory.

But then Oraios returned to reality and gazed upon the form of the Morningstar, suspended with chains above a mystic circle drawn in his lifeblood and fortified with the dirt of providence. The Archon felt his dreams sadly slip away, resigning himself to his fate.

"It is only a matter of time now," he mused aloud, watching as his brothers continued their preparations, the images of Heaven in his mind already starting to fade.

\* \* \*

"I don't think you understand what I'm trying to say," Scholar said to the savior of Aerie, dipping his tea bag again and again in the steaming cup of water just poured from the electric teapot. "Malakim are mysteries even to us."

"So they're a mystery, fine. I'm cool with that," Aaron said, a twinkle of optimism in his eyes. "All I need to know is if they can help Vilma."

Scholar sipped his drink without removing the bag. A good, strong brew was required for *this* conversation. "Yes, I would imagine. If there are any beings of an angelic nature out there that might have the knowledge to solve Ms. Santiago's problem, it would be they, but—"

"No 'buts,'" Aaron said with a quick shake of his head. "This is the closest we've come to a solution and I'm not about to lose it."

"But it isn't close enough," Lehash said. Aerie's constable had helped himself to a cup of coffee and a seat, leaning the chair back on two legs against the wall. Ignoring Scholar's looks of disapproval, he continued. "The Malakim have become legends to us—like Merlin or Paul Bunyan and his blue ox to the humans."

Aaron closed his eyes and took in a deep breath. "So are they real or are they made up?"

The gunslinger slurped the remainder of his coffee and brought the front legs of his chair down upon the floor with a thud. "There might be some truth in all the tall tales, but it's been jumbled together over the years, and it's hard to tell fact from fiction."

Lorelei spoke up from a workstation tabletop where she sat cross-legged, reading through an ancient text where the Malakim were briefly mentioned. "It says here that they were the arch mages of angelic magick and keepers of forbidden knowledge." She flipped her snow-white hair back over her shoulder and out of her face. "Knowledge known only to God."

"What we do know for certain," Scholar continued, "is that the Malakim were created to be extensions of God, the receptacles of all His wisdom and knowledge—forbidden or otherwise."

"It's that knowledge thing I'm interested in," Aaron said. "Where can we find these Malakim?" he asked. "Do you know—"

"The Malakim supposedly came to Earth after the war in Heaven," Scholar interrupted. "To study and record the changes caused by the fallen."

"How can they be contacted?" Aaron asked, his patience clearly wearing thin.

Scholar set his mug down, immediately craving another cup. "That's what I've been trying to tell you, Aaron. The Malakim have hidden themselves away. There hasn't been any contact between our kind and them for thousands upon thousands of years."

"I can't believe this," the Nephilim said, sitting down on

the bare floor and running his fingers through his hair. His voice was heavy with disappointment. "Have you ever actually seen one?" he finally asked, looking up at Scholar.

"No, but—"

"Have *any* of you seen one?" Aaron prodded, climbing to his feet.

"Well, it might have been a Malakim," Lehash began, rubbing his stubble-covered chin. "But I can't say for sure."

Scholar quickly turned and walked to farthest end of the room. Aaron wanted proof of the existence of the Malakim, and proof he would have. It was kept in a glass case along with all the other treasures of Aerie. He carefully opened the lid and removed the ornate cylinder from its resting place upon a red velvet pillow.

They were all staring as he returned, still startled by his abrupt departure. He held the canister up for Aaron to see.

"You want to know how we are sure the Malakim exist?" he asked, heading for the workstation where Lorelei sat. She hopped down as he approached. "Belphegor gave this to me for safe-keeping," Scholar said, slowly unscrewing the end piece from the tube.

"I can probably figure out where he got it," Lehash said, watching with the others.

Scholar gingerly tipped the canister, allowing the rolled scroll to fall out into his waiting hand. "It was given to the Founder when he established the first safe haven for our kind."

Slowly he began to unroll the scroll, revealing the angelic script upon the golden parchment.

"It's a spell," Lorelei said, bending over to examine the writing.

"Yes, it is," Scholar said. "The first spell of concealment ever to be placed upon our sanctuary. The Malakim who visited approved of what Belphegor was doing and gave us his blessing, which meant God's blessing."

"Well, I'll be damned," Lehash said, pushing closer for a look. "A real live Malakim gave that to Belphegor." The gunslinger smirked. "Always wondered if we had God on our side; didn't know we had the paperwork to prove it."

Aaron came closer, moving past Lehash's bulk to stand next to Scholar. He gazed down upon the scroll, a strange look in his eyes. "A Malakim wrote this?" he asked, his index finger tracing the shape of the heavenly alphabet in the air above the scroll.

"Yes," Scholar answered.

"Then that means he touched it," the boy said dreamily, his thoughts seemingly someplace else altogether.

"Of course he touched it," Scholar responded testily. "How else could he have written it?" He lifted his hand, allowing the scroll to roll shut.

"I have an idea," Aaron said, turning to leave. "It's probably a long shot, but it can't hurt to try."

"Where you going, kid?" Lehash asked, following close behind.

"To see Gabriel."

# CHAPTER EIGHT

"Time is short," Verchiel hissed, his voice echoing through the abandoned church. "Find the last of the Malakim."

Katspiel convulsed violently upon the unconsecrated altar of Saint Athanasius Church. His eyeless gaze stared blindly at the fading image of Heaven painted on the high rounded ceiling, his face wan, twisted in a mask of agony. The magicks the Archon attempted to command were wild and unruly, leaching away his life force in exchange for the location of the last of Heaven's magick users.

"So elusive," he grunted, reaching up with clawed hands as if to rend the air. "Quicksilver—moving from here, to there, across the world of God's man, then gone, like darkness chased away with the coming dawn."

The angel curled into a tight ball. "I must rest," he slurred.

But Verchiel would not hear of it. He flew from his perch on the back of a wooden pew and landed upon the altar beside the quivering Archon. "There will be no rest until the Malakim is found," he screeched, grasping Katspiel by the scruff, yanking him, flailing, into the air.

"Mercy," the angel mage begged, his voice trembling. "All I ask is for some time to—"

"Don't you understand, worm?" Verchiel growled, pulling the Archon closer to his snarling face. "Surprise is lost to us. Our prey knows he is being hunted."

"So tired . . . ," Katspiel groaned as he dangled limply in his master's grip.

"There will be plenty of time to rest once the Malakim is found and the final piece of knowledge is extracted from his skull." Verchiel dropped him to the dusty floor. "Continue," he ordered.

Slowly Katspiel raised his arms, a spell of summoning upon his lips, the drone of his feeble voice drawing down magickal forces eager to partake of his already depleted life force.

Verchiel watched intently until the sound of someone entering the church distracted him. He turned and saw Kraus heading down the center aisle toward him. The human moved differently now, his newly regenerated sensory organs taking in everything, devouring the sights around him.

Kraus approached the altar, and Verchiel watched curiously as a look of horror slowly spread across his face. "What is it, healer?" And then he, too, realized what the healer saw.

Verchiel had started to bleed.

New wounds had appeared, and old wounds, long since healed, had reopened, dark blood raining down to spatter upon the altar and puddle at the angel's feet.

*"Time is short,"* he had told the Archon.

Truer words were never spoken.

The air around the sleeping girl crackled with a subdued supernatural energy, and Aaron could feel the hair on his arms and the back of his neck stand on end. Vilma was lying on a bare mattress on the floor, placed in the basement of an abandoned house on the outskirts of Aerie, away from the citizens' homes. She looked small upon the king-size mattress—fragile, as if the power inside her was consuming her mass, eating away at all that was human so only the angelic would remain.

A sheen of sweat was on her brow, and she grumbled in her sleep. But the language she spoke was neither English nor her native Portuguese. It was the language of angels, and Aaron knew that the essence inside her was growing stronger despite the supernatural restraints placed upon her.

Gabriel lay faithfully by Vilma's side, his dark brown eyes never leaving her as she slept. His burns had already begun to heal, the scorched patches filling in with new golden yellow fur.

"How is she?" Aaron asked, reaching out to stroke the dog's head.

*"It's hurting her,"* he replied, his voice full of concern. *"I'm trying with all my might, but I can't seem to calm it down. It wants to get out—it wants to run wild."* The dog looked away from his charge to hold Aaron in his soulful gaze. *"But I'm not going to let that happen."*

"You're a good dog, Gabriel," Aaron said, and leaned down to kiss the top of his hard, bony head. "What would I do without you?"

The dog seemed to take the statement literally. *"What a horrible thought."* He tilted his head to one side, considering the alternate reality. *"What* would *you do without me?"*

Aaron smiled, amused by the animal's strange perception of things. But the humor was fleeting as they again found themselves staring at the unconscious Vilma, locked within the grip of a power older than creation.

*"What are they doing to help her?"*

Aaron sighed. "That's just it, Gabe," he began. "They have no idea what to do. Normally, when something like this happens they . . ." He couldn't bring himself to say it.

*"They what?"* Gabriel asked. *"They wouldn't hurt Vilma, would they?"* He climbed to his feet. *"I won't let them, Aaron."*

"They don't want to, but it might come to that if something can't be done," Aaron explained. "She's becoming dangerous, Gabe, and to keep her from hurting someone . . . there might be no choice."

The Lab sniffed at the girl's sleeping body, his tail beginning to wag. *"She doesn't want to hurt anybody, and neither does
the thing inside her. It just needs to be trained."*

"I know that. Look, Gabe, there is a slim possibility that
certain angels called the Malakim might be able to help Vilma,
but the thing is, nobody knows where they are."

Aaron could practically hear the gears clicking in Gabriel's
square head as he tried to process the information.

*"We have to find them, then,"* the dog said matter of factly.

"Exactly," Aaron replied. "Since your accident," he continued, "since I made you better, your senses have gotten more
powerful, haven't they?"

*"Yes."*

"Do you think you could track an old scent from something?" Aaron asked.

The dog thought for a moment. *"How old?"*

Aaron shrugged. "I'm not sure. A few thousand years maybe."

*"Is that all?"* the dog responded, a mischievous twinkle in
his dark brown eyes. *"And here I was thinking you were going to
give me something tough."*

Something was drawing Lucifer out of his inner self, pulling
him away from the retreat he had created deep within his
subconscious. He didn't want to leave, struggling against
the current threatening to wrench him from his internal
world and the woman he loved, but it was to no avail. So he

left Taylor standing nervously before the locked vault door and promised to return as soon as he was able.

He allowed himself to be drawn upward, the powerful force dragging him through multiple layers of consciousness, and the closer he got to the surface, the worse the pain became. But he endured, embracing it, for it had been his constant companion since his fall. It was his penance, and he deserved no less.

Lucifer's eyes opened, dried discharge crackling as his upper lid pulled away from the lower. He blinked away the blurriness, his burning gaze focusing upon the mystical circle that had been drawn on the parquet floor beneath him. An aching pain in his arms and legs diverted his attentions elsewhere, and he realized that he was suspended by chains, hanging over an arcane protective circle, the subject of some kind of ritual.

It was more than mere physical pain he felt; this unpleasant sensation went far deeper than that, and he came to the frightening realization that Verchiel was somehow succeeding with his mad plans—that the angel had found a way to undo God's Word. The image of the large vault door within his mind—its locks falling away—filled his head, and he recoiled from it.

"You can't do this," he said aloud, struggling pathetically against his bonds, his body swaying with his useless efforts.

"Oh, but I can," said a disturbing voice from close by, and Lucifer lifted his head to look upon Verchiel, or at least he believed it to be him.

Clad in armor that once shone like the sun, the figure that shambled toward him was a nightmare to behold. The exposed flesh of the angel's face, arms, and legs was wrapped in bandages, bloodied by oozing wounds.

"Is that you, Verchiel?" Lucifer asked, struggling to keep his head up, the muscles in his neck beginning to cramp. "What happened? Cut yourself shaving?" Then he saw the eyes that raged from between the gore-stained bandages and knew exactly who it was before him.

"Insolent even in the face of your own demise," Verchiel hissed.

In all his years of existence, Lucifer had never seen such hate as he now saw in the Powers leader. Here was a being birthed by God that had somehow lost touch with everything that made him a creature of the divine. Even Lucifer still remembered what it was like to serve God, after all that he had been through.

"Believe it or not, Morningstar, I asked the Archons to awaken you," Verchiel said, his voice a rasping whisper through the bandages that partially obscured his mouth. "I want you to be fully aware of the next catastrophic act you will be party to." The angel stepped closer, careful not to disturb the mystical circle, and grabbed Lucifer's chin, lifting his face to gaze upon Verchiel's disturbing visage. "I thought we might have a private discussion first, while the Archons rest. They have been working so very hard to complete their task."

"What's happened to you?" Lucifer asked. The sickening smell of decay wafted from Verchiel's body, and he wanted to turn his head away, but the Powers commander still held his chin firmly in hand.

"This is yet another example of how the Lord rewards those who serve Him faithfully," Verchiel growled bitterly. "All my wounds, received in service to His holy cause, open again and weeping."

Lucifer directed his gaze to Verchiel's cold eyes. "Do you think maybe He's trying to tell you something?" he asked, hoping to reach even a sliver of sanity in the Powers commander.

"Yes," Verchiel said with a slow nod of his bandaged head. "Yes, I do believe that He is attempting to commune with me. Through His actions, or lack thereof, He is telling me that the sinful have won, that the wretched and the cursed, the criminals and the abominations whose taint has poisoned the heavens above and the earth below, hold indomitable sway over all."

Verchiel leaned his face closer to Lucifer's, the smell of rot nearly suffocating. "But I will not hear of it," he said, squeezing his prisoner's chin all the tighter, refusing to allow him to look away. "I will not surrender to those who should have died beneath my heel. I shall see it all turned to Hell before I give it away."

And with the last pronouncement of his rage, Verchiel released his grip and backed from the circle. "And to think, the one that began it all—who brought war to Paradise, and still had the audacity to believe that his sins could be forgiven—shall be the instrument of my defiance." Verchiel studied the first of the fallen, the hint of a grotesque smile beneath the soiled wrappings. "It brings me a certain satisfaction to know that the prophecy will never be brought to term, that the founder of our misery will never find forgiveness at the hands of his son."

Lucifer couldn't bear to hear any more of the angel's rantings. He wanted to return to the darkness of oblivion, to the comfort of a precious memory in the shape of a love long lost. But there was something that Verchiel said that he did not quite comprehend. He strained to lift his head and look upon the Powers commander to ask the question.

"Forgiveness at the hands of *his son?*"

Verchiel chuckled, a wet rumbling sound. "Don't tell me that you didn't know, or at least suspect, Morningstar," he teased.

"What are you saying?" Lucifer struggled to ask, the Archon spell used to return him to consciousness wearing thin.

"Why, the Nephilim of prophecy, the one called Aaron Corbet—he is your son."

# CHAPTER NINE

"*This place is much bigger on the inside,*" Gabriel observed as he strolled deeper into the seemingly endless room, his nails clicking on the bare, hardwood floors.

"At that first stack, take a . . ." Aaron started to tell him, but the dog was already on his way to finding the others.

*"Don't tell me, Aaron,"* Gabriel said, his nose skimming the surface of the floor. It sounded like a Geiger counter searching for dangerous levels of radiation as he followed the scent. *"Let me find them on my own."*

Gabriel hadn't wanted to leave Vilma, fearing that his absence would cause the essence to awaken again. But he had finally agreed when Aaron explained that it was the only way left to help the girl. Besides, Scholar wouldn't allow the scroll to leave his house.

Aaron followed the dog through the multiple winding corridors of bookshelves as the animal tracked his quarry. He was pleased with how well Gabriel was doing, but were the Lab's olfactory senses really good enough to find an angelic being that had left his scent on a scroll thousands of years ago? That was the million-dollar question, and a chance they were going to have to take.

Scholar had scoffed at the idea, saying that he'd never heard of anything quite so ridiculous, and the others weren't quite ready to go along for the ride either. Aaron defended his theory, giving examples of his dog's ability to track. Being able to find a slice of cheese hidden somewhere in a house didn't have quite the impact that he had imagined, but the example of Gabriel being able to track the scent of fallen angels was at least met with a begrudging curiosity. He explained that Gabriel's senses had intensified since he had been healed and that he was no longer just a dog. Gabriel was special and was capable of amazing things.

The dog suddenly stopped short, sniffed the air, and reversed his direction. *"Almost lost it,"* he grumbled. *"Lots of other smells around here, but I can smell that cigar stink above them all."*

And with that final statement, the dog quickened his pace, Aaron almost jogging to keep up. At a closed door he began to bark, his tail wagging furiously.

"Good dog," Aaron said, patting his head and opening the door to allow the animal to confront his prey.

They were waiting, sitting around a circular table. Lehash and Lorelei smiled as Scholar scowled.

"There's our mighty bloodhound," the gunslinger said, reaching out to give the dog a pet.

Gabriel licked his hand. *"I'm not a bloodhound. I'm a Labrador retriever, and I found you very easily because of your stink."*

The constable jokingly sniffed beneath his arms. "Didn't think I was that ripe, but maybe I was mistaken."

"I'm not impressed," Scholar said, adjusting the cuffs on his starched white shirt. "Sure, he was able to find us in here, but I'm curious to see his level of success when taking on the whole world."

Gabriel walked around the table until he was standing in front of Scholar. He sat down at the fallen angel's feet, never taking his eyes from him. *"We'll never know until we try, will we?"* the dog said, his voice filled with far more insight than Aaron would have imagined.

"He's right," Lorelei said, trying to hide her amusement. "We've gotta at least let him try. What can it hurt?"

The scroll had been returned to its protective canister and Scholar tentatively reached for it. "I feel just as strongly about the presence of animals in my place of work as I do about cigar smoke."

Lehash rolled his eyes, folding his arms across his chest. "Just let the dog sniff the damn scroll."

Scholar carefully slid the piece of parchment out of the

tube and into his hand. Gabriel's head craned toward it, sniffing the air, and Scholar recoiled, pulling the scroll away.

"That's close enough," he snapped.

*"No, it isn't,"* Gabriel told him.

Aaron stepped forward, holding his hand out to Scholar. "Give it to me," he said firmly.

Scholar started to object, but Lehash shifted in his chair, his steely gaze intense. "You heard the boy," he drawled menacingly.

As if it was the hardest thing he ever had to do, Scholar placed the rolled parchment in the center of Aaron's hand. The Nephilim knelt down beside the dog and began to unroll the scroll.

*"That's much better,"* Gabriel said as Aaron placed it beneath his wet, pinkish nose. *"It smells very old."*

Aaron could feel Scholar's tension behind him as a bead of moisture began to form beneath one of Gabriel's nostrils, threatening to drip onto the priceless document.

"Easy there, Scholar," Lehash warned, "or you just might piss yerself."

*"I'm done,"* the dog said, and Aaron moved the scroll away just as the glob of moisture rolled from Gabriel's nose and dripped harmlessly to the floor.

"That wasn't so bad, was it?" Lorelei chided as Aaron handed the parchment back to Scholar.

The angel said nothing, quickly rolling the scroll up tightly and placing it back inside its protective container.

"Well?" Aaron asked for them all as he turned to Gabriel. The anticipation level in the room was extremely high. Much was riding on the dog, and Aaron wasn't quite sure how he would handle the situation should Gabriel fail. What would happen to Vilma then? He didn't want to think about that. Instead he focused on the Lab.

The dog ignored his question, getting up from where he sat and walking around the room in a circle, head bent back and sniffing the air.

"The anticipation is freaking killin' me, dog," Lehash growled, but Gabriel didn't pay him the least bit of attention as he continued to wander about the room.

Suddenly the dog let out an enormous sneeze, paused, and then sneezed again. *"I have it,"* he said, his voice flat, and Aaron was about to get excited when he noticed that the hackles had risen on the back of his friend's neck.

"What is it, Gabriel?" he questioned, kneeling beside the dog. "What's wrong?"

*"I know where the Malakim is."* The dog looked nervously about the room, his ears flat against his head. *"And it is someplace very strange."*

Katspiel did not know how much longer he had.

The magick had given him the information he so desperately sought, but now it demanded payment, and he no longer had the strength to hold it at bay. The forbidden was in him, moving about freely, completely unhindered, partaking of flesh and blood, bone and spirit—all that defined him.

He was an Archon, an angel endowed with the facility to wield the mystical arts of Heaven. Not all were seen fit to wear this mantle, only a few selected by the mighty Malakim. Katspiel was one such being, and over time he learned the protean nature of the power he would attempt to tame.

It was killing him now, but he was left with little choice. It was either die as the conjuring nibbled away at his life force, or be brutally killed by the displeased rage of Verchiel. Either way, Katspiel knew it was only a matter of time now before his life came to an end.

The Archon rose unsteadily to his feet upon the church altar, swaying in the darkness that had become his world since the magicks he sought to sunder, bound to the fallen angel Lucifer by the hand of God, lashed out and took away his eyes. He and his brethren should have stopped then, heeding the Creator's warning, stepping away from Verchiel's mad plan. But they had come to call the Powers leader "master," their existences inexorably intertwined, their fates becoming as one.

The location of the last Malakim burned in his mind, and Katspiel summoned his wings before it was too late. Enshrouding himself within their feathered embrace, he went to his master, all the while trying to imagine what the world would be like after the Word of God was undone and Lucifer's punishment was set loose upon the land. And as his wings opened in the school and he sensed that he was in the presence of Verchiel and the first of the fallen, Archon Katspiel realized that he was glad he would not be alive to experience it.

"Master Verchiel," he announced, hearing the sounds of an angelic being in the grip of torment, and the low, rumbling laugh of his master. "The last of the Malakim has been found," he managed, and slumped to the floor, the muscles beneath his decrepit flesh no longer capable of sustaining his weight.

"You have served me well, Katspiel," Verchiel said, an eerie calm in his voice, perfectly at ease with the horror his command would soon unleash. "And your loyalty shall be remembered long after the punishment is meted and order is restored to the heavens above and the earth below."

Oh yes, Katspiel was certain that the commander of the Powers was correct in that. He and his brothers would indeed be remembered for what they had done.

*Remembered in infamy.*

It nearly killed him to see her this way.

Aaron carefully sat down on the mattress beside Vilma. She had kicked away the light covers they had provided for her, writhing and moaning as if caught in the grip of a bad dream. Her breathing was shallow, and the golden manacles covering her wrists sparked and hummed as the power inside her tested the limits of angel magick. She had become more restless since

Gabriel had gone, but his canine friend was needed elsewhere if they were going to help her.

The girl let out a pathetic cry and thrashed her head upon the pillow. A single tear broke loose from the corner of one tightly closed eye and trailed down the side of her face. He felt a hitch of emotion become trapped painfully in his chest and reached out to take hold of one of her hands. It felt warm and dry in his, and Aaron tried with all his might to infuse some of his own strength into her.

"Hey," he whispered, not wanting to startle or scare her. "Just wanted to stop by and see you before I leave. But I'll be back as soon as I can. I promise."

He wasn't sure if she was even able to hear him, but it didn't matter. He needed to talk to her, needed to show himself why he was doing what he was about to do. If there was any doubt, he didn't recall it now.

"We're going to look for an angel—a Malakim, they're called—and I think he might be able to help you."

Vilma seemed a little calmer, and he liked to think that maybe it was because of his presence. Aaron knew it wasn't his fault, but he couldn't help feeling a certain amount of guilt. This wasn't what a beautiful, eighteen-year-old woman's life was supposed to be like. She should have been thinking about finals, graduation, and the prom, not about whether an angelic force from Heaven living inside her was going to cause her to go insane.

He rubbed his thumb gently across the back of her hand. "So I need you to hang on for me, to be strong, 'cause there's still a lot of things we need to talk about once you get better."

Vilma's life had been turned upside-down by her association with him. He felt like a kind of super virus, infecting anybody that got too close. *The casualty rate of the Aaron Corbet disease is pretty high,* he realized, thinking about all those who had died just for being part of his life: his foster parents, his psychologist, Stevie, Zeke, Camael, and Belphegor. Squeezing her hand tighter, Aaron decided that he wasn't going to let Vilma become part of that depressing statistic. He would rather die himself than have anything else bad happen to her.

Aaron released her hand, letting it gently fall to her side. He had to leave; the others would be waiting for him. He leaned forward, placing a tender kiss upon her forehead. "I'm so sorry for this," he whispered. "And I'm going to do everything that I can to make it up to you."

She offered no response and that was fine with him. Vilma seemed to be resting peacefully at the moment, and he took that as a sign for him to take his leave. Quietly he stood, his eyes never leaving her sleeping form, and backed away. He turned and just about jumped out of his skin when he saw that Lorelei was standing at the foot of stairs, her plastic makeup case, filled with angelic remedies, in hand. He hadn't heard her come down, and he put his hand against his chest to show that she nearly gave him a heart attack.

"Sorry," she whispered. "I didn't want to wake her."

Aaron looked back to the girl upon the mattress. "That's okay. She's sleeping pretty well now." He continued to stare at her, his heart aching.

"I don't want to state the obvious, Aaron," Lorelei said, "but you *do* know that this isn't your fault, right?"

He didn't answer, not fully believing that what she said was true.

"What's happening to Vilma would have occurred whether you were in the picture or not." She reached out and laid a supportive hand on his shoulder. "She's a Nephilim, Aaron, and you didn't make her that, no matter how guilty you feel."

He thought about all that Vilma had been through. "Verchiel used her to get at me. I should have—"

"Verchiel just made an already complicated situation a little more complicated," Lorelei interrupted. "No matter how rotten you think you are, Vilma's better off having you in her life than not. We all are."

He took his eyes from Vilma and looked at the Nephilim with the snow-white hair whom he had learned to trust as a friend and confidant. "Do you really think so?" he asked, the weight of his responsibilities feeling perhaps the tiniest bit more manageable.

She laughed softly and smiled at him. "I'm Lehash's daughter, for Pete's sake. I wouldn't say it if it weren't true."

He took it for what it was worth, and at that moment its value was quite high. "Thanks," Aaron said, turning back to

Vilma for one final glance. "Take good care of her until I get back, would ya?" he asked Lorelei as he started up the stairs.

"You just worry about finding the Malakim and getting what we need," Lorelei responded. "Right now Vilma should be the least of your worries."

And she was right, Aaron knew as he walked down the hallway and out the front door. They were waiting for him on the front walk, Gabriel wagging his tail as the boy pulled the door closed behind him and stepped off the porch.

"Ready?" Aaron asked, a nervous sensation forming in the pit of his stomach.

"I was ready about fifteen minutes ago," Lehash grumbled, finishing up the last of a cigar. "Now I'm just plum chompin' at the bit."

*"What's 'chompin' at the bit'?"* Gabriel asked the angel.

"Ants in my pants," he responded, flicking the smoldering remains of his cigar to the street.

*"You don't really have ants in your pants, do you?"* the dog asked, confused by this new expression. *"If you do, you should get them out before they bite you."*

"Thanks for the advice," Lehash snarled, not having the patience to explain to the animal any further.

Aaron decided that it was time and called upon the power that was his birthright. Flexing the muscles in his back, he eased his wings from beneath the flesh and opened them to their full, impressive span.

"Group hug," he said, surprised at his own attempt at levity. "Let's do this."

The gunslinging angel and dog huddled closer. And he took them within his wings' ebony embrace, departing Aerie on a mission most dire, the fate of the woman he loved hanging in the balance.

# CHAPTER TEN

"Hard day at the office?" Taylor asked.

Lucifer found himself back within his psyche. It was good to be away from the physical pain, even though he was beginning to feel an uncomfortable sensation in his chest. He wondered how long it would be before the pain found him, even this deep within the psychic landscape of his own fabrication.

They were sitting at a small kitchen table, very much like the one at which they had shared many a pleasant meal. And as in the past, this Taylor, this creation of Lucifer's fevered mind, had made a nice candlelit dinner.

The first of the fallen shuddered as the light of the twin candles illuminated a large door floating in the darkness around them. He studied the thick steel monstrosity created by his psyche to keep at bay the horrors of what he had done in Heaven. *Has it lost more of its padlocks and chains?* he worried.

He was sure it had.

"What, you're not going to answer my question?" Taylor asked as she picked up her napkin and placed it on her lap.

"I think Verchiel is succeeding," Lucifer said, eyeing the door. He could have sworn he heard movement on the other side. "He's found a way to undo the Word of God."

Taylor cut into her meal as she spoke: steak with mushrooms and thick, brown sauce. He loved mushrooms. "We can't allow him to do that." She primly placed a large piece of meat into her beautiful mouth, and he watched her chew as he considered his response. She was thin—dainty, really—but the girl could eat, and enjoyed doing so without the slightest hint of concern, he remembered fondly.

"No, we can't. But I don't know how long we'll be able to hold out." He knew the meal was only a fabrication of his thoughts, but it looked fabulous, and he dug in hungrily. "It's only a matter of time before he has everything he needs to set it free," he said, hearing another padlock fall.

Two glasses of red wine appeared on the table, and Lucifer watched Taylor pick hers up in a delicate hand and take a small sip. "Not that that isn't enough," she said, setting down her glass. "But is anything else bothering you?"

Something on the other side of the door pounded three times, and another lock clacked open to dangle uselessly from the end of a link of chain. "He told me that I sired a child. I have a son."

Taylor didn't respond; she simply cut another piece of meat. How could anything he said to her be a surprise? After all, she *was* a creation of his imagination.

"How did I not know this?" he asked, pushing his plate away, his appetite suddenly gone.

"Remember, there was time when you no longer wanted to be the Morningstar, when you attempted to abandon your true nature," Taylor responded as she picked up the napkin in her lap and dabbed at the corners of her mouth. She had cleaned her plate.

"It was when I was with you," Lucifer said. The door suddenly trembled, and he felt the vibrations of the assault as something hurled its weight against it.

Taylor smiled at him and nodded. "And you almost did forget," she said, crossing her long legs and letting the simple sandal she wore dangle from her foot. "We were happy—at least, I thought we were."

Lucifer felt a pain blossom in his chest and almost mistook it for God's Word coming undone, until he realized that it was the agony of his heart breaking yet again with the memory of leaving her. "I started to have dreams—about what I had done, the lives that were lost because of me—and I feared for your safety."

He stood and moved around the table toward her. She

rose to meet him and they gently embraced. "It was never my intention to hurt you," Lucifer said, holding her tightly. "But I was insane to think that I could ever experience happiness after what I'd done," he whispered. "My penance wasn't finished, so I *had* to leave, for your sake as well as mine."

The door shook upon its hinges and more locks fell as Taylor looked up into his eyes. "You've seen him, haven't you? Our child."

Lucifer remembered the vision he'd had soon after being captured by Verchiel and becoming aware of the Nephilim prophecy. It was the image of a young man, a big yellow dog faithfully at his side. "Yes," he answered dreamily. "I think I have."

"His name is Aaron," Taylor said, laying her head against his chest. "It means exalted—on high."

Lucifer smiled and kissed her gently on the top of her head.

And the door vibrated threateningly as the punishment of God raged upon the other side.

Aaron had always believed that he shared a special, almost psychic bond with Gabriel, and that had only been intensified after the emerging power of the Nephilim saved the dog's life. The boy was testing this theory as they traveled through the void between an angel's place of departure and its final destination. The two had already shared dreams, so Aaron figured sharing thoughts in the waking world wasn't all that farfetched.

As they left Aerie, he had asked the dog to think about

what he had seen while sniffing the ancient scroll and to direct those thoughts to him. It was an overwhelming experience. Aaron's mind was bombarded with Gabriel's thoughts. At first they were simple, dealing with base needs like food, shelter, warmth, and companionship. But then they became more complex: recollections of places, events, important moments in the Labrador's life. Aaron had never imagined how much a game of fetch at the park had meant to the dog, or having his stomach rubbed, or that piece of steak in the doggy bag from a fancy restaurant.

And Aaron saw himself through the eyes of his dog, and through those loving eyes he could do no wrong. If only he could be half the person the animal believed him to be, then he would be truly worthy of such adoration.

He was finally able to focus enough within the labyrinthine twists of Gabriel's thoughts to find what he needed. Here was where the scent from the scroll had brought them. It was a place unlike any other on Earth. In fact it wasn't on Earth at all, and he could see why the dog had been so spooked. Aaron took the image and made it his own—and he felt a hint of dizziness, like the descent from a great height in an elevator, before his wings opened to reveal their location.

"Would you look at that," Lehash said in awe.

"Are we in Heaven?" Aaron asked. He gazed with wonder over the rolling plains of golden grass, at the richest of royal blue skies. The gentle winds filled with soft, traipsing melodies were the most beautiful sounds he had ever heard.

"No," Lehash said, tilting his head back and sniffing the air. "Maybe a little piece of it, but not Heaven in its entirety."

*"The person who wrote the scroll is over that hill,"* Gabriel said from beside Aaron, his snout pointed into the breeze.

"Where do you think we are, Lehash?" Aaron asked as they turned and followed the Lab up a small hill.

"Looks to me like somebody built a little hideaway smack dab between the here and the there." The fallen angel removed his Stetson, combed back his long white hair with his fingers, and returned the hat to his head. "I'm surprised the dog was able to find it."

*"I'm very special,"* Gabriel reminded him.

"That you are," Lehash agreed, chuckling.

"I didn't expect anything like that," Aaron said suddenly. They had reached the top of the hill and he was pointing down toward a tiny cottage with dark brown shingles, tarpaper roof, and a rock foundation. Clouds of thick gray smoke billowed out of a stone chimney, and he had the impression that it was probably quite cozy on the inside.

"After all you've seen lately," Lehash said, leading them down the hill, "you can still be surprised?"

They stopped in front of the heavy wooden door.

*"He's in there,"* Gabriel assured them, his keen nose twitching as he sniffed the air.

"Should I knock?" Aaron asked the fallen angel beside him.

Lehash shrugged. "Can't hurt to be polite, I guess," he answered, and Aaron rapped his knuckles on the door.

They waited, and when no response came, the gunslinger leaned forward and added his own two cents. Still nobody answered.

"We don't have the time for this," Aaron said impatiently. He reached out, grasped the knob, and pushed the door open. It was very dark inside. "Hello?" he asked, his voice echoing strangely, and he quickly realized why. The room they entered was enormous, and he was reminded of Scholar's library, although the size and opulence of this room put the fallen angel's residence to shame.

"Son of a bitch," Lehash said, looking at the curved, hundred-foot ceiling and then the marble floor beneath their feet. "But then, what did I expect from a Malakim?"

Gabriel sniffed around the entrance, his claws sounding like tap shoes on the smooth stone floor, while Aaron admired the great stone pillars that flanked them on either side.

"How tall are these Malakim?" he asked, taking note of the gigantic double doors at the end of the hallway before them. The knockers, enormous lion heads holding thick metal rings, were at least thirty feet from the floor.

"They're extensions of God, fer cryin' out loud," the gunslinger growled. "They can be as tall as they like."

And as if on cue, the double doors were flung wide with a

thunderous clamor that caused the great hall to tremble, and a creature the likes of which Aaron had never seen or imagined came barreling down the hall toward them. It was at least fifty feet tall and wore armor that shimmered and bubbled as if forged from molten metal. Its head was that of a gigantic ram, and it had wings the color of a desert sunset. In its equally prodigious hands, it clutched a fearsome battle-ax that Aaron guessed was at least three times as big as him. They barely leaped away in time as the ax descended in a blurred arc to cleave the marble floor. Though it missed them, the aftershocks of the impact shook the floor beneath them as if they were in the grip of a major earthquake and they struggled to stay on their feet.

"I will not be caught as my brethren were," the great beast-man roared as he yanked his weapon from the broken marble and prepared to strike again. "The knowledge you wish to pilfer shall remain with me and me alone!"

"Stop!" Aaron begged moving toward the Malakim, hands outstretched. "We just want to—"

But Lehash had summoned his pistols of angelic fire, and as the beast turned to deal with this new threat, one of its mighty wings lashed out and swatted Aaron away. He saw a galaxy of stars as he landed upon the stone floor, fighting to stay conscious. Seeing his master down, Gabriel leaped at the fearsome giant, sinking his fangs into the molten metal of the creature's armor, only to let go with a cry of pain as his mouth began to smoke and smolder.

Lehash's guns roared to life and bullets of heavenly fire exploded upon the berserker's armor, miniature explosions across the surface of the sun, but to little effect. The monster spread its wings wide and soared at Lehash. The fallen angel continued to fire his weapons as the armored beast swung his ax, the flat of the blade catching the gunslinger and sending him rocketing through the air into one of the great pillars. The constable lay still upon the cold, stone floor among pieces of the broken pillar as the beast touched down in a crouch beside him. Tossing the mighty ax from one hand to the other, it lifted the weapon above its head with a bellow of rage and prepared to finish its fallen foe.

Aaron struggled to his feet, feeling the transformation of his body to a more fitting form for battle. He didn't want it to be this way. All he wanted was to ask for help, but they were beyond that now, and combat was the only answer. He propelled himself forward, landing between Lehash and the ax. He listened to the great blade whistle as it cut through the air, his own sword of heavenly flame igniting in his hand to meet it. The sigils burned upon his flesh and he felt his wings explode from his back as the two awesome blades connected with a clamorous peal, the explosive force of the two weapons meeting tossing them apart. Aaron's ears rang. Quickly he struggled to his feet, ready to meet the next assault from the armored monster.

But the beast simply stood, the great battle-ax lowered to

its side. It was staring at him, its cold animal gaze intensely scrutinizing. "It's you," it said, a strange smile briefly appearing upon its savage features.

"We don't mean you any harm," Aaron said carefully, and watched as the mass of the giant before him began to change, to diminish, the battle-ax fading away in a mellifluous flash of brilliance. No longer was there a fearsome warrior before him; it had been replaced by a tall, striking figure with silvery white hair and skin the color of copper.

"I am well aware of that . . . now," said the angelic being. "I am Raphael of the Malakim, and I beg your forgiveness." His voice was like the wind outside: melodic, strangely soothing. "I thought you to be servants of the renegade Verchiel, but of course you are not. There is no mistaking the sigils upon your body, son of the Morningstar."

Aaron allowed his weapon to dissipate. "You know about the whole Lucifer thing too, huh?" he asked as he walked over to check Gabriel. The dog's mouth was slightly blistered, but he appeared to be fine.

"The Malakim have known of your coming for a very long time," the angelic creature said simply, turning to walk back through the towering doorway. "In fact, we were responsible—my brothers and I—for providing the seer with the vision that described the prophecy of which you are such an important part."

Aaron watched the figure disappear into the room beyond

as he hurried to Lehash's side. The fallen angel was sitting up amidst the rubble of the damaged pillar, rubbing the back of his neck and wincing in discomfort.

"Did you hear him?" Aaron asked excitedly as he helped the gunslinger to his feet.

"Always was curious as to who got the ball rollin'," Lehash said, beating the dust from his clothing with his hat. "Makes sense it was them."

Raphael again appeared in the doorway. "Do hurry," he said, motioning with a delicate hand for them to join him. "We haven't much time, and there is still much to discuss." He disappeared again into the room beyond the enormous doors.

The three cautiously entered the room beyond the great hallway. Aaron couldn't believe his eyes—another bizarre example of angelic magick. From the regal majesty of the hall, to this: It was as if they had wandered into an old-fashioned parlor. The Malakim was sitting in the far corner at a small wooden desk, rummaging through one of the drawers. "Please, make yourselves at home," he said, busily searching for something.

"Impressive place you got here," Lehash said, looking about the room. The decor was warm and rich: lots of dark wood, and long velvet curtains that covered two sets of windows, the thick, red material draping down to the polished hardwood floor.

Gabriel hopped up on a sofa, upholstered in the crimson material and framed in shiny, dark wood.

"Gabriel, get down!" Aaron ordered automatically.

*"But he said to get comfortable,"* the dog protested as he slowly slunk from his place upon the furniture.

"That's quite all right," the Malakim said, shutting the drawer and rising to approach them. "That's what our little hideaway has always been about," he said, lifting his robed arms and gesturing about the room. "A place for my brethren and I to get away from our duties, to relax and ponder what we have seen."

Gabriel lay down upon an embroidered area rug and with a heavy sigh placed his snout between his paws and closed his eyes. No matter where they were or what they were doing, that animal could always find the time to steal a little nap.

"Please, sit, relax. Use this place as it is supposed to be used."

Lehash politely removed his hat, and he and Aaron sat down upon the sofa vacated by Gabriel. The Malakim chose a leather chair across from them.

Aaron leaned forward tentatively. "You said something about your brothers and Verchiel?"

The Malakim nodded and lay his head against the back of the chair. "He killed them both, taking from them knowledge that is not meant for an angel of his caste."

Lehash appeared stunned. "Verchiel killed two a' you?" he

asked incredulously. "He actually killed two Malakim? How is that even possible?"

The bronze-skinned creature closed his eyes, his face twisting in pain as he recounted the tale. "They took us by surprise, using powerful magicks that we ourselves taught the mages in his service."

For a moment the room was uncomfortably silent; Gabriel's heavy breathing was the only sound.

Raphael continued, smiling sadly as he opened his eyes. "With our ability to glimpse the future, you would think we should have been able to prepare for this. But then, maybe because it was inevitable, subconsciously we chose not to see it."

Aaron squirmed in his seat, images of Vilma in the throws of painful transformation filling his head. He was torn by the reason he had come on this mission and by what Verchiel was up to. Although his loyalty was to Vilma, he found it extremely disconcerting to learn that both he and the Powers commander seemed to be searching for the same thing.

"What does he want?" Aaron asked curiously. "What is he trying to take from you?"

The Malakim shifted in his chair and crossed his long legs. "At first I had no idea, but now it makes perfect sense." He reached inside the folds of his robe and brought forth a vial of glass, its ends sealed with ornate golden metal. Aaron could see that there was liquid inside as the Malakim passed it to him.

"Before our time is up, however, this is for your mate," he said as Aaron took the offering.

Aaron blinked repeatedly, unsure if he had heard the angel correctly. "Mate?" he asked.

Raphael nodded as he sat back in his seat. "Yes, your mate. And may I be the first to say that your children will be absolutely magnificent."

Fifty thousand volts of electricity could have passed through Aaron's chair and it would have had pretty much the same effect upon him.

"My children?" he yelped, shocked by the Malakim's words.

Gabriel sat up suddenly, awakened by his master's exclamation. *"What's happening?"* the dog questioned in a grumbling bark, looking about the room. *"What's going on?"*

"I think your master just got a little peek at the future," Lehash said, amusement in his gruff voice. He reached down and patted the dog's head. "That's all."

*"No,"* Gabriel said emphatically. *"Can't you hear it?"* he asked, his nose twitching, hackles of fur rising around his neck. The dog rose, his body trembling in anticipation.

The Malakim sighed, standing from his chair. "It all seems so brief," he said sadly, brushing the wrinkles from the front of his robe, "when finally confronted with your inevitable demise."

Aaron was about to ask for an explanation when he heard it as well. He knew the sound; it was the noise made when an angel traveled from one place to another, implosions of sound as the fabric of reality was torn open for a brief instant and allowed to flow shut. Only this time he heard it multiple times, and understood exactly what it meant.

"We're under attack," he blurted out as winged shapes exploded into the room from beneath the velvet curtains in a shower of glass and fire.

"No kidding," Lehash growled. His pistols flashed to life in his grasp and he began to fire.

The sigils had risen upon Aaron's flesh and an idea for a weapon had entered his thoughts, when he felt a powerful grip upon his arm. He turned to confront Raphael, who was shaking his head.

"You are to leave here now," he said above the roar of Lehash's guns and Gabriel's frantic barks.

Aaron started to protest, but the look upon the angelic sorcerer's face rendered him speechless. "There is nothing you can do for me now. Return to Aerie, help your mate, and meet your own destiny," the Malakim ordered.

Aaron chanced another look at his friends. The Powers soldiers had momentarily stopped their charge through the windows, but Gabriel and Lehash stood at the ready, just in case. *The calm before the storm.*

"Take your friends and go," Raphael told him.

And though it pained Aaron to leave the heavenly being, he knew that things far larger than him were at work here. "C'mon.

We have to go," he called to his friends as the black wings that would take them back to Aerie emerged from his back.

The Malakim bowed his head to Lehash and Gabriel as they passed him, his body already changing, his gentle features becoming more animal, the molten armor again appearing on his expanding form.

Aaron was about to take his companions into his winged embrace when the wall of the room exploded inward and more Powers soldiers surged in. Raphael met the attack with unbridled fury, Powers soldiers dying beneath the bite of his monstrous ax.

And then Aaron saw him, the focal point of the young Nephilim's rage, portions of his body not covered in armor wrapped in bandages stained with gore. Verchiel entered the room behind his troops, spear of fire clutched in his hands, tattered wings beating the air as he searched for his chosen prey. Aaron knew he should have left then, but he hesitated, held in place by his hatred for the leader of the Powers host.

The Malakim turned, as if sensing that they had not yet gone. "Go," he bellowed in a voice like the roar of a jungle cat. "It is not time for the final conflict. Go!"

And as Aaron closed his wings, he witnessed the most horrible of sights: The Powers swarmed upon Raphael, cutting down the Malakim in a senseless flurry of savagery. Verchiel strode past the violence, fixated upon the Nephilim.

"Leave!" Aaron heard the last of the magickal trinity cry

out from beneath the angelic swarm. He finally did as he was told, taking his companions within his wings' embrace.

"Not this time," Verchiel screeched, letting fly the javelin of fire with all his blistering rage and fury behind it.

Aaron wished them back to Aerie.

But the angel's spear was faster.

# CHAPTER ELEVEN

Kraus awoke curled beneath a tattered blanket on the floor, a scream of terror upon his lips.

For a moment he thought the darkness had claimed him again, that perhaps Verchiel had taken back his wonderful gift, but then realized that it was only the night collected around him. Empty bookcases and stacked metal desks emerged from the gloom as his new sight adjusted to the inky black of nighttime.

He had been dreaming, vividly recalling a time before his service to his lord and master, Verchiel. A time of woe and suffering.

Tossing back his blanket, he climbed to his feet and stood in the darkness of the room. Something was wrong; he could sense it. There was an unnatural hum, a pulsing throb like the beat of some prehistoric monster's heart in the air around him.

The sound was everywhere—it *needed* to be everywhere—and he felt the desperation of it worming inside him, bringing forth further memories of the dark times before he swore his fidelity to God's warrior and his holy mission.

Kraus left the room, seeking to escape the recollections of his early days of torment, to distract himself elsewhere, but the alien thrum was with him, no matter where he went, rousing memories of a past long suppressed.

Before serving the Powers, all he had known was darkness and pain, the pity and the disdain of the sighted. He had been raised in a place very much like this one, very much like the Saint Athanasius Church and Orphanage had been before its doors were closed.

The Perry School for the Blind. It was the only home he had ever known.

Kraus moved down the darkened corridors, riding the intensifying waves of unease. He could not keep the past at bay; the memories escaped, bursting up from layers of time, as vivid as if they had occurred only moments before.

There had been others like him at the Perry School, born without sight, given up to those who cared for the less fortunate. And care they did. Oh yes, he remembered their care indeed.

Kraus approached an open door and a staircase that led down into deeper darkness. The feeling was stronger here, and he descended, drawn toward the wellspring of despair, all the while remembering.

The staff at the school for the blind treated them as lesser life forms, below even the ferocious dog kept by Mr. Albert Dentworth, the head administrator. Kraus relived the terror that would grip him every time he heard the rattling of the animal's chained collar and its nails clicking and clacking on the hardwood floors as it drew closer. They were nothing but burdens to the world and to the personnel whose job it was to care for them, and were often told as much. For the majority of his existence he lived in Hell, and every night he prayed to be brought to Heaven.

The stairway took him to the gymnasium and into the lair of the Archons. At the moment, they were gone, off with Verchiel on his latest incursion. An intricate, mystical circle had been drawn upon the floor with what looked like dirt, and above it, from thick chains, the prisoner hung. A deep, vertical gash had been cut from the prisoner's chest to his stomach, the wound held open with metal clamps, and Kraus wondered how it was even possible that the prisoner still lived.

As a child, his every waking moment, and before going to sleep at night—exhausted from chores that left his fingers stiff and bleeding—Kraus had prayed for God to take him away. He didn't think himself more deserving than any of the others who lived beneath the roof of the Perry School, it was just that he'd had his fill and wanted it to stop. He couldn't live like that any longer, and each night he begged the merciful Creator to end his life.

The first of the fallen moaned pitifully, and a strange, red-colored cloud puffed from his open chest to be trapped within the confines of the mystical circle beneath. Kraus found himself driven back by an overwhelming sense of desolation that suddenly permeated the atmosphere. He had found the source of his waking malaise, and whatever it was, it came from within the body of the fallen angel Lucifer.

Kraus heard the angel that he would later call his master, as he had those many years ago—Verchiel, whispering in his ear, telling him he had been sent by God, and that because of his fervent prayers, he had been chosen to aid the soldiers of the Lord in the most important of missions.

Kraus remembered the incredible joy, the sheer euphoria of knowing that God had heard his pleas, but at the time he had been filled with great sorrow. He knew that only he would know this happiness, and those brothers and sisters in darkness with whom he had shared the hell of the Perry School would continue to know only suffering. How could he do the work of God, knowing that others like himself still suffered?

And the angel Verchiel had offered him a solution. *"You can end their suffering,"* he had said. *"All you need do is command me, for this will be my payment to you, for the fealty you will swear to me. All you need do is ask."*

So Kraus had begged the messenger of Heaven to release the others of the Perry School from their lives of suffering and sorrow.

And Verchiel had obliged.

The memory of that night drove Kraus to his knees. He was trembling, awash in the raw, unconstrained emotions of that moment long ago. Whatever was leaking from the body of Lucifer, it was quite proficient in dredging up the echoes of the past.

Kraus recalled the night he was reborn as a servant of the Powers, pulled from the relative warmth of the school into the heights of the cold night sky, the sound of Verchiel's beating wings almost deafening. And he heard the cries of other heavenly creatures around him as he was carried higher and higher.

*"They shall know suffering no longer,"* the angel who would be his master had roared, and the sky around them rumbled as if in agreement. The flash of lightning that followed somehow permeated the darkness that was his existence. He remembered the searing white light and the roar of thunder that shook the air.

Kraus gulped for air, his body sliding down the cool concrete of the gymnasium wall. The memories were unmerciful, his senses raw. Somehow he could feel the lightning strikes upon the school, the smell of it as it burned filling his nostrils, the cries of those trapped within filling his ears.

He had always told himself that it was for the best. The students of the Perry School had been freed from a pathetic existence; he truly believed that. But lately he had begun to see things more clearly, and was filled with horror. Since Verchiel's gift to him, his perceptions were slowly changing, revealing the ugly reality of it all.

The air around him shimmered and quaked, and Kraus knew that his master had returned, but he did not feel joy as he would have in the past, only apprehension.

The angels appeared before him. There were fewer Powers soldiers, and those who remained mere shadows of their once glorious selves. They appeared haunted, the armor they wore hanging loosely upon their diminished frames.

And then there was Verchiel, the sight of him filling the healer with a strange mixture of sadness and fear. His once golden chest plate was tarnished almost black with the blood of his prey, and the freshly opened wounds continued to weep, saturating the bandages the healer had used to dress them.

Verchiel fell to his knees before the mystic circle. "The time is nigh," he said, and the remaining Archons scurried about their preparations.

*But for what?* Kraus wondered, an overwhelming feeling of dread reaching down to the depths of his soul. He wanted to ask the angel that was his lord and master, but he feared what the answer would be.

Aaron thought it had missed him.

He had hesitated for only a moment as he struggled with the idea that he could finally put this madness to rest once and for all. But the look upon the Malakim's face—the intensity in his dark, soulful gaze—had told him that he should leave, that perhaps a being that had lived for millions of years might have a better idea of the big picture than he did.

He honestly believed that Verchiel's spear of fire had passed harmlessly through the air where he and his friends had been standing moments before, confident his new abilities were far superior to the fiery weapon of the Powers commander. Aaron remembered closing his wings, hugging Lehash and Gabriel tightly against him and thinking of Aerie—seeing it as clear as day in his head. They had gotten away, free and clear.

Or so he thought.

With deadly accuracy, the spear made from the fires of Heaven had found its target.

He had made it back to Aerie, unfurling his wings and releasing his friends, before falling to his knees. Aaron couldn't seem to catch his breath, his body strangely numb, but he could hear everything they were saying. Lorelei was there, demanding to know what had happened as she knelt over him in the street. Lehash was close by, explaining the attack upon the Malakim's lair.

Aaron guessed that Lorelei was using some kind of magick on him, for he could feel her hands upon his chest probing at where *he imagined* the spear had nailed him. It really didn't hurt too badly; in fact he didn't feel much pain at all. *Maybe I'm just tired from all the running around,* he thought.

Gabriel was with him, nervously panting in his ear. Aaron

wanted to tell his friend that everything was going to be all right, that he was fine, but for some reason he couldn't talk.

Everyone around him seemed to be in a panic.

*Maybe I should be worried,* he thought, but then dismissed it as foolish. He was fine; they would have him fixed up in no time.

They were carrying him now, bringing him to Lorelei's house. That was good, he thought as a heavy fatigue closed in around him. All he needed was some rest, and then he would be fine.

*All he needed was rest.*


*"He looks dead,"* Gabriel said flatly, sitting beside his master's bed. He had been by Aaron's side since they'd returned from their mission, scrutinizing every twitch, every movement—of which there was very little. This worried the dog, for Aaron was a very restless sleeper, and to see him lying so still was greatly disturbing.

"But he's not," Lorelei said, reaching down to scratch behind the dog's ear.

Gabriel moved his head away, too distracted for the affection of others. *"I know he's not dead,"* he replied, his eyes never leaving Aaron. *"Believe me, I'd know. I'm a dog; I'd smell it. Death has a very strong smell."*

They both fell silent. Lorelei leaned over to check Aaron's bandage as Gabriel watched closely. There had been very little blood, the intense heat of the spearhead cauterizing the wound almost instantly. She had put something on the injury, something that smelled very strange, very bitter. She had told him that it was an old medicine made from a root of the Tree of Knowledge, from a place called Eden. Gabriel didn't care for its scent—it made him sneeze and his eyes water—but if it was going to help Aaron, it was fine with him.

Vilma, on the other hand, was doing much better. The contents of the vial that Raphael had given Aaron seemed to be exactly what the girl had needed. The angelic essence had calmed almost immediately, and it appeared that she was going to be all right.

Gabriel was suddenly frustrated. He loved Vilma very much and certainly did not want anything bad to happen to her. But if she got well and Aaron didn't, how would he feel toward her then? The dog pushed the thoughts aside, returning his attentions to his master.

*"When will we know if he'll live?"* Gabriel asked Lorelei as she continued to examine Aaron's wound.

The Nephilim gently replaced the bandage and moved away. "He's comfortable," she said with a slight shrug of her shoulders. "I'm keeping the wound clean to prevent any infection."

*"But when will we know?"* the dog barked, his demeanor far angrier than he had intended. He lowered his head, ashamed, his ears going flat against his blocky skull. *"I'm sorry I barked,"* he apologized. *"I'm just worried."*

"It's all right," Lorelei said with understanding, reaching to stroke his head again. This time he didn't pull away. "We've done all we can do."

*"So we have to wait?"* Gabriel turned to her as she continued to pet the short, velvety fur atop his head.

Lorelei nodded. "Afraid so."

He went back to watching Aaron, the very faint rise and fall of his chest, wishing with all his might for him to be well again.

"I'm going to go grab something to eat," Lorelei said. "Would you like to come with me?"

*"No, thank you. I think I'll just stay here with him."* Gabriel slowly lowered his face to rest his chin upon the bed near Aaron's frighteningly still hand. *"I'm not feeling very hungry."*

The door that held back the outcome of the Morningstar's hellish folly shook violently on its psychic hinges.

It wanted out.

The great vault door moaned as it slowly began to bulge outward. All that remained was the steel itself: the locks, bolts, and chains, all broken by the fury of the maelstrom railing behind it.

Lucifer was alone now. Taylor was gone. She had left him when the pain in his chest had become too great, as if she couldn't bear to see what was going to happen.

*No,* he thought, on his knees before the psychic blockade. *I can't let it out.*

He concentrated upon the battered door and saw that

there were new locks, sliding bolts, and thick black chains, all strong—or stronger than what had been there before.

*Hell will not be released this day*, the first of the fallen angels told himself, finding the strength to climb to his feet before the obstacle that separated the world from holocaust. All the pain, misery, and sorrow that he was responsible for would stay within him, where it belonged, where it had been placed. He'd always found it strangely amusing that the punishment given unto him by God had somehow managed to become a thing of legend in the human world—an actual place of eternal damnation for those who sinned against their chosen religious faith. Gehenna, Sheol, Ti Yu, Jahannam, Hades, Hell—so many names for what was his and his alone to bear.

The force upon the other side intensified, and he was hurled backward by the savagery of its furor. His new, stronger restraints were ripped away, tossed into the darkness, ineffective against the relentless onslaught delivered against the psychic representation of God's Word.

The Morningstar crawled to his feet, trying again to reinforce the barrier, but the sharp, biting agony in his chest drove him to his knees. He looked down and saw the wound. A bloody, twelve-inch gash had appeared there, and the sight of it filled him with trepidation. He was growing weaker, his strength draining from the vertical opening carved in his center.

The door shuddered and vibrated within its frame, and Lucifer watched in mute horror as the top right corner started to bend outward, the steel moaning and squealing its objection.

"Please, God, no," Lucifer hissed, throwing himself at the door, pressing his body against it. The pain, guilt, and sorrow of what his jealousy caused had grown stronger through the millennia, and he had always found the strength to keep it at bay within himself, for this was his designated burden. Now he tried with all his might to will that barrier stronger, to add his mental strength to God's original penance, but could feel the awful vibrations of an unstoppable force through the many inches of what should have been super-strong metal.

From the twisted corner he first saw it, a tendril of luminescent vapor. Lucifer knew this thing intimately. It had been a part of him for what seemed like forever, fused to his angelic essence since his fall from grace. He knew its rage, its sorrow, and its infinite cruelty, and despaired for the fate of God's world if it were allowed to be free.

"Don't let this happen," he prayed, his faced pressed against the trembling metal, and he was glad that Taylor, even though a creation of his mind, was no longer there to witness his horrendous failure. "Please," he begged as the door buckled and the metal twisted. And he had just about given up all hope of stopping the deluge of Hell from flooding the world.

When there came a voice.

"Looks like you could use a hand here," it said, and Lucifer turned to gaze into the face of salvation.

It was a nice face—with *his* eyes.

# CHAPTER TWELVE

Verchiel listened intently to the powerful arcane words stolen from the minds of the Malakim as they spilled from the lips of the Archon faithful. *It is only a matter of time,* the Powers commander thought, amused that he was actually even aware of time's passage. He had existed since the dawn of creation and had never really given the concept much thought, until now.

The three remaining Archon magicians stood within the mystical circle beneath the suspended form of Verchiel's prisoner, his instrument of retribution. Everything was proceeding smoothly, the pieces of his mechanism for vengeance falling ideally into place, almost as if it were meant to be. *As if He knows that He must be punished for what He has allowed to transpire.*

The Archons droned on, the pilfered knowledge of the

Malakim helping to unravel the edict of God. Lucifer moaned in the grip of unconsciousness as the magickal obstructions holding back his punishment were methodically peeled away. The first of the fallen angels was fighting them, but Verchiel would have expected no less from one that had been the Creator's most beloved—and greatest disappointment.

The Powers leader stepped closer to the arcane ritual, careful not to open his own wounds that had finally stopped bleeding. "Give in, Morningstar," he urged the fallen angel. "Accept your responsibility, not only for the fall of Heaven, but now for the ruin of mankind as well."

He strolled around the mystical circle, around his despised adversary, the one whose corruption had acted as a cancer, eating away at Verchiel's holy mission—at everything that defined his purpose in The Most Holy's blessed scheme of things. "The pain you must have experienced these countless millennia, my brother," Verchiel cooed. "Now you have a chance to be free of it—to let your punishment be shared by all who have sinned."

Lucifer thrashed in his chains, droplets of perspiration raining from his abused body to be absorbed by the soil of Heaven that comprised the magickal circle below him. His mouth trembled as he strained to speak.

"What is it, brother?" Verchiel asked in a soft whisper. He leaned closer, eager to hear his prisoner voice his agony, perhaps even a plea for mercy. "Speak to me. Share with me your woes."

The fallen angel spoke. It was but two words, and spoken

so softly that the leader of the Powers was not quite sure that he had heard it correctly.

"What was that again, Lucifer Morningstar?" Verchiel asked, leaning even closer to the first of the fallen's cracked and trembling lips.

"Thank you."

Verchiel recoiled as if struck. *Is this some kind of perverse game the criminal is playing?* he wondered. *Some bizarre way to show his strength? His superiority? It is all for naught if that be the case.*

"You thank me for this, monster?" he raged, feeling his own wounds begin to weep again. "For the torment you now endure?" His voice trembled with fury.

Lucifer was struggling to remain conscious, his eyes slowly rolling back in his head as the lids gradually began to fall.

"Tell me!" Verchiel shrieked, reaching in to the confines of the magickal circle to grab the fallen angel by his short, curly hair and yank his head toward him.

Lucifer's eyes snapped wide and a demented grin bloomed upon his tormented features.

"Tell me," Verchiel hissed again.

"If not for this . . . for you," the Morningstar whispered, "I would never have met my son."

The mouse's stomach ached from hunger. It had not foraged for food since its friend had been brought here to this room. It couldn't, not while the man was being tormented so.

In the shadows the mouse cowered, afraid to move. There was something in the air here, something unnatural that made its tiny heart flutter like a moth attempting to escape the spider's web. Every one of its primitive instincts screamed for it to run, that here was certain death. But it remained—afraid to abandon the one who had befriended it. Loyal to a fault.

They were hurting its friend again. The mouse did not want to watch, but could not tear its eyes away. It yearned to do something, anything to help the one who had shown it such friendship, but its tiny mind could not even begin to fathom what that something might be. It did not have the size or ferocity to frighten the larger, more powerful creatures, or the strength in its jaws to gnaw upon the thick metal chains. So it cowered in the shadows, watching and afraid.

Too small to matter.

Aaron wasn't sure what he expected of the fallen angel that was his father. He was *Lucifer*, after all, and all kinds of crazy stuff had passed through his mind: red skin, pencil-thin mustache, goatee, cloven hooves, horns, pointed tail, pitchfork. He was curious but never expected the answers to be imminent.

He knew that he was unconscious, in some dark, inner place, alone, or so he had believed. He had wandered through the shadows for quite some time, descending deeper and deeper into the inner world of darkness, until he heard the cries for help.

*"Please, God, no."*

Instinctively Aaron moved toward the sound of the plaintive voice, cutting through the ocean of black.

*"Don't allow this to happen."*

In the distance he saw a man standing before an enormous metal door, pressing himself against its surface, as if trying to keep it from opening.

*"Please,"* the stranger begged as something pounded and railed upon the other side.

Aaron felt compelled to help the man and tentatively approached. But as the man turned to face him, a smile that could only be described as euphoric spread across his handsome yet strained features. And in that moment Aaron knew this stranger's identity.

This was Lucifer Morningstar, the first of the fallen.

*His father.*

"I'm not sure how long he can hold out," Aaron muttered, opening his eyes and gazing up at the cracked and stained ceiling of the bedroom where he had been staying since coming to Aerie.

*"You're awake,"* Gabriel said over and over again, licking his face, head, ears, and hands with abandon. *"You're awake. You're awake. You're awake."*

He wasn't sure how long he'd been unconscious. Gabriel's affection could not be used as an accurate guage. There were days Aaron had gone out to get something from his car and been met with the same kind of exuberant greetings, as if he had not seen the Lab in months.

Aaron pulled the dog's face away from his, scratching him behind the ears. "Hey, fella," he said. "Nice to see you, too. How long was I out?"

"About two days," answered a voice as the bedroom door opened and Lorelei walked in carrying a tray loaded with medical supplies. She placed the tray atop the dresser and retrieved a bottle of antiseptic, bandages, some cotton balls, and a roll of tape.

*"I thought it was at least a week,"* Gabriel said as he lay down beside his master, rump pressed tightly against Aaron's side.

"It really is true what they say about animals having no concept of time," Lorelei said, sitting on the bed and carefully peeling the bandage from his bare chest.

"He has a tendency to exaggerate," Aaron said. "Will I live?"

"It was touch and go there for a while," she said honestly, examining the wound. "But it seems that you've healed up pretty well." She dabbed at the still-tender puncture in his chest with a cotton ball soaked in antiseptic. "Lehash told us what you did, hanging around a bit too long after the shit hit the fan. Very stupid, Aaron Corbet. If you're not careful, they'll revoke your savior's license." She placed a new bandage over the wound and taped it down.

"How's Vilma?" he asked, throwing off the thin sheet that covered him, starting to rise from the bed.

"Hey," the female Nephilim protested. "She's resting comfortably, which is exactly what you should be doing." She halfheartedly tried to push him back, but had little success.

Aaron felt a bit weak and dizzy, and placed his hand against the wall to steady himself. "There's no time for that," he said, waiting for the room to settle. "I'm not sure how much longer he can hold out." He moved to his duffel bag to dig out a new shirt.

*"You said that before."* Gabriel was still lying on the bed. *"Who are you talking about?"*

Aaron slipped a red T-shirt over his head and gently pulled it down over his chest, so as not to disturb the bandage. "While I was out, I went someplace," he said, putting on his socks and sneakers. "Inside here," his hands fluttered around the sides of his head before beginning to tie his sneakers. "And I met my father—I met Lucifer."

"You met the Morningstar?" Lorelei asked in shock.

Gabriel bounded from the bed to join Aaron by the door. *"Was he nice?"* he asked, tail wagging.

"I met him, and now I know what Verchiel is up to," Aaron said, leaving the bedroom. "And it's pretty horrible."

"Are you up for this, Aaron?" Lorelei asked as she followed him to the front door. "You almost died, and here you are running off again."

He stopped and stared at her, not really sure what to say.

"There's an awful lot riding on you and—"

"And none of it will matter if Verchiel has his way," Aaron interrupted.

Lorelei looked as though she might protest, but clearly thought better of it. "Promise me you'll be careful," she said instead.

"I'll be careful."

The woman nodded. "Good. You're the first savior I've ever had for a friend, and I'd hate to have to find another."

# CHAPTER THIRTEEN

It had been a good visit.

Lucifer only wished that they could have done something a bit more pleasant, a few drinks perhaps, a nice dinner, conversation that went well into the wee hours of the morning. Holding back Hell was not the activity he would have chosen for his first meeting with his son.

*He seems like a good kid,* Lucifer mused. Eager to help, and he had his father's eyes, but there really wasn't much he could do about the Morningstar's current situation. He had only helped to delay the inevitable for a little while longer.

Things were bad. Vechiel's magicians had almost succeed in breaking down all his remaining barriers, and the pain was becoming unbearable. Lucifer hadn't wanted his son to see him this way, so he had sent him away, urging him to put his strength to use elsewhere, for his was a lost cause.

But deep down, the first fallen angel didn't want to believe that was completely true. The prophecy of forgiveness had come to fruition because of him, because he had hoped that someday the Lord God would understand how sorry he was and give him the chance to apologize.

Unfortunately Verchiel would do everything in his power to make certain that Lucifer never had the chance to utter those words of atonement, and would make him responsible for yet another heinous crime against God and what He holds most dear. The leader of the Powers didn't believe that Lucifer had the right to be forgiven, and there were days when he believed that Verchiel could very well be right. But it wasn't up to them to decide. God would forgive, or He wouldn't. It was simple as that—or at least it used to be.

Fight as he did, Lucifer knew he could not keep the door closed for much longer. Hell raged at his back, the pain at the core of his being, methodically peeled away like the multiple layers of an onion.

The Morningstar was ashamed, believing that he should have been stronger, able to restrain that which had been such a crucial part of him for so long. Hell had come to define him, showing what his petty jealousy and arrogance had been responsible for.

In the world of inner darkness it sounded like gunfire as the first thick metal hinge exploded from the vault door. It was followed by a second, and as he pressed his back flat against the cold surface of the door, he felt it shift within its frame. *It won't be long now,* Lucifer knew. The gaseous discharge of the accumulated misery on the other side wafted up around him.

It made him see it all again, experience it as though it were happening. It was Hell incarnate.

"I'm so sorry," he cried aloud as the door fell, trapping him beneath its tremendous weight.

And that which came to be known as Hell surged out from within him, a geyser of rage, pain, sadness, and misery garnered from the most horrible event ever to befall the kingdom of God.

*"So sorry."*

*She looks much better,* Aaron thought, watching Vilma as she slept peacefully. Silently he thanked the Malakim for what he had done for her—for him—and swore that Verchiel would be made to pay for his crimes.

He reached down and pulled the blanket up over the girl. It was damp in the basement, and she had enough problems without catching a cold to boot.

*"She's much better, thanks to you,"* Gabriel said from nearby.

Aaron couldn't stop watching her.

*"You love her, don't you?"*

Aaron's first impulse was to deny it; he'd never admitted it out loud before. But the fact was he did love Vilma Santiago, and as he watched her sleep, he couldn't imagine his life without her. Aaron remembered the Archon's words about his mate, and the beautiful children they would have together. Vilma was part of his future. He just hoped she wanted him to be a part of hers.

"Yep, I guess I do," he finally responded. He looked at the dog that was lying on the concrete floor not far from the foot of the mattress. "Is that cool with you?"

Gabriel was staring at Vilma as well, and Aaron could feel the emotion emanating from the Labrador's dark, soulful eyes. *"It's cool,"* he said, blinking slowly. *"She'll be good for our pack."*

Aaron smiled. "Won't she though?" he agreed, rising from her side.

*"Do you have to go?"* the Labrador asked, climbing to his feet as well.

Aaron nodded, knowing his options were few and time was growing slim. His father had been weakening, and who knew what kind of power Verchiel now had at his disposal. If what Lucifer told him was true, the leader of the Powers wasn't just gunning for Nephilim and fallen angels anymore; he had a score to settle with the whole planet.

"This is it, Gabe," he told the animal. "Verchiel is going down for good this time."

"My sentiments exactly," Lehash said as he walked down the stairs toward them, Scholar close behind.

Aaron had been waiting for them to arrive, certain that Lorelei would have gone to them as soon as he'd revealed his intentions.

Scholar looked pale as he maneuvered around Lehash. "Lorelei told us what you learned," he said, a tremble in his voice. "Verchiel has lost it completely. It was bad enough that he wanted *us* dead, but to intentionally unleash that kind of force upon the earth . . ." The fallen angel stopped, speechless for the first time that Aaron could recall.

Lehash's pistols flared to life in his grasp and he spun them on his fingers in true cowboy fashion. "Never met a son of a bitch that deserved two in the brain pan more," he proclaimed.

Vilma stirred at the sound of their voices, rolling onto her side before returning to the embrace of healing slumber.

"I'm doing this alone," Aaron said softly.

Lehash's heavenly weapons dispersed in a flash. "Must be the acoustics down here," the gunslinger said, sticking a finger in his ear and wiggling it around. "But I'd swear you just said you were going to face Verchiel alone."

Aaron nodded. "That's what I said."

Lehash scowled and Aaron prepared for the onslaught that he knew would be coming. "You're not going anywhere alone, boy," he snarled. "Look at you," the cowboy said, throwing out one black-gloved hand toward him. "Yer lucky you can stand, for pity's sake. You just got stuck with a spear—and almost died! This ringing any bells?"

Aaron's hand instinctively went to the bandage on his chest. The wound was still painful, but he was healing quickly, another perk of being a Nephilim. "It's not that I don't want your help. In fact nothing would make me feel safer than to have you guys at my side when this finally goes down."

Lehash studied him, slowly folding his arms across his chest while Scholar simply stared.

"But I've come to realize that I have to do this alone."

Lehash shook his head. "It ain't true," he grumbled.

"It is," Aaron answered. "This has been about me from the start. Verchiel lost it because of the prophecy." He pointed to himself. "I'm that prophecy, I'm the physical manifestation of all that he hates. It's got to be me that takes him down."

*"He almost killed you, Aaron,"* Gabriel said, his gruff animal voice filled with concern.

"Key word being 'almost,'" Aaron responded. "I wasn't ready before. I didn't understand what all this angel stuff was about. But I do now. I know how much is at stake. It's not just fallen angels and Nephilim that are in danger. It's the entire world."

Lehash rubbed his hand across the rough skin of his face. "He won't go down easy. An animal's at its most dangerous when its back is up against the wall."

*"He's right about that,"* Gabriel said, fortifying the gun-slinger's words.

"Believe me, I know that I could very well be killed, but I also know that it's for me to do, and me alone. *I've* got to be the one who ends this."

The room became very still, the only sound Vilma's gentle breathing as she slept.

"'And the one shall come that will bring about the end of their pain, his furious struggle building a bridge between the penitent and what has been lost,'" Scholar said, his stare vacant, as if he were looking beyond the room, perhaps into the future. "That's a line from the prophecy," he said, his eyes focused on them again. "Your prophecy."

And Aaron knew it was time to go. He reached within himself and drew upon the power of angels, feeling the names of all those who died fighting for Lucifer's cause rising to the surface to adorn his flesh. *This is for them, as well,* he thought. His senses grew more keen, the fury of Heaven thrumming in his blood. He brought forth his wings of blackest night, unfurling them slowly, fanning the air in anticipation.

"I have to go now," he said in a severe voice he had come to recognize as his own, a voice filled with strength and purpose.

He looked at them all, perhaps for the last time, and an unspoken message passed between them. This was hard enough without the hindrance of final words, and even though they would not be by his side in this last battle, they would in fact be with him in spirit, providing the strength he would need to fight.

"See you when this is done," Aaron said, Vilma's peaceful sleep his last sight before departing to fulfill his destiny.

It had never known such a connection to another living thing.

Its tiny heart beat rapidly; its respirations quickened as it listened to the furtive moans of its friend in agony.

The others of his kind were hurting him again, their droning chants making him writhe and cry out. They sat around the outside of his circle, rocking from side to side as they repeated their hurtful song.

Something leaked out from the tortured creature's body. The mouse was reminded of the morning fog on the river outside the mountain monastery that used to be its home, only that fog was not the color of dried blood and did not bring with it such feelings of unease. Something was coming into the world that did not belong, and the mouse's friend cried out in abandon, a mournful song filled with shame at not being strong enough to prevent it.

The one called Verchiel impatiently paced before the hanging figure, his gaze fixed upon the tortured one. It was he who was behind it all, he who was responsible for all the pain.

The rodent could not bear to hear it any longer, did not want its friend to think that he suffered alone, and against all instincts it scampered across the wooden floor, no longer caring if it was seen or not. The mouse passed between two of the chanting ones, reaching the ring of foul-smelling dirt. It stifled the frenzied urges to flee, its tiny eyes fixed upon the face of the one called friend. It had but one purpose now.

The dirt on the floor was cold and damp and stank of death, but it did not hinder the mouse as it forced its way through the mire, interrupting the perfection of the circle's curve. It had broken the circle and the patterns beyond, without notice, conquering its fear and reaching its friend.

Standing upon its hind legs, the mouse raised its pointed face and reached up with its two front paws to the sad figure hanging above it. *"You are not alone,"* it squeaked in the most rudimentary of languages.

Triumphant, yet unaware of what it had truly done.

Verchiel was mesmerized by Lucifer's suffering.

He could not pull his gaze away, watching as the greatest of sinners strained to keep God's punishment within him.

"Let it go, damn you," Verchiel hissed, the anticipation almost more than he could bear.

*Soon they will all pay,* the angel thought with a perverse sense of satisfaction—the human monkeys scurrying about thinking themselves so much more, the fallen angels and their Nephilim spawn, and the Lord God. *How sad that it has come to this,* the Powers commander ruminated as he watched the first of the fallen writhe. Verchiel was surprised that one such as Lucifer could care so much for the primitive world to which he had been banished. He himself could no longer hide his distaste for the place and its corrupting influence over his Father in Heaven.

"I shall show You the error of Your ways," he spoke aloud, hoping that the Almighty would hear his words and know how wrong He had been to discard him. Verchiel would show the Creator the madness of it all.

Suddenly Lucifer, the first of the fallen, let loose a scream that spoke of his final resignation. The collected horror that was his punishment flowed from his body, pouring from the opening cut into his chest—a thick, undulating vapor eager to make the acquaintance of the world.

"How utterly horrible you are," Verchiel whispered with a kind of twisted admiration, moving closer to the magickal circle that acted as the punishment's cage. "What terror you shall reap under my command."

He looked about the room at the last of his soldiers, bloody and beaten by a crusade gone to seed. Once they had numbered in the hundreds, but now less then twenty remained under his command. And once they would have fought hard against a threat such as this, not unlocked its cage to set it free upon a thankless world. The angels fluttered their wings nervously, sensing the fearsome virility of the power that was being unleashed. They remembered it—the war—and what it had done to them all, the scars it had left.

"Do not fear, my brothers," Verchiel proclaimed, "for with this force we shall be vindicated, and every living thing, whether of flesh and blood or of the divine, will know that our mission was righteous, and will beg for our forgiveness."

The Archons began to scream, and Verchiel looked toward the angelic magicians. Somehow the power leaking from Lucifer's body had managed to break free of its containment, moving past the mystical circle of Heaven's soil and his adversary's blood, swirling around his faithful sorcerers like a swarm of insects. The Archons' screams were frantic, unlike anything he had ever heard before.

Archon Oraios ran toward the Powers commander, his head enshrouded in a shifting cloud that clung stubbornly like a thing alive. "How could we have been so foolish!" the magician wailed, arms flailing in panic. "To think that we had the right—to think that we could erase His Word!"

Verchiel grabbed the angel by his robes as he passed, throwing him violently to the gymnasium floor, and still the cloud remained. A sword of fire came to life in the commander's grasp. "What is happening here?" he spat, watching as the punishment of God continued to leak from Lucifer's body, past the circle of containment, and into the room.

"It's loose," Oraios cried, thrashing upon the floor as the cloud expanded to engulf the magician's body. "Somehow the circle was broken and now it is free. How could we have been so stupid as to think we could control it!"

The gymnasium erupted in a cacophony of screams and moans as the Lord's punishment acquainted itself with the others in the room. Verchiel watched aghast as warriors he had fought beside in the most horrendous of battles were reduced to mewling animals. They cowered in the scarlet cloud—the embodiment of all the suffering caused by the war in Heaven. It laid waste to them all, driving them to destroy themselves. One tore out his eyes, while others turned their own fiery weapons upon themselves. Their screams were deafening.

"You must do something," Verchiel barked at the Archons as an angel of the Powers host repeatedly flew into one of the room's concrete walls, as if trying to shatter all the bones in its body.

The three Archons crowded together in the far corner of the gymnasium, trying to hide from the force they had unleashed.

"Do something!" Verchiel screamed again, but they only huddled closer, trembling violently.

"They're afraid," said a voice, little more than a whisper.

Verchiel looked to see that Lucifer was awake, even as the power continued to leak from his body. "*You* did this," Verchiel said with a snarl, pointing his fiery sword at the prisoner. "*You* caused this to go awry."

Another of the Powers host took his own life, his mournful wails reverberating horribly off the cold walls before falling silent.

Lucifer laughed painfully, the rumbling chuckle turning into a wet, hacking cough. "I'm the one hanging over a mystical circle with his chest cut open, and this is my fault," he said in wonder. "How is that?"

Suddenly Verchiel caught movement from within the circle's center and noticed the prisoner's pet vermin, cleaning dirt and blood from its dirtied stomach. He was about to snatch up the bothersome creature and squeeze the life from its body, but then he realized that it wouldn't matter.

There was a sudden searing flash of heat and Verchiel looked back to see that the Archons had set themselves ablaze. He could hear their voices raised in unison as the mystical fire consumed them, begging the Creator for forgiveness. They remained alive far longer than he would have imagined possible, before their piteous pleas ceased and they collapsed to the wood floor in a pile of fiery ash and oily black smoke.

"Set me free," Lucifer said as Verchiel returned his attentions to his prisoner. "Do the right thing. Redeem yourself. Let me reclaim my punishment. Let me put it back where it belongs," the first of the fallen pleaded. "There's a chance we might still be able to stop this."

Verchiel gazed out over the gymnasium where the broken, bleeding forms of his remaining followers littered the floor. The cloud of misery was expanding, rolling inexorably toward him. It had finished with his soldiers and now wished to feast upon their leader. He tensed, waiting for its dreadful touch with a strange anticipation.

"Who said anything about wanting to stop it?" Verchiel replied as he was engulfed in the hungry red mist. He felt it cling to his body, worming its way inside him through the open wounds that adorned his flesh. He waited to feel the unrelenting horrors of the Almighty's punishment, but instead felt the same ever-present sense of rage he'd had since being abandoned by God.

And then the leader of the Powers came to a startling realization. *I'm already living the torments of Hell.*

# CHAPTER FOURTEEN

In his mind Aaron saw his destination, a barely legible, weather-beaten sign that read SAINT ATHANASIUS CHURCH AND ORPHANAGE: ESTABLISHED 1899. This was where the final battle would occur. There were multiple buildings, including a church, but he knew he needed to be inside the school. That was where his father was being held. That was the image Lucifer had placed within the Nephilim's mind.

The picture of the gymnasium inside his head made him think briefly of his own school, Kenneth Curtis High, and all he had given up—graduation, college, a human life. He had been so angry in the beginning, that his once normal life had been turned on its head by angelic prophecies and blood-thirsty angels, circumstances beyond his control, a destiny he had known nothing about. And even though time had allowed him a begrudging acceptance of his fate, it hadn't made his sacrifices any less difficult.

He parted his wings like the curtains on a stage pulled back to present the last act of some great production. *This is it,* he thought in nervous anticipation, the final chapter of a story that began on the morning of his eighteenth birthday, the day his life changed forever.

He furled his great black wings beneath the flesh of his back, their movement stirring a strange, reddish fog that drifted above the floor of the gymnasium. An atmosphere of danger permeated the room, and the hair at the back of his neck prickled, a sword of fire springing to life in his hand. He was ready for this to end.

His eyes scanned his surroundings. The mist was thick, but he was able to make out the features of the old gymnasium, the hard parquet floor covered with years of dust beneath his feet, a skylight in the ceiling above, spattered with bird droppings. He moved his hand through the dense vapor, wondering what it was, knowing it couldn't be good. It made the bare flesh of his arms tingle, his chest ache as he reluctantly took it into his lungs.

Then it hit him with the force of a storm driven wave. His weapon of fire fell from his grasp as his body was wracked with violent spasms. *What's happening?* Aaron wondered on the brink of panic as the synapses in his brain exploded like fireworks on the Fourth of July. It was as if every emotion—rage, despair, love, joy—had come alive at once, more incapacitating than any physical attack. He was numb, stumbling through the billowing red fog, trying to regain control of his runaway passions. He had no doubt now as to what this was. He was too late. His father's curse had been unleashed.

The punishment of God was free.

Try as he might, Aaron could not wrest control of his emotions. The mist cajoled them, inflamed them, drawing them out like infection from a wound. Raw, unhindered feelings that ran the gamut from sadness to rage to joy were released within him. Again and again he lived the moments that had created them, the mundane and the profound, the joyous and the miserable.

Fear flashed through him as he saw the first foster home he could truly remember, horrible people who had taken him in only for the meager allowance the state paid for his upkeep. He felt the loneliness and anger, relived the abuse and neglect. Then that experience was viciously torn away to be replaced with another, and then another still. It was as if all the defining emotional moments of his life were happening simultaneously: the early endless stream of foster homes, the fights at school, his discovery of Gabriel—a filthy puppy tied to a tree in a gang member's backyard—the first time he saw Vilma Santiago, and the deaths of the Stanleys, the only true parents he ever knew.

Aaron tried to block them out, to hold them at bay, but the experiences were relentless, an assault upon his every sense. His confusion turned to rage, and then to panic. He lashed out with a newly summoned blade of fire, futilely cutting through the swirling crimson vapor, doing anything to fight back, but to no avail.

The fog grew thicker, hungrily closing in around him. And suddenly, as if his own emotional turmoil hadn't been enough, every aspect of the war in Heaven bombarded his already torn and frayed senses. He saw the crystal spires of Heaven stained crimson with the blood of discord, smelled the sickly sweet aroma of burning angel flesh, and listened to the cries of brothers, once comrades in the glory that was Heaven, locked in furious combat. *How easily it all fell apart,* he sadly observed as he experienced the woe of God, a despair the likes of which he could not even begin to describe. It was all encompassing, a sucking void that pulled him in and devoured all hope.

At that devastating moment Aaron fully understood the magnitude of his father's crimes and the fallout that followed. To go against the Creator, to strike at God—it was the pinnacle of sin, the saddest of all things. He could think of no way to escape the anguish of it. The malaise was like an enormous hand pushing him down to the ground, crushing him, and he came to the sickening realization that nothing mattered, that the struggle of the fallen angels for forgiveness was to no avail.

It was hopeless.

All his sacrifice and struggle had been for naught.

With a trembling hand Aaron brought his weapon of fire to his throat and prepared to end it—to make the misery stop.

He felt the searing bite of the blade's flaming edge upon the flesh of his neck, but did not pull away. It was a blessed relief to feel something other than the sorrow of the Lord God.

*"Stop,"* begged a voice riding upon the churning mist of crimson.

And strangely it stayed his hand, the fiery blade faltering. Aaron stumbled through the unnatural fog, stepping over the bodies of others who had released themselves from the pain of Heaven's fall, drawn toward the voice, an island of hope in a sea of desperation.

The image of a man hanging from the ceiling in chains appeared in the roiling vapor. Aaron moved closer and could see the glowing, archaic symbols etched upon the dark metal restraints, symbols infused with the ability to sap away the strength of the angelic.

He reached up to help the man down as further waves of drowning emotion washed over him, and he again found himself contemplating his sword. *It'll be quick and relatively painless,* he thought, raising the blade of fire to his throat. *Anything to take away the hurt . . .*

"That's not the way," the hanging man croaked, and raised his head of curly black hair to look upon Aaron with eyes deep and dark, old eyes filled with centuries of pain.

Aaron knew this man, so long associated with all that was evil and wrong with the world. He was pulled into Lucifer's gaze, unexpectedly feeling as though he had been tossed a life preserver, adrift in a furious sea of rabid sensation. "It . . . it hurts so much," he said, clutching a prized moment of solace, fearing he would not have the strength to endure the next pummeling wave.

"But think about how good it will feel when it stops," Lucifer whispered, his head slowly falling forward again.

The red cloud churned around the fallen angel, emanating from a gaping, vertical wound that began in the center of his chest, the horrible gash splayed open with metal clamps. Aaron was reminded of the cat he'd had to dissect in his junior year biology class, only this subject was somehow still alive.

"You've got to use it," Lucifer murmured. "The pain. Use it as fuel to move past the torment, to the light at the end of the tunnel—punishment to absolution. It's what's kept me relatively sane since the Fall." He strained to smile. "It's good to see you in person, son. Only wish the circumstances were a bit less hairy."

Aaron moved closer to the prisoner, fighting to keep his feelings in check. "Let me help you," he said, preparing to use his heavenly blade to sever the debilitating chains and release the fallen angel that was his father.

Lucifer's head rose. "Watch your back," he croaked in warning, and Aaron spun around, his sword instinctively raised, blocking another weapon of fire as it descended out of the mist to end his life.

"You'll do no such thing," Verchiel screamed, emerging from the deadly fog.

Aaron was momentarily shocked by the angel's decaying appearance. The heavenly armor that once gleamed like the sun was now dirty gray. The usually firm and modeled flesh of his arms and legs was wrapped haphazardly in blood-stained bandages. His face was like a single, open wound.

Their weapons hissed as they bit into one another, shrapnel of heavenly fire cutting through the air. Aaron cried out in sudden pain, his cheek glanced by the sword's fiery embers.

"The end is upon us," the leader of the Powers rumbled as he bore down upon his weapon, attempting to drive Aaron to his knees.

"That's probably the first and last time I'll ever agree with you, you son of a bitch," Aaron snarled, calling forth his wings, pushing forward, driving his attacker back, using the rabid emotions as his father ordered.

The two angelic entities glided across the gym, locked in a furious struggle, the Creator's punishment flowing around them, becoming darker, thicker, as if egging them on. It was taking all that Aaron had to ignore the multitude of emotions that made him want to drop his sword, to give in to the sadness and despair all around them. He raged against the disparaging feelings, reminding himself of all those who were depending on him.

Verchiel pressed his attack, his sword coming dangerously close to severing Aaron's head from his shoulders. The

Nephilim flapped his powerful wings, sending himself up toward the muted light from the skylight, Verchiel in heated pursuit. Then he suddenly spun around, arcing downward, plowing into the angel and sending them both plummeting to the gymnasium floor.

They hit the hard wood with incredible force, boards splintering and popping from the impact. Verchiel shrieked, thrashing beneath him. He reached up and dragged a clawed hand across Aaron's face, barely missing his eyes. The Nephilim leaped away and noticed that he was covered in blood. It took him but a heartbeat to realize that it was not his own, but Verchiel's. The injuries beneath the angel's bandages were bleeding profusely and he stank of rot.

Verchiel climbed to his feet, his great wings flexed, feathers shedding like falling leaves. He glanced down upon himself, the blood from his injuries running down his body in rivulets to pool at his feet. "This is what it's come to," the Powers leader said, a despair in his voice that only added to the anguish roiling about them. "It's all been taken away from me." He glared at Aaron with black, hate-filled eyes. "*You've* taken it away from me—you and the monster that spawned you."

"Do you honestly believe that we're entirely to blame?" Aaron stared hard at the angel, his gaze unwavering. "That we've somehow pulled one over on God, and you're the only one who knows about it?" He shook his head in disgust. "What a load of crap."

Verchiel seethed, fists clenched before him, black blood oozing between his fingers to patter like gentle rain upon the floor.

"Sins were committed," Aaron continued. "Crimes so unimaginable that they could never be forgiven. Or can they?"

The fog swirled about Verchiel, as if somehow attempting to comfort him. "You know nothing of what we experienced," he growled.

Aaron extended his bloodstained arms, showing the Powers leader the black sigils that adorned his flesh. "But that's where you're wrong," he said. "I wear their names, those who died fighting for Lucifer's cause. And inside of me lives a piece of each and every one of them."

The angel's horrible face twisted in revulsion. "You're more of a monstrosity than I thought," he snarled with disgust.

"A monstrosity who knows their jealousy," Aaron countered. "That feels what it was like when God seemed to turn away from them to embrace another creation on a new world. I know how desperate they were to regain his favor. Desperate enough to do something foolish."

Vechiel glanced down at the blood pooling at his feet. "They broke His holy trust and for that they deserved a punishment most severe." He looked back to Aaron. "I was doing what I was told to do. It was my holy mission to bring them down."

"The fallen eventually realized that they were wrong, but

have you?" Aaron asked. "If God told you, right now, that they were to be given a chance to do penance—to prove they were truly sorry—would you even be able to hear Him?"

"I followed my commands."

"Exactly," Aaron agreed with a slight nod. "You followed *your* commands."

Verchiel turned suddenly, stalking away from him. "I'm tired of all this . . . living," he said.

Aaron noticed that one of the angel's blood-covered hands had begun to glow, and he readied himself for the next round of conflict. "Then let's see what I can do about putting you out of your misery," he replied, sword of heavenly fire burning righteously in his grasp.

The leader of the Powers turned, his right hand glowing with incredible heat, the blood running down from the wounds upon his arms, hissing snakelike, evaporating to smoke before it could drip upon the white-hot hand. He laughed, a sound void of any humor. "I wonder if He's listening now?" He turned his eyes toward the heavens and raised his burning hand. A tendril of living flame erupted to explode through the skylight and illuminate the night beyond it with the glow of Heaven's fire.

"What is that disparaging statement humans often make to each other?" the angel asked, as jagged pieces of the broken glass rained down upon him. "Go to Hell?"

And Aaron realized what was happening. He watched in

stunned horror as the crimson mist coalesced, snaking across the floor like some prehistoric serpent, over the bodies of those felled by its malignant touch, eager to invade the world beyond these walls.

"Yes, that's right," Verchiel said with an obvious glee. "You can all go to Hell."

Kraus tried to squeeze himself deeper into the darkened corner of an abandoned classroom, a cacophony of emotions bringing him to the brink of insanity. All the anguish, anger, and loneliness that had been part of his early life was with him again, the intensified feelings bombarding him threefold.

With his new eyes he had watched the angelic ritual performed upon the fallen angel Lucifer. Even before the last of the rite was completed, the healer knew that nothing good would come from it, and he attempted to hide himself away.

For decades he had served the angelic host Powers, developing a certain preternatural sense for things beyond the norm. As most humans were oblivious to the paranormal, Kraus found that he had become keenly sensitive. Those senses were screaming now, and he attempted to fold himself tighter into a ball, to protect himself from the forces that had been turned loose this day.

*How could I have been so blind?*

Though a force from Heaven, Verchiel had become twisted,

obsessed with the completion of his holy charge no matter how high the cost. And Kraus had helped him. How strange it was that it took the leader of the Powers host rewarding him with the gift of sight for him to truly see how things actually were.

*I was blind, but now I can see.*

Kraus heard the cries of his classmates at the Perry School as they were consumed by fire, and he shuddered in the darkness. There had been no act of mercy that fateful night, only murder.

He was suddenly reminded of something Lucifer had said to him only days ago, and fought an unrelenting wave of fear to remember exactly what had been said. The healer had found himself drawn to the prisoner's cage, although he had been instructed never to enter the room in which the Powers' captive had been imprisoned. Somehow he sensed that he was needed, that his skills as a healer were being called for. Still condemned to darkness, he had gathered his instruments and healing potions, feeling his way to the schoolroom where the personification of all that was evil was imprisoned.

*Evil personified.* Kraus would have laughed if he weren't so afraid.

The Devil had welcomed him into the room, and Kraus stood strong against him. He knew he had to be on guard, for the prisoner's manipulative ways were legendary. He had bravely informed the prisoner that he was a healer and had come only to administer to the fallen angel's wounds. Lucifer had said he understood, and although most of his burns had healed, he wished for Kraus to treat a few stubborn patches.

The healer had stoically obliged. It was his duty, after all, to care for the angelic creatures around him, whether they were soldier or prisoner. But he found himself in awe of this prisoner's demeaner. Here was the Prince of Darkness, the Lord of Lies, imprisoned by the forces of Good, and all he could talk about was how much he enjoyed the springtime, and could he please have some bread for his friend, a mouse.

*Was it then that the first seeds of doubt were planted?* Kraus wondered. Or had it been with those final words, as he completed the application of healing salve upon Lucifer's burns?

*"It's going to get worse around here before it can get better,"* Lucifer had warned. *"That's the way it has to be, but I thought you might want to know."*

He had wanted to ask the prisoner to explain, for he had already begun to suspect, to feel, that the near future was ripe with the potential for danger. The words were at the tip of his tongue, ready to fall from his mouth, when Verchiel returned from his latest defeat at the hands of the Nephilim. He had been lucky that the Powers commander hadn't slain him then and there, but the angel had been preoccupied with his plans for the future and Kraus had quickly fled.

*The future.*

Lucifer's words again echoed through his mind. *"It's going to get worse around here before it can get better."*

Kraus uncurled himself and leaned back against the cold plaster wall. He remembered the last time he had seen the prisoner, hanging from the ceiling in chains, his torso cut open and something unspeakable leaking out into the world.

"Very bad indeed," he muttered, afraid to move, afraid to incite another pummeling wave of the supernatural force that seemed to have subsided for the moment, allowing him to gather his wits about him.

"Why would he have told me that?" Kraus asked the oppressive gloom.

In his mind he saw the mist leaking from Lucifer's wound—saw how he fought to keep it inside—and Kraus knew he had to do something.

The thought of leaving his hiding place filled him with mortal terror. What was happening beyond the walls of this classroom was not meant to be seen by mere man. And besides, what could he possibly do to prevent it?

*"That's the way it has to be."*

Kraus finally found the strength within himself to stand, and before he could question the sanity of his actions, went to the door.

*"But I thought you might want to know."*

He moved through the darkened school, the eerie vapor that had once been contained within the first of the fallen becoming thicker as he neared the gymnasium. Kraus tried with all his might not to let it affect him, not to be reduced to quivering human wreckage by its touch. It was the hardest thing he had ever done, plunging headlong into that debilitating mist. He waited for it to overcome him, to crush him beneath the overpowering weight of its despair, but it did not happen. *Perhaps more than the ability to see was bestowed upon me by Verchiel's restorative touch,* Kraus considered.

It was like being blind again as he felt his way through the swirling mist, stumbling over the bodies of those who had already fallen victim to the full extent of the vapor's malignancy. He could not bring himself to look at them, for they had been his charges for decades, their well-being his responsibility, and it hurt him deeply to know that there was nothing he could have done to ease their pain.

A limp human shape, hanging from the ceiling's metal girders by thick links of metal chain, loomed out of the drifting mist before him. But now that he had reached his goal, Kraus was unsure of why exactly he had come. He could hear sounds within the fog, voices raised in rage, and he suspected that the Nephilim had come to challenge Verchiel's insanity.

"It's bad," Kraus muttered to the unconscious figure, clutching his satchel of healing tools to his chest as if they could somehow protect him. The deafening sound of an explosion and the shattering of glass made the healer wince, and he shielded his head from possible hurt. "Very bad," he whispered, and he felt the cool touch of the fresh night air invade the stagnant atmosphere of the gym.

He noticed that the mist was being drawn toward an opening in the ceiling where a skylight had been, and the nightmarish images of the vapor expanding across the globe filled his head. "I can't imagine it any worse," Kraus muttered.

And Lucifer slowly raised his head.

"Help me down," he said. "I think that's my cue."

Aaron watched in terror as Verchiel rose up alongside the integrated fog, wings beating the air as he followed the seething mass on its undulating course toward the open skylight, toward its freedom.

Then instinct took over and Aaron spread his wings and leaped into the air. The manifestation of Heaven's grief had become something akin to a single great tentacle, slithering through the air pointed at the gaping hole in the ceiling.

"You have to stop this!" he screamed at Verchiel, his blade of fire passing uselessly through the gaseous mass. At one time the Powers leader must have been a rational thinking being, and he hoped to somehow appeal to what remained of that creature, if anything remained at all. "You claim to be a loyal servant of God, and yet you're going to allow this to happen? Think about what you're doing!"

Verchiel hovered just below the shattered framework of the skylight, his tattered wings flapping furiously to keep his form aloft. His dark, horrible eyes were riveted to the snake of fog. Night had fallen outside, and despite the horror of what was happening below, the stars in the sky twinkled beautifully. If the mist were allowed to escape, Aaron wondered if the night sky would ever look this beautiful again.

"He has to be shown," Verchiel said dreamily, beckoning for the deadly vapor to flow all the faster. "If I'd only been allowed to complete my mission, this never would have happened." He shook his head sadly as if there was nothing more that he could do. "It is too late—too late for us all."

Aaron flew at the Powers commander, thoughts racing. There had to something he could do to stop it. Anything. "It'll be the death of us *all*!" he shouted at the angel, desperately trying to reach any hint of the divine still lurking within Verchiel. He had turned this monstrous haze on; he had to know how to shut it off.

The leader of the Powers brought forth his own sword of fire, swiping at Aaron, driving him back. "Yes, it will be our death!" he cried out, his face a blood-covered mask of open sores, "and *He* will be forced to bear that guilt."

Aaron narrowly avoided the bite of Verchiel's burning blade, riding dangerously close to the hellish mass. The angel came at him again, his bandaged hand closing about the Nephilim's throat, forcing him back into the punishment of God.

Aaron struggled violently to be free, but Verchiel's grip was like steel. He felt as though he were drowning, every fiber of his being invaded by the experience that was the War in

Heaven. Finally he managed to break away, falling toward the ground, unable to function—barely able to cope with what his body was experiencing. He landed with a sickening thud and painfully rolled over on his back, looking up at the ceiling. He thought of the world beyond the gym. He had seen what Lucifer's hell had done to the angelic, heavenly beings of amazing power and strength, and shuddered to think of the horrors that would soon befall the people of the world.

Struggling to collect himself, Aaron yelled at the angel hovering near the ceiling above him. "You have to stop it!"

Verchiel simply smiled, the marble pale skin of his face hidden in blood. "I can't," he said with a shake of his head. And his smile grew all the larger and twice as terrible.

Verchiel recognized some of the misery emanating from the body of the condensed vapor as his own. Anger turning to rage, sadness to overwhelming despair; all of them he had experienced during the Morningstar's war in Heaven and during his own recent abandoment. He had contributed mightily to this swirling miasma of experience, and now it was to be released upon the world.

The angel's black eyes gazed up through the open ceiling from which Hell would escape, through the cold light of stars above, and attempted to see Paradise. He had always imagined that his mission, his private war, would eventually end and that he would return to Heaven a hero of the cause. Things would be as they had been: chaos squelched, order restored, and the memory of Lucifer Morningstar and his atrocities purged from the memories of all divine beings. Verchiel saw himself basking in the celestial light of his Lord and Heavenly Father, the favored child of God, and all was right in Heaven and the universe.

*But it's not meant to be,* the angel forlornly reminded himself, averting his gaze from the wide sky above to the snakelike monstrosity writhing in the air below him. Here was the personification of his *own* rage, his way of punishing all those who had hurt him. A horrible but necessary way to make things right again.

The Morningstar had not been forgotten. His presence had continued to infect the heavenly domain like some malignant growth, blossoming into the cancerous prophecy of forgiveness, and eventually the state in which Verchiel currently found the world. He could take it no more; the denigration had to be stopped.

"Are you watching, my Lord?" he called to the open space above him. The stars winked as if in response. "You may have been able to forgive them their trespasses, but I cannot."

He soared up and out through the damaged skylight into the night, gazing down as the probing tip of the gaseous appendage cautiously reached beyond the skylight into the cool night air.

"That's it," the angel encouraged, a perverse satisfaction

the likes of which he had never known empowering his decaying form. "This world of sin belongs to you now. Let them feel what we felt—how horribly we suffered for His love."

Verchiel looked out over central Massachusetts, his gaze traversing beyond New England to look upon the whole planet of man. "Will You forgive *me,* Heavenly Father?" he whispered. "When *my* sin is committed and my penance is done, will You take *me* back into Your embrace?"

He again looked upon the monstrous thing that had been the bane of Lucifer as it prepared to make its way into the world.

But something was wrong.

It hesitated.

Verchiel flew closer and watched in surprise as the hellish mass began to recede into the building. "Come back!" he roared pitifully, his cries of disappointment echoing through the still of the night.

He descended, following the serpentine form back into the building, Bringer of Sorrow ignited in his grasp.

There was Lucifer Morningstar kneeling upon the floor of the gymnasium, his own fingers now holding open the gaping wound in his chest, an expression of unadulterated suffering etched upon his features, as he gradually drew the thick crimson vapor back within himself. Standing beside him, a supportive hand upon the first of the fallen's bare shoulder, stood Verchiel's own healer, the monkey Kraus.

"What is this?" the angel growled aghast, not so much that the Morningstar was free, but that one who had served him so faithfully, on whom he bestowed such a great gift, could be party to Verchiel's own betrayal.

"I'm taking it back," Lucifer said, struggling to his feet with the help of the human animal. "It is not the world's burden." The enormous volume of swirling mist slowly burrowed back inside his body. "It is my punishment. I am its master, and it is mine alone to bear."

"You always were a selfish one, Lucifer Morningstar," Verchiel ranted as he dropped from the ceiling, placing all his might behind what would be a killing blow.

# CHAPTER FIFTEEN

Time slowed as Verchiel's blade fell toward him.

For a glorious few moments Lucifer had experienced what it was like to be free of his burden. It had been bliss, and for an instant he considered the possibility of life again without his punishment.

*I've done more than enough penance,* he thought, trying to convince himself that it wouldn't be such a bad thing to let God's chastening of him go. *I'm truly sorry for all my sins. He must know that,* Lucifer rationalized. *Maybe this is how it was supposed to be. Is this how I'm to be freed from the Lord's wrath?*

He looked up now and saw Verchiel above him, armor tarnished, skin covered in tattered, blood-stained bandages and open sores, decaying wings spread wide as he fell toward him, hissing weapon of fire falling toward his face. *Is this a messenger from God?* Lucifer asked himself. *One that the Creator sent to tell me I am forgiven?* But no matter how hard he tried to convince himself, Lucifer knew the answer.

It was not yet his time for absolution.

Wearily he began to take it back, all the pain, sorrow, anger, and misery spawned by his jealousy. The chore was daunting and excruciating, and the first of the fallen wasn't sure he had the strength left to finish it. But the human healer, Kraus, had lent him some of his own strength, and Lucifer had managed to complete his task.

Hell churned inside him again. It belonged to him and nobody else. It would be his until the day he was forgiven, or his life was brought to an end.

And not before.

Which brought him back to the here and now. Verchiel's blade was dangerously close. Lucifer thought of conjuring his own weapon of choice, a fiery trident that could have easily challenged Verchiel's blade of sorrow. But in his millenia on Earth he had developed an aversion to violence, and it had been so long since he last summoned a weapon from Heaven's arsenal. The image of the three-pronged weapon began to form in his mind.

He was not as fast as he once was, and he could feel the heat of Verchiel's blade upon his face as sparks of heavenly fire filled his hands. Hopefully he would not be too slow. It would be sad to have come this far only to die now.

Although he had difficulty with the details, the trident

began to take shape and Lucifer raised his arm. The weapon wasn't quite ready, and he feared that it would not have enough substance to prevent the sword of sorrow from cleaving his skull, but there was no time left. He had to try. He pushed Kraus away, out of harm's reach, and prepared to meet Verchiel's attack.

Bringer of Sorrow cut through Lucifer's weapon as if it were not there, and the first of the fallen readied for the blade's searing bite. He was sorry that it had come to this, sorry that he hadn't more time to spend with his son, sorry that he hadn't been forgiven. Then it stopped less than an inch from his nose, an equally impressive blade of Heaven blocking Verchiel's strike with a resounding crackle of divine fire.

Lucifer turned to see his son in all his Nephilim glory, wings of raven black, body adorned with the names of those who had sworn allegiance to the Morningstar and died for his cause. He certainly was a sight to behold.

"Thank you," Lucifer said with a sigh of relief.

*"De nada,"* Aaron replied before turning his full attention to the Powers commander.

"Let's finish this," the Nephilim said impatiently, and the angel Verchiel appeared eager to oblige.

Blades still touching, opposing forces sputtering and sparking angrily, Aaron placed himself between Verchiel and Lucifer Morningstar. It was his turn now.

He remembered the first time he had seen the angelic creature that would unmercifully steal away so much that was important to him, immaculately dressed in his dark suit and trench coat, gliding into his foster parents' house on Baker Street as if he belonged there. *He actually believed that what he was doing was right,* Aaron thought bitterly. Killing his parents, burning down their home, and kidnapping his little brother. *Oh yes, that was exactly what God wanted, for sure.*

The sight before Aaron now was nothing short of pathetic—filthy, blood-covered, and ragged—but no less dangerous. He thought of asking the creature to give up, providing him with a chance to put away his sword and stop the inevitable, but he knew it wouldn't happen.

"So, we going to do this?" Aaron asked, his steely gaze unwavering.

Verchiel spat upon the floor, a thick, bloody phlegm that, by the sound of it, was filled with teeth. "Oh yessss," he hissed as he wiped his mouth with the back of a bandaged hand, and attacked.

Aaron parried his assault and followed through with one of his own, driving the last of the Powers away from the still recovering Morningstar. *It's like fighting a wild animal,* he thought, the angel growling and spitting with each opposing move as they hacked and slashed at each other across the gymnasium floor.

Aaron's back struck up against the cool concrete wall and

he managed to duck as Verchiel's blade cut across its surface, leaving a deep, smoldering furrow in the building stone. The angel moved in to strike again and the boy saw his opportunity, a memory of countless fights while growing up. Using his wings, he propelled himself forward and slammed his fist into the face of his foe. It was like hitting melting ice, wet, on the verge of yielding, but not yet ready to crumble. Verchiel flipped backward, wings flapping wildly as he landed on the floor.

Certain that at least two of his knuckles had been broken, Aaron shook the pain from his hand. "That was for Doctor Jonas," he said, remembering his psychiatrist, the first victim of the Powers' hunt for him.

Verchiel's face was a bloody mess, a combination of blood and teeth oozing from his swollen mouth as he rolled to his knees, beginning to rise. Anger flared in Aaron and he surged toward the angel again, preparing to deliver a powerful kick to his side.

The Powers commander caught his leg, twisting it savagely to one side, and Aaron fell to the floor. The angel scrambled across the floor toward him, a horrific, blood-stained sight, the insane jagged grin of a jack-o'-lantern on his once pristine features.

The Nephilim lashed out with the heel of his shoe, connecting with the side of the angel's face. It did little to slow him down as he scrabbled atop Aaron, wings flapping, long, spidery fingers winding about his throat and beginning to squeeze.

"I've longed for this moment, *monster*," Verchiel gurgled, bloody saliva dripping from his injured mouth and running down Aaron's face. "To kill you with my bare hands, to watch the accursed life leave your eyes."

Vibrant blossoms of color exploded before Aaron's eyes as the angel's viselike grip grew tighter. Instinctively a weapon of fire began to form in his hand, but he couldn't concentrate, the images in his head a jumbled mess. Darkness began to creep in around the edges of his vision. He thought of a knife, a simple thing made for only one purpose.

With failing strength he drove the blade into Verchiel's side. The tip of the knife deflected off the angel's armored chest plate, sparks of fire exploding between them, but it was enough to distract his foe, and his grip loosened. Aaron managed to pull a knee up beneath his attacker, and with the last of his reserves, he flipped Verchiel over and behind him. He flexed his wings and sprung up from the floor, whirling around as the burning knife grew into a sword of fire.

Verchiel was already up on his feet, charging, Bringer of Sorrow held aloft in both hands. "The prophecy dies with you, Nephilim!" he screamed as he brought the blade down upon Aaron. "I can be satisfied with that victory alone."

The force of the blow was devastating, driving Aaron to his knees as he blocked the blazing sword's descent. "Hate to disappoint you," he snarled as he leaped to his feet, pushing Verchiel away with his sword, "but the only victory today is

THOMAS E. SNIEGOSKI

for the fallen angels, when I put you down once and for *all*." He could feel the strength of the angel warriors whose names adorned his flesh surge through his body. Never had he felt so sure of anything as he did at that moment, perfectly attuned to what he was and what he was supposed to do.

Verchiel attacked again, his sword of heavenly fire dropping again and again as it attempted to cut him down, but his blade did not—could not—touch the Nephilim. It was as if Aaron was anticipating the Powers commander's every move, countering each parry with one of his own. Verchiel's attacks became more wild, more frenzied, but still the Nephilim did not fall.

His patience waning, Aaron finally lashed out on his own, swatting Verchiel's weapon from his hand. The angel snarled, summoning yet another instrument of death, but Aaron responded in a similar fashion, disarming the angel commander with perverse ease.

"It's done," he said, his voice filled with confidence.

Suddenly the angel warrior seemed to wilt before his eyes, as if the fight had finally been stolen from him. Verchiel dropped to one knee, his head bowed.

"Do it," he spat, refusing to look at the Nephilim.

Aaron clutched the hilt of his own blade all the tighter, feeling the heat of his weapon course through his arm. The warrior's essence housed inside him screamed in rage. Here was his enemy kneeling before him in supplication, an enemy that had taken away so much, and still he stayed his hand. If he were to strike at Verchiel now, it would be no better than murder.

Verchiel raised his swollen, blood-covered face to fix him in the most horrible stare. "Kill me now," he demanded.

Though Aaron wanted to raise his blade and cut the monster's head in two, he restrained himself. "I may be an abomination in your eyes," he said, "but I am not a murderer."

Verchiel moved like lightning, surging up from the ground, a knife of fire in his grasp. "Mercy from my most hated foe," he hissed serpentlike, lashing out at Aaron's exposed throat. "It would have hurt me less if you had taken my head from my shoulders."

Aaron blocked with his hand, the knife slicing through his palm rather than his throat. He jumped away from the enraged angel.

Verchiel swayed upon his feet, knife of fire still clutched in his hand, but he did not attack again. "This is far from over." He spread his wings and soared toward the open skylight. "Perhaps another time," he called as he escaped into the night with the flapping of mighty wings and a snowfall of molted feathers.

Aaron knew what he had to do.

"Be careful," he heard a voice say from across the gym, and he saw that his father was watching. The human healer knelt by his side and was stitching closed the vertical wound in his chest with a rather large needle and what looked to be thread spun from gold. "We've got quite a bit to discuss when this is all over," Lucifer said.

Aaron nodded as he spread his wings for flight. "We certainly do." Then he soared through the hole in the ceiling, in pursuit of the angel Verchiel.

The night air was cool upon his skin, a kind of balm to his injured hand, and it reinvigorated his senses, clearing his head as his eyes perused the evening sky in search of his prey.

*He can't have gone far,* Aaron mused. *Wouldn't have gone far. Verchiel must know that I will chase him.* He doubted that the Powers leader would pass up the opportunity to take him out once and for all. It didn't look as though the angel would be alive for much longer. This had to be Verchiel's last chance to ruin it all, to stop the prophecy from becoming reality.

Aaron heard them first, the hungry crackle of heavenly fire as it cut its way through the air. He dove to the side as four daggers of flame passed harmlessly through the spot he had been hovering mere seconds before. But a fifth had been thrown in anticipation of his reaction. The fiery blade penetrated his upper thigh with a bubbling hiss, burning through his pants, plunging beneath the flesh to the very bone. It was as if someone had poured molten lava inside the wound. Aaron cried out, gripping his injured leg, attempting to stay aloft.

Then, like something out of the worst of nightmares,

Verchiel dropped from the sky. The angel actually appeared to be in even worse shape, flesh in various stages of decay, wounds ripe with infection. Even as they hovered in the open night sky, Aaron could smell the nauseating scent of rot. It was as if all the evil and insanity that had shaped this once heavenly creature into what he was today was bubbling to the surface, showing the world his true face.

They fought, their powerful wings pounding the air unmercifully. It was hard to focus above the pain in his leg, and Aaron's endurance was rapidly waning. The bitter conflict had to end soon. A sword of fire flashed in Verchiel's grasp and Aaron lashed out, kicking savagely at the angel's wrist and making him drop it, but another was already forming to take its place. Aaron kicked again, this time with his wounded leg, and explosions of jagged agony sliced through his body.

Verchiel seemed to sense the Nephilim's dwindling fortitude. Aaron could see it in his red-rimmed eyes as yet another sword of fire appeared in his hand. "You will know your better!" the angel screamed, flecks of blood flying from his mouth as he soared across the short distance of sky, sword arcing downward toward the Nephilim.

Aaron wasn't sure why he thought of it then or why he hadn't thought of it before, but the inspiration came to him suddenly, fully formed, and a weapon the likes of which he had never wielded before burst to existence in his hand. It was a gun, much larger than Lehash's pistols, the barrel long and thick. It had none of the delicate beauty of the gunslinger's twin weapons, reminding Aaron more of the guns he'd seen in some of his foster father's Friday night action movies, something that would have been used by Arnold, or maybe even Clint. Something used to take the bad guys down once and for all.

Aaron almost found the change of expression on Verchiel's twisted features comical as he raised the fearsome weapon forged from his imagination and heavenly fire. Almost. If only the whole situation hadn't been so damn sad.

He pulled the trigger, and a sound like what he would have imagined from the Big Bang erupted from the weapon. A tongue of fire at least a foot in length lapped eagerly at the air as the force of the blast tossed Verchiel back. He began to spiral down toward the church below, a tail of smoke trailing from a grievous hole in his shoulder. The once fearsome angel crashed through the large, circular, stained-glass window at the front of the Saint Athanasius Church.

Still clutching the hand-cannon forged from his imagination, Aaron followed, cautiously entering the church through the broken window ringed with jagged teeth of multicolored glass. It was dark inside, the only light thrown from the stars and the half-moon above.

As Aaron touched down upon the altar, he checked the landscape. Most of the church's religious trappings had been removed. Rows of benchlike seats were spread out before him, and a bloody trail ran up the center aisle to end with Verchiel as he crawled laboriously toward the front doors and escape. Aaron allowed his wings to catch the air and glided down the aisle, favoring his injured leg, the powerful weapon still at his side.

Verchiel sensed his presence, halting his progress and slowly rolling onto his back. The angel's breath rattled wetly in his lungs. Shards of stained glass clung to the sticky surface of his gore-covered body. Aaron gazed into the darkness of the circular wound that had been blown into his right shoulder and imagined that he was gazing into the angel's soul. It was as he suspected: nothing there but a yawning blackness.

"What are you waiting for?" Verchiel gasped through his swollen and bloody mouth. "This is your chance to destroy the one that wished with all his heart to see you wiped from existence."

Aaron raised his weapon, sighting down the barrel, taking aim at the one that had caused him so much grief. He was repulsed by this creature lying on the floor before him, the furthest thing from a being of Heaven he could possibly imagine.

Verchiel chuckled, bubbles of blood forming at the corners of his mouth. "I would have purged the world of your taint," he taunted. "Burned the ground you walked upon with heavenly fire."

But Aaron also felt something else: a certain pity for the

being that had once been a soldier of God, then became so twisted and poisoned by his hatred and his inability to forgive that it had turned him into a monster.

"There would have been no one to mourn your passing," Verchiel continued, shaking his head from side to side, "for I would have slain them as well."

Aaron knew that angel was trying to goad him into action, and he decided he would not play the game. He lowered the weapon, allowing it to disintegrate in a flash.

Verchiel's face twisted in confusion. "What are you doing?" he asked, a quivering rage evident in his question. "I'm prepared to die now. Kill me."

Aaron shook his head slowly, a now familiar sensation beginning to build in the center of his chest. It was the beckoning of a higher power to release those imprisoned within cages of fragile flesh—to allow them the opportunity to stand before their Lord God and beg for absolution. It was the power that defined him as the savior of prophecy, and it coursed up from his center and down the length of his arms, emanating from his outstretched hands.

"Kill me," the angel demanded again, struggling to rise to his feet.

And though it pained him greatly, Aaron knew exactly what he was supposed to do with Verchiel. He had to let go of his anger, of his hate for the pathetic monster that had caused him and the ones he loved so much hurt. And he was better for it, experiencing the true meaning of his God-given gift.

"It's not my place to judge you," he said, his voice calm, showing not a trace of anger.

Verchiel's black, soulless eyes bulged as Aaron reached out to him. Suddenly the angel knew what was about to happen. He wasn't going to be slain by his most hated enemy.

This was a fate far more horrible than that, and he tried to flee.

Aaron reached out, taking hold of Verchiel's head in his hands, and let the power of forgiveness flow through him and into the leader of the Powers host.

"I forgive you," he whispered as the Powers commander struggled to be free of his hold. "But will *He?*"

Verchiel shrieked in fear, his sword, Bringer of Sorrow, appearing his hand. He attempted to lash out at Aaron but didn't seem able to control the fire. The sword lost its shape, the flame instead flowing down to consume his arm, eating away the wounded flesh and continuing on.

Verchiel thrashed in the Nephilim's grasp, trying with all his might to escape, but the fires of Heaven hungrily devoured his shell of flesh, leaving behind a being of muted light, one that did not shine like the others Aaron had set free. This one was different.

Aaron released the creature and stepped away from the angel in its purest form. Verchiel knelt upon the floor of the church, quivering as if cold, but Aaron suspected it was fear that brought this reaction. The frightened creature raised its head, gazing up at the ceiling, seeing far more than the images of Heaven's glory painted there.

"It was all for you," Verchiel muttered in the tongue of the messengers. The glow of his body began to intensify, and soon he was enveloped in a sphere of solid, white light, as if a star had somehow fallen from the sky to lie upon the floor of the church.

Aaron shielded his eyes with his wings, saving his sight from the searing intensity of the light. *"I am so sorry"* were the last words he heard uttered by the terrified Verchiel as he was taken in a flash.

Taken up to Heaven to face the judgment of God.

# CHAPTER SIXTEEN

I t was as if some great burden had been lifted from her.

Vilma Santiago opened her eyes in the semigloom of the basement room where she had been confined. She felt better than she had in days. She couldn't describe it exactly. The only thing she could even vaguely compare it to was waking up the morning after taking a really important test at school, the sense of relief she felt when she realized that the test was behind her. It was a really stupid comparison, but it was the best she could manage at the moment.

She sat up, waiting to feel the ominous stirrings of the angelic power within her, but felt nothing other than an extreme sense of calm.

The golden chains attached to the manacles upon her wrists rattled as she climbed off the mattress and padded barefoot across the concrete floor to the stairs. Slowly she climbed the steps, listening carefully, curious if there was anyone else in the house with her, but she heard nothing.

The girl stepped out into the hall and turned toward the kitchen, vaguely recalling that Lorelei and Aaron had given her something—some kind of medicine. But deep down she sensed that that was only partly responsible for the peace she was feeling.

She found Gabriel lying on the floor in the kitchen, staring out at the night through a broken screen door.

"Hey, boy," she said, happy to see the animal, strangely relieved that she hadn't been left completely alone.

Gabriel, startled by the sound of her voice, sprang to his feet, tail starting to wag when he realized that it was she. *"You scared me,"* he said as he trotted to her, nuzzling her hands for affection.

"I'm sorry," Vilma told him, stroking the soft fur of his head. The chains between the manacles jangled.

*"I don't think you're supposed to be up and around,"* Gabriel cautioned. He leaned heavily against her, accepting her ministrations with relish. *"They told me to make sure you stayed in bed."*

"I feel better," she told him. "Much better, really." She put her arms around his neck and gave him a serious hug. "I don't know what it is, but I all of a sudden feel like everything is going to be okay."

Gabriel twisted in her grasp so that he could look into

her eyes. *"Is he all right? Do you know if Aaron is safe? I was feeling something too, but I couldn't tell if it was a good feeling or a bad one."*

"I don't know," Vilma told the Labrador, looking at her reflection in his dark gaze. "I just woke up feeling that things had finally been set right." She smiled and shrugged her shoulders. "I really don't know what it means. It's just how I'm feeling."

Gabriel tilted his head quizzically. *"I guess that's a good feeling, then."*

"I guess so," she said, standing and walking toward the door. "Where are the others, Gabe?" she asked the dog as they stepped out into the cool, spring night.

The streets of Aerie were deserted. It was eerily quiet, no signs evident that this *wasn't* a neighborhood abandoned during the nineteen seventies, even though she knew otherwise.

*"Lorelei said something about going to the center of town to wait."* The dog gazed down toward the end of the street, nose twitching as he sniffed the air.

"To wait for what? You mean for Aaron to come back?"

Gabriel slowly nodded his blocky head. *"Or maybe for something bad to happen."* His voice sounded small, tinged with fear.

Vilma took in a deep lungful of the damp night air as she gazed up at the stars, reaffirming the peace she had felt since awakening. She wasn't sure exactly how she knew, but she was certain that something about the world had changed.

"No," she said, heading toward Aerie's center with Gabriel close at her heels. "I don't think this is bad at all."

The citizens had gathered in the center of what had once been called the Ravenschild Estates, now known to them simply as Aerie. Lehash wasn't sure exactly why they had decided to congregate not far from the twisted rubble that had once been their place of worship, but they were all here.

It was probably for the same reason that he had come, an almost palpable feeling in the air that something big was about to happen. Nobody was talking really, both fallen angel and Nephilim alike. All were standing around, gazing off into the distance or at the night sky above them. They didn't seem to know the direction from which it was going to arrive, but they knew it was coming nonetheless. He wouldn't have disagreed with them.

Legs crossed at the ankles and leaning against a broken streetlight, Lehash sucked upon the moist end of his cheroot, letting the smoke leak from his nostrils to swirl in the air about his face. He studied the gathering crowd. How their numbers had declined, thanks to the Powers' attack just weeks before. How many of them had been struck down, only to be freed from their mortal shells by the touch of the one they had come to think of as savior. *Will the rest of us be as lucky?* he wondered.

"Fancy meeting you here," called a voice from across the street, and Lehash watched as his daughter approached. She strolled down the street, careful to avoid the gaping holes that had been caused when the full fury of her angelic spells had been unleashed upon the Powers, the magick of angels igniting pockets of explosive gas trapped beneath the toxic-waste-tainted ground. She had brought a weather-beaten beach chair with her, one that had belonged to Belphegor, and she unfolded it to sit down as she reached him.

"I kind of wondered if I was the only one feeling it," she said, crossing her legs, nervously wiggling her foot as she gazed around at the center and all who had gathered there. "Guess this answers my question."

Lehash silently pulled upon the end of his foul-smelling cigar, his preternatural vision scanning the entire surroundings, as well as hundreds of miles beyond it.

"That's one thing I never could stand about you," Lorelei suddenly said from her beach chair. "You never let me get a word in edgewise."

His daughter thought she was pretty funny. It was a trait that she definitely shared with her mother. The gunslinger remembered the human woman he had fallen in love with, fooling himself into thinking that he could live like them. But the joke had been on him. It hadn't been one of his prouder moments, but he had left the woman, for her own good he had told himself, knowing full well that she had been with child as he headed out again alone—until he found Aerie, a place where he could belong.

"Don't know why I ever admitted to bein' your daddy," he said dryly, blowing smoke into the air to punctuate his statement.

Lorelei chuckled, grabbing hold of the long, snow white hair the hung past her shoulders. "I don't think you could've denied it," she said, shaking the hair at him. "The family resemblance is unmistakable."

Lehash removed his Stetson and ran his fingers through his own snowy hair, pushing it back on his head before replacing his hat. "Yer probably right," he drawled, the crack of a smile appearing at the corner of his mouth. "Should'a dyed my hair."

His daughter smiled, and he continued to smoke his cigar, and they waited, as did all the other citizens.

Waited for something to happen.

"What are we going to do if he fails?" Lorelei asked quietly.

Lehash looked down at her sitting in her lounge chair beside the streetlamp as if waiting for a nighttime parade to pass by. It was a question he had been thinking since Aaron left Aerie in pursuit of his father and Verchiel. The kid was good, there was no doubting that, but the gunslinger had also seen the savagery of the Powers commander many times throughout the centuries. And if there was one thing that Lehash had become in his millennia on the earth, it was a realist.

He took a long, hard pull on his cheroot before answering.

"We'll do what we've always done. We'll survive, fight if we have to," he said. "But the world's going to become a pretty inhospitable place if the boy—"

"I'm not talking about that," Lorelei said cutting him off. "I'm talking about the prophecy. What happens if he dies before fulfilling the prophecy?"

Lehash dropped the remains of his cigar to the street, crushing out the burning ember beneath the toe of his leather boot. "I guess we're out of luck," he said, feeling an icy grip of hopelessness the likes of which he hadn't felt since descending from Heaven and first setting foot upon this world.

The jangling of chains distracted them, and father and daughter both looked up to see Gabriel trotting down the damaged street beside Aaron's friend Vilma.

"I told that dog not to let her out of bed," Lorelei said, standing up as Vilma and Gabriel approached the center.

"I guess she felt it too," Lehash said. From what he could see, the girl seemed healthy, no signs of the furious internal battle she had been fighting earlier. The Malakim's potion appeared to have done what he had promised it would. Furtively he hoped that her struggle hadn't been for nothing.

Lehash felt it before it actually happened, as if somebody had taken a cold metal spur and rolled it down the length of his spine. And by the expression he saw upon his daughter's face, he knew that she, too, had felt it. He lifted his hands and allowed his guns of heavenly flame to take shape.

"Dad?" Lorelei questioned.

She stumbled and he let go a gun to grab her arm, keeping her from falling, all the while scanning the neighborhood and beyond, searching for any hint of trouble. Whatever it was—whatever they were feeling—was coming now, and there wasn't a damn thing any of them could do to stop it.

Gabriel began to bark crazily, his tail wagging. The dog seemed to be staring at a spot in the center of the street, across from the rubble of the church. Something was manifesting in the air there, something black and shiny, and Lehash lowered his guns knowing full well what he was seeing.

"He's back."

The gunslinger left his post and headed toward the disturbance. Lorelei followed closely at his side, and before he knew it, Scholar, Vilma, and Gabriel had joined them. Citizens from all around were converging on Aaron Corbet.

Lehash raised his hand, signaling for those around him to stop where they were, as he carefully inched his way toward the boy. He wanted to be certain that everything was all right before exposing the others to potential danger.

Aaron stood, unmoving, head bowed as if in deep reflection, his enormous wings closed about him like a black, feathered blanket. Slowly the wings unfurled to reveal that the boy had not returned alone. Two men were with him, one on either side of the young Nephilim. Lehash didn't recognize the older of the pair. He was human, with the taint of angel magick about him. But there was no mistaking the identity of the other, even with the odd addition of a mouse perched upon his shoulder.

"Hello, Lehash," he said in a voice as smooth as smoke, and the gunslinger suddenly found himself wrestling with conflicting emotions.

"Been a while, Lucifer," Lehash responded tersely, not sure whether he wanted to embrace the angel or put a bullet of fire through his head.

Aaron returned his wings to beneath the flesh of his back, a wave of exhaustion washing over him with the realization that he had made it home.

*Home.* He couldn't believe that he actually now considered this decrepit neighborhood built upon a toxic waste dump his home. It was kind of sad, but at the same time it filled his heart with happiness to know there was a place where he belonged.

Before he left Saint Athanasius, there had been some protest from his companions when he suggested they return to Aerie together. The human healer, Kraus, did not feel he deserved the kindness of Aerie's citizens after having served the Powers for so many years. And Lucifer Morningstar, well, he suspected that many of Aerie's fallen residents would still have issues with him.

Aaron would hear none of it. He was tired, and he wanted

to return to his friends. Giving them little choice, he had wrapped his father and the healer in his winged embrace and brought them back to Aerie with him.

"Since you two already know each other," Aaron said, trying to divert the constable's attention, "allow me to introduce Kraus. He was the Powers' healer."

The old man bowed his head in reverence to the angelic gunslinger. "I am truly honored to be in your presence," he said.

Lehash moved closer, sniffing at the man. "He has the stink of Verchiel on him. The Powers commander changed him somehow."

Kraus lifted his head and gazed at the formidable angel before him. "He gave me the gift of sight," the human said, touching his face. "I was blind from birth, but now I am able to see."

"A healer, then," Lehash said, looking the man up and down. "I guess the citizens could use the help of a healer."

Lorelei moved around her father and tentatively approached Aaron. "So it's over?" she asked, as if afraid he was going to tell her otherwise.

Aaron nodded. "Verchiel's the problem of a higher power now."

A yellow streak bounded from the crowd and Aaron found himself knocked backward by the impact of his best friend. He stumbled, his injured leg barely supporting his weight, as

Gabriel braced his front paws on the boy's chest and frantically, affectionately, licked his face.

*"I'm glad you're back and that you're not dead,"* the Lab said between sloppy laps.

Aaron hugged the big yellow dog, letting his tongue wash over every inch of exposed skin on his face and neck. "I'm glad I'm not dead too, pally."

Gabriel dropped back to all fours, tail wagging wildly as Aaron continued to heap affection upon him. "How's Vilma, Gabe?" he asked. "Did you keep an eye on her for me? Is she doing any better?"

*"Ask her yourself,"* the dog replied, looking into the crowd just beyond where he was standing.

The full meaning of the animal's words didn't quite sink in until Aaron followed Gabriel's gaze and his eyes locked immediately with hers. He practically ran toward Vilma, taking her into his arms and holding her as close as he possibly could. If he could have opened himself up and placed her safely within, he would have done so. The girl reciprocated, burying her face in his shoulder, her arms wrapped tightly around her neck.

"I knew you were all right," she whispered in his ear. "I knew you wouldn't leave me alone."

They kissed then, their lips pressing hungrily together, and Aaron finally understood what had been absent from his life thus far. He had been incomplete, a piece of him missing without him ever truly realizing it. Sure he had felt the emptiness from time to time, but he'd chalked it up to feeling sorry for himself, never knowing that there was another half out there in the world waiting to be joined with him. Vilma was that half, and at that moment, as he held the woman he loved in his arms, Aaron Corbet knew for the first time what it was to be whole.

*"Is that your father, Aaron?"* he heard Gabriel ask, and let go of Vilma long enough to see Lucifer moving through the crowd, talking to those who had gathered, heralding his arrival.

"Yes, it is," he said, no longer afraid to admit it.

A silence had come over the center, and only the voice of the Morningstar could be heard.

"I'm sorry," he said to each and every one of the gathered. "I'm sorry for all that I have done, and for all that has happened because of me."

He moved among them. Whether they were fallen angel or Nephilim, all were deemed recipients of his soulful regrets. Some embraced the angel that once sat at the right hand of God, tearfully accepting his words of apology, while others snarled, turning their backs, not yet willing to forgive him his sin, or themselves their own.

Lehash, Lorelei, and Scholar were the last to receive the Morningstar's words of atonement, and Aaron wondered if he was going to have to get involved. The air became charged with tension as Lucifer approached them, and he readied himself just in case.

"Tumael," Lucifer said, bowing to the angel that Aaron had only known as Scholar.

Tumael bowed back, accepting the first of the fallen's apology graciously.

He moved on to Lorelei.

"I accept," she said before the words even had a chance to leave his mouth, and Lucifer smiled.

And then the Morningstar turned his attention to Lehash.

Aaron wasn't sure what history had passed between them, but he guessed that Lehash had at least once been a follower of the Morningstar, and the gunslinger didn't appear to be the kind of angel that easily forgave and forgot. Time seemed to have frozen as the two fallen angels stared at each other, and Aaron got the distinct impression that the two had at one time been close, maybe even friends.

"We had to be out of our minds to follow you," Lehash said, his eyes dark and intense.

Aaron watched the constable's hands, looking for the tell-tale spark of potential danger. The pistols were gone at the moment, but they could easily return in less than a heartbeat.

"I think we all went a bit insane," Lucifer answered, his watchful eyes never leaving the angel in front of him.

Lehash casually scratched the accumulation of stubble on his chin.

*Do angels even need to shave?* Aaron wondered as a bizarre afterthought, intensely watching the scene playing out before him.

"Do you think we're any better now?" the constable asked.

Lucifer thought for a moment, turning his gaze away from the gunslinger and looking at those gathered around the center of the blighted neighborhood. His mouse nuzzled the side of his face affectionately, and he reached up to gently stroke the top of the rodent's head. "I do believe we are," he answered, and he bowed his head to Aerie's keeper of the peace. "I am sorry, Lehash, for all that I have done, and for all that has happened to you because of me."

Lehash scowled as he reached inside his coat pocket. Slowly he withdrew one of his foul-smelling cheroots. "After all this time, that's the best apology you could come up with?" he asked as he placed the end of the cigar between his waiting teeth.

Lucifer stepped closer to the gunslinger and Aaron tensed, his wings ready to launch him into the air toward the two fallen angels. His father raised a hand, causing Aaron to twitch in anticipation, but he stayed where he was. The tip of one of the Morningstar's fingers began to burn white with the heat of heavenly fire, and he gently touched the tip of the cigar protruding from the gunslinger's mouth, igniting its end.

"It was kind of short notice," Lucifer said as Lehash began to puff upon the cigar. "And I never really thought I'd have this chance."

Lehash brought a hand up to his mouth, momentarily removing the cigar. "Things do have a way of working out, don't they?" he asked the angel that had led him down the path to the fall from Heaven.

"They certainly do," Lucifer responded, and the almost palpable tension that filled the air dispersed like a fast-moving summer storm, the atmosphere suddenly fresh and clear.

Everyone just seemed to be milling about, basking in a strange sense of closure. Aaron knew they were all feeling the same thing. With the threat of Verchiel and his thugs removed from the equation, the citizens were now free to think about things other than their day-to-day survival—namely their forgiveness. A special freedom had been given to them this new day, and Aaron allowed himself to take a small measure of pride in the fact that he had played a large part in bringing this part of the story to a satisfying conclusion.

"It's strange," Aaron said, his arm still around Vilma, Gabriel standing loyally by his side. "This is the first time I've ever seen them happy." Even the human healer, Kraus, seemed to be fitting in, already beginning to administer to those who had not yet healed after Verchiel's attack on Aerie.

*"It's nice,"* Gabriel said, and his tail began to wag.

Vilma gave Aaron an affectionate squeeze, resting her head upon his shoulder. "And it's all because of you," she said. "You did this. You gave them something that they'd only dreamed about."

She pulled away and studied his face. Her stare was

intoxicating, and if all he did for the rest of his days was to look into those eyes, it would be a satisfying life indeed. She tapped the center of his chest with her index finger.

"You, Aaron Corbet," she said, her voice like the beginning chords of the most beautiful song he'd ever heard. "You made their dreams come true."

He couldn't have imagined a more wonderful moment, but as everything else in his life had, that too was about to change. For he was the messenger, and he had a purpose that took precedence over everything else.

Aaron felt it begin to grow deep within his chest. It was calling to him in a voice that was growing louder and stronger with each passing second.

"Aaron, what's wrong?" Vilma asked. She stepped away from him as he began to tremble.

"Nothing's wrong," he said in a voice void of any doubt. This was it; through all the battles with monsters and renegade angels, this was what it had all been leading up to. "Everything's exactly as it's supposed to be."

Aaron called forth his wings as the glow began to emanate from his hands, a store of supernatural power never fully tapped, until now. The citizens saw him—saw what was happening—and they began to smile, and some to cry tears of joy. The power that was his and his alone to wield called out, and he went to them, as they were drawn to him, seeking the absolution that had been so long in coming.

And as he walked among them, his touch forgiving them of their sins, Aaron Corbet thought of who he was and what he had become. Never would he have imagined that a foster kid from Lynn, Massachusetts, could command the power of God's forgiveness. Yet this was how it was supposed to be—how it was *always* supposed to be. Yes, there had been hardships, the loss of loved ones, and seemingly insurmountable obstacles, but from all the pain and suffering, a thing most wonderful had been achieved.

The fallen angels of Aerie glowed like gigantic fireflies, dancing in the air above him on iridescent wings that made a sound like the gentle stroking of harp strings as they flapped. Aaron turned and saw that Scholar now waited before him. The fallen angel looked anxious, gazing wistfully at Aaron and then back down the street toward his workplace.

"Don't worry," Aaron reassured him, reaching out to touch the front of his crisp white shirt. "We'll take good care of your books. I think I know just the guy to do it."

They both looked toward the man called Kraus. He had fallen to his knees, staring in awe at the constellation of angels hovering above. "I think he'll do an excellent job," Aaron said as the power surged from his fingertips into Scholar.

The fallen angel's shell of flesh, blood, and bone was burned away in an explosion of white light, and the angel Tumael was welcomed by his brethren in the air above the center.

Aaron smiled as he saw Lorelei and Lehash slowly walking toward him. The gunslinger was one of the last, and looked as though he just might burst from his skin even without the Nephilim's touch.

"This is it," Lorelei was saying as she held onto the arm of her father's coat.

Lehash kept his eyes on Aaron, saying nothing as father and daughter tentatively walked toward the constable's absolution. The other Nephilim affectionately touched him as he passed, thanking him for his protection, and wishing him well on his journey home.

The cowboy angel stopped before Aaron and respectfully removed his hat. The Nephilim raised his hand toward Lehash, the outline of his fingers barely visible within the corona of the pulsing, white power he now wielded.

"Wait," Lehash suddenly said, his own hand going up to block Aaron's touch. "I can't go," he said, and turned to look at the faces of the Nephilim that eagerly awaited his ascension. "Somebody's got to watch out for them, protect them." He looked to Aaron. "There's still so much they have to learn."

Lorelei squeezed her father's shoulder, leaning in to place a kiss upon his grizzled cheek. "We'll be fine," she said, and Aaron nodded in agreement.

Lehash took what would be his last look at the children of angel and human, and then stared into his daughter's emotion-filled eyes. "You probably will be," he said, reaching out to cup her cheek in his hand. "But there's no harm in trying to stay for just a bit longer." They both laughed, and embraced for the final time.

Then Lehash released his daughter and turned to Aaron, puffing out his chest. "Well, c'mon, savior boy. I ain't got all day."

Aaron smiled broadly, laying the flat of his palm against the gunslinger's chest, and watched in awe as Lehash's true form gradually took shape, the human shell shucked off like a thick layer of dirt and grime. The angel that was Lehash propelled itself skyward with a succession of powerful flaps, dipping and spinning in the air in an amazing display of aerial acrobatics, before joining the others.

"Show-off," Lorelei said, wiping tears of happiness from her eyes.

Aaron looked up at the angels of Aerie, committing each and every one of them to memory. It was an amazing sight to behold, as if the stars had come down from the sky for a closer look. He knew that he would remember and treasure this moment until his dying day, but he also knew that it was time for it to end—time for those above him to leave.

He spread wide his great wings and held his arms aloft toward them. "You're forgiven," he called out.

And one by one they left this earthly plane, returning to the place of their creation, a place long denied them, but that now took them back into its celestial embrace.

Heaven welcomed them home.

Slowly Aaron lowered his gaze from the early morning sky and saw with a combination of shock and shame that there was one that he had forgotten.

Lucifer stood alone, a beatific smile upon his dark, handsome features as he looked to where his brethren had gone. There was a longing in his stare, but also a happiness for those who had finally completed their penance and were allowed to know the glory that was Heaven again.

"Is this for you as well?" Aaron asked, startling the first of the fallen from his meditations beyond the sky.

Lucifer held the tiny mouse in the palm of his hand, tenderly stroking its fur. "I don't know," he said sadly with a slight shake of his head. "I'm afraid to find out."

Aaron stepped toward him and gently laid his hand upon his father's chest. He felt the power at his core rise, and for a fleeting moment, believed that *it* was about to occur, that it was to come full circle, and the final forgiveness was about to be bestowed upon the one who had started it all.

But it wasn't to be.

The divine power receded deep inside him, dwindling away to but a burning ember in the center of his being.

"I'm sorry," Aaron said sadly, removing his hand from his father's chest, and the first of the fallen smiled at him. It was a sad smile, but one full of understanding and immeasurable patience.

"So am I," Lucifer said, returning his gaze to the brightening morning sky above Aerie, gently stroking the tiny animal nestled within the palm of his hand.

*"So am I."*

# EPILOGUE

Lucifer Morningstar stood outside the Saint Athanasius Church and Orphanage and listened for the sounds of Nephilim. There were more of them out there in the world, he knew, children of the dalliances of angels, their birthrights gradually blossoming upon their eighteenth year of life.

*Happy birthday to you.*

The temperature had dropped considerably in the past hour, and it had started to snow. Lucifer turned his attention to the change in weather, studying the intricacies of each individual flake as it slowly drifted down from the sky. The mouse on his shoulder curiously sniffed at the winter's rain as it fell, its tiny pink tongue darting from its mouth to lick at the water as it melted upon the jacket of the fallen angel's dark blue suit.

The summer in the northeast had been brutally warm,

and it looked as though the New England winter was going to be just as extreme. But the weather did not bother the first of the fallen angels. He quite enjoyed the seasonal changes. If he hadn't, he would have suggested that the new Aerie be established in San Diego, California, instead of western Massachusetts.

The fallen angels of Aerie were gone, but the Nephilim remained. They were to be the new protectors of a world rife with paranormal dangers. Verchiel and his Powers had ignored their true purpose, choosing to focus their energies on a personal vendetta rather than the job they had been assigned to do.

As he could sense the emerging Nephilim, so could the fallen angel detect the presence of things that had no right to be upon this world, things that wished Earth and its inhabitants harm. It was now the responsibility of the Nephilim to clean-up after the Powers' irresponsibility and to keep the world of God's chosen creations safe from harm.

But there was much they needed to learn before they could take on such an enormous task, much that he, Aaron, and Lorelei would need to teach them.

They had been here for a little more than six months, the new Aerie established within the former roost of Verchiel and his ilk. The Ravenschild Estates had quite simply become too large for their lesser number. With the fallen angels gone, this was a new time for the Nephilim, a new history waiting to be

forged for them as individuals, rather than victims of a geno-
cide perpetrated by Verchiel and his host.

As for himself, Lucifer looked upon this as yet another test
from his most Holy Father above. He would help to train those
who would protect God's human flock, and finally, hopefully,
achieve absolution for his most heinous sin.

The snow now fell harder, a whipping wind creating
swirling vortexes of white that danced around the expanse
of unkempt lawn in front of him. He could sense the small
animals that lived in the overgrowth around the church and
orphanage, hunkered deep within their burrows, primitive
instincts telling them that this would be the first major storm
of winter, that soon everything would be covered in a cold
blanket of icy white.

*And from this season of death there would be rebirth.*

All Lucifer wanted was a chance to apologize to his Father,
as he had to the brothers that had sworn to him their allegiance
in Heaven so very long ago. But he knew that opportunity had
to be earned, and would come at a heavy cost indeed.

The mouse on his shoulder whispered in his ear. It was
cold and wanted to go inside. Lucifer obliged his tiny friend,
taking him indoors and out of the storm. After all, there was
still much to be done to prepare the Nephilim for the tasks
before them.

He thought one more time of his brethren, basking again
in the glorious radiance of the Almighty, and longed for the

day that he, too, would be allowed to experience the Blessed Majesty once more. Was that a hint of envy he felt growing in the deep inner darkness of his psyche? Quickly he squelched it before it had a chance to take root, before it could do any harm. The first of the fallen had had more than his fill of jealousy's bitter fruit.

The price of forgiveness was indeed a costly one, but it was an amount that Lucifer Morningstar was willing to pay.

Aaron and Gabriel trudged through the quickly accumulating snow in search of the newest of Aerie's citizens.

The boy had lived with them for a day over two weeks. His name was Jeremy Fox, and he'd come from London, England. Aaron had found him living on the streets of the great, old city, begging for change and eating from Dumpsters. To the casual passerby he appeared to be just another sad example of a mental health system in desperate need of an overhaul—muttering and crying out, talking to himself as he wandered the streets of England's largest city. He hadn't been difficult to locate; the power of the Nephilim was strong inside him, and it practically cried out to be found.

Now Aaron found the youth behind the abandoned school, in the snow-covered playground. He was sitting atop the monkey bars, sneakered feet dangling, the top of his sandy blond head and shoulders covered with collecting snow. He had not been adjusting well, and Lorelei was worried.

"Hey," Aaron said as he walked closer.

*"Hey,"* Gabriel repeated, not wanting to be left out of anything.

The youth remained silent, as if attempting to tune out the strange world in which he had come to live. Aaron could sympathize; it hadn't been all that long since he was in the very same frame of mind.

It had been Lorelei who convinced the youth to listen to the story told by the two crazy Americans who seemed to appear from out of nowhere, a fantastic tale about angels having relationships with human women and the children that were born as a result. Jeremy had looked at them as if they were out of their minds, and Aaron was certain that he was trying to decide whether they were in fact real or just manifestations of the insanity that had taken hold of him since his eighteenth birthday. They had told him that they could help, and Aaron had watched a look of cautious hope fill the boy's eyes.

Taking that as a yes, not giving him a chance to refuse, the Nephilim savior had taken the troubled youth within the confines of his wings of shiny black and had transported him back to the safety of Aerie.

He had been here since, but did not seem to be adapting to his new life, clinging to his humanity, refusing to accept the reality of what he was becoming.

"Lorelei's worried about you," Aaron said, looking up

at the boy sitting on the top rung of the monkey bars. "She thought I should find you—just in case you needed to talk or something."

Gabriel sniffed around the various pieces of playground equipment, his nose melting furrows in the two inches of snow that had already fallen.

The wind suddenly whipped up, causing the powdery snow to drift, making it seem that more of the white stuff had fallen in some areas than in others. The winter wind had a bite to it, but it didn't bother Aaron as it once had. *Just another perk of being Nephilim,* he thought. Hot or cold, it was all the same to them, perfectly adaptable to any climate upon the planet.

Jeremy remained unresponsive, immobile upon his metal perch.

"Guess not," Aaron said, putting his hands inside the pockets of his spring jacket. "Well, if you should need to, you know where I . . ."

The boy turned to look at him, the snow atop his head sloughing off to fall to the ground below his dangling feet. "They say that you're some kind of bloody savior," he said, his accent thick and full of repressed emotion. "What's that like, then?"

It was something Aaron tried not to think about very often. He knew that he had a job to do, a purpose and a destiny. But the moniker of savior was one that he did not wear comfortably.

Aaron came closer to the jungle gym. "Don't believe

everything you hear," he said, casually taking hold of one of the horizontal pipes in both hands. "There's very little difference between me and you," he told the boy. "It wasn't too long ago that I was thinking the same thoughts you are right now."

Jeremy's features grew angry, and he let himself drop from his seat to the snow-covered ground. He came at Aaron then, chest puffed out, eyes wild. The older Nephilim held his ground.

"And *what* am I thinking?" Jeremy asked in a hiss. "Use your angel powers and tell me what's going on inside my bloody head, mate."

Gabriel had come to stand by Aaron, his nose covered in snow from his explorations beneath the cold, winter covering. *"You shouldn't talk to Aaron that way,"* the dog warned, hackles of fur rising around his neck. *"He's just trying to help."*

Aaron reached down and thumbed the dog's side in assurance. "It's okay, Gabe," he said. "Jeremy and I are just talking. He's a little upset."

The Lab grumbled something and then became distracted by a squirrel, and he bounded off in pursuit of the animal with an excited bark.

"You want me to tell you what's going on in your head?" Aaron asked the new Nephilim. "You're thinking that the world has become insane, that everything you've known, everything you've taken for granted all your life, has been flipped upside-down since your last birthday." Aaron paused. "How am I doing so far?"

Jeremy seethed with an inner rage that Aaron was all too familiar with. "You don't know anything," the boy growled, sparks of heavenly fire shooting wildly from his fingertips.

"You know how I know this?" Aaron asked. "Because I thought the exact same things when it was happening to me, when the power that was inside me—something that I didn't want or ask for—decided to take my normal life away from me." Aaron placed one of his own hands upon his chest, his gaze never leaving Jeremy's. "I thought the exact same things."

The boy's anger seemed to drain away, as if he were suddenly no longer strong enough to hold on to it. It slipped away from him, and he seemed to diminish in size, the outrage he was feeling over what his life had become seemingly all that was sustaining him.

"I don't know how much longer I can fight it," Jeremy said pathetically, the snow melting upon his face, mixing freely with the warm tears that now fell from his eyes. "I can feel it inside me—clawing to get out."

"You don't have to fight it," Aaron told him. "That's why you're here: to learn about what you truly are—to learn about your destiny."

The boy chuckled then, wiping away the moisture from his face and snuffling. "Destiny?" he asked. "Didn't know that I had one of those."

"Bet there's a lot you don't know about yourself," Aaron said. "Let us teach you."

Sometimes it wore on him.

Aaron scooped up a handful of the fresh snow and began to make a snowball. "Here it comes," he warned. The last of the snowfall had been mixed with rain, creating a slushy mix perfect for snowballs.

Across the expanse of front lawn, Gabriel crouched. *"I'm ready,"* he growled.

Most of the time these days, Aaron felt like Gabriel at that moment, tensed, ready to confront the latest obstacle head on.

He let the snowball fly, and as it fell, Gabriel leaped up into the air to capture it in his mouth. "Good catch, boy," Aaron said, clapping his hands and praising the animal for his skills.

Gabriel proceeded to eat the snowball, crunching upon the firmly packed snow, pieces falling from the sides of his mouth as he chewed. *"Make another one,"* the Labrador urged between chews.

It was so easy to get caught up in the flow of it, to become the ultimate leader, the weight of the world upon his shoulders. He needed moments like this to remind himself that there was more to life than being the leader of the Nephilim.

Gabriel had finished his icy snack and was waiting for the next, tail wagging happily. *"C'mon, Aaron,"* the dog urged. *"Throw another one."*

He squatted down and grabbed some more of the wet white stuff. "You'll never be able to catch this one," he said in mock warning, making his best friend all the more excited.

Aaron knew that his was a great responsibility, that the protection of the world had been placed in his hands and the hands of others like him. It was up to him to make sure that they were ready for this chore, a daunting task, yes, but one that he was more than capable of performing.

"Here it comes," he warned the animal, and tossed the ball of snow as hard as he could up into the air in an arc, watching as it began its descent. Gabriel bounded across the snow in pursuit, his eyes upon the plummeting prize.

Was it the life that he would have chosen for himself? No, not a chance, but he no longer resented the fate that had been unceremoniously thrust upon him. It was his destiny, and he had learned to accept it as that.

Gabriel returned to him, snowball clutched in his mouth, and dropped it at his feet.

"What, that one didn't taste so good?" he asked the dog.

*"I'm full,"* Gabriel said, deciding to lie down in the snow and roll upon his back. Aaron laughed at his dog's antics, kicking snow onto the animal's pink exposed belly.

They both felt it in the air, a familiar disruption that foretold of a Nephilim's arrival, and recognized it as someone special.

*"She's coming,"* Gabriel said excitedly as he shot to his feet, shaking snow from his fur as Aaron scanned the open space before him for signs of her arrival.

No more than five feet away the air began to shimmer and ripple, a darker patch beginning to form at its center. Gabriel began to bark happily, tail wagging like mad. Aaron sometimes wondered who loved her more.

Vilma Santiago emerged from the ether, her downy white wings the color of freshly fallen snow parting the substance of space around her. It was amazing how far she'd advanced in such a short period of time. She, too, had come to accept her heritage, embracing the angelic nature inside her.

Gabriel could barely contain himself, galloping through the snow to see her. *"Vilma's here!"* he said over and over again, and she knelt down to accept his excited affections. She seemed just as happy to see him.

It had been a few days since they'd last seen each other, what with getting ready to start classes at a nearby college in spring and gradually getting her aunt and uncle to accept the fact that she was going away to school. Vilma Santiago was taking control of her life, and of that Aaron was very proud.

Not long after Aerie's fallen had been forgiven, she had returned to Lynn, to her aunt and uncle. He guessed that it had been difficult, their relationship now strained by her abrupt departure from their home, but they had come to begrudgingly accept her explanation of needing some time away to find herself. Aaron chuckled with the thought. *She'd certainly done that.*

Vilma finished showering the excited Labrador with affection and proceeded toward Aaron, a sly smile upon her face. He watched as her beautiful wings receded on her back, only the slightest expression of discomfort on her features.

"I missed you," she said, leaning forward to plant a big kiss upon his lips.

He met her halfway, his own lips eagerly pressing against hers. The two embraced, and he was positive that there wasn't anything that felt better than having her in his arms. If there was, he didn't remember it.

Upon returning to Lynn, she had contacted the superintendent of schools and had worked with him and her teachers to make up the finals and projects that she had missed with her sudden absence. In no time she had completed the necessary requirements and had received her high school diploma with honors, albeit without the pomp and circumstance of a graduation ceremony, but Vilma had what she needed to continue her dream of a college degree.

*Maybe I'll complete my own high school requirements someday,* he thought as he held the young woman that he loved and respected so much. But if he didn't, that would be okay as well, for he was certain that life had other things in store for him.

Gabriel attempted to squeeze his blocky head in between

their embrace. *"Hi, remember me?"* the dog asked, often as ravenously hungry for affection as he was for food.

Vilma laughed, a light airy sound that Aaron had learned to adore, and bent down to hug the animal as well. "How could we ever forget you, Gabriel?" she asked in mock horror.

*"I know,"* the Labrador responded, accepting her additional attentions. *"I am pretty special."*

"That you are, my friend," Aaron said as he took Vilma's hand in his and began to lead her toward their new home within the old orphanage.

"And how is everything here?" she asked, walking by his side through the snow.

"Fine," he answered her, "especially now that you're here." And he gave her hand a gentle squeeze to stress how glad he was to be with her.

Vilma responded in kind with a smile that was pure magick. He doubted that Lorelei could summon anything quite as powerful.

Aaron needed moments like this, for it helped him to put it all in perspective.

*"When are you two going to have babies?"* Gabriel suddenly chimed in, a look of seriousness upon his canine features.

They were completely taken aback by the question, and Aaron felt a flush of embarrassment blossom upon his cheeks. Vilma fared a little better than he, covering her mouth to stifle a laugh. Gabriel did not care to be laughed at. The dog waited for his answer. She had no idea what to make of the question, but Aaron suspected that it had something to do with what the last of the Malakim had said to him before he had been taken by Verchiel.

*"May I be the first to say that your children will be absolutely magnificent,"* the angel sorcerer had said in that strange place between worlds.

Lehash had said that the Malakim had the ability to look into the future, and had seen that he and Vilma had children—magnificent children. Aaron had never bothered to share this information, not wanting to pressure her in their relationship in any way.

"Where did that come from?" Vilma asked the dog.

*"Just curious,"* Gabriel answered. *"I'm certain that they would be magnificent."*

Aaron felt her gaze upon him as they reached the entrance that would take them inside the building.

"And what do you think, Mr. Corbet?" she asked as he reached out to pull open the door. "Would they?"

He held the door against his back, allowing them to enter before him. Vilma waited just inside, arms crossed, as he let the door slam shut behind him.

"Well?" she chided.

"Yes," he told her, a smile upon his face that he couldn't control. When they decided to take that next step, to marry and eventually have children, he knew that it would be the most amazing thing in his life. To have a family with her was something to look forward to.

Something for the future.

"Yes, they will most certainly be magnificent," he told her.

Until then, there was still so very much that needed to be done.

# ABOUT THE AUTHOR

THOMAS E. SNIEGOSKI is the author of more than two dozen novels for adults, teens, and children. His books for teens include *Legacy*, *Sleeper Code*, *Sleeper Agenda*, and *Force Majeure*, as well as the series The Brimstone Network.

As a comic book writer, Sniegoski's work includes *Stupid, Stupid Rat-Tails*, a prequel miniseries to the international hit *Bone*. Sniegoski collaborated with *Bone* creator Jeff Smith on the project, making him the only writer Smith has ever asked to work on those characters.

Sniegoski was born and raised in Massachusetts, where he still lives with his wife, LeeAnne, and their Labrador retriever, Mulder. Visit him on the Web at www.sniegoski.com